RONIE KENDIG

NIGHTSHADE

DISCARDED HEROES #1

BARBOUR
PUBLISHING

For more information about Ronie Kendig, please access the author's Web site at the following Internet address:
www.roniekendig.com

Cover design: Müllerhaus Publishing Arts, Inc., www.Mullerhaus.net

Published by Barbour Publishing, Inc., P.O. Box 719, Uhrichsville, OH 44683, www.barbourbooks.com

Our mission is to publish and distribute inspirational products offering exceptional value and biblical encouragement to the masses.

 Member of the
Evangelical Christian
Publishers Association

Printed in the United States of America.

DEDICATION

To A.—whose story did not end happily.

ACKNOWLEDGMENT

Special thanks to:
    Brian Kendig—you are *my* hero. I love you!
    My agent, Steve Laube—for sage advice, friendship, and Ledge Talk
    John Olson—for believing in me and brainstorming this concept
    Chuck Holton—for your invaluable advice on making this plausible among the military
    Andrew Kendall—for the excellent Nightshade symbol design
Beloved friends: "Twin" Dineen Miller, Kimberley Woodhouse, Robin Miller, Sara Mills, and Lynn Dean. Love you ladies!
Brainstorm help: Camy Tang
Pre-readers: Colonel and Mrs. Thomas Dean, MSgt. and Mrs. Troy McNear, Brandt Dodson
Research help: Trish Perry, Sydney Wiley, MaryLu Tyndall, Steve Miller, Patricia Carroll, Victoria Kendig, and Mike and Deirdre Ramsey

Characters/Glossary

Nightshade Team

Max "Frogman" Jacobs—former U.S. Navy SEAL

Colton "Cowboy" Neeley—former U.S. Marine Corps Special Operations Command, sniper

Griffin "Legend" Riddell—former U.S. Marine Corps Special Operations Command

Canyon "Midas" Metcalfe—former Army Special Forces Group

Marshall "the Kid" Vaughn—former U.S. Army Ranger

Oscar "Fix" Reyes—former U.S. Air Force Pararescue

General Olin Lambert, aka "The Old Man"—Chief of the Army, member of Joint Chiefs of Staff

Camelbak—a hydration system that allows the user to access/drink water without using their hands, accomplished via a plastic, pliable water bladder and a hose with a bite-valve.

MARSOC—Marines Special Operations Command. MARSOC is tasked to train, organize, equip, and, when directed, deploy task-organized, scalable, and responsive U.S. Marine Corps Special Operations Forces worldwide. (source: http://www.marines.mil/unit/marsoc/Pages/about/About-MARSOC.aspx)

PJ—Air Force Pararescue—Mission is to recover downed and injured aircrew members in hostile and denied environments; PJ term derived from pararescue jumpers.

Special Forces—U.S. Army forces organized, trained, and equipped to conduct special operations with an emphasis on unconventional warfare capabilities, often referred to as the Green Berets.

Special Operations—A broad term used across military branches to refer to operations conducted in hostile, denied, or politically sensitive environments to achieve military, diplomatic, informational, and/or economic objectives
(Source: http://www.militarywords.com/result.aspx?term=special+operations)

SEAL—U.S. Navy SEAL—acronym for **SE**a, **A**ir, **L**and

Sitrep—situation report; a report of the who, what, when, and/or where, etc.

SEAL CREED

In times of war or uncertainty there is a special breed of warrior ready to answer our Nation's call. A common man with uncommon desire to succeed. Forged by adversity, he stands alongside America's finest special operations forces to serve his country, the American people, and protect their way of life. I am that man.

My Trident is a symbol of honor and heritage. Bestowed upon me by the heroes that have gone before, it embodies the trust of those I have sworn to protect. By wearing the Trident I accept the responsibility of my chosen profession and way of life. It is a privilege that I must earn every day.

My loyalty to Country and Team is beyond reproach. I humbly serve as a guardian to my fellow Americans, always ready to defend those who are unable to defend themselves. I do not advertise the nature of my work, nor seek recognition for my actions. I voluntarily accept the inherent hazards of my profession, placing the welfare and security of others before my own.

I serve with honor on and off the battlefield. The ability to control my emotions and my actions, regardless of circumstance, sets me apart from other men. Uncompromising integrity is my standard. My character and honor are steadfast. My word is my bond.

We expect to lead and be led. In the absence of orders I will take charge, lead my teammates, and accomplish the mission. I lead by example in all situations.

I will never quit. I persevere and thrive on adversity. My Nation expects me to be physically harder and mentally stronger than my enemies. If knocked down, I will get back up, every time. I will draw on every remaining ounce of strength to protect my teammates and to accomplish our mission. I am never out of the fight.

We demand discipline. We expect innovation. The lives of my teammates and the success of our mission depend on me—my technical skill, tactical proficiency, and attention to detail. My training is never complete.

We train for war and fight to win. I stand ready to bring the full spectrum of combat power to bear in order to achieve my mission and the goals established by my country. The execution of my duties will be swift and violent when required yet guided by the very principles that I serve to defend.

Brave men have fought and died building the proud tradition and feared reputation that I am bound to uphold. In the worst of conditions, the legacy of my teammates steadies my resolve and silently guides my every deed. I will not fail.

PROLOGUE

Crazy lights swirled against the evening sky. Day morphed into the merriment of night. Cotton candy and hot dogs. Teens decked out in goth gear contrasted sharply with young couples dragged from ride to ride by squealing offspring. White smeared over a man's face as red encircled his mouth. Like a giant maraschino cherry, his nose squawked when a child squeezed it. He threw his head back and laughed. The little boy stood perplexed, as if uncertain whether to laugh or break into tears.

Olin Lambert shifted on the park bench as a parade of kids trailed the balloon-toting clown through the park. He glanced at his watch. His contact was la—

The boards under his legs creaked. A man dressed in a navy jogging suit joined him.

"You almost missed the fun." Olin tossed a few kernels of popcorn into his mouth.

Rolling his shoulders, the man darted his gaze around the carnival insanity. "You know how dangerous this is? What it took for me to get out here without being seen?"

The danger and risk to his contact were no greater than what was stacked up against Olin. They both had a lot to lose—careers, reputations, families. . . . "We could leave now."

9

"You know this has to happen."

After a sip of his diet cola, Olin stuffed the half-full bag of popcorn on top of the overflowing trash bin. He wiped his hands and turned back to the man. "So, the body count's finally high enough?"

Blue eyes narrowed. "I'm here. That should tell you something."

"Indeed." Olin waited as the ice cream vendor wheeled his musical cart past. "I need full autonomy for me and my team."

Music burst forth as swings whirled occupants in a monotonous circle. A performer tossed flaming sticks and maneuvered one down his throat, swallowing the flames. *Oh*s wafted on the noisy, hot wind from the audience gathered around him. A scream pierced the night—a woman startled by another clown.

"Okay, fine. Just get on with this. I'm a sitting duck out here." He rubbed his hands and glanced around.

Olin swiped his tongue along his teeth, took a draught of his soda, then slumped back against the slats. "I want it in writing. Two copies. Mine. Yours."

The man shook his head. "No trails."

The corner of Olin's mouth quirked up. "You've already got one." He nodded to the ice cream vendor, who reached over the register and tapped a sign with a hole in the center where a camera hid.

A curse hissed through the night. "You'd bleed me out if you could."

"Whatever it takes to protect these men."

Eyeing him, the man hesitated. "The men? Or you?"

"One and the same. If they're protected, I'm protected. Whatever happens out there, we're not going to take the fall for it."

"If it goes bad, someone will get blamed."

Olin pursed his lips and cocked his head to the side. "More dust has been swept under the proverbial Capitol Hill carpet than anyone will ever admit. You have to decide: Is the cost high enough? How many more lives are you willing to sacrifice?"

"Seven."

On his feet, Olin tugged up the hood of his jacket. "Then we're through."

The man caught his elbow. "Sit down."

Teeth clamped, Olin returned to the bench. He bent forward and rubbed his hands together, more than ready to forget he'd ever tried to deal with this man, the only man with enough power on the Hill and the right connections to both fund and authorize black-ops missions. Missions nobody wanted to acknowledge.

The din of merriment swallowed the silence between them. A beat cop worked the scene, glancing their way as he walked, no doubt making a mental note to watch them.

"Get me their names. I'll write a carte blanche."

Olin's gut twisted. "Not happening." If he revealed the names of his elite, he would essentially place them on individual crosses to be crucified by some politician who got wind of this or by someone far more dangerous—media—if something went south. "Project Overlook happens under my guidance with all the freedom and resources I need, or it doesn't happen and you have one heckuva mess to clean up."

"If I do this, I could get put away for a long time, Lambert."

"And a million people will die if you don't."

"We should sit back and let Congress grant the authorization to go in there."

A deep-chested laugh wormed through Olin. "You've been around too long to believe that. Thick bellies and big heads crowd the halls of the Hill. They want the power and none of the responsibility." Had he been wrong in talking to the man next to him? What if he went to the Hill and spilled the news about Project Overlook? They'd be dead before the elite soldiers he had in mind could get their feet wet.

He let out a long exhale. "If you aren't going to pony up, this conversation is over. You contacted me because you knew I could take care of this little snafu. So let us go in and quell this before it destroys more and the body count rivals 9/11."

He eyed Olin, a slow grin cracking his lips. "You've always impressed me, Lambert, even though you're Army."

"Navy lost the last game, Admiral." Olin let his gaze rake the scene around him. "These men are fully capable, and the situation can be tamed before anyone is the wiser. We don't have time to wrangle the pundits. Let's get it done, Mr. Chairman, sir."

Chairman Orr stood and zipped his jacket. "You'll have it by morning."

CHAPTER 1

Cracking open the throttle ignited a wild explosion of power and speed. Zero to sixty in less than three seconds left Max Jacobs breathless. Gut pressed to the spine of his Hayabusa, he bore down the mountainous two-lane road away from civilization, away from...everything. Here only pine trees, concrete, and speed were his friends.

His bike screamed as it ate up the road. The thrill burst through him. He needed the rush. Craved it. *Stop running, Max.* Her words stabbed his conscience. Made him mad.

Rounding a bend, he slowed and sighted the drop-off in the road—remembered a full 10 percent grade, straight down. His gaze bounced between the speedometer and the cement. Common sense told him to decelerate. The boiling in his veins said otherwise.

He twisted the throttle.

Eighty.

Max leaned into the bike and felt the surge.

Ninety.

He sucked in a breath as he sped toward the break.

The road dropped off. The Hayabusa roared as the wheels sailed out. He tried to grip the handlebars tighter as nothing but tingling Virginia oxygen enveloped him. Silence gaped.

This could be it. This could end it all. No more pain. No more life without Syd . . .

Take me. Just take me.

The Hayabusa plummeted.

Straight down. Concrete. Like a meteor slamming to earth.

The back tire hit. A jolt shot through the bike. Then the front tire bounced. Rattling carried through the handlebars and into his shoulders. He grabbed the brake—

Stupid! The brake locked. Rear tire went right. He tried to steer into the skid but momentum flipped him up. Over. Pops snapped through his back as he spiraled through the air. In the chaos his bike gave chase, kicking and screaming as it tore after him.

Crack! Pop! The sound of his crashing bike reverberated through the lonely country lane.

Scenery whirled. Pine trees whipped into a Christmas-color frosting. Tree bark blurred into a menagerie of browns, drawing closer and closer.

Thud! His head bounced off the cement. He flipped again.

Finally. It'd be over. He closed his eyes. No more—

Thud! "Oof." The breath knocked from his lungs. Pain spiked his shoulders and spine. Fire lit across his limbs and back as he slid from one lane to another. Down the road, spinning. Straight toward the trees.

He winced, arched his back. Kicking, he tried to gain traction. If he wasn't going to die, he didn't want to end up paralyzed. *Just like you not to think it through.*

He dumped into a ditch.

Smack!

Everything went black.

He blinked. Pain shrieked through his body, his thighs and shoulders burning. "Argh!"

Max pried himself onto all fours, hanging his head. A crack

rent the face shield. A wicked throb pulsed through his temples and . . . everywhere. He fought with the helmet. Growled as he freed the straps. He pawed it off, cursing at the thing for saving his life. Those head whacks as he somersaulted through the air should've punched a hole in his skull. Warmth dribbled down his brow. He pressed a palm against his forehead. Sticky and warm. Blood. He grunted and strained to look across the road. Mangled. Twisted. His bike. Him.

Why couldn't God just let him die? Humanity would be one up, and he wouldn't have to face his consummate failures in life. "Just let me go!" he growled and pounded a fist against the pavement. He'd do anything to go back to the Middle East, pump some radicals full of lead, and unleash the demon inside. Anything that told him he still had purpose in life.

But that wasn't an option anymore. Another bad choice. Could he get anything right? Maybe his father had been right to up and leave them. Just like his mother.

A glimmer of light snagged his attention. Less than a mile down the road, a black SUV barreled up the road from town. Max tensed. He'd seen a vehicle like that three times in the last week. But out here? In the middle of nowhere, invading his self-inflicted punishment? This wasn't a coincidence. And he didn't like being hunted.

Max dragged himself into the trees, wincing. Using his forearm, he wiped the blood from his face. Why? Why couldn't he just die? Nothing here for him. No reason.

Sydney. . .

He banged the back of his head against the tree. Pain drove through him like an iron rod. Good. It felt good to hurt. A relief to the agony inside.

Glass popping and crunching snapped his attention to the road. The SUV sat like a giant spider. He wondered who was in the vehicle as he eased farther into the foliage. A carpet of pine

RONIE KENDIG

needles concealed his steps. He glanced back to the intruder.

The SUV shifted as a man climbed out. Large, African American, and an expression that said he didn't mess around. Whatever the guy wanted, he wouldn't take no for an answer. At least not easily.

Even from ten yards away, Max could see the muscle twitching in the man's jaw. He swallowed and licked his lips, readying himself for a confrontation. He swung back and gazed up at the canopy of leaves. Could he hoof it back to his apartment? Gathering his strength, he shrugged out of the shredded leather jacket, wincing and grunting as it pulled against raw flesh.

"You through? Or you want another go at it?"

What? Max peered around the trunk, surprised to find the man at the edge of the road, hands on his hips as he stared into the trees.

"We took you for stronger." The man glanced back at the bike. "But maybe you're nothing but broke and no use to no one."

Heart thumping, Max jerked back and clenched his teeth. Who was this joker?

"So, what's it going to be, Jacobs? You ready to face a little reality?"

How does he know my name? "Who are you?" Max hissed as the tree rubbed his raw shoulder. "What do you want?"

"You."

Max drew the SOG knife from his pocket and opened it. Holding it down, he pushed into the open, making sure his injuries didn't show him weak. "What's the game?"

The man's eyebrow arched. He angled his left shoulder forward, tugged up his sweater's sleeve, and flexed his oversized bicep. A tattoo expanded across his muscle. Marine. MARSOC, if Max made out the symbol correctly. Marine Recon Special Operations—impressive.

An ally? As he struggled out of the ditch and back onto the

16

road, Max collapsed the blade. Heat rose from the cement, aggravating the exposed flesh on his back and legs.

"Navy and Marines, you and me. Almost brothers. It's the Rangers I don't like. So, I forgive you for coming at me with a blade. This time."

Max stared. Confusion—and pain—wrapped a tight vise around his skull.

"What's it going to be, squid?" The guy pointed to the wreck of a bike on the road. "You don't have a ride back to town. So why don't you climb in and listen to what I have to say?"

Might ignore the nickname jab, but the guy assumed too much. "You flash a tattoo and think I'll just bend my knee? I don't think so." A silent brotherhood had closed Max's knife. But he didn't want company. The oaf's or anyone else's. But how else would he get home?

"What? You think you're going home? To your can opener and mattress?"

Mr. Recon had a point. Still, he knew too much, and that made Max stiffen—fiery shards prickling his back.

"No obligation. Show me a little respect, and just hear me out."

At least, as the man had said, he'd have a ride. Eyes on the large man, Max pocketed the knife as he trudged to the other side of the SUV and opened the door.

He paused at the plastic covering the seat. He jerked his gaze to the driver.

Mr. Force Recon grinned. "You're predictable, Jacobs."

Max lowered himself onto the seat, cringing as new fire crawled over his back and legs. He buckled in, the irony of the seat belt crossing his mind. "So what's this about? Why have you been following me?"

A crisp cologne swirled in the air-conditioned interior as Mr. Recon folded himself behind the steering wheel. "You've been recruited, Lieutenant Jacobs."

Max snorted. "Already did my time. I'm out." He gulped against the flurry of emotions within.

"Yeah? How's that working out for you?"

Glaring, Max resisted the urge to thrust his SOG into the guy's gut. He'd left the service for Sydney. Only it'd been too late. And in one fell swoop, he lost everything. "Why don't you tell me? You seem to know everything."

Mr. Recon pursed his lips and nodded. "Okay." He rubbed his jaw. "You were discharged ninety days ago. In that time, you've been arrested twice, once for fighting. The second time—less than three days ago—for assault against your now-estranged wife."

The words cut deeper and stung worse than his now-oozing flesh. Max looked at his hand and flexed his fingers.

"Yesterday you were hit with a permanent protective order by said wife. She filed for separation." He leaned on the console and again arched that eyebrow. "How am I doing?"

"If you knew anything about me, you'd dull your edge."

Wrist hooked over the steering wheel, Mr. Recon continued unfazed. "The military discharged you. Honorably. A veteran of two wars. Untold combat situations and medals. They tried to put you out medically two years ago, but you fought it."

"And won."

"Yessir." The man nodded for several seconds. "So, why now? Why'd you let them put you out this time?"

Max shoved his gaze to the heavily tinted windows. That was a story nobody needed to hear. Bury it six feet under and walk away.

"You're a discarded hero, Lieutenant Jacobs."

Head whipped back to the driver, Max fought the urge to light into the guy. But something in the amused eyes betrayed a camaraderie. An understanding. Acceptance.

"Who are you? What's your story?"

"Name's Griffin." He bobbed his head as they pulled onto

the highway, driving east toward the Potomac. "My story. . . ?" A toothy grin. "Let's just say I got smart."

The sound of crinkling and rustling plastic pervaded the cabin as Max shifted to alleviate a pinprick fire shooting down his leg. He hissed and clamped a hand over his thigh. "So, what's the gig?"

"The gig is whatever nobody else will do. What you should ask about is our group—and I do mean *our* group, Lieutenant. Because you are fully a part of this. Are you ready to step out of the medical trappings of your discharge, of the devastation that has become your life since you've returned from your last tour?"

Max grunted. "Yesterday."

"That's what I like to hear." Tires thumped over docks as Griffin steered into a warehouse. "Then this is where it starts."

CHAPTER 2

"Y ou did the right thing."

Sydney Jacobs traced the knot patterns in the oak tabletop without looking at her mother. Vanilla-scented steam spiraled up from the mug of hot tea cradled in her hand. Maybe she *had* done the right thing.

Maybe not.

The only certainty right now was how miserable she felt. Despite the receding pain in her cheek and jaw, her emotional scars hung thick and heavy around her heart. It wasn't supposed to be like this. . . .

Pushing the depressing thoughts away, she took a cautious sip and set down the drink.

Her mom slipped into the chair next to her with her own coffee and a basket of pastries. "I know it's hard to see outside the bubble that has encased your life, but you needed to do this." Reaching between the mug and pastries, she touched Sydney's shoulder. "For you."

Sydney traced the lip of the mug then sighed. "It's been a week, and I can still see the fury in his eyes." She fought the tremor slithering through her lips. A piece of her resented the man who was supposed to protect her—her husband! Another piece understood that war had ravaged his mind, his soul.

He'd always been intense. That very attribute had drawn her to his dark eyes and smile. Max never did anything halfway. Full throttle to the end. But he'd gotten worse with each tour, with each stint away from her. Proof of his volatility lay in the telltale yellow, slightly swollen bruise on her cheek. She shouldn't have tried to break up the fight. Now she looked like a victim, and Max an abuser. The thought twisted her heart.

Her mom nudged the basket closer. "Go on. I got apple fritters, your favorite."

Sydney wrinkled her nose. "Not really hungry." With a shuddering sigh, she lifted her tea and took another sip.

"You have to eat. I won't watch my daughter waste away."

"I'm far from that." Sydney rose and headed to the sink with her mug. "I'm going to head in to work. I need to get my mind on something productive." She dumped her coffee. The liquid raced around the stainless steel basin. Brown. Swimming. Just like her muddied marriage. Right down the drain.

Why couldn't she save it? Where had she gone wrong?

"Please eat something. You're rail thin."

She whipped toward her mother to argue—but her world spun. Dizzy. Hollowness devoured her hearing. She held her forehead and blinked.

"You okay?" Concern flooded her mother's voice as she joined her, touching Sydney's shoulder. "I am really worried about you, sweetie."

Hands on the sink, she squared her shoulders. "Well, don't. This isn't exactly where I wanted to be with my life, but. . .I'll be fine."

How *had* she gotten here? From a lavish wedding, through five years of marriage, building a beautiful home with Max, one she'd thought would draw them back together. . .and now, he was gone. Not allowed within fifty feet.

"How about if I meet you for lunch?" Her mother's gaze bore into Sydney. "I'd like to check out that little Chinese restaurant we passed on the way home yesterday."

Max doesn't like Chinese.

Sydney's eyes burned, and she bit her lip against the quivering. "Yeah." Drawing herself up, she donned a faux air of confidence. "I'd love some orange chicken."

"Sweet and sour for me."

"Okay." She could do this. "One o'clock at Chang's." Sydney gave her mom a quick hug and strode toward her bedroom, anxious to be free of her presence. Although loving and caring, her mother also knew how to smother. Like right now. And Sydney needed time and room to think. Odd that she'd head to work at a busy newspaper in Virginia to do that.

She pushed open the door—and stopped. The bed she'd shared with Max for the last five years gaped, opening a cavernous hole in her heart. They would never share a bed again. She'd never again lie in his arms, feeling warm and safe. Sydney eased the door closed and leaned against it, her hands still on the knob. Head propped on the wood, she blinked back tears and looked up at the ceiling.

God, why?

After mentally shaking off the question, she shoved away from the door. Not going to mope. Wouldn't get her anywhere. She stomped to her closet where clothes flanked her, and she ran her fingers over the fabrics. Her hand rested on a silky top, one Max had always called sexy.

A pang knifed her heart. The same top she'd worn when he'd erupted. Anger lashed out. Hadn't she done everything possible to save their marriage? And what had he done? He'd walked away. He sure didn't have a problem fighting for his military career, but when it came to her and their marriage, the hero she'd fallen in love with had vanished. Argument after nasty argument with her begging him to seek help. Their pastor had even volunteered to do it for free. But Max only roared louder. Somehow he seemed to think it made him less of a man. Or weak. God forbid he be weak—after all, the SEAL creed demanded perfection.

With a sigh, she bent and retrieved a black turtleneck from the lower shelf. Then gray slacks. An ensemble to give her a conservative, got-it-together appearance.

If only she did.

In the bathroom she worked a straightening iron through her hair then added some pomade to limit the frizz that would kink her strands in the moist Virginia air. Fingering the long strands into place, she noted how the fluorescent lights hit the bruise marring her cheek. Maybe a little more makeup. After dabbing some flesh-colored base onto the spot, she appraised herself in the mirror. Not bad. Hopefully enough not to draw attention.

She turned sideways, gauging her weight. Hmm, perhaps Mom was right. But since when was "a little thin" bad? She grabbed her tote and headed to the front door. After yet another promise to meet her mother for lunch, Sydney made her way to work. Funny how every turn, every signal felt…different. Yet inanely the same. She tilted the rearview mirror and eyed herself. Double-checked the puffy cheekbone—concealer worked wonders. Would anyone notice? Would they stare?

God, please just let me have a quiet day. She swallowed hard and climbed out of the Lexus. She paused as she considered the SUV, remembering Max's adamancy that she could have whatever she wanted. He'd been like that. Always giving her the best, as if he thought he could make up for the one area he failed—giving of himself. With a huff, she headed up the steps toward the glass atrium at the *Virginia Independent*, wishing she'd stopped for some backup. A two-pump mocha. With caramel.

Her heels hit the high sheen of the foyer as she hurried to catch the closing elevator doors. She whizzed inside with just seconds to spare and punched number six.

"Sydney? You're back?"

She spun at the voice, surprised to find LaDona Fletcher leaning against the mirrored wall. The woman pushed past two men.

"Hey," Sydney managed, suddenly realizing how unready she'd been for this day. "How're you?" She gripped the bar as the elevator lifted, nausea washing over her.

"Great. Now that you're back Kramer will get off my case. He's been ranting about not having a decent editor in the building."

Even to her, the smile felt wan. "I guess that means I have job security."

A quiet *dong* sounded, and the doors slid open. LaDona hurried out and waved. "Let's do lunch soon."

Following the features editor, Sydney blinked as the woman rushed off without another word. Since when did Fletcher have time for lunch with anyone? She shrugged and stepped into the fluorescent light–humming mall of cubicles. She wove past the monotonous maze of squares, smiling as old friends' eyes widened and some staffers said hi.

An electric hum bathed the office as the staff launched into another busy day, keyboards clicking, cooling fans thrumming. At her desk, she breathed a sigh of relief that she'd not been inundated with cheery welcome backs or the doleful looks that said they knew of her problems. Her separation. She dropped into her chair and settled in to work.

During the first few hours, she managed to get her voice mail cleared, e-mails organized, and mail sorted—most into File 13.

"Jacobs!"

She jerked up and met the hardened gaze of Buck Kramer across two rows of cubicles as he stood outside his office.

"Let's talk." He hiked his thumb over his shoulder before storming back to his desk.

Stomach knotted, Sydney pushed out of her chair and strode

across the room. In his office, she almost smiled at the familiar stacks of papers piling up on the conference table. Awards, mementos, steins, and memorabilia covering his twenty years as managing editor weighted the oak bookshelves. Even the dank smell of cigarettes from his smoking years still lingered.

Hunched over his desk, he flipped through several files, his thick head of hair belying his sixty-plus years. "Sit down." Without looking up, he pointed toward the cozy chair opposite him then slid the papers aside and met her gaze. "So. You're back."

"Yes, sir."

From beneath bushy brows, he considered her. "Is your mind here?" His head cocked to the side, eyes narrowing "Or is it on that bruise?"

Her fingers automatically went to her cheek. Heat rushed into her face.

Buck cursed and mumbled. He shook his head, apparently composing himself. "Sorry, Syd." He tossed down his pen. "I promised your father I'd watch after you, and I just. . ."

Licking her lips, she waited for him to finish, silently willing him not to go into the incident, her past, her failure.

"I could kill that—"

"I'm fine." Her heart thumped as she plastered a smile onto her face. "I know you have strong feelings about what happened— as do I—but let's just. . .leave it in the past. Okay?"

Somber gray eyes met hers. A single nod. "Fair enough."

On her feet, she scooted around the chair. "If you don't mind, I'm going to get back to work. There are a million e-mails to wade through." Without waiting for a reply, she hurried back to the safety of her cubicle.

Over the next hour, she sat a little lower in her seat and avoided looking over the carpeted divider. Better a mouse in its hole than a mouse in the trap. Would she always feel like cowering? The blessing of working for one of her late father's best friends seemed less than ideal at the moment. Kramer knew too much. Cared too much. She closed her eyes and pinched the bridge of her nose.

"Hey, how's my favorite editor?"

She whirled around and felt the first ray of sunshine touch her day. "Lane."

Propped against the divider, he held out a paper coffee cup with a recycled cardboard protector. "Two-pump mocha." Winking, he grinned. "With caramel."

Widening her eyes, she seized the cup. Held it up to her nose and savored the deliciously sweet aroma spiraling through the puncture in the lid. "Mm. How did you know I needed this?"

Lane slid onto the small chair inside her L-shaped desk. "I saw you head into Buck's earlier." He sipped from his own cup. "How'd that go?"

She shrugged.

"Did he swear to kill Max?"

"Yeah."

"Should've seen him the day he got word about it."

Sydney let out a sigh and ran a hand through her hair. Yawned.

"Tired? I thought you just had a week off."

"Ha ha." She wasn't bothered by his teasing and knew she didn't have to explain her stress-related exhaustion. He was one of the few who knew exactly what happened that night. Experienced firsthand what Max was capable of when enraged.

"Look. . .I. . ." He bent forward, elbows resting on his knees. "I feel responsible for the fight with Max last week. I—"

"No. Stop." Sydney held up her hand. "You got caught in the middle. And *I* am the one who's sorry for dragging you into my own little disaster. So." She pursed her lips, faking courage she didn't have. "Let's leave it there." Sorrow dug a hard line into her heart. One she vowed she'd never cross—the line between life with Max and life without. "He's gone." The words burned the back of her throat.

Lane dropped his gaze.

Sydney wouldn't take the pity sitting down. "I needed to do it." That's what her mother had said. And she was right, wasn't she? She hurried on, not wanting the answer to that. "Besides, the only way I could get Bryce off my back was to file a protective order."

Her brother had hounded her for months to leave Max, but the fight had put him over the edge. Every time she thought she could move on, get past the nightmare that had invaded their lives, it slapped her in the face again.

Heavy silence coated the air as they sat sipping their too-expensive drinks.

"Oh!" Lane looked up. "Are you still interested in getting out of editing?"

"Interested?" She grinned, so very grateful for the change in topic. "Of course I am. Think I want to spend the rest of my life correcting everyone else's fun?"

"Good. Then you've got a new job."

Quiet wrapped around her small square in the *Virginia Independent* as they held each other's gazes. Finally, Sydney found her voice. "What do you mean?"

Lane set down his cup. "I talked to LaDona about the idea you had—"

"The human interest pieces?"

"Yep. And she said that's exactly what she's looking for."

Exhilaration raced through her. "You're kidding!"

"Nope. She wants to talk to you about it today. There's a story Culpepper picked up, and she wants to run something about it, too."

"Cul. . ." Sydney nearly choked on the name of their largest competitor. If Culpepper had picked it up, then it'd be huge, especially for their small-town paper. "This is great—and right at the holidays." The populace loved to read human interest stories around Christmas—sort of reminded them of the good in humanity. That the Scrooges could be overcome. Her smile grew, inside and out. This was just the distraction she needed. "Yeah. . .this is perfect."

Lane's green eyes sparkled, a slow smile seeping into his lips. "It's nice to see that light in your eyes again."

Her joy tripped. And fell over his comment. Had she really been *that* glum that he needed to mention it? Would this always be the proverbial elephant in the room?

"I should be going." He stood. "You have plans for lunch?"

"Huh?" She glanced up at him. "Oh. Yeah. My mom."

His smile waned. "Well, I'll see you later."

Why did he seem down about that? Lane had always said family was important. Shrugging off his reaction, Sydney swiveled her chair back to her computer. She surfed through their competitor's online paper and found the human interest story.

"This must be it. . . ." A local firefighter had held a fund-raiser for a single mom whose home had burned over Halloween. In the middle of the ongoing effort, an anonymous donor had promised to match the funds. With that, the small neighborhood rallied—so much that the mom and her two children had just moved into a fully furnished home. And married the firefighter. The heroic firefighter saved the day—and rescued the girl!

It read more like a fairy tale. Chewing the top of her pen, she considered the story. What must it have been like for that woman to be rescued in every hurting part of her life? To have some gallant hero care enough to step in and effect change and healing?

Sydney had a hero. Once.

In a way, he'd died. Right along with their marriage.

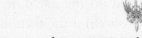

Elite soldiers stood in a semicircle, waiting. For what, Max wasn't sure. And he wouldn't ask. If his guess was right, then time would

tell—because Griffin seemed to be the guy in the know, and his relaxed posture against the SUV said things were going according to plan.

"Hey, dude, want me to look those over?" A blond guy dressed in khaki shorts, a faded tank, and a pair of flip-flops motioned to Max's scrapes and lacerations.

Right. Beach bum wanted to play nurse. "I'm good."

"About as good as a dog in a meat grinder," the guy said.

Max clenched his teeth. Whatever kind of circus Griffin was running. . .

A diesel engine growled, the sound reverberating off the aluminum in the cavernous space, preempting the shiny blue dualie truck pulling into the dank building. The engine cut. A guy stepped out and donned a black cowboy hat that added about five inches to his six-foot-two frame.

Griffin's laugh rumbled as he pushed off his SUV. "Colton."

A broad grin spilled under the rim of the man's Stetson. "Hey." The two clasped hands and patted backs. "How's Dante?"

A quiet dialogue carried between the two for several minutes that effectively cut out the rest of those gathered. Yeah, they had a friendship, one that said they trusted each other with more than superficial things. Something about the tight bond rankled Max. Hit deep.

"Why are we here?"

Max's gaze bounced to the shortest and youngest of the six men in the building. The Kid had read his thoughts. A warehouse full of warriors? This setup smelled rotten.

"If you'll be patient—" Griffin paused and glanced behind him. "I think it's time."

A black Chrysler 300 glided into the middle of the grouping. The hollow clunk of an opening door echoed off the steel rafters and grime-laden windows. A man emerged. White hair feathered back. A sun-bronzed nose sported dark-tinted sunglasses. The thud of the door almost swallowed the crunching of his squeaky shoes. New, expensive shoes. Maybe even tailor-made. He gripped the rim of his glasses and drew them off.

Was the old man supposed to mean something? Be someone who mattered? Irritation skittered along Max's shoulders as the old man shook hands with Riddell and the cowboy.

"Who's the hoo-hah?" Max mumbled to himself.

"You kidding me, man?" The blond look at him and smirked. "That's—"

"For those not enlightened," an authoritative voice cut through the surfer's explanation, "my name is General Olin Lambert. I am a member of the Joint Chiefs. But among the seven of us, I am merely a citizen of the United States just like you." Blue eyes probed each man.

Right into Max's soul.

"With Mr. Riddell's help, I've hand-chosen each and every one of you for a very specific purpose. There isn't anything about you or your lives that I don't know." Lambert paused, as if to let his words sink in, but Max just wished he'd get on with it. Scabs were forming on his scrapes.

"Chosen us for what, *ese?*" asked the Hispanic man.

"A black ops team."

And that meant two things: military and that this meeting was over. Max turned and started walking.

"It's not military, Mr. Jacobs."

Hesitation held him at the large, garage-style door he'd entered. "How can you do black ops without military aid, intelligence, and backup?" He turned around, ignoring what felt like glass stuck to his calves and thighs.

"I didn't say we wouldn't have aid or intelligence." Creases pinched Lambert's eyes at the corners. "I said it's not military."

"Come again?" the beach bum asked, disbelief coloring his words.

"Let the general explain." Griffin leaned back against the truck with his cowboy buddy.

"Thank you, Mr. Riddell." Lambert tucked his sunglasses in his left breast pocket, then threaded his fingers in front of him. Impressive and commanding. "Each of you has returned from combat changed, affected."

Nervous glances skidded from man to man. Max glued his attention to the general, refusing to acknowledge the truth of Lambert's words.

"You're what I've dubbed discarded heroes."

Grunts of approval rang through the building, and the group seemed to tighten in around the old man. Being a general, he knew what it was like to have slanted glances of pity from those who knew where you'd been, what you'd probably done, and what it was like to go against a politically correct ideology and fight for freedom on foreign soil. Or to have some tree hugger spit in your face and call you a murderer.

"You served your time, saw and experienced things no normal person should have to endure. Sure, you were trained. Taught to expect evil. Demanded success. However, when confronted with the true terrors of war, no human mind can dissolve the images embedded in memory for all time.

"Then it's time to get out. They yank you back here, give you a once-over, and toss you out with a 'thank you very much and have a good life.' So you go home, try to reintegrate into society, and—"

"It's screwed up," the Kid said. He shrugged when the others scowled at him. "Well? I'm right, aren't I? From what I heard you saying earlier," he pointed to the beach bum, "you've spent time in Afghanistan—a lot." Then to the Latino, "You probably did your tours of duty in Panama or the like." His gaze came to Max.

"Don't." Fists balled, Max willed his feet to remain in place. He didn't want anyone digging in his brain.

"Mr. Vaughn is correct," Lambert said. "You've all seen combat.

You've all been trained to kill; then you come back, and what do you do with those skills but go out of your mind?"

Max shifted. Was it over yet? He eyed the wide-open berth to freedom behind the blue dualie.

"Max Jacobs."

Hearing his name felt like a detonation that blasted his attention back to the general.

"You served eight years with the SEALs. Your experience in command and combat no doubt left indelible scars. Watched your best friend toss himself on a grenade to save the team."

Bile pooled at the back of Max's throat as the memory surged. He flared his nostrils, pushing the images back into the pit from which they'd been drawn.

Lambert stalked the inner perimeter, as if prepping troops for war with a pep talk. "Lieutenant Jacobs is the man I've chosen as team leader, but his position is no more valuable than anyone else's. You've all seen war. In this building are years of tactical experience. Incredible wisdom. And one element that makes each of you vital for this to work."

"What's that?" Cowboy asked, his arms folded over his thick chest.

"Loyalty, Mr. Neeley. Your duty with the Marine Special Operations Team is bloated with exemplary conduct, commendation after commendation." He waved his hand around the cozy circle. "I've reviewed all of your files and found the same thing in every one."

Awkward silence cooled some of the tension in the room, and once again Max eyed the exit.

"Mr. Reyes, your career as a pararescue jumper, specifically your medic skills, saved dozens of lives."

"Pair o' what?" Cowboy taunted.

"Hey," Reyes grinned. "You're just jealous. I'm a PJ. Why you think they call me Fix?"

"Because you put everyone in one?" Griffin chuckled, eliciting more laughter.

"Nah, man. It's 'cause of this," he said as he drew out a crucifix from his shirt and kissed it. "My crucifix. They called me Cru at first, then since I'm a medic, they started calling me Fix."

Swallowing his groan, Max ran a hand through his short crop. Religion and military. This was starting to feel worse than an AA meeting. And there wasn't a point. "This is a lot of flowery, moving discourse, but what do you want from us?" Max mentally shook off the way the others looked at him. Was he the only one who was still waiting for the boom to lower?

"Mr. Riddell, if you please." Lambert pointed to the black SUV as Griffin opened the tailgate. "Give each man one."

Griffin handed out small black packs that bore a lone symbol. A strange star backed by a sword and wings. The Kid, the Beach Bum, and the Latino dug into the packs, almost excited. In seconds, a black phone, keys, a watch, and a set of duds spilled across the gray cement floor in front of them.

Max remained in place, his pack dangling from his clenched fist. He didn't like being played. And this definitely felt like a setup.

General Lambert faced him. "Is there a problem, Mr. Jacobs?"

He dropped his pack onto the floor. "Not seeing the point."

Behind the general, Griffin seemed to grow several inches as he towered over the aged officer. "What?" he growled. "You want to take another nose-dive off that hill? Hope this time there's only enough of you left to fill a baggie? Want to make that estranged wife of yours a widow before you can be called a failure?"

Hands coiled, Max drew up his shoulders. Saw red. *No. No.* He wouldn't give in to the goading. He dragged his attention back to the general.

"Ease up, Legend," Cowboy said, patting Griffin's chest. "Give the guy a chance."

Lambert remained unwavering. "The point, Lieutenant, is to establish a team that can penetrate hostile situations without any entanglements, without any blame on the good ol' US-of-A or any other entity or government. You returned from two tours in Iraq, one in Afghanistan, and a covert mission nobody in this room will ever know about. You were the best, a natural, your CO said. But you were so volatile after those experiences took their toll they tried to discharge you, and your compatriots nicknamed you after a volatile chemical. Somehow you held it together. Then jumped ship without warning." More than recitation of information lurked behind the general's blue eyes. A knowing—no, an understanding, quiet and unnerving. "Tell me, Mr. Jacobs, what are you doing with your life now?"

"Minding my own business," Max answered through tight lips.

Lambert laughed. "And that's exactly what you'll be doing as part of my team. Funding isn't a problem. You'll have unlimited resources."

"That'd be a change," the Kid grumbled.

"To go where?" the Beach Bum asked.

"Doesn't matter," the Kid interrupted. "Man, how is this any different than military? I got out for a reason."

"You'll go wherever needed." The general turned toward the younger man. "Yes, Mr. Vaughn, you did get out for a reason. Tell me, did abandoning the one thing you loved the most give you the love of your father after all?"

The Kid paled.

"Why?" Max couldn't stand it anymore. "Why are you doing this? What's this thing to you?"

Lambert lowered his head then looked back at Max. "I am. . .discarded just like you."

"Bull." Max tucked his hands under his arms. "You sit in a cushy chair in a carpeted office. You're paid, you're connected—"

"I know what you guys have been through." The general

tapped his temple. "MAC-V SOG in Nam. Two tours."

Max's eyebrows shot up. That meant the man before him had likely seen more carnage than the rest of them put together.

"Heard the phrase 'peace with honor'?"

Max shrugged. "Yeah, sure. Who hasn't?"

"It was a platitude." Lambert's eyes flamed under his passion. "The armchair generals lost the war, not the grunts on the ground. We won every battle they let us win. But that doesn't make it any easier when you're the only guy who comes home from your unit with all his parts and pieces still connected where God put 'em.

"I may not be young, I may not have done combat tours in Iraq like you, Lieutenant, but I was tossed aside, too. For years I languished." The general pushed to his feet, his voice thick and his eyes weighted by the story. "But I slowly remembered that I'd joined the military for a reason—I wanted to be a *man*. A real man willing to defend my country with life and limb. I knew then I could screw up my career or I could do my best to make a difference in the lives of those who came after."

Silence hung rank and thick in the abandoned warehouse. Something akin to admiration leaked past Max's barriers as he watched the indignant rise and fall of the general's chest. A smile threatened his resolve as the old man glared at the hulking men around him.

Lambert's lips tightened over a clean-shaven jaw. "What's it going to be, gentlemen? Do you have what it takes to finish the fight with the gift God gave you? Or are you going to turn tail, accept what the government stamped on your papers, and leave— go quietly into the night?"

"Whoa-hoa!" Laughing, Beach Bum stepped forward. "Old Man's got some fire under that shiny dome."

Lambert spun toward the bum. "What's it going to be, Sergeant Metcalfe?"

The blond pursed his lips, considered Lambert, then nodded. "I'm in."

The bright blue eyes shifted to the Latino.

"You need some CPR, ese? You look worked up."

A half smile slid into Lambert's face. "A little passion never hurt, eh, Mr. Reyes?"

"You all right, old man." He hooked Lambert's hand and patted his back. "You all right." Reyes leaned in toward the general's shoulders and looked at the Kid. "But I don't know about this kid. He don't look like he's out of diapers yet."

"That's wrong. That's just wrong." The Kid's face flushed. "I spent six years in the Rangers. I have enough—"

"Rangers." Max couldn't help but grunt his disapproval. "That explains a lot."

The Kid's chin jerked up in defiance. "I'm in."

It seemed Lambert grew with each affirmation. He shifted to the cowboy. "Mr. Neeley?"

Cowboy gave a slow, firm nod, his hat shading his eyes. "I'm ready."

Lambert smiled. "Good. Good."

They were all crazy. Joining a group like this meant more problems. "What if we get in trouble out there?"

"Then get out of trouble," Lambert said. "Understand that this team does not exist. If anyone comes looking, there will be nothing to find. Only one man besides those of us in this facility knows it exists, and he'll pay the highest cost if that confidence is broken. No one—and I mean *no one*—will know your names."

"So our orders are coming from on high?" Metcalfe asked.

A twinkle brightened Lambert's eyes and gave silent assent to the question, although he gave no answer. Instead, he continued. "Any mission, any activity will be utterly and completely disavowed by the United States. *You* will be disavowed. If you get into trouble, Mr. Jacobs, count on your ingenuity to get out. If you are killed, no one will know."

"Or care." The Kid shrugged, a sick smirk in his face.

Max wanted to punch him.

"Or maybe that's where Sergeant Metcalfe, call sign Midas, will come in with his golden touch." Lambert ambled toward him.

The beach bum made a *tss* noise and shook his head. "Nothing golden, just hard work."

The general's smile disappeared behind a stern facade. "What is your answer, Lieutenant Jacobs?"

"This is crazy." What else could he do? Flip burgers at the nearest fast food? What was worth staying here for? No wife. No family. "Fine." The separation papers told him he had nothing left here anyway. "I'm in."

"Good." General Lambert's smile softened his commando persona. "Look around. The men here are your new brothers, your family. Only they will understand when the horrors of war invade your sleep. Only they will be there when you're pinned down and need an extraction.

Arms wide, Lambert smiled like a proud father. "Gentlemen, welcome to Nightshade."

CHAPTER 3

This was her worst idea ever.

Okay, maybe not *ever*, but it sure ranked high on the stupidity scale.

But she needed closure.

Maybe that wasn't really it, either. She just needed. . .no, she *wanted* to see him. Just one more time. To let him know she didn't hate him, that he would always have a place in her heart—if he changed.

Sydney gripped the steering wheel tighter as she sat at the red light, her heart thrumming as she glanced at the collage box on the leather passenger seat. Row after row of Max's medals glared back at her. He never cared about the awards, leaving them scattered over his dresser in the closet. He'd always groused that he'd done his job and didn't need a shiny piece of metal to tell him that.

But she was proud of him and wanted to do something special, so she'd had them framed for his birthday last year. When she came home from work the next day, it didn't surprise her to find the box hung—in the closet.

A strange dichotomy worked in Max Jacobs. Pride as hot and pure as molten gold ran through his veins. But not in the way one would think. He didn't flaunt things. Instead, he held his head high, wouldn't accept defeat, and resisted counseling for his anger.

She chewed her lip, wondering if she should just turn around right now and head home. Bryce would rake her over the coals if he knew she'd visited Max. While she understood her brother's protective nature, he didn't understand her feelings for Max.

Honk! Honk!

Sydney jolted out of her somber thoughts. The light had turned green. With a furtive glance at the delivery truck behind her, she pressed the gas pedal. Winding her way through the tangled streets to Max's apartment, she swallowed the metallic taste darting over her tongue. A queasy stomach beaded her lip with sweat.

Maybe she should tell him. . . . If she was right, he deserved to know, didn't he?

She frowned as she turned onto Parker Drive. Unease skittered down her spine as she took in the rundown street. Surely this wasn't where Max lived. He'd never approve of such a place and had been downright hostile when she suggested living downtown, stating it wasn't safe or nice enough.

Chain-link fence separated the street and sidewalk from the apartments. Small cement buildings looked wounded and bleeding with their peeling paint and cracked windows. She licked her lips as she eased the car along the curb in front of a red-brick building. Holding up the paper she'd written his address on, she confirmed the numbers with the weather-worn numbers hanging over the mottled wood.

"Oh, Max," she whispered, guilt riddling her for living in luxury on the other side of town in their four-bedroom home with granite countertops. Eyes roving the street to verify her safety, she lifted the collage from the seat.

What if he wasn't home? Maybe she should've called.

No. Because if she'd called, she would've talked herself out of this. Framed medals clutched to her chest, she climbed from the car, shut the door, and clicked the key fob. The *tweak-tweak* of her alarm gave little confidence the gray crossover would be there when she came back.

As she reached the top step, Sydney stared at the keypad and speaker. She'd have to buzz him to let her in? She blinked. What if he refused? Her gaze traced the dark green paint that split and peeled in more places than not. Just as she turned to press the button, the front door flung open. A man rushed out with barely a glance in her direction as he shouted on a cell phone.

Heart in her throat, she caught the door before it closed and slipped inside the building. Stairs rose directly in front of her, begging her farther into the dank structure. With a breath for courage, she climbed the stairs, cringing at each pop and creak as she made her way to the second floor in the hopes of finding apartment 214.

A minute later, she stood before the black door. Clanging and grunts slithered under the doorjamb in a repetitive fashion. What was he doing in there?

Better knock before you talk yourself out of it. Rapping on the wood, she held her breath.

A heavy thud was soon followed by three smaller ones. For several seconds, silence reigned. Her gaze flipped to the peephole. It looked new compared to the beaten and worn brass numbers. No doubt Max had installed it—and was looking at her right now. A smile bobbed and fell from her lips. A chain rattled, then a *click*, and the door opened.

Max stood there, shirtless and breathless. "Syd," he said, his chest heaving—a sheen over his well-toned torso. Behind him, she saw his all-in-one gym. He'd been working out. And it showed. "What're you doing here?" He frowned and glanced down the hall.

"Don't worry. I'm alone."

Now that he wasn't in the service, he looked so good with his longer hair, sweat dripping off a few strands. Stubble lined his jaw, adding to his rugged appearance. Curse the way the man left her weak in the knees, her stomach churning.

His face darkened. "You're alone?"

"Don't worry. Bryce doesn't know."

Max hissed. "He's the last thing I'm worried about. I'll get my shirt and walk you out." He turned back into his apartment.

And that's when she saw it—the streak of still-red scabs down his back and shoulders. She winced and gasped. "What happened to your back?"

"Nothing. Don't worry about it." Stuffing his arms into a T-shirt, he moved into the hall and locked his door.

"That's not 'nothing.'" She stilled when he stepped closer to her. "You had a bike accident, didn't you?"

One side of his mouth curled upward as he hooked her elbow and led her down the hall. "Something like that."

"Did you see a doctor?"

He stopped and cocked his head to the side, his dark eyes penetrating her reserve. "You're worried about me."

"Of course I'm worried. Just because this. . .this thing is happening doesn't mean I don't care about you."

Max tucked his chin, tension radiating from him. "This *thing* is divorce. A petition *you* filed."

Ignoring the way her chin quivered, she shoved the collage toward him. "I brought this over. It's the last of your things. I thought you'd want it."

Max glanced down at the box then at her. Irritation crowded the concern that had lingered only moments earlier. Slowly, he took it. "Syd," he said, his voice barely a whisper.

She quickly shook her head and pursed her lips, knowing full well she'd cave if he tried to talk her out of this. "Please, Max." Gaze on his bare feet, she tried to blink back the tears. "Don't. . ."

His rough, calloused hand came to her cheek, and he swept his thumb over her face.

Smooth and creamy, her skin was as soft as he remembered. Every pulse of anger he experienced over the fact that she'd come into this high-crime disaster he lived in, every muscle that knotted at finding her on his doorstep, drained at the silkiness of all that was Sydney. She'd violated the court order—the very one *she* had requested—to bring him a collage, one she knew he didn't want, one he'd said she could keep.

No, Sydney wasn't here because of a box of medals. She'd come to see *him*.

Oh, he wanted her back, wanted their life back, wanted things to be right. Good. The way they were before.

But that hope vanished when she stepped out of his reach. "Please," she said, her throat processing a nervous swallow as she avoided his gaze. "I just. . ."

His anger vaulted over the hurt and took control. "You just what?" *Keep it cool, man. Keep it cool.* He held up the medals. "Brought me something I told you I never wanted?"

Sydney leaned against the wall, her shoulders hunching.

Max ground his teeth. "I want you, Syd. I don't care about things. I don't care about my job. You. That's all I want."

Tears spilled from her eyes. "You get mad. . . . You lose control." Sorrow filled her face and carved a gaping hole in his heart. "I can't live like that anymore."

He balled his fist, hating the painful truth of her words and how his anger took over. Always took over. Hating that she'd resolved their marriage couldn't work without him changing. Changing what? He had been like this the day she'd vowed to love him till death parted them. And as far as he knew, neither of them had died. "Then why are you here?"

A sob ripped through her. "I can't. . ."

His chest tightened. *Get it together.* He choked back the anger and frustration. Let out a huff. His entire life was slipping down a one-way track to hell, and he was utterly powerless to stop it. "Let's get you back in the car and on your way to safety."

She pulled out of his grasp. "I don't need you to walk me out like a child."

"What?" He ran a hand through his hair. "I—fine. Okay." Hands up, he sighed. "Fine. Go, leave."

Everything in him railed as she disappeared down the stairs. He waited until he heard the creak of the door then hustled down the steps after her. Watching through the rectangular block of glass, he waited until she climbed into her car and started the engine before he released the tension. What was she thinking coming out here, a place where there were more guns than people?

He glanced down at the collage box. She'd been so proud of it when he opened it at his birthday barbecue last summer. Their guests had *ooh*ed and *ahh*ed over the dozen awards. What good were awards when everything in you, everything in your life, was falling apart? About all they were good for was to make empty frames look good. Still, he'd thanked her. And he knew she would expect him to hang it up, but he didn't want it in a high-traffic area. Matter of fact, if nobody saw it, he'd be happy. Thus the prime location at the back of the closet next to his cleaned, pressed, and stored duds.

In his apartment, he slid the box across the counter and grabbed a bottle of water from the fridge. For the first time, he considered that closet—it had contained all his SEAL equipment, his uniforms, the gear, and his medals. Nicely and neatly contained. Tucked out of view. Sort of how he dealt with everything. Neat little closets nobody could see into, not even himself unless he needed to.

It was the only way to cope.

Ain Siro mountains loomed in the darkness, cutting off the small village from the somber glow of moonlight. Shrouded in the anonymity of night, Max huddled among a group of firs at the base of the mountain. Rushing water cascaded over rocks and tumbled southward fifty yards north.

Armed with his M4 and a rucksack full of adrenaline, he crept along the perimeter of the village huddled near the vital river. Each step purposefully placed. Each breath measured. Nestling against the tree gave him the temporary cover he needed. Using his night vision scope mounted on his weapon, he visually confirmed each member of the team was in place. Their first mission, yet after months of training, they operated seamlessly.

Shifting to the right, he swept his gaze over the interior of the village where Janjaweed forces reclined around a small fire pit. The spiked drinks Nightshade anonymously donated to the forces had the necessary effect. Talk and laughter drifted on the hot winds and invaded the tranquil setting. The underlings remained clustered around one man. Colonel Paka. Nightshade's primary objective.

Even now as Max watched the man, he understood the neutralize order. According to the recon Legend and Cowboy had gathered, the man had raped and butchered more than a dozen of the villagers huddled in structure one-eight in the last twenty-four hours. This mission wouldn't end soon enough.

Sweat dribbling down his back, Max monitored the progress of Fix as he hustled to the last vehicle in the parked convoy by the creek. Just one more device to plant before his man would scurry back into the trees with the Janjaweed none the wiser. Listening to the gentle swish of Fix's tactical pants ten yards east, he knew the time had come.

So it begins.

At the signal, Legend slipped out of the trees and snuck to the lone Jeep between two mud-and-stick homes. Waving Midas into action, Max glanced at the Kid, who hovered behind him. He nodded, and they both sprinted into the dwelling northeast of Legend.

Laughter spirited from the campfire at the center of the oppressed community. Easing into point, he stared down his scope and fixed his attention on the leader of this group, his round belly the result and proof of the easy life compared to the swollen, malnourished bodies of the women and children. Thirty soldiers to Nightshade's six.

Now to even the odds. With a quick flick of his hand, Max gave the signal.

Thud!

One tango down. Seeing Cowboy's sniper precision impressed Max. He kept his sights on Paka, waiting.

Thud.

Behind the leader, two and three dropped.

Why hadn't Cowboy taken out Paka, yet? The felled soldiers were too close. Max glanced into the woods even though he knew he'd never spot Cowboy's sniping position.

Still, if the colonel saw them before—

Shouts rang out.

Max's adrenaline spiked. "Blow the trucks!" He pushed away from the hut and rushed into chaos.

Shots cracked the night.

Boom! Boom! White rent the darkness, illuminating the Janjaweed darting through the camp. Max squinted against the brilliance of the explosion. They had to make it to the structure in the center, to the women and children. Fifty humans packed into the smallest dwelling.

Half bent, he hurried toward the target.

Ping! Sparks flew.

He flung himself backward, pressing his shoulder to the hull of the Jeep. With a breath, he peeked up over the hood—

Tzing!

Max jerked to safety. Cordite stung his nostrils. "Taking fire." With the accuracy of those shots, someone must've taken cover and targeted him. Testing his theory, he slowly nudged his weapon up.

Crack! Glass shattered, raining down on him.

"Cowboy, I've got a little problem."

Behind him and past the Jeep, he heard the heavy thumps of soldiers shuffling around. Scrambling, most likely, for safety. Grunts and the hollow sound of hand-to-hand combat filtered through the night. Max reveled in the realization that the Janjaweed wouldn't be safe. Those men would fight. So would his. And the wicked would pay for their crimes.

Smoke snaked out from the fire and billowed toward Max. He had to get to the women and children in structure one-eight, but he couldn't move until Cowboy cleared his path.

"Target acquired." Cowboy's voice carried smoothly through the coms. "Tango down."

Trusting the sniper's call, Max rolled around and hustled to the next hut. The Kid's steady movements followed him. As Max neared the marked location, Midas fell into step with him.

"Frogman, we've got a situation." Legend's tone hissed through the coms and pushed Max against the prickly branches of the hut, his pulse pounding.

"Go ahead."

"All but one scum accounted for."

Max ground his teeth. "Let me guess: our primary?"

"Roger that. The man we thought was him is his second. We are minus one bad guy."

Where had the colonel gone? Hiding? The only possible scenario presenting itself rankled Max deeply. A man like Paka wouldn't hesitate to endanger anyone and everyone in close proximity if it meant he could live another day to kill and rule. Which pointed Max toward structure one-eight, the one he leaned against.

"Cowboy," Max whispered.

"Go ahead."

"You got my twenty?"

"Affirmative."

"Am I hot or cold on our objective?" He hoped the infrared technology gave Cowboy a line of sight through the wild brush that formed the walls of the home.

A low chuckle seeped through the line. "Red-hot, Frogman." Cowboy's smile bled into his words. "One coward hiding behind women's skirts targeted . . . and acquired."

After sending Midas and the Kid back one hut, Max crouched out of sight but close enough to charge Paka if he showed himself. "You know what to do."

Silence gaped through the coms. Was he asking too much? Were Cowboy's skills *that* good? Or would it end in a bloody mess, like the rest of Max's life?

Finally, "Roger that."

"Do it."

Seconds ticked by. Bark splintered to Max's right.

A scream pierced the air.

Max bolted into the hut, weapon at the ready. Two seconds dragged by as his gaze struck the screaming, churning sea of bodies until he spied the hulk of a man spread out on one side.

"Out! Out! Out!" he shouted to the women and children. He scissor-stepped toward the body. No movement. Not even a twitch. Was it too much to hope for?

Bodies bumped and jostled him as the women rushed the children from the hut. Gaze locked on the colonel's body, he waited until the cramped space emptied. The door flapped shut.

M4 hoisted to his shoulder, Max inched closer. Sweat sped down his temple.

"Whatcha got, Frogman?" whispered Midas.

Anticipating an ambush, Max nudged the body with his toe.

A hand flashed out.

Max pulled the trigger.

His leg flipped up, sending him backward. His head slammed into the hard-packed earth. *Smack!* Stars sprinkled through his vision. He flung himself over. Where was his weapon? He slapped his hand to the right, groping as he shook off the ringing in his ears. His fingers tracked over the muzzle—the pressure of his touch pushed it out of reach.

"Frogman?"

Metal glinted from the side.

Rolling right, Max called, "Kill him! Take him!" He heard the colonel's unsteady moves behind him. He pawed for the M4—felt warm steel.

Fire seared through his shoulder from behind. "Argh!" He drove his elbow backward. Made contact with the guy's gut. Max spun with his arm drawn back to pummel the man.

Crack! Crack!

The colonel stilled. Dropped. Crumpled on the ground, two dark stains smeared through his uniform shirt. Max flipped the man over. Straddling the fat body, he waited with his fist poised to strike as he watched the lifeless eyes, waiting for the man to come to or steal a second life to finish off Max. Finally satisfied the guy was dead, he dropped him and staggered to his feet.

Max stumbled away, clutching his left shoulder. "He's down." He swiped his weapon from the ground and stepped into the hot night.

Exultant cheers burst out, stopping him. He gazed at the fifty-plus villagers smiling as they pumped fists in the air amid shouts of victory. A tall, lanky woman ambled toward him with a small boy perched on her hip. She gave Max a medallion and kissed his cheek, mumbling something in her language.

A man came forward. "She thanks you for saving her, the children. All of us."

Max nodded, disconcerted as he stared at the medallion, then tucked it in his pocket. Someone touched his shoulder—pain ripped through him. He hissed and jerked away.

"I'll get this taken care of, Frogman."

Max tightened his muscles and glared at Fix. "I'm good."

"Sorry, ese." Fix grinned. "You don't make that choice. As the only certified medic, I'm the doc. I outrank you in this case."

He considered challenging the medic.

But the nod from the PJ reminded him they were a team. They'd successfully freed not only this village, but every other one along the river's edge, from the tyranny of a gluttonous, perverted Janjaweed leader.

They'd done good. Real good. For the first time in a very long time, he experienced a sensation almost lost to him. Pride.

No, he wouldn't challenge his own men. They were a team.

They were Nightshade.

DAY ONE

A village near the island of Mindanao, Philippines

Moonlight skidded and danced over the night-darkened waters of the Indian Ocean. Like a meditation fountain in one of the nearby villages, water lapped softly against the rocks below. Jonathan Harris lowered himself to a moss-covered boulder and rested his forearms on his knees. The thick air pressed upon him as heavily as the daunting awareness of what the sun's rise would bring. Departure.

Back to the States. Plucked from the missionary life, from the hearts of the people he'd grown to love as his own family. All thanks to the guerilla coup overrunning the villages. Island Hope Foundation had been given two days to clear off the small island. The U.S. Embassy had ordered them out immediately, or they would be abandoned to their own devices.

Leaving wasn't an option. When the notification came, Jonathan had talked with his wife, Kimber. They both agreed God had brought them here for a reason. Jonathan just hadn't figured out what that was yet.

But then IHF received the daunting news that if any of their team stayed and lost everything in an attack, their primary pockets in the States and Britain would wash their hands of the project. Sometimes, Peter Jordan had muttered over the webcam, God uses common sense as much as the divine. And to Peter, common sense was clearing out until things settled.

This would be a good time to pray. Jonathan let out a long sigh and closed his eyes. Mentally, he trained his mind to silence, preparing to set his cares and heart before the Lord. With another breath, he...slumped.

Pray. How could he? They'd come to one of the many small islands surrounding the larger island of Mindanao to stay, to make their home among the inhabitants and be a witness, a living testament to God's love. Now they were supposed to just walk out? Where was God in that?

Frustration pressed on him as he gazed over the lush tropical vegetation. The dull glow of the moon peeked through palm fronds waving under the tease of an ocean breeze. Kimber had given birth fifteen months ago to Maecel, the first of the children they hoped to have and raise on the island. This was home. Their home.

Jon rubbed his knuckles. *I don't understand, God.* He smirked and let out a soft snort. Wasn't that the way? Despite the Bible clearly stating the impossibility of comprehending the mind of God, humankind persisted in trying. So maybe man was essentially trying to drag God down to his level.

God in a box.

His heart twisted and knotted. *Forgive me, Lord.* He propped his forehead in his hand.

Snapping twigs drew him round.

Emerging from between two palms trunks, Kimber glided toward him. Even after four years of marriage, she still set his heart racing. "I thought I'd find you here," she whispered and drew closer.

"You should be in bed," he mumbled, turning back to the ocean glittering before them. "Is Maecel asleep?"

"Finally. Imee took over for me about an hour ago; you know how she loves Maecel."

"She's a good woman." A friend they'd made, and now God would tear them apart.

Kimber eased down on the stone sloping gently up behind him and pressed her soft form against his back. Arms wrapped around his waist, she rested against him. "God knows what He's doing, Jon."

Brushing his palms together, he nodded. "He always does." Still didn't make any sense. Rarely had since the guerilla uprisings. "We wanted to make our lives here."

Kimber sat quietly.

He'd always treasured her gift and ability to listen, to see beyond the surface. "Why would He send us out here then yank us back before we can get the orphanage built? Or stock the school?"

"I don't know," she mumbled.

Jon looked over his shoulder and eyed her. She sounded down—she was rarely down. "You okay?"

After a lengthy pause, she sighed. "I've wrestled with Him—with this relocation—long enough." The sparkling water reflected in her eyes. Eyes that pooled with tears.

Jon shifted on the rock and reached back for her. "Kim, what is it?"

Nuzzled into his shoulder, she cried.

She'd been his rock, his strength. Even when things had become tough, Kimber always remained steadfast. To have her trembling in his arms, to feel the fear he'd been battling shaking her body tore at everything in him. Jon gritted his teeth. He drove his gaze to the star-littered sky. *God, where are You in all this?*

Warm wetness soaked his shirt as his beloved clung to him. "I. . ." She shuddered, sniffling. "Why do I feel like I'm never going to see them again?"

"Shh." He stroked her soft blond hair. "We'll only be gone until this chaos settles. We'll return as soon as the U.S. okays it."

"But what if it's too late?"

He pulled back and cupped her face, peering into the dark eyes that had long captivated him. "You're the one who always tells me God is never late."

Head hung, she leaned into him. "I know. I'm not sure why I'm having such a hard time with this. Something just feels different."

He hated the worry lacing her words and face. Desperate to ease the tension, he changed the subject. "The last time you said that, you were pregnant."

She slapped his side playfully. "That is not the case this time, Jonathan Harris."

Shouts from the hidden path yanked them both to their feet. Instinctively, he tucked Kimber behind him, bracing himself. Had guerillas already found them? Was it too late for them? Was the only key to survival surrender?

"Jon! Jon!" Datu rushed from the bushes, his eyes wide and a fist clenching a machete. "You must come. Fast!"

Tension kinked Jon's muscles.

"Come. Hurry! They here." He shuffled back to the path and waved Jon with him.

Grabbing Kimber's hand, Jon followed the tribal chief's son up the winding path into the hills. "What is it?" he asked, using their ancient tongue.

"They kill many. Everywhere in village. Kill all. Hurry!"

The guerillas. After all these months, the guerillas had finally set upon the village? Jon broke into a sprint, darting around vines, shrubs, and bushes, his heart already engaged in the fight. He prayed, his heart seeking the courage of David in battle; his mind, the wisdom of Solomon.

Screams pierced the night. An odd thick haze swarmed through the bushes. *Fire!* Crackling trailed his realization, the sounds of the fire licking and no doubt consuming the bamboo huts.

Jon leaped over a large rock—the last barrier into the village. In that airborne second, he saw and heard a dozen armed gunmen snaking through the raised huts shouting.

Pop! Pop! Pop! Pop!

Gunfire punctured the chaos and stabbed into Jon's awareness as his feet skidded across the dirt path between two huts. He dropped to a low crouch, ducking behind a large basket. On his knees, he squinted under a hut toward the hub of the village.

A nightmare unveiled before him. Two men dragged Leili, a girl of no more than twelve, around a corner. She screamed and kicked, tears forming dark rivulets down her face. Jon's stomach churned—only to threaten to heave when he made out the still form of Leili's brother prostrated and. . .decapitated.

Jon jerked his gaze down. *Father!* Shouts pulled him out of his desperate cry. His heart leaped into his throat at the sight of a woman cowering under the powerful grip of a guerilla who aimed an AK-47 at her face. Imee!

Oh no. If that man had Imee, where was Maecel? At that instant, Imee locked eyes with him. And she darted a look toward the hut he'd shared with Kimber for the last two years. A burst of adrenaline shot through his veins at the hope that Maecel was still alive. Slithering around the large fire pit, he made his way toward his home. Less than twenty feet separated him from his daughter.

An infant's wail sliced through him.

Two gunmen swung around, AK-47s seemingly sniffing the air for the infant's scent.

Jon dove for cover as Maecel's cries shattered his careful approach. He scrabbled under a hut and worked his way to the other side, hoping the soldiers didn't see him. Dirt poofed into his face with each labored breath as he shimmied toward the steps and dragged himself halfway up the plank that formed a ramp into the hut. Amid the flurry of noises and scents, he peered into the darkened hut, past the thick smoke plumes from a nearby hut engulfed in flames. No soldiers. No Maecel. Nothing moved.

Oh, please no. They couldn't have found her. He dropped to his knees, the wood digging into his flesh. With his hands, he probed the blankets and simple furnishings for his plump daughter. Heavy breaths pounded his chest. Acrid odors filled his nostrils. His throat burned.

Maecel wailed. Near!

Where was she? He scampered to the far side, in the direction of her cries. There, in the oversized bassinet behind the rocking chair! He scurried to her writhing form beneath a small blanket.

As Jon scooped her into his arms, boards creaked behind him and a beam of light fractured the dark void. Someone had joined him.

Holding Maecel tight, Jon silently prayed as he turned. Two soldiers stood at the opening, machetes and AK-47s in hand. Another tramped up the plank, shouting.

One sneered at him, a rotted tooth mingling with the gray smoke. "Allah say kill all who will not convert."

CHAPTER 4

"Mangeni Zisero?" Sydney stood on the stoop of the row house, shivering even beneath the warmth of her thick wool coat.

An ebony-skinned woman nudged the door open. "Yes?"

"My name is Sydney Jacobs," she said, offering her hand. "I'm with the *Virginia Independent*."

"You very pretty."

"Uh. . .well, thank you. May I come in?"

Another woman wedged into the doorway. "She expected you to be mean and ugly. Most others have been interested in twisting the story to make those who helped her look bad." The woman crossed her arms and glared down at Sydney.

"I assure you, I am here for Mangeni's story. She said she wants to thank these men, so the first thing we need to do is get information about who they are, but to do that, I need details about the attack. When and where." Sydney smiled. "Can I come in?"

Without taking her brown eyes off Sydney, the woman spoke to Mangeni in a foreign tongue—Ugandan probably. Mangeni nodded and waved Sydney into the house.

Swirls of a heady scent assaulted her as she wove through the narrow hall and over worn carpet. *Thunk*. Her heel hit a bare patch where cement showed through. Sydney hugged herself, trying to avoid touching the walls, which looked as if they'd been greased recently. The noxious odor thickened as she moved farther into the house. Around a corner. Space tightened.

Mangeni stopped and smiled a true, heartfelt smile as she pointed through a doorway into a closet. "My home."

Holding her stomach, Sydney gazed at the cramped quarters. Not a closet, but a makeshift room. Pushed against the wall, a mattress laden with tattered blankets coddled two small, sleeping children, their dark skin standing out against the dingy, pale sheet. A lone chair sat in one corner with piles of clothes huddled around it.

Mangeni began speaking in her native tongue again.

A voice from behind Sydney gave the translation: "In my country, I have nothing. No home. No bed for my children. Only a space in a tent. Here, I have a room, electricity, water, a bed. Everything we need. God is good to me, yes?"

Sydney pushed her gaze to Mangeni's. She nodded. What else could she say? God was good—to some people. Not to her, but that was another matter altogether.

"The children, they will not remember the war. I am glad. Their father was murdered. I thought me and the little ones would die next, but the men came."

Struggling to maintain her concentration with the pungent odor accosting her, Sydney rubbed her forehead. "How many were there?" She dug through her purse, tugged out the digital voice recorder, and turned it on. "How many soldiers?"

Mangeni shrugged. "Six, maybe ten."

"That's all?" Why hadn't there been more? With such small numbers, she guessed the team to have been special ops. Who else would brave such danger with so few?

Her mind darted to Max and his work with the SEALs. The ache still felt raw. And now—

No. She just couldn't go there. Couldn't consider the possibility.

It's more than a possibility.

"Um. . ." Sydney looked at her notes. Where was she? "I. . . you. . .when did this take place?"

"In October," the other woman answered. "She came to America just before Halloween."

Just in time for the debut of the For Human Sake column. "So the incident was about a month ago?" A cold wave of nausea pressed Sydney against the wall as she scribbled down the information. She supported herself, determined not to show how awful she felt. "What did these men look like?"

Wide, dark eyes held hers. "Soldiers." Mangeni's hand rested on her arm. "You sick?"

Sydney shook her head. "No, I'm fine." But she'd be a lot better if she could escape the odor permeating this house and her senses. She backed out of the room, only to have another wave hit her. What was it? She glanced toward the kitchen and saw a pot on the stove, steam pouring out. Discreetly, she wiped her nose, trying to shield it.

Her stomach roiled. Churned. She was going to be sick if she didn't leave now. "Thank you for your time. I'll see what I can find and call you."

After hurried thanks and good-byes, she rushed into the crisp night air. She hauled in a deep breath. Light spilled from the front door onto the path. They were watching. She pushed herself to her SUV, climbed in, and started the engine. Music roared to life along with the heater. She flipped it off and opened the window. Cool air raced around her.

They were still watching. She had to get moving. She pulled away from the house, drove down the street, and yanked into the first parking lot she could find before she lost it. Forehead against the steering wheel, she blew out a thick breath from puffed cheeks. What had happened back there?

That was a question she didn't need to ask. She knew the answer.

Please, God. Don't let this be. . . . Not this. Please.

Tears streamed down her face. Two days before Thanksgiving, and she had only pain and heartache.

Just let me know You're there. That it'll be okay.

Her phone rang.

Wiping her tears, she fumbled through her purse until she wrapped her fingers around the device. "Hello?"

"Hi, sweetie. Where are you?"

Mom. Sydney cleared her throat. "Uh. . ." She glanced at the building in front of her. A church. "I. . .uh, I had an interview in Richmond."

Light sparkled through the stained-glass windows of the church with a warm, cozy glow as if the colorful panes had a life all their own. Heat speared her heart when her gaze hit one in particular. Jesus. Words etched at His feet read, "Lo, I am with you always."

She snatched the thin thread of hope. How she'd ached for this—to know God was still there. That He loved her. Hope lit anew.

"How long before you get home?"

She shifted into drive and eased her car into traffic, peering into the rearview mirror, once again looking at the stained-glass window. *Thank You, Lord.* "I'm on my way, so about a half hour. Why? What's up?"

"Nothing." The pitch in her mother's reply betrayed her.

"Mom, come on. I know you. What's going on?"

"I just hadn't heard from you, so I was worried."

"Did you need something? Should I stop by your house on the way home? Or the store?"

"No, no. Just come home. I'm here cooking the pies."

Sydney's pulse raced. "You're at my house?"

"Mm-hmm."

That meant— Oh no. Had she really left it out in the open?

She wasn't ready to deal with this. She'd wanted time. "I'll be home soon." She hung up. Sweat coated her palms. She smeared them along her slacks. Every mile, every minute weighted her courage, dragging her into a deep, dark sea of despair.

The stained-glass window rushed into her thoughts. She gripped the thread of hope tighter and turned onto Willow Drive. She slowed at the vehicle out front. A red F-250.

Dread plunked into her stomach. Her mother *had* found the box. That was the only reason her brother would arrive early for Thanksgiving dinner with the family. Parked in the driveway, she stared at the house.

Mom, Bryce, his wife and daughters. . .and the little box in the bathroom.

"I can't do this."

Flickering light from the porch snagged her attention. The front door opened. Bright light spilled across the paved sidewalk. Max's pride and joy. He'd spent an entire weekend on that brick-lined path.

There was so much of him still here.

Broad and muscular, Bryce stepped onto the porch, his hands tucked in the front pockets of his jeans. Just seeing her brother. . .

She tilted her head and fought the swell of tears. Maybe, just maybe, they *hadn't* found the box. Maybe her secret was safe. The hope pushed her out of the SUV.

Huddled against the cold, she hurried to her brother. "What're you doing here so early? What a great surprise!" She threw herself into his arms and hugged him. She'd be fine as long as she didn't look into his blue eyes.

"Vic and I wanted to see you. See how you're doing."

"Aw, you're too sweet." Okay, that felt convincing. Was he buying it? She grabbed the screen door handle and whisked it open. "Let's get inside before we freeze to death."

In the dining room, Sydney dumped her purse and keys on the table. A bubbly three-year-old's voice drifted from the back den. "Hey, wow! Is Libby talking that much already?" She smiled at Bryce, but her heart caught.

Somber blue eyes watched her, steady and sympathetic.

Her smile faltered. "I can't wait to see her." Without another word or the chance to fall apart at the seams, she started for the den.

He caught her arm. "Syd."

Her eyes shuttered closed. "Please, Bryce. It's been a rotten year. I want to have a nice Thanksgiving. Okay?"

"You can't ignore it forever."

Was he talking about the divorce or the box? She eyed him. "Ignore what?"

"We know." He stepped closer. "Mom found it when she came over to prep for tomorrow's dinner."

Footsteps shuffled behind her.

Although she wanted to yell at them for invading her privacy, Sydney knew the anger swirling through her stomach wasn't aimed at her family, but at the deep pain and unfairness of life. "I...I didn't look at it." Her vision blurred beneath the tears. "The thought of it." She sniffled. "I couldn't even read the results."

He hugged her. Kissed the top of her head. "It's positive."

She moaned, grateful for his strength. "Why would God let this happen now? We were married almost six years! Why did he wait until Max was gone?"

"So, it is Max's?"

Sydney jerked out of his hold, affronted. "What? Of course it's his! What kind of question is that?"

"That's not what I meant. It's just that your marriage has been rocky for the last couple of years, especially the last six months. I wasn't—didn't think you'd been intimate with him."

"He's my husband. I love him." Defiance flashed through her

chest. "The only reason I filed is because you made me."

Bryce's brow furrowed. "You filed because Max wasn't ready to get help and you didn't want to end up dead."

"He would never do that, and you know it!" Heart slamming against her indignation, she stomped into the kitchen. "You've never liked Max."

"This goes beyond liking, Sydney." Her brother followed her, rapping his knuckles against the counter. "He's out of control and isn't dealing with the trauma he endured in combat. He hit you!"

She whirled around. "He hit me because I tried to interrupt a fight. He's a trained, skilled fighter. I might as well have stepped in front of a weapon he was firing. It was *my* mistake."

Sadness clung to his shadowed face. "Domestic abuse victims rarely blame the abuser."

Her hand flew out and struck his cheek before she had time to stop it. She covered her mouth, stifling the tears and fury.

"For pity's sake, you two!" Her mother came around the counter from the den. "You'll wake Madison." She shifted her attention to Sydney. Her shoulders drooped and her expression oozed sympathy. She held out her arms.

Sydney rushed into the hug. Face buried in her mother's shoulder, she let loose the tears she'd held captive. Real tears. Gut-birthed and wracking. Not the trickling tears that had been more like letting off steam. As she cried, her mother led her to the sofa.

"Auntie Sydney, are you okay?"

Sydney wiped her cheek and found little Libby staring at her with those large, round blue eyes. She swept her hand over her niece's porcelain face and smiled through blurry vision. "Yeah, baby." She gulped at the endearment that suddenly held new meaning. "I'm okay."

Bryce lifted his daughter and passed her over to Victoria, who hustled the little one out of the room. He then joined them, sitting on the coffee table in front of her. "I'm sorry. I've been pushing you to leave Max, but I should've been supporting you. Period."

She twisted a loose thread of her coat around her finger.

"We're here for you. Whatever it takes. If you want me to move back here, Vic and I talked, and we'll do it."

She smiled and shook her head. "That's not realistic, and you know it."

"Doesn't matter. Family sticks together." He rubbed the top of his knuckles, his gaze surfing the carpet. "Does Max know—"

"No." Sydney's breath caught in her throat. "I'm not going to tell him."

"Syd—"

"I don't want him coming back without real change. If he came back now, it'd be for the baby, but how long would that last? It'd be for the wrong reason."

"I don't want him near you again. Not after the way he assaulted you!" Her mother's voice pitched. "You have more than just yourself to protect now."

"Mom, he didn't assault me."

"A right cross into your face is assault," Bryce challenged.

"It was an accident! He was fighting with Lane, and I tried to stop him." If only they could've seen the mortified expression on Max's face.

Bryce fell silent, but his eyes screamed at her. "I still think he has a right to know about this. You'll want child support and alimony."

Sydney's heart broke. "Please." She swallowed the grief and tears. "Just let me handle it."

"He'll be ticked that you didn't tell him." He looked at her stomach. "How far along do you think you are?"

She gave a light snort. "I can tell you the very night I conceived." The day Max returned from his last tour of duty. "Almost four months."

"You'll be showing soon, so you'll need to be prepared for when he finds out."

"Well, he's gone. He said he has a job that has him traveling." She wiped her nose with the tissue her mother pressed into her hand. "I don't need Max here to have his baby."

CHAPTER 5

A *whistle rent the night.*

Max ducked, his M4 held close as his gaze swept the field before him.

Boom!

He flew into the dirt face first, the concussion scraping him over the ground. Scrambling for safety, he spit dirt and mud.

"Eagle One, request immediate evac. Taking heavy fire."

Turning, Max searched for his teammate radioing for the extraction. Thick smoke clouded his view. Flames danced along a thatched room, quickly consuming the small hut shielded beyond the smoke. Arm covering his mouth and nose, he coughed.

What was that? He'd heard something. . . .

He squinted. Blinked through the gritty air. His eyes watered.

Again, the noise teased the air. It sounded like a child.

There aren't any children here, *he thought.*

A scream.

Max jogged forward, tugging his bandana over his face, leaving his eyes to suffer the torched atmosphere. "Where are you?" With several deep breaths, he pumped his lungs full of air and rushed into the burning hut.

A shadow scampered into the corner.

He reached out across the open area and clutched a limb. Pulled. The child came easily. They had to get out of here before the next assault. "Come on," he urged the child. But when he looked down...

Max leaped back. Dropped the limb. Only a limb.

He jerked awake. Sweat drenched his pounding chest. He raked a hand through his hair.

"You okay?"

Max blinked. A sidelong glance told him Cowboy had seen everything. "Yeah." His gaze skated down the line of men waiting in the hangar for the chopper. The others chatted or slept. Nobody else seemed to have noticed. "How much longer?"

"About fifteen."

The rumble of the chopper vibrated through his boots. Max's hand slid over his right leg pocket where he felt the curling edges of the photo through the material. Still there. Comfort wound around his heart.

But *she* was gone. For good.

Elbow propped on his knee, he cupped his forehead. With Christmas only two weeks away, he had nobody and nothing to come home to.

"Got your new bike yet?"

"No," Max said, straightening. "It's getting carbon-fibered."

Cowboy cocked his head. "Come again?"

"Carbon fiber—changing some of the fiberglass out for lighter, stronger material."

Deep and taunting, Cowboy's laugh seeped past the heavy drone of the rotors. "Speed."

"What else?"

"Bet that's expensive."

Max shrugged.

"I suppose you don't have any other financial obligations. Like child support or alimony." Cowboy tugged off the rag from his sweat-laden hair.

"Not yet." But he would once the attorneys finished the paper-work. He'd instructed his lawyer to let Sydney have whatever she wanted. He didn't need it. This was his fault anyway. Let her have the entire paycheck if she asked.

The chopper arrived, and the guys loaded up. Max tried to shake off the dreams and prying curiosity of Cowboy. Soon the noticeable descent of the helo seemed to rouse everyone. All glad to be home—in one piece. Gently the wheels touched down. Nightshade disembarked and headed into the hangar.

Showered and changed, Max stored his weapons and tactical gear in the below-ground locker and spun the dial. He stuffed his clothes and dirty duds into his duffel then donned his leather jacket. As he yanked the zipper, he remembered the small gift nestled at the bottom of his sack. He paused and reached into the bag. Drew out the box. He flipped the lid, a smile sneaking into his face at the sight of the pendant.

He hung his head. Threw a hard right into the metal door.

The loud bang crackled through the locker room.

Max ground his teeth. *Your anger is out of control*, she'd said. She was right. But he just couldn't touch that vault unless he wanted to unleash the demons of his past. He'd seen and done too much. Lost everything.

"Let's grab dinner at Jolly's Tavern." The Kid buttoned his shirt as he glanced around.

"I'm outta here." Pack slung over his shoulder, Max started the two-mile hike to his apartment. If he could call it that. With only a cot and a lawn chair, it wasn't much. He didn't care.

The throaty rattle of a diesel rumbled behind him.

He glanced back.

The truck slowed, and the window slid down. "Wanna ride?" A wide-brimmed Stetson concealed Cowboy's eyes. "Unless you're a glutton for punishment."

"I joined Nightshade, didn't I?"

"That you did."

"Look, man," Max mumbled, glancing down the ice-slicked road. "I appreciate the offer, but I'd be miserable company."

Cowboy smiled. "Misery loves company, right?"

What was it about this Cowboy? Didn't he get the message? Then again, there was something about him that made Max want to reconsider the offer. The gift in his bag seemed to burn against his back. Maybe. . .

He grabbed the handle and tugged open the door. "Could you give me a lift somewhere?"

"I think you missed the point, Frogman. That's what I offered."

Settling into the passenger seat, Max shifted. "Not my apartment. I want to check on something."

Just as Cowboy steered away from the curb, a black SUV ripped past them, horn blaring.

"Griffin has entirely too much enthusiasm after a mission and this late at night." Cowboy eased his truck into traffic. "So, what happened to your marriage?"

Max stole a glance at the thick-chested man. He didn't mince words. Then again, that was the way with spec ops guys. You lived and died together. No secrets. "I screwed it up."

For a moment, Cowboy didn't respond. Then, "I understand."

"Yeah?"

"I have a three-year-old daughter."

Curiosity piqued in Max. "You were married?" He motioned out the widow. "Take the next right."

"Nah, had a head bigger than a bale of hay. Thought I was too good for everyone." With his wrist hooked over the steering wheel, Cowboy pulled up to the light. He guided his truck around the turn. "I was in the service by the time I knew about her pregnancy. Then my girlfriend took off with another man shortly after McKenna's birth. They found Meredith a month later, overdosed in a motel five miles north of the Texas-Mexico border."

"Tough break." He pointed out the streets as they wove through town.

"Yeah, I'm doing Nightshade because it allows more time with McKenna. I missed the first three years of her life; don't plan to miss many more."

"I thought your family was in Texas."

"My folks picked up and moved out here this summer. Left Humble to start over." Cowboy grinned. "Bought some farmland."

Max gave a slight nod—but his gaze shot to the row of houses on the right. Mentally measuring out the distance between the road and the front door as the big truck slid past the home he'd bought with Sydney, the house they'd shared four of their married years, he tried to steady his breathing. He was far enough out, wasn't he? This couldn't be considered a violation of the protective order, could it?

Agitation wound tightly through his gut. Protective order. Against him. He hated himself for that night. She'd done the right thing. He didn't deserve mercy for hurting the very person he was supposed to protect.

Lights flicked on in the living room.

His heart hiccupped. Four months. He ached for what he'd lost. For what he'd done. His mind cranked through a laundry list of things he'd never have with her again. Dinner. A movie. Endless rounds of Uno with more laughter than points.

What have I done? Why did he let things get so out of hand?

Cowboy eyed him. "Love covers a multitude of sins."

The words carved a long line through his heart. "Not in my life."

Icy blackness spread a sheen across the roads. Olin clutched the collar of his wool overcoat tighter as he left the comfort of his car and slipped into the rear passenger seat of the waiting Suburban. Warmth bathed him in a cozy embrace.

The dome light between the two front seats cast a spotlight on the tan leather interior. A manila folder slid toward him. A new mission. He wanted to grin. Instead, he maintained his stiff facade and took the folder. As he perused the contents, pleasure coursed through him with the knowledge that his brainchild had become the new government pet. "I take it Nightshade exceeded your expectations?" He flipped a page and eyed the details. "What's the timetable?"

"One week."

He cast a glance at the chairman. "Our fees increase with the difficulty of this mission."

"You're already bleeding me dry." The chairman tapped the paperwork. "If Nightshade can eliminate this problem, then my expectations *will* be exceeded."

"I have a feeling you won't ever admit to being impressed."

"I don't need to explain to you the delicate nature of this scenario. The political backdrop and repercussions are enormous. Nobody will touch it."

A grin split Olin's lips. "Nightshade loves a challenge."

He looked good. He always had.

Sydney's stomach twisted as Max entered the conference room with his attorney and a man in dark jeans and a white button-down, a black Stetson clutched in one hand. Dressed in his typical black leather jacket and jeans, Max hung back, his gaze never meeting hers. But she could tell he wasn't the vibrant man she'd fallen in love with seven years ago. The downturned lips and dark rings under his eyes bore witness to the many nights he'd had bad dreams. Nightmares. Ones he refused to talk about or get help with. How she ached to know what ate her husband up from the inside out.

She lowered her head. Should she offer him another chance?

"You okay?" Bryce's whispered words skated into her indecisiveness as he wrapped an arm around her.

Sydney nodded and cleared her throat. Her brother had insisted on coming for "moral support." Really, she knew he wanted to pummel Max. But in her grapple for courage and strength, she'd relented.

"Mr. Fielding, thank you for coming and bringing your client," her attorney, Jonas Whittier, said as he shook hands with Max's lawyer.

Seated on one side of the long conference table, Sydney smoothed her hands down her slacks and watched as her husband and the other two men took their seats. She twisted the ring on her finger. Her wedding ring. By the laws of the state of Virginia, she was still married to Max and would be for another ten months. Unlike some states, the divorce petition wouldn't be filed until after a year's separation.

"As we're all aware, we are here to work out the details of the marital separation agreement." Jonas drew out two copies of the trial MSA they'd drafted yesterday and slid them to Max and his lawyer.

Mr. Fielding snatched it from the table, his eyes darting over the information as if greedily devouring the requests.

Would they fight her over the alimony and other financial points? Money had always been a sore point with Max.

"I think my client and I will need time to discuss this," Mr. Fielding said as he flipped to the second page, then the third. Finally, he glanced at Mr. White over the paper. "You sincerely expect my client to pay all of this?"

Sydney glanced toward Max—and their gazes collided. Unyielding. Strong. Warmth swished through her stomach.

Her lawyer removed his glasses. "What we've asked for is reasonable and—"

"I'll sign it," Max said without breaking eye contact. Sitting to the left and leaning toward his friend, he roughed a hand over his jaw then let his gaze drop.

Silence devoured the room. Sydney looked from one attorney to another.

His attorney argued. "Now, Mr. Jacobs, I don't think—"

"I said I'll sign it." Max grabbed a pen and dragged the MSA closer.

Mr. Fielding yanked the papers up before ink met paper. "I'd like a moment with my client."

Tension flooded Max's face.

Sydney swallowed. Would he fight his own lawyer?

"There's nothing to discuss," Max groused. For a moment, he held her gaze. "Sydney's never done me wrong. If she thinks this is fair, then it's done. I want her taken care of."

"Then why didn't you do something sooner?" Bryce asked.

Max glared at her brother. "I see you're speaking for her again."

Bryce was on his feet.

So was Max.

Heart in her throat, Sydney yanked her brother's arm. "Bryce, sit down!"

The cowboy rose, bent toward Max, and whispered something in his ear. Almost instantly, Max's clouded expression lightened, and he returned to his chair. Attention back on the MSA, he scribbled his signature then slapped the pen down. He looked to Mr. Whittier. "Anything else I need to sign?"

How like Max to walk in and take control. Yet she wondered at this turn. He wanted her taken care of—sure, he'd always taken care of her. *The best for my girl,* he'd said time and again. But was it that, or was he so anxious to be divorced from her? Did he already have a girlfriend ready to take her place?

Maybe it was good that she hadn't told him about the baby. Their baby.

"Uh. . ." Mr. Whittier paused as he perused his files. "No, no, I don't think so. That's it—for now." He peeked at Sydney, his face stricken. Clearly he'd never dealt with a man so used to getting his way or maintaining control.

Max shoved to his feet. "Then we're through here." His dark eyes bore into hers. "Merry Christmas, Sydney." He pivoted and stormed out the door with his friend.

Before she could stop herself, Sydney rushed after him. "Max, wait!"

"Sydney, no. Don't," Bryce called from behind.

As she hurried around the corner, she could only pray Max didn't notice the slight curve to her stomach. "Max, please wait." Her voice seemed to echo down the hall, chasing him to the exit, where he hesitated.

She strode past the big cowboy, who'd paused and stepped back, and stood before her husband. "Max. . ." She hung her head. Could she tell him about their baby? She wanted to with everything in her. But she'd also wanted their marriage to work. Wishful thinking.

"I should go," he said, his voice low. And husky.

"I—" She slowly raised her head and gazed into the licorice eyes that always seemed a mirror of her own soul. Tears burned the back of her eyes. "I never wanted this."

"Then why are we here?" The question wasn't sharp or accusing, but probing and filled with more pain than she'd ever heard in his voice.

She squeezed closed the thin crack in her defenses and swallowed. "Max. . ."

His hand swept her cheek. "I'll always love you."

"Then get help and bring back the man I love."

He patted his chest, the leather making a poofing sound. "*This* is who I am, Sydney. You didn't have a problem with me when we got married." His brow dug toward those dark depths. Stubble lined his jaw and mouth.

Why had she hoped—even tried to talk to him? It was always the same. He argued this was how he was, that she didn't have a problem with things until her brother got involved. "You've changed, Max. For the worse. There was a day you never would've hit a man who was helping me."

His gaze hardened. Lips flat-lined, like her heart. "He stepped in where he didn't belong."

Staring at each other, neither moved. She saw some of her own haunting torment in his eyes. Maybe if she just told him, that would be the tipping point. "I'm—"

"Time to go, partner." The man behind him patted Max's shoulder.

Max tore his gaze from hers and walked out the door.

She looked down. Then hung her head, cupping her face in her hands. Tears welled up again, this time rising over her barriers and spilling down her cheeks.

Familiar, warm arms embraced her.

"I just wanted things to be different, for *him* to be different." She slumped into Bryce's arms. "I wanted to tell him about our baby."

"This is why I insisted you file. Even the baby won't change him. He's too set in his ways."

She pulled out of his hug. She didn't need Bryce's lectures anymore. Didn't need to hear that her husband was too self-absorbed to see the damage he inflicted on their marriage. And most importantly, she didn't want to deal with the fact she was about to become a single mother.

A blur of white slid past the glass doors. Max's friend.

Her heart skipped a beat.

Had he heard her talk—about the baby?

DAY ONE

"Thou shalt have no other gods before me." Jon's heart thumped as if in cadence with the staccato firing of a nearby weapon. A courage he hadn't known he possessed rose up within him with a ferocity that surprised even him. These men probably didn't even know the verse. But he was pretty sure by the darkening expressions that they got the point.

The shorter of the three stepped forward and raised the weapon, his brow knotting. "We will test your God." He snickered. "He raise you from the dead?"

Jon tensed and tightened his hold on Maecel, who protested with a squeak. His mind danced to Shadrach, Meshach, and Abednego. "He is more than able, but if He does not, I will not bow."

Malice deepened in the man's face. "You make you choice." He seemed to be enjoying it as he peered down the muzzle.

The faint movement of his finger to the trigger well pooled acid at the back of Jon's throat. Is this why God had sent him here? To die? How many times had he prayed *Not my will, but Yours, Lord?* But the words were easier spoken than standing here with palms almost too slick to maintain his grasp on the bright-eyed daughter God had blessed him with.

Thud! Thud!

The two men who flanked the third dropped like dead weights—right out of the hut. The third spun, and met the solid right cross of Datu.

"Hurry!" Datu leaped down and rushed around the side.

It took a split second for Jon to gather his wits. Then he grabbed his sat phone and backpack they kept ready for emergencies and darted after the man. His feet had no sooner touched the ground than shouts erupted.

Bullets whizzed past him, the pungent smell of cordite bleeding into the air. He zigzagged into the dense jungle, searching through the branches and trees for sign of the chief's son and Kimber. The late hour and smoke made it next to impossible to see more than a few feet ahead. Chest heaving, he tried to listen over Maecel's whining to decipher which direction to take. He *shh*ed his daughter, knowing better than to stop moving lest he end up with a bullet or machete blade in his back.

Voices skated into the darkness ahead. He aimed in that direction, ducking under low-lying branches and climbing over fallen trees. Minutes later, he met up with Datu.

Kimber rushed to him, tears streaming down her cheeks. "He wouldn't let me go into the village. I was praying so hard! And then when he brought her, I couldn't leave."

"Her? Brought who?"

Her frantic barrage of partially slurred words slid over his mind, dousing him in confusion. With both his daughter and wife wrapped securely in his arms, he whispered a quick prayer of thanks for their safety. Kimber kissed Maecel, who finally puckered her lower lip, then burst into tears and lunged for her mother.

"You help," Datu said, motioning to something behind a log.

After handing Maecel off to Kimber, John strode toward the man—and stopped cold. A young girl sat huddled on the forest floor, arms hugging her knees as she rocked. Tattered clothes hung from her petite frame. Ebony hair dumped over her shoulders, concealing her face in shadows—but still, the bruises screamed.

When Jon reached to brush aside her hair to assess her injuries, she yelped and jerked away.

Datu rattled off something in Tagalog, his voice and demeanor nervous, but pleading and urgent. "She the one. They rape, beat her. She escape." He squatted before the girl. "This Jon. He good man."

Sniffling and shaking, the girl dragged her gaze to Jon. "You're a Christian, yes?" she asked, her words colored with typical smatterings of a Filipino accent.

Surprised by her near-perfect English, Jon knelt and casually inspected her injuries. "That's right," he mumbled, scanning her face. "You know English. How?" The darkness worked against him, shielding her in the black void of night. Her right eye looked nearly swollen shut. Blood glistened on her lower lip, probably still bleeding because of her crying.

"My father is a missionary, like you. They. . ." A sob wracked her, and she burrowed in on herself, once again rocking. Eventually, she raised a battered hand to her lip and winced. "They butchered him! Then they did things. . .and killed my mother and sisters." Anger bit an edge into her broken words. "I should be dead, too. I should be dead!"

Jon touched her smooth olive skin, now bruised and marred, feeling the stickiness of the drying blood against his palm. "God saw fit to keep you alive. And I'll do my best to make sure you have time to figure out why."

"We go, meet others at safe place." Datu prodded. "Her leg broke. You carry?"

Jon looked at the girl again, wondering if she'd panic at his touch. It was the most reasonable choice to have him carry her. Datu bore the short stature of his people. And Jon, blessed to be from a line of long-legged ancestors, had height and strength on his side. He bent closer to her. "What is your name?"

She regarded him again with those dark, penetrating eyes. So like Kimber's. "Kezia."

"Okay, Kezia," he said softly, shifting to a better posture and for balance. "I'm going to lift you. I don't want to hurt you any more than you've already been hurt. Is anything else broke?"

Tears swam in her eyes as she shook her head and lowered her gaze.

Crack! Crack!

The nearby sound of gunfire swirled adrenaline through Jon's limbs. He slid his hands under her and hoisted her up, tensing when she whimpered again. He turned, and Datu guided them uphill. Staying off the cut path, the group would have a better chance of avoiding the guerillas. But they'd also have a better chance of encountering other unfriendly life forms—snakes, venomous critters, and the often irritable lemurs.

An hour into their trek, they came upon a small creek rushing over rocks and trees. Datu stopped, glanced around, then sloshed through the water and toward a gathering of large boulders.

Jon, lifting Kezia above the fast-moving water, worked his way across with Kimber's guidance and help. Together they stood on dry land—and froze.

"Where'd he go?" Kimber drew closer and gripped his arm.

Tension balled in the pit of his gut as he searched the shoreline for sign of the chief's son. "I don't know." He squinted, hoping to see through the darkness, but only shadows and the gurgling sounds of the creek came to him.

Then a shadow rose up out of the rocks like a specter.

Jon's heart sped.

"This way," Datu hissed. "Hurry!"

Sucking up the frantic chill that darted through him, Jon nodded, urging Kimber ahead of him. "Go." They climbed over the rocks, Jon ever so careful with his wounded charge. Only as he crested the last large boulder did he see the darker-than-dark void amid the cluster. A cave!

He crouched and waddled into the darkness. But the deeper he maneuvered into the cave, the brighter it grew.

"There's light ahead," Kimber whispered.

A man's face appeared. Then another. Jon recognized some of the men as belonging to Datu's clan. A few, however, were not familiar. Where had they come from? Four came toward him and motioned to the girl. Kezia whimpered and snuggled into his hold.

"Over here." Datu stood over a blanket where another man waited with what looked like a medical kit.

Jon delivered her safely to the blanket and set her down. When he straightened, he gaped, unbelieving that he could stretch to his full six-foot-two height. Portions of the ceiling were charred, apparently from pit fires. How long had this cave been used as a place of refuge?

The doctor crouched over the girl, probing her side and leg.

Kezia's eyes darted to the ceiling, and even from a distance, Jon saw her trembling chin and moved closer. He eased himself into her line of sight. "It'll be okay, Kezia."

Black and swimming in tears, her eyes begged for hope.

"Back, back!" the doctor groused.

When Jon obeyed and scooted away, Kezia cried out, "Don't leave me!"

Her words, strangled by her tears, stilled him. "I'm not going anywhere, Kezia. I'm here. I won't leave you."

As torches flickered nearby, the light revealed the extent of her injuries. A jagged, bloody line stretched from her chin to her ear, where the lower portion of the lobe had been sliced off. In his periphery, Jon saw the doctor reaching for her leg.

Kezia screamed—then went limp.

Jon's heart seized. Soft cries behind him yanked him back to reality. His wife. He stumbled over to Kimber, where she huddled in a corner with Maecel. He slid along the stone wall to the ground, pulling his girls into his arms. Holding them seemed the only normal thing he had left. He kissed the top of Kimber's ash-covered head, his eyes on the frail girl who'd survived atrocities no human should experience.

Father. . .why?

Once Kezia's leg was set and her face stitched, the doctor shifted and nodded to him, as if saying all would be well.

"*Salamat.*" Jon whispered his thanks, careful not to disturb his daughter, now sleeping in Kimber's arms. Gaze fixed on the young girl, he did not want to relax despite the good prognosis. He must keep vigil, keep his promise to be there for her. Yet his eyes drooped, heavier than the rocks surrounding them. Sleep claimed him greedily. Fleeting, frightening images darted through his dreams. Screams, the glint of machetes, blood dripping like a waterfall. Abu Sayyaf soldiers—both terrifying and wicked. One leaning over Kezia as she slept in a pain-induced coma.

Jon jolted awake—then flung his arm up against the shadow looming over him.

Datu hovered. "We talk."

Extricating himself from Kim, who was propped against him, Jon yawned. Head tucked so as not to graze his thick skull on the sloping ceiling, he joined Datu beside a small table. A woman handed him a ladle of liquid. He thanked her in Tagalog and sipped it.

"Kezia see General Mauk."

The ladle wobbled, water sloshing over the lip as Jon stared at Datu. "Mauk? How? Where did she see him?"

"He hurt her. Try to kill her."

A cold chill darted across his shoulders. "You realize. . ." Jon couldn't say it, couldn't give breath to the unspeakable things Mauk would do to a girl like Kezia.

"Yes. She Christian. They no want her talk."

A girl with firsthand knowledge of the atrocities the guerillas perpetrated against the villagers was a mouth that could potentially bring them down completely if she'd seen something powerful—and gruesome—enough. No guerilla would tolerate that. Especially not a Christian witness.

To silence the voice of hope, the evil one would do anything, including slaughtering an entire village. All because missionaries wanted to bring hope and love, God's love. Missionaries. Him. Everyone knew the truth about what the guerillas did. But knowing and proving it were two different things. And stopping it was nearly unfathomable. This was the last thing they needed. Mauk and his mercenaries would hunt her down and kill without regard. Their being Americans only increased the pleasure with which Mauk would kill Jon, Kimber, and Maecel, for not only helping her but for their very existence on an island Mauk sought to control.

"We climb hill." He trudged through the cave, motioning Jon to follow as he moved into the open.

"Hill?" Jon tensed, his gaze skipping upward, taking in the thick cluster of trees that blended into one mind-bending blur of green. Up the hill meant heading straight into the dark heart of the area. "Isn't that where the *Higanti* live?"

Datu blinked, startled. His determination slipped back into place quickly. "No, we no go there. Just up. . .hill."

Kimber joined him, cradling Maecel. They shared a nervous glance.

"Come. Hurry, they follow." Datu pointed behind them, and sure enough, Jon saw the forceful swaying of branches as the radicals climbed after them.

Still, his mind wasn't settled. The Higanti warriors were nested deep in the jungle, building their forces to exact revenge against the radicals and take back land that had been stolen from them. The plan unseated what little of Jon's confidence remained that they'd get out alive. Fiercely loyal and brilliant in fighting, the Higanti were not to be trifled with. Mighty fighters. Strong-bodied, despite being short.

They were a small clan on the island. But they were also the only clan who'd mustered enough anger and determination to fight Mauk once before. The world had considered the battle a civil war and had ignored both it and the Higantis' plea for assistance. Not an official tribe, they did not even gain the ear of their own government. Thus they fought with rage and hated Mauk and his militia.

There was just one problem.

The Higanti hated Christian missionaries more.

CHAPTER 6

Something was wrong. Max stared out the side window, his thoughts on the conversation at the attorney's office. Syd's voice...he played her words and intonations over in his mind. He detected stress. But there was something else. And her eyes—

"You okay?"

"Yeah. Sure." Max's gaze bounced from the rain-mottled window to Cowboy—but not even all the way before flipping back to the street puddles and what happened at the MSA meeting.

Was she hiding something? No. One thing he could say about her in all their years of marriage: Syd had always been forthright. He rubbed his knuckles over his lips. What was going on? The balance in that room had tipped, and not just because it was a divorce meeting.

He let himself wonder what their lives would be like without all the problems, without the anger and arguing. Would they be a regular *Leave It to Beaver* family? Maybe have kids and live happily ever after? She'd always wanted a baby, but he'd reasoned against it, especially with his job taking him away so often. Maybe he should've gone easier on that.

"Here we are."

Max tensed. Had they already made it to his apartment? He blinked and cleared his throat. "Thanks for the ride." He grabbed the handle and pushed on the door.

"Hey."

With a glance back, he slid from the cab.

"You need company tonight?"

The comment hit Max sideways. He didn't need anything. Isn't that what he'd always said? He was a SEAL. He could take care of himself and an entire platoon. "I'm good."

Uncertainty lurked in Cowboy's eyes.

"Night." Max slammed the door before the guy could start the spiel he felt coming on. He trudged across the parking lot to the front door. Pulling the key from his pocket, he once again felt a familiar weight encircle him. Breathing became a chore. He looked at the door, the brass numbers tacked into the faded paint, slightly off-center. Like his life. Why bother going in? He was alone with his latest purchase—a single mattress that he'd pushed against the wall in the efficiency. The TV was propped on the kitchen counter right in front of the mini microwave. The dingy room might as well be a padded cell for all the good it did him.

Forget it. He needed white noise. Crazy noise. He spun and crossed the lawn to the storage building he'd rented as a garage. Within minutes, he streaked down the rain-slicked roads on his bike. Up one side, down the other. Searching. . .for something. Whatever it was, he'd know it when he found it. Or when it found him.

But all he found in the next hour was aggravation and damp pant legs. He wove into a gas station and ripped off his helmet. As the tank filled, he leaned against the frame, arms crossed over his chest. Once again, his mind wandered back to the meeting. Was that moment the final rivet in the steel trap of their marriage? He had to accept it, right? Their marriage ended. She was gone. Really, truly gone.

You could've stopped this.

He shifted off the bike and finished pumping. Key stuffed in the ignition, he reached for the handles—

Laughter burst out at him, snapping his gaze to a three-story brick building across the street. A couple swaggered from the entrance, arms wrapped around each other, their merriment skidding over the road and into his chest like the bullets of an AK-47. Every staccato note a thump against his pride. He'd been happy like that once.

He swallowed. Glanced back at the building and the sign hanging over the door. FOOLS GOLD. He'd fit right in.

No. Bad idea.

Cranking the engine, he looked back. What would it hurt? He let the engine rip and aimed the bike to the opposite side, where he parked. Helmet under his arm, he leaped off. He hustled to the door and pocketed the key to his Hayabusa in his leather jacket.

Dim lighting danced over a haze of smoke circling the interior. Clinking and more laughter filtered into his awareness as he scanned the split-level bar. An upper balcony area sported a pool table, video games, vinyl chairs, and a dart board. In the center of the lower floor, the bar sparkled with neon signs and lit-up liquor displays.

Head tucked, he strode to the bar. *Just one.* Enough to take the edge off the perpetual fire in his gut. The dull pain that throbbed through years of a failing marriage. Hands on the slick surface, he hunched his shoulders and kept his head low.

"What'll ya have, handsome?" the bartender, a buxom blond, asked.

"Jack Daniels." He set his helmet on the empty stool next to him.

"Bottle or glass?"

"Gl—"

"Ginger ale," Cowboy's voice cut in from behind.

Where had the guy come from? Was he following him? Heat

blasted Max's neck and shoulders as the meaty man slid onto the stool next to him. "Leave me alone, Cowboy."

"Ginger ale, darlin'. Two." Cowboy shifted on the seat then leaned toward Max. "Not going to let you do this, man."

Staring at his flesh turning white around his knuckles, Max ground out, "Not your choice."

Cowboy chuckled. "Actually, it is. I don't want you showing up hungover some day and slumping into my line of sight." The burly man nudged his elbow. "Course, maybe you *do* need another hole in that thick head if you think this is the answer."

"I don't need lectures."

The bartender set two glasses in front of them. The swirling, sparkling liquid masked its true identity—a nasty carbonated drink. If only Max could mask himself.

They sat for several minutes without speaking. He concentrated on the pain shooting through his jaw and neck as he ground his teeth together. Amazing how with music and laughter blasting through the bar the silence settling between him and Cowboy proved deafening.

Cowboy took a sip of his ale. Set the glass down. "I know what you're doing."

Score one for Cowboy. But it didn't exactly take a genius to know what Max was doing in a bar.

"Drowning the pain isn't the answer."

"Yeah, what do you know?" Max grabbed the drink and gulped—anxious to have a reason not to talk. The ginger ale stung. Almost as good as liquor. Only it didn't last as long.

"I tried the bottle for a while—and found out what it's like to wake up and have no idea if you made it home without killing someone. Or to find yourself in bed with a woman you don't know." Cowboy's head sagged a little under the confession. "It's not worth it."

Score one more for Cowboy. So he had a history. Didn't mean

he knew what Max was going through. Didn't mean he understood consummate failure. Obviously the guy had a good life—nice truck. Family—a daughter and parents who were still around. Things had turned out okay for him.

Max had pain—gouge out his heart, slice and dice it, skewer and flame-broil it pain. "Look. . ." He let the words die on his tongue, struggling to be civil. "I appreciate your noble effort to rescue me, but I'm a lost cause. Round up some other pathetic soul to save."

When the bartender made her rounds, Max signaled her.

"Jack Daniels."

"Look, Emerie," Cowboy said as he leaned across the counter, speaking to the bartender. "I just feel compelled to inform you that my friend here has a rare disease. And if you serve him alcohol, it's going to bring on a violent reaction."

Max thrust himself upward. "What? What're you talking about?"

"See?" Cowboy winked at the girl. "It's already starting, just being around the stuff. If I were you, I'd mosey on away and pretend you never saw him. That way, when the law arrives, you aren't responsible. Right?"

Max saw red. Pure red—Cowboy's blood spilled all over the floor. He'd kill the guy!

But he couldn't. Wouldn't. He'd severed his marriage with a wrong move. Wouldn't do it this time. He snatched his helmet and drove himself out the front door, tension piling on top of the knots at the base of his neck. Chest puffed out, he drew his fist to his side, ready to pummel someone. Anything! He stomped past the trash can—and drove a hard roundhouse kick into it. Metal clanged against metal, drawing out more of the demon caged within. Only then did he notice the chain holding the trash bin to a steel frame. With a bounce, he spun and planted another straight into it. The chain snapped.

"Sure am glad that's not me."

Max spun around with a solid, hard right.

Cowboy ducked. Then he grabbed Max's forearm and spun him against the wall, one arm pinned behind his back, the other pressed to the crumbling bricks. His helmet clattered against the sidewalk. Mortar dug into his cheekbone.

Max cursed. "Stay outta my life!"

With a slight nudge forward, Cowboy scraped Max's cheek along the brick.

"Get off me!"

"Get it under control, sailor."

"I'm not a sailor. I quit." *I'm a loser. Class-A failure.* He wriggled against the steel-like hold, his breathing coming in gulps as the tension dribbled out.

Slowly, Cowboy's grip eased. Max flipped around, his back against the wall the cowboy nearly made him eat. Blood trailed down his cheek. He wiped it away.

Hands on his hips, Cowboy let out a heavy grunt. "So what happens in the field when someone crosses you? Going to point that M4 at their skull?"

Glowering, Max kept his trap shut. Knowing what's right and doing what's right was a game he'd always lost. He raked both hands through his hair. "I can't do this."

"Not alone, you can't."

But he *was* alone. Utterly. His best friend, the most incredible woman he'd ever met, was gone. And it was all his fault. *I don't want to live. I don't want a life without her.* He clenched his eyes and sucked down the adrenaline spurting into his throat. Suddenly aware of the small crowd lingering by the still-open door, he straightened. Braved a glance at Cowboy. "I. . .I better head out."

"Why don't you come over and shoot some pool?"

Temptation mingled with relief at the thought of not going

home to an empty apartment and being alone with his thoughts. "Why? You want to put my head through another wall?"

Cowboy grinned. "If that's what it takes, *sailor.*"

The word wasn't lost on Max. With an accepting nod, he bounced the keys to his bike in his hand. "I'll follow."

Forty pothole-jarring minutes later, Max rolled to a stop outside a pristine, ranch-style home situated on vast acreage. A front porch, complete with double swing and porch light, proved he and the cowboy had next to nothing in common. *I tried the bottle for a while. . . .* He glanced to the side as Cowboy parked his truck in a massive garage. What shadows hid behind the guy's sunny disposition?

Once inside a small enclosed entry, Cowboy led Max down a darkened hall and banked right—then straight up a narrow flight of stairs where he flipped on a switch. Light bathed a large, converted attic. A pool table devoured the bulk of the room; a leather couch sat against a lone window in the far wall.

"When I had the house built," Cowboy said as he chose a pool stick, "I wanted a place I could come and spend sleepless nights without disturbing anyone." He grinned and pointed to the rack on the wall, indicating for Max to make his pick. "It's right over my bedroom, so no one's the wiser."

With a pole in hand, Max squeaked the chalk over the tip. "How often are you up here?"

Cowboy shrugged. "Don't keep track." After he racked the balls, he shifted to the far end of the table. "Wanna break 'em?"

"Go ahead."

That was his first mistake. Cowboy slaughtered him in minutes. A few more rounds, and Max began to realize the enigmatic cowboy had probably logged enough hours up here to rank as a professional pool player.

Close to midnight, Max rolled his shoulders and accepted the soda Cowboy offered. "I take it you've done a lot of steam burning up here."

Cowboy grinned. "A lot more than I'll ever admit."

Stroking the sweat beads on the soda, Max slumped against the pool table. "I'm going crazy with the divorce." His gut twisted into knots with that revelation. "I–it's what I deserve, but. . ." The back of his throat felt raw—like everything else in him. He roughed a hand over his face then rubbed his eyes. Maybe he should just get some rest.

Cowboy pitched his empty Sprite can and joined him, arms folded over his thick chest. "I think there's hope, Max."

The surge of energy made him almost giddy. But he knew better. He squished the flickering flame of hope. Wouldn't let himself be fooled. Wouldn't be a fool. That thread of hope dangling before him morphed into a viper.

Hope was dangerous. Deadly.

Static hissed through the line as the voice mail connected. Sydney tapped a pencil eraser against her desk, waiting for her voice mail message to play.

"Ms. Jacobs, this is Deidre Hicks from the Pentagon Public Affairs Office. I just wanted to inform you that the incident you asked about in—uh, Namibia? Well, ma'am, I'm afraid there's no record of any such incident. Maybe you have the wrong date. Or country. Thanks for checking with us at the Pentagon. I'm sorry we couldn't be of more help."

I bet you are. Sydney flung the pencil at the carpeted cubicle divider and pursed her lips. Yeah. Right. No records. Having been a military wife, she was used to the Potomac two-step. Ask one question, get the answer to another—or nothing at all. Convenient for them. Altogether frustrating for her. Sitting up, she laced her fingers through her hair, propped her forehead on the heels of her hands, and let out a long, slow breath as she stared between her arms at the names on her list. With a groan, she dragged the pencil back and sliced through General Snow's name. Strike four. Olson, Dean, and Woodhouse had all said the same thing.

But Mangeni had sworn vehemently that the soldiers had come in October. And that they were American.

Uncapping her bottle of water, Sydney studied the spreadsheet where she'd listed all the vital information. She worked the names, dates, and notes. Dead ends. Every single one.

"How is that possible?" she asked herself.

"What's that?"

Sydney jumped at the sound of Lane's voice. "Where did you come from?" She laughed and swiveled her chair toward him as he plopped down in the spare seat.

"In case you forgot, I sit about three rows back, two over." A smile twinkled in his eyes.

"Ha. Ha." She slid the file shut and let out another sigh. "It's a bit hard to do a human interest feature when you can't track down a human with interest in talking."

"You still don't have anything?"

She glared at him. "Don't rub it in. It's impossible. Every lead flops." She fanned the pages of notes and incomplete information at him, rustling his sandy blond hair. "I really don't get it. I mean obviously *someone* knows when a group between six and ten purportedly American soldiers enters a village, demolishes it, and according to Mangeni, rescues the villagers from a notorious Janjaweed leader. A leader who it just so happens turned up downriver two weeks later sprayed with a dozen bullets."

He looked at the closed folder. "Maybe the woman didn't recall the facts correctly. Or maybe it's a translation error."

Sydney wrestled with his suggestion. "I've gone back and questioned her twice in the last two weeks, hoping that's the case. But her story hasn't changed."

Lane's gaze locked on something behind her—actually over her head.

"Uh, Syd. . ."

She furrowed her brow and glanced over her shoulder. A dozen reporters hovered below a television monitor mounted in the corner of the office. The ticker feed read: LIVE FROM MOZAMBIQUE.

Behind the attractive reporter, a smoldering village lay in ruins. *". . .just joined us, I'm Rorie Mills, live in Mozambique. To be precise, I'm standing in the middle of a small village that, less than twenty-four hours ago, endured a brutal and bloody battle."*

The words pulled Sydney from her chair. "You seeing this?" she mumbled, wandering closer to the monitor and hugging herself.

"Yeah." Lane's breathy words skated down her neck. He peeked around from behind her. "Sounds just like Namibia."

"While the government has made vast improvements here in Mozambique, there is still a battle raging against drug lords transporting their illegal wares through this area, which has been a central transit point for South Asian hashish and, to some degree, the drug methaqualone for export to South Africa." The reporter shifted so that she stood sideways and pointed. *"These villagers claim local guerillas have taken their family members, literally dragging them out in the middle of the night, to work the drug fields. Fear and terror have reigned here."* She turned back to the camera. *"That is, until last night. Reports are that a team of elite soldiers—some villagers claim they were American—swarmed in during another kidnapping raid and successfully prevented the seizure of the able-bodied men and women. However, soon after—"*

"It's the exact same thing." Sydney spun and strode back to her cubicle. With the pages spread over her workstation, she pointed to it. "Look. A village in trouble. Elite soldiers. This isn't a coincidence, and who knows why they're going in there, but I bet someone is getting thick pockets for this." She grabbed her phone, pressed her fingertips under the number for General Snow, and punched it in. "Let's see what the good general reports now."

"Easy there, Syd." Lane reclined against her cubicle, his green eyes searching hers. "You don't want to stir up trouble."

"Trouble?" she scoffed, then whipped her attention to the line. An automated voice filtered into the reception. "Ugh. Voice mail." After leaving a message requesting an explanation and whether the incident was truly related to Namibia, she tossed her phone. "Why would they hide this?" She peeked at the screen. "This is a good thing. Helping those who can't help themselves."

"It's a political hotbed."

She blinked at Lane. "What?"

"Syd!" Buck Kramer's voice boomed across the maze of cubicles, yanking her around. He stood just outside his door, his bushy eyebrows drawn into a deep scowl. "In my office, now!"

"Uh-oh. That doesn't sound good," Lane said, looking over his shoulder.

Dread swirled in her stomach. "The last thing I need right now is to lose my job." Especially now that her doctor had confirmed the pregnancy. She needed the insurance if she wanted to avoid having to file for reimbursements with TRICARE, which undoubtedly meant Max would find out.

As she stepped away, Lane gently caught her arm. "Let's do lunch afterward."

About to agree, she saw something in his gaze that unnerved her and doused her casual consent. Did Lane have romantic notions? Even if she were officially divorced from Max—which she wouldn't be for many months—it would take much longer than that to heal. To stop hurting. To stop loving Max.

"Sorry, I can't." She scrambled for a plausible excuse. Her gaze shot to the monitor that still rambled about the chaos in Mozambique. "I'm going to head over to Mangeni's to see if I can get anything else out of her." She slid her arm free with a mumbled explanation of not keeping Buck waiting.

Discomfort bombarded her. Between Lane's not-so-subtle interest, the exhaustion that came from carrying a precious new life inside her, and the stress over this stupid humanitarian piece that proved to be much harder than it should be, Sydney longed for the days when she was a housewife with a part-time job.

At Buck's office, she found the door shut. She peered through the glass and saw him rubbing his temples as he spoke on the phone. With a gentle knock, she motioned, asking if she could enter. Instead of waving her in, he shot her a heated glare. The look blasted into her chest, worrying her. After a few more nods to whoever had fouled up his mood, Buck hung up and shouted for her to enter.

Hesitation guarded her steps as she entered. "Is everything okay?"

"No, it's not okay! Shut the door." He huffed and pushed out of his creaking chair. "I thought you were working on human interest pieces."

"I am. LaDona assigned me the For Human Sake column. I've been—"

"Then what in Sam Hill are you doing calling the Pentagon again?" His round face reddened. Sweat beaded on his brow.

"I. . .I was. . . ." She drew in a breath, steadied herself. *I will not cower. I have done nothing wrong.* "The woman I'm doing the first piece on wants to thank the men who saved her village last October. I'm trying to find out who they were."

"So what do you need the Pentagon for? Why are you harassing the top brass?"

"Harassing!" The accusation slid down her spine like a steel rod, straightening her. "I haven't harassed anyone. I've been—"

Shaking a finger at her, he stormed around his desk. His entire body rippled with the anger leeching out in liters of sweat. "You are not to call anyone at the Pentagon again unless you have my express permission."

"But—"

"Is that clear?" he shouted, his double chins jiggling.

Mentally and physically, Sydney drew back. He'd never been so. . .frightening toward her before. Working to calm her ramming heart, she nodded.

He grumbled some curses as he waddled back to his desk and dropped into the chair with another epithet. "You're going to be the end of me."

"I'd think you'd be thrilled with a hard-hitting reporter."

"Not when you get caught and draw every politician down my back!"

She pulled her waning courage up off the floor and stood. "May I ask what they said?"

He scowled at her with a look that dared her to ask again.

Licking her lips, she accepted the grating answer and left, fighting the urge to sprint from the building. As she neared her cubicle, she heard her cell phone's distinctive ring belting out "Jesus Take the Wheel." She darted the last few feet and snatched up the phone. The caller ID didn't register a number.

Brushing aside her frayed nerves, she pressed TALK. "Sydney Jacobs." When no response came, she hunched her shoulders and burrowed into the minute privacy of her cubicle, straining to hear. "Hello?"

"First and only warning. Leave it alone."

DAY TWO

Dawn rose like a specter of doom. Each sprinkle of daylight shattered what little possibility they had of staying hidden. With Datu and seven men from the cave, Jon and Kimber struck out on their journey into the hills. To the Higanti. Ahead of him, four villagers who'd constructed a stretcher conveyed Kezia through the lush landscape. Their dark figures almost blended with the scenery under the tease of light. With each foot he put in front of the other, Jon felt the atmosphere thickening. Soon the skies would let loose their bounty. And they had no shelter, no umbrellas to protect against the inevitable drenching downpour. He smoothed Maecel's hair, wondering how he'd keep her warm so she wouldn't catch a cold or worse.

He flicked his wrist and checked his watch. Six thirty. They should've been at Zamboanga International Airport by now. Jordan would go ballistic when he found out they'd missed the flight. Shifting Maecel to his left arm, he dug in his pack for the satellite phone.

"Oh no," Jon mumbled as he tried to navigate terrain with Maecel, the phone, and the uneven path.

Kimber glanced over her shoulder, dark ringlets dangling in her face. She brushed the strands aside. "What's wrong?"

He met her gaze and held up the phone. "Battery's low. I've got to call Jordan, let him know we're not going—"

"No! No, no!" Datu snapped, rushing toward Jon. "You no call."

Jon paused, considering the chief's son. "I have to. They're expecting us."

"No!" Datu shook a stubby finger. "You no call. You call, Mauk come."

"What do you mean? I'm calling our mission board. They have to know. They might even be able to help Kezia."

"No. Mauk see all. He know all—he own all."

"He doesn't own Island Hope." Jon glared down at the fierce brown eyes. Yet dread swirled in his gut. He didn't want to believe what Datu was saying. Didn't want to believe that a deadly foe could intercept his phone call to IHF. But it made sense. Yet how else would they get help? And if he waited, the sat phone would be dead and there would be no chance.

"Jon," Kimber said as she took Maecel from him. "Let's just keep moving. Maybe we can figure something out."

Figure something out? Was she kidding? If they didn't make that call now, they never would.

"God will work it out. He'll show us." She strapped a blanket around Maecel, effectively creating a sling.

How was it that she always had the peace, the inner strength that he longed for? Would that he could be as confident in God's ways as she was. *God, help me trust You.* He stuffed the phone back into his pack and followed her. He'd think after eight years of missionary work, three immersed completely in the culture, he'd have that part down pat.

Far from it. Every day, every breath brought him to his knees.

And then there was Kimber. Kimber Leigh Stanton, home-schooled, eldest of six children, heart of gold. Many times she'd told him that God had given her everything she ever wanted in life. To have a godly husband, to be a mother, and to work the mission field. Living as an example of Christ's love fulfilled Kimber in ways that still boggled his mind. Then again, she ministered to the wounded hearts. His job was leadership.

Maybe I just have to figure it out my way.

He grunted. For as long as he could remember, his way had been the hard way. That's exactly what he'd done before stepping onto the mission field. Growing up as a preacher's kid did weird things to him. He wanted to make his father proud but somehow found himself doing everything *but* making the man proud. Kinda hard to live up to the gigantic reputation of a wildly successful, megachurch pastor-father when you're sliding out of jail on drug-related charges. Two years later, Jon had set out for the Philippines, determined to prove his mettle, his worth as a son of Stephen Harris. A son of God.

And his father would climb the steel rafters of the sanctuary when he found out Jon and Kimber never made that plane.

No. Jon had to find a way to get word to his father or IHF about what was happening. He'd make a call. Just a short one.

But what if Mauk *did* intercept it and learned Jon and Kimber had escaped? Not only escaped, but had Kezia. The sky would unleash more than rain. What hope existed if they got embroiled with the Higanti, who would make sure Jon and Kimber never left alive? Was there any hope to get out of this?

He wiped a hand over his face, swiping the sweat from his skin. Aches dug into his shoulders and back, kneading a hefty dose of tension into the very marrow of his bones.

"We take break," Datu finally called.

Resting against a palm trunk, Jon dug into the pack and retrieved an energy bar. Maecel's face lit up. "Me, me, me," she said with a throaty grunt and motioned for the food.

Jon smiled and broke the bar in two, handing one piece to Maecel and the other to Kimber. He then gave them a water pack.

He shifted his position and nudged closer to his wife. Head tucked, he whispered, "I have to call Jordan." He skated a glance around the makeshift camp. Nobody seemed to be listening, including Kimber, who ate and talked playfully with Maecel.

Was she listening? Had she heard? "I'm concerned he's taking us to the Higanti, and if *they* learn we're Christians, we're dead."

"You don't know that's where he's taking us." Her hissed words warned him of her feelings.

The heckling sounds of the tropical forest pervaded the silence that hung between them. Jon lowered himself to the ground, his back to Datu and the others. "But what if it is?"

Kimber locked eyes with him then lifted Maecel up, effectively blocking her face. "Why? Why would he do that? He could just kill us here and get it over with."

Why, indeed? That was the question plaguing him. Again, the smartest thing was to try to call IHF. "If I can call Jordan, he might be able to get us out, but it's going to take some time to put together the plans. Until then. . ."

"We're on our own."

His nod felt curt to even him. "We just have to stay alive."

Her eyes darted to his. "And what if the call brings Mauk?"

"I have to try." He swallowed the doom hovering over it. "Either way, we're dead."

CHAPTER 7

Y ou have a problem."

Olin slid a mint into his mouth and looked over the park, appreciating the beautiful sunshine and cool breeze. He unbuttoned his suit jacket and relaxed, his words aimed at the man sitting behind him. "I have many problems, but none that concern you."

"A woman is inquiring about the missions. She called within two days of Moz. How does she know about that?"

A shallow laugh worked its way through Olin's chest. "It was on the news."

"But her questions are detailed. She knows about Namibia, too."

"Relax, Chairman. My team is well-hidden and will not be blown."

"If they're blown, you're blown. Then I'm blown."

Olin sighed and watched a green kite soaring overhead.

"I'm not going to let that happen. I won't go down. You promised me—"

"And I keep my promises." He leveled a firm gaze at the man. "I assure you, were this a problem, it would be eliminated already. If you overreact, mistakes will be made. Trust my men. Trust me." Olin smiled at a woman as she walked her fluffy white dog past. Once she was out of earshot, he cleared his throat. "I'll take them off the grid for a while, but that also means you're out of luck with any black-ops necessities. Just understand, Chairman, that keeping them out of sight and mind is done in exchange for your promise to leave this alone and not leap without looking."

Without a word, the chairman stood and walked down the path toward the Potomac.

Welcome to Paradise Gardens. Max stared out at the diamond-encrusted water. Unbelievable. He'd been ready for another long stint in the jungle hunting bad guys, equalizing pressure. . .but this? A pristine beach on a private island for two weeks? He crossed his legs, bent over, and stretched. The only thing in the last four days since the helo deposited him on the hot sands that had saved his sanity was tearing up the beach until he felt like he would drop.

After a few more stretches, he started his run. The first day, he'd been so ticked he'd completed the first circuit in under an hour. Now he ran a fast clip, but since there wasn't anything else to do on this godforsaken island other than crawl the walls, he made several circuits. At least it ate up the hours. The rigorous workout of running in the sand tamed his mind and strengthened him.

Someone had it in good with Lambert. How else could the general manage sending a team of six onto a private island for fourteen days with free rein? And not just an island, but a fully stocked and loaded home that rivaled the Taj Mahal with its ornate detail and luxury. It was too much. Far too much for a group of soldiers. Besides, what was the point? Were they supposed to unwind? Like that could ever happen.

As the sun rose higher and beat down on him, Max completed a lap and slowed. Laughter rumbled from the volleyball pit. Fix jumped and slammed the ball hard—it pinged off the compacted sand and burst up at Cowboy and Griffin. Even amid the triumphant shout of victory, Fix high-fived the Kid. They were laughing, acting like they didn't have a care in the world. Lucky them.

Dripping sweat and disgust, Max climbed the steps to the house.

"Max!" The Kid jogged toward him, wearing those stupid Hawaiian shorts and a goofy grin. "We need another player for the match."

He considered the sand pit but shook his head. "It's even. You don't need me."

"Actually, we talked Legend into playing finally. And Midas is just coming in from a swim."

Griffin lumbered onto the sand court with a taunting grin. "This why they call you Legend?"

A laugh seeped through Griffin's chest. "Let's find out."

Midas sloughed his way up the shore, wiping the salty water from his short crop, and jabbed his board into the sand. With a grin, he stepped onto the court—on Fix's team.

Ah. A challenge.

Max almost grinned as he plodded toward his new teammates, Cowboy and Legend. They patted his back and took up positions. Crouching, Max peered under the net at Midas.

"Ready to eat sand, Frogman?"

"You first."

Cowboy served, and the ball sailed over the net, straight toward Fix, who bumped the ball toward the Kid, who in turn set it up—

Midas leaped into the air and pummeled the ball.

It streaked straight toward the ground. Max dove hard. But a blur of white told him he'd been too late.

His opponents cheered his failure. Max pulled himself off the beach.

"That's all right. That's all right," Legend said, clapping and swiping palms with Max. "We'll stomp them. Bury them six feet under." His laugh seemed to echo over the waters.

Rolling his shoulders, Max returned to his spot and readied himself for the serve, this time coming from Reyes. The man served effortlessly, and Max began to wonder if he'd been set up. Midas hooted when Cowboy intercepted and bounced it up. Max jumped and slammed the ball back over the net.

A plume of sand burst up—and only seconds before he made out Midas's long frame sliding toward them. The ball was still in play! And back on their side.

Legend once again bumped it to Cowboy, who set it up. On his feet, Max again leaped and spiked the ball. This time the Kid missed—and it smacked the hot sand.

"Score!" Cowboy and Legend cheered, slapping Max on the back. An hour and two games later, with the points tied and both sides set to win, a truce was called for lunch. Max appreciated the way the guys played, the way even though they were on opposites sides and willing to drive a ball hard into each other's chests, they were a team. It was good. Real good.

As they trudged into the house to shower and change for lunch, the Kid sidled up next to Max. "D'ya hear?"

"What?"

"Oberly is having a massive party tomorrow night. Guests are going to be flown in."

With a check on the rest of the team, who'd slowly gathered, Max couldn't help but be surprised. Guess this wouldn't be quite as solitary as they'd thought. More people, more noise. That should be a good thing. So why did it bug him so much?

"Probably be women." The Kid's grin grew bigger, if that was possible. "Loads."

That's why. A party meant revelers, happy drunk idiots. He tucked aside the urge to knock the Kid upside his head. Marshall was young, inexperienced. Didn't have a clue about life. Rich kid.

Had daddy foot the bill for anything he wanted, like parties with loose women and booze. Not only would there be drunks, but there'd also be people who would question why a half dozen well-muscled grunts were holed up on a secluded island.

"A party?" he asked, looking to Cowboy.

The cowboy shrugged. "Seems so. They're setting up tents and decorations by the pool, which is why we're out here. Gettin' outta the way."

Max chewed the information.

"Rumor has it," Legend said, "the team's invited. One caterer even said it's a group of models coming in for a photo shoot."

"Yes!" the Kid shouted, then laughed. "See? A party unlike any other. Maybe they'll want us to pose with the ladies." The Kid turned sideways, flexing his biceps, then rolled his abs.

Midas shoved the Kid. "You haven't got a prayer, Scrappy Doo."

"Yeah, a party—with professional photographers who could slap your ugly mug all over the front of a magazine and blow our cover." Max could tell by the seriousness in Cowboy and Legend's faces that they had already thought about that. "Steer clear. Lambert told us to lie low, get some R&R. Avoid attention." He headed to his room.

Cleaned and marginally refreshed an hour later, Max returned to the main floor, where marble and ornate statues ruled the cavernous room. Sparkling chandeliers spun light into the living area and the foyer. Max banked right and strode down the slick floors to the grand dining hall on the northeast corner, its wall of windows overlooking a small inlet. Two round tables skirted in burgundy and topped with mounds of mouth-watering food were almost concealed behind the bulk of the muscular men already scavenging. Max grabbed a plate and joined his teammates.

"Hey, you worn a track in the sand yet?" Cowboy popped a grape in his mouth as he shifted to the right one step and scooped some creamy stuff onto his plate.

Had anyone else asked that question, Max might've smacked them. But it was Cowboy. His new ally. The man who saved him from getting stupid. . .*stupider.* "I'll have it ready by the time we leave."

Cowboy grinned, chewing. "Thought you might."

Quiet descended on the group as they chowed down, anticipation over the arrival of the models still clogging the air. Almost as if on cue, a man in a wait-staff uniform appeared in the doorway, standing with his arms stiff at his side and his chin parallel to the floor. He cleared his throat.

As one unit, the team turned toward him.

"Mr. Oberly has graciously extended an invitation to a quiet gathering, poolside this evening, to meet his guests."

The Kid and Fix slapped a high-five.

Steer clear did not mean steer straight into the target.

Max clenched his fist, watching as the Kid danced with two women, whooping and hollering. Less than a half dozen feet away, Fix did the same. And surrounding the entire party, a throng of photogs.

"This is a bad idea," he mumbled.

Cowboy lifted a bottled water from the buffet table. "Can't do much about it, so let's just blend."

"Blend?" Max glared at the cowboy who, dressed in a pair of dark jeans and a button-down shirt, didn't know the meaning of the phrase.

"What?" Cowboy grinned broadly. "Hey, it's my style. I'm comfortable with who I am."

Chuckling, Max slid his hands into the pockets of his slacks, silently cursing Olin Lambert for telling the team they'd be spending a few days doing recon in an upscale setting. *Be sure to pack appropriately.* Yeah, Olin had seen this coming.

He considered the drinks, wondering which ones had the wrong kind of punch.

A warm hand rested on his chest, snapping his attention to the blond leaning into him. "You look lonely," she purred. Pretty platinum hair curled around a young face, framing her chocolate eyes. "Dance with me?"

Tensed at her touch and seductive manners, Max tried to keep his attention on her face. He was married—well, at least technically. But Syd had closed the door, hadn't she? Besides, what could one dance hurt? He let her lead him onto the dance floor set up under the tent. She turned into his arms and set a hand on his shoulder. "So, what's your name?"

"Max." Why did this feel like junior high?

"I'm Tawny."

He resisted the urge to groan, and just when he thought better of agreeing to this, she closed what space remained between them and curled into him, her cheek against his. Something inside him curdled. But it felt good to hold her, to feel her soft curves against him. Yet it made him miss Sydney—the shape of her body, her full curves, the way she fit perfectly into his arms and embrace, unlike the woman in his arms now.

You're an idiot.

"Go, Max!" the Kid called over the noisy din of the crowd.

His teammate's cheer snapped Max out of his stupor. Clutching her shoulders, he held her at arm's length. "Sorry, this. . .it's not working."

Her startled expression pushed him back through the sea of partygoers. He gulped the adrenaline. What was he thinking? How could he consider something like that? He knew exactly what he'd been thinking—that he could find something to soothe the pain of missing Sydney. But in truth, he wasn't thinking. Because *nothing* could replace his wife.

Wife. In less than a year, he wouldn't have a wife, according to the courts. Weaving through the crowd, he made his way to the beach. A cool breeze drifted off the water, swirling around him as he walked the sandy stretch and headed to the dock, where he sat on the edge, watching the sparkling waves ebb. He'd be a liar if he said a part of him didn't want the girl. To have the soft feel of a woman in his arms...

"Did I do something wrong?"

Max bolted to his feet, irritated the woman had followed him. "No." He held out his hands. "Look, I'm sorry, but I'm not interested."

She did a good job of burying how much that hurt, but not enough. He saw it dart in and out of her carefully applied face. "Hey, it's not like I want a commitment. I mean, this is a bachelor-bachelorette party, right?"

"Which is exactly why I don't belong in there."

Her face went slack. "Oh. So you're married."

Until the divorce was final. "Yeah."

"She must be a really lucky lady."

Max snorted. Besides being a horrible pick-up line, if she knew the truth about him, knew what he was really like, she'd run as fast as she could back to the luxury jet that had plopped her onto this island.

She gave him a wistful smile then started back to the party.

Only then did Max see Cowboy standing at the end of the dock. The cowboy nodded as Max strode toward him. "You handled that well."

"You have no idea."

Within minutes, the rest of the team had gathered on the sand.

"What is this, intervention?" Though sarcasm coated his tongue, Max was stilled by the somber expressions of the team. His pride took a beating. "I'm fine."

"I don't know," Midas said. "You looked pretty rattled when

you stormed off that dance floor."

"Look, I don't need to discuss my business with anyone."

"You're right," Legend said, his tone calm and even. "But we're a team, and you need to know that we got your back covered. Anytime. Anywhere."

Pride swallowed, Max nodded, ashamed that his entire team had witnessed him taking that girl into his arms—disrespecting his wife and their relationship. Weak fool, that's what he was. "You can go back to the party. I think I'm going to skip out."

"But *we're* not skipping out, right?" The Kid spun around in front of them, walking backward. "I mean, come on, guys. *Chicks.* I've been locked up here for almost a week with no phone and no girlfriend. I say we dive in."

"We're supposed to be keeping it quiet," Cowboy said.

"Maybe it's that you're too old," the Kid taunted the much larger man.

"Come here. I'll show you who's old." Legend popped the Kid.

Even though the others were teasing Marshall, Max noticed they didn't argue with the idea of returning to the party. Like they needed the trouble of company, *female* company.

"What do you guys say?" the Kid persisted.

Fix shrugged, his eyes on the glistening ocean. "Why not?"

When the two high-fived again, Max tensed. Surely he could count on the MARSOC boys to choose the wiser path, the path of least estrogen.

"I'm for hanging here, might even turn in early," Legend mumbled. "I mean, who knows how long the partying will go on? I need my beauty rest."

Cowboy laughed. "Yeah, you do. But I'm thinking it's too late to start now."

"Aww. That's low." Legend and Cowboy continued laughing.

Marshall turned his attention toward Max. "Come on, man."

"Not interested." Maybe he'd do some running, burn off the

weight of what just happened. The knots in his muscles kinked and threatened a revolt. He started away. "I'm going to take a walk."

"For the love of. . ." The Kid groaned loudly. "Look, just let her go."

Max stilled. Exactly what *her* did the Kid have in mind?

"Hey." Cowboy's quiet, stiff voice carried a warning to Marshall. "Leave it alone."

"Nah, man. He's gotten meaner. And I think it's because he's obsessed with his ex-wife."

The world tilted. Spun. So did Max. His left eye twitched. "Excuse me?" He took a step back toward the team, his focus locked on Marshall Vaughn.

"She ain't worth it. Just let her go. Get on with your life."

Fingers curling into fists, Max lowered his head and voice. "That's none of your—"

"So what if you screwed it up?" The Kid shrugged and tossed up his hands. He gave a halfhearted, almost mocking laugh. "Or is she just too dumb to appreciate what you've done for our country, for freedom? I mean, I see those tree huggers who don't get it. Is she like that? Ya know? Is that the problem? Does she even have a heart? What kind of sick—"

Rage drove Max head first into the guy's chest. The Kid landed with a thud. Pinned to the ground. His arms and legs flew out. Max yanked onto his knees, straddling the puke. He slammed a hard right cross into the Kid's face.

Crack! Blood spurted.

Another punch.

The Kid's fist jabbed out. Nailed Max's mouth. They rolled. Flipped. On his feet, he waited. But Marshall came up with a growl. Max planted a solid right uppercut and lifted the Kid off the sand. Marshall doubled.

He'd make the Kid eat every word about Sydney. "She's my

wife!" He grabbed the back of the Kid's high-and-tight head and shoved it hard into the packed white sand. Grains puffed out as the Kid clawed for air, a groan ebbing through his chest and back. "Keep your mouth shut!"

Pressure hooked both of Max's arms and jerked him backward. He hit the ground with a jarring impact. *Oof!* Spots sprinkled his vision. For all of two seconds, he saw a clear black sky and started to pull himself up, but Cowboy and Legend dropped on him, stretching his arms to the side.

"Let me go!"

"Max!" Cowboy hissed, his mouth near Max's ear. "Get it under control."

"I'm going to kill him," Max growled. "No one—*no one* talks about my wife like that. *Ever!*" With everything in him, he lurched forward, his momentum started by the two musclebound Marines whose feet slid backward in the sand but held.

"Reyes, Midas," Legend shouted. "Get Vaughn out of here."

Max struggled against them, cursing and vowing to hurt the Kid. Somehow he managed to free a hand and land a solid punch against the side of Legend's head.

The barrel of a man shifted. With a grunt, he drove a fierce jab straight into Max's face.

Darkness devoured him.

Warbling and distant shouts echoed through his head. Max shifted, something rubbing his neck and shoulders raw. Where was he?

"You need a doctor?" Hollowness swallowed the question.

"We're good," Legend's gruff voice boomed nearby.

"You sure? He doesn't look as bad as the other guy, but—"

"Thanks, we've got it."

Bright light tore through his skull. Max groaned and lifted himself up. Everything in him throbbed. "What. . . ?" He pressed the heel of his hand against his jaw joint then propped his arms on his knees. Stretching his neck, he groaned again as the memory of the fight stole into his awareness. "How's the Kid?"

"Broken nose. Couple of busted ribs. Maybe a concussion."

Humiliation crowded him. Holding his head, Max pried himself off the beach. He started walking. The quiet crunch of sand nearby warned him he wasn't alone. Legend? Cowboy? He couldn't look back. Instead, he stumbled toward the house, noting the party was all but abandoned. How long had he been knocked out? He lowered himself to the steps and cradled his pounding head in his hands.

Boards creaked on either side of him. *Great. Both of them.*

"Look, I got to be straight with you," Legend said, his words quiet and stern. "What happened out there—that can't happen again."

"Tell the Kid to keep his trap shut." Max knew it wasn't the Kid's fault. And he knew the point Legend was making without threatening. But he just couldn't own up to it, not in front of these guys. Not here. *Failure.*

"Marshall might have the experience for Nightshade, but the Kid lacks maturity. Nobody's arguing that. But Max. . ." Cowboy let out a long sigh. "Your anger is a problem."

How many times had Sydney said the same thing?

Flexing his fist, Max winced at the tightness of his skin under the dried blood. His blood. Marshall's blood. His mind careened back to the night he'd knocked Lane Bowen out cold. And accidentally clipped Sydney in the process. At the stinging reminder, his gut churned.

Sydney was right—he was out of control. His temper had shattered their marriage. Tear-filled eyes had pleaded with him, but it was her words that scalded his heart. *I'm afraid of you, Max.* He clenched his eyes and swallowed the bitter truth filling his mouth.

"How's your head?" Legend asked.

Max shot him a sidelong glance. "You coldcocked me. How do you think it feels?"

"Maybe that will teach you to think before you try to go at it with me." On his feet, Legend patted Max's shoulder and volunteered to get some painkillers. But Max was well aware of the silent conversation that had taken place between the two buddies, a chance to let Cowboy give it to Max straight.

"When you hit Legend, I think he wanted to pound you to China and back."

Max stretched his jaw, pain flaring up through his skull. "I'm sure he would've if you hadn't been there."

Cowboy rubbed his hands together. "What're we going to do about this?"

His own wife. His own team. He'd failed them all. "Better off dead."

A low chuckle. "Not an option. Plan B?"

Max ran a hand along his neck. "I don't know, man. It's...I..."

He shrugged, hating that he couldn't sort it all out. That he couldn't figure out what demon possessed him. "Syd said I had to get help, but I told her this is how I am, this is who she married." The retort sounded as empty today as it had each time he'd barked it at her.

"Do you believe that?"

"No. Yes." Max's eyes slid shut. "I...I don't know. The things in here," he said, tapping his temple, "are things I can't explain to a woman who's never seen the backside of a jungle or riddled a twelve-year-old with bullets because he aimed a fully automatic weapon he knew how to use at me." He met his friend's gaze. "I don't want her to know about those things. I don't want those images in her mind. She's good, pure." *She's Sydney.* "But it's clawing me apart—I can't sleep. It screwed *me* up. Why would I give her that misery?"

"Because in barricading that pain, you've also bricked up your heart and soul."

CHAPTER 8

N<small>o, no!"</small> The woman waved her dark hand at Sydney, shooing her out of the small, cramped apartment. "Mistake. All mistake."

Sydney blinked. This couldn't be possible. "I'm sorry? I spoke with Anisia not two hours ago, and she—"

"Trauma too much. Say things she no mean," the woman insisted, again nudging Sydney from the darkened hall.

Casting her gaze around the sparse living quarters in hopes of finding a reason to stay, to speak with Anisia herself, Sydney spotted a little boy coloring on the floor. It wasn't his brilliant eyes against his near-black complexion that froze her. It was the art-work. A five-pointed star inlaid on a sword. Mangeni had mentioned a similar symbol.

She quickly detoured from the path the women urged her on and crouched next to the boy, turning his page slightly so she could see it better. What was it?

The other woman, Anisia's aunt, snatched the paper away. "You go! Only trouble come."

Rising, Sydney frowned at the woman. "What do you mean?" Maybe she should hold her ground, insist on speaking with the woman who'd witnessed the intervention.

"Nothing. You go now." She took Sydney's arm and led her to

the door. "No come again. No come."

Shuttled to the small stoop, she stood staring back into the house. In the seconds before the door closed, a woman's wrought face appeared around the corner at the end of the hall. Sydney shoved her foot into the door. "Wait!"

"I call police!" the aunt yelled and pushed Sydney.

Anger slithered around her chest. The woman didn't want her talking to Anisia. Why? What had changed in the two-hour span since she'd left the *Independent* and driven across state lines to meet with this refugee? There'd been no mistake, as Anisia's relative insisted. The boy's drawing convinced her of that.

Back in her Lexus, Sydney sat staring up at the third-floor apartment. The curtains parted, and the same young, dark face appeared. Anisia wanted to talk but wouldn't. Was she scared?

First and only warning. Leave it alone.

Her intestines churned, forming a knot. Had they threatened this family, too? The thought brought Sydney's hand to her mouth. What would she do if the woman who'd survived brutalities in her uncivilized world came here—only to get killed? The thought forced her to start the car and leave. She certainly didn't want to cause anyone more pain.

Yet her mind dragged back to Anisia's son. He'd obviously seen the intervention as well. Maybe she could find a way to talk to him. No. He likely spoke no better English than his mother.

Her stomach rumbled, reminding her she'd not eaten in several hours. With the baby, she'd inhaled more calories in the last few months than she probably had all year. Wouldn't Max get a kick—

She choked back the thought and pulled into a Mexican fast-food place. Order placed, she eased her car forward and waited for the food. Her cell phone spewed the country song into the air. Sydney dug through her purse and located the vibrating device. "Hello?"

"How'd the interview go?"

"Hi, Lane. I'm fine." She giggled. "How're you?"

"Touché. Sorry. I deserved that."

"Yes," she said as the bag of preservatives-carbs-calories-laden food passed through the window to her. "Thank you," she said to the worker and left the restaurant.

"Where are you?"

"About two hours out."

"No. I meant the restaurant. Are you eating fast food?"

Guilty pleasure lapped at her hunger. "Yeah, I am. I'm starving." As she steered the car onto the highway, she rummaged in the bag for the first burrito and took a bite. "It's wonderful, too." She let out a soft moan. "Oh man, I'm hungry."

"You never eat fast food!"

"Well. . ." She swallowed the mouthful of beans, beef, and cheese—and her pride. She hadn't told Lane about the baby. And probably wouldn't until it was impossible to hide because it'd only bring up sympathy or Max. Neither of which she wanted. "Call me desperate. So, you asked about Anisia. Total bomb out."

"What?"

"Yeah. Her aunt insisted there was a mistake, that nothing of the sort had happened."

Lane was oddly silent.

"I don't buy it, though," she said, wolfing another bite and talking around the food.

"Good, but what makes you certain?"

"Her son drew a picture of a sword and five-pointed star. It looked just like what Mangeni described in her interview."

"So you think they're connected?"

Sipping her water, she finally—fully—embraced the idea. "Have to be. And I think someone wants it kept silent. Anisia looked terrified when I saw her. Then you factor in the threatening phone call I got earlier, and I can't see how they *aren't* connected."

"Wait. The *what* you got earlier?"

Boop-boop. Boop-boop. Sydney glanced at her phone face. Saved by the mom. "Oh! Lane, my mom is calling. I better take this." She quickly ended the call and switched over. "Hello? Mom?"

"Hi, sweetheart. How're you doing? Did you get to see the doctor?"

"I did." She looked at the second burrito, one bite removed, and felt nausea sweep her. Had she really eaten an entire, nasty, fast-food burrito? Ugh! She dropped it in the bag and wiped her hand on an imprinted napkin. "Everything looks fine, Mom. He listened to the heartbeat and examined me."

"Did he give you a due date?"

"He did." She gripped the wheel tightly and drew in a breath. "June first." Max's birthday. Could the timing be any crueler?

"Oh, sweetie," came the long, sigh-breathed near apology. "Do you know what the sex is?"

"I have another appointment in a month for an ultrasound."

"I'm just so excited about this baby. My baby girl having a baby! It's so wonderful. I mean, I know things weren't planned, but why don't we go shopping tomorrow for some maternity clothes and baby things? That'll be fun." Her mom's chipper voice grated against her.

It wasn't that her mother was insensitive, but Sydney didn't feel like celebrating. "My clothes are fine. I still haven't had to let out the buttons yet, so I don't want to go big until I really am." Which would buy her some time at work. And with Buck. And Lane.

"Look, Sydney, this child is a precious gift—"

An eerie whistle rent the line.

"Ack!" Sydney yanked the phone away, cringing. Carefully, she tested the line to make sure it was gone. "Mom, what was that noise?"

A busy signal rattled her.

She pressed END and redialed. The phone rang and rang. No answering machine. Unease snaked around Sydney. A chill draped her shoulders. She tried again. Again. Adrenaline spiking, she dialed her brother.

"Hey."

"Bryce, I think something's wrong."

DAY TWO

Hours later

The viper dropped like a rope in front of him. *Thump!* It slithered and pulled itself into a coil. Jon stopped and flung out his hand to the side, protecting Kimber from stepping into the snake's path. He eased the machete handle up and gripped it tightly between both hands. As he lifted the weapon up, the snake slithered closer.

Huddling a sleeping Maecel closer, Kimber's quick intake of breath and the rustling of jungle litter as she took shelter behind him spurred him on. He had a family to protect!

Flexing his biceps, he hauled it up—

"No!" Datu's snapped word slammed into Jon, who nearly stumbled forward as he tried to stop the inertia.

Regaining his footing, he looked at the chief's son. "What do you mean, 'no'? That thing can kill us. I'm going to do whatever it takes to protect my family."

"If soldiers find carcass, they find us."

The logic was flimsy, but a margin of truth remained in it.

"This way. We go this way. No kill snake." Datu waved Kimber and the others to the side and around trees and bushes, avoiding the snake and apparent proof of their whereabouts.

Jon watched as the group filed single file in a wide arc.

Something ate at him about the way Datu seemed so adamant about leaving no trail. They were in the middle of a dense tropical jungle on an island and hours away from any cities. What was he afraid would draw trouble? The smell of one snake's rotting corpse?

With one last look at the banana-colored snake, he trudged behind the others. Maybe it was just exhaustion settling in that made him feel so edgy. Trust had never come easy to Jon, but eking out a living in a village with natives who were nothing like you—they bore the olive skin, dark eyes, and short stature of their lineage, and he bore his own blond hair, blue eyes, and near-basketball-player height—presented its own challenges, not unlike the ones he'd battled in Colorado and by not being a basketball player in a college of state champions. But here? Here he'd found happiness and peace. And a deeper level of trust in God's sovereignty and ability to provide, always provide.

No, this concern wasn't the result of his spiritual journey, the journey that restored him to his father—for the most part—and to God the Father, eventually bringing him here. A journey that proved to him that he didn't deserve the love of those who'd become a part of his life. Kimber. Maecel.

Or maybe it was because of his spiritual walk. Perhaps this nagging was a warning. Of the supernatural kind.

Yeah. As the delicate realization took root in his gut, he grew to understand the guidance of the Holy Spirit in this instance. A sweet, soft voice never raised over the din of life's chaos. A gentle word, a slow breeze.

Show me, God. What do You want me to see?

Almost instantly his eyes skimmed the dozen feet stretching between him and the last man in the group. Weeds bent and snapped. Grass and jungle litter crushed flat. A shrub's branches broken. With a half dozen of them slogging up a hill, anyone with a brain could find the trail.

Pausing, Jon drew back. No, something wasn't right. As a matter of fact, this was very wrong. They were heading much farther north than necessary. Getting up and away from the village made sense, but this route? Wasn't this the way Igme had warned them about? The blue-streaked jungle warriors lived up this way, didn't they? But as Kimber had asked—why? Why would Datu take them into the jaws of the lion?

He considered the man he'd allowed to lead them into the heart of darkness. What did he really know about Datu? He knew Igme, Datu's father, well enough—a very reputable and honorable chief among those on the island. There wasn't a clan or village that didn't know Igme or his fair rule. When IHF first made contact and offered education and financial assistance, Igme had readily agreed. It had been an amazing experience for Jon to lead the man through the prayer of salvation.

Over the last two years of living with the clan, Jon had grown to love Igme, staying up late discussing matters within the village and outside. Even now he remembered the chief's concern about his second-eldest son, Datu.

His soul wanders. It was the only thing Igme had said of his second born. Not being the eldest and not having the blessing of his father yet, Datu had not been granted a seat during clan meetings. Jon had thought Datu had been a bit restless because of this, but was it more?

And where was Igme?

The thought stopped him cold. He pivoted, as if he could see through the miles of vegetation they'd already traversed and back to their village.

Only as he considered the chief's son plodding uphill with confidence and determination did Jon realize there might be something more sinister at work. What if he was leading them to the Higanti for a specific purpose? But what? What would he...?

Jon's stomach clenched as a thought took hold. *A trade.*

He locked his gaze on the slight form of Igme's second-born. Had his soul wandered to the darkness? Jon's thoughts swam as a sizable distance grew between him and the group.

"Jon?"

He looked up the incline, grateful to see Kimber slipping back through the ranks to him. Good, he could share his concerns with her.

From the front, Datu's brow furrowed as he stared down at him.

"I'm right behind you," Jon said, hoping to reassure the man and not draw attention to himself or his suspicions. As Kimber dropped behind with him, he nodded for her to start back up the incline. "Keep moving and listen."

Her blue eyes widened. For a second, she seemed to study him, then nodded and hiked.

"Something's not right," Jon whispered.

Over her shoulder, she said, "I can sense it now, too."

Relief flooded him at her simple words.

"What do we do?"

Several steps filled the gap as he tried to figure out the best way to effect his plan. "I'm going to fall back some and try to contact Peter to see—don't turn around!"

She whipped back to the front, and he could see her arms automatically embrace the sling with their sleeping daughter. Still, he noticed the way her movements became mechanized, stiff.

"Try to act natural, Kimber. We need to buy as much time as we can."

When the lead was enough that he felt Datu wouldn't detect his actions, Jon eased the sat phone from his pocket. Holding it low, he scrolled to Peter Jordan's information. Gaze bouncing to the others, he pressed SEND and watched the connection symbol, waiting for it to sync up. A second later, he stepped off the path and stood behind a tree. He tugged up the hood on his shirt and tucked his chin, eyes on the group.

The ringing tone sounded like a screeching monkey in his ear. His pulse ratcheted.

The line picked up. Clanking. Had the phone been dropped.

"Hello? Jon, is that you?"

He pulled in closer to the tree. "Yes, Peter, it's me."

"Thank You, God! Jon, where are you? Did you miss your flight?"

"No. Yes."

Peter laughed. "I know you weren't ready to come back, but for pity's—"

"Peter, listen! Things are bad. Kimber and I are on the run with Datu."

"Igme's son?" Peter's voice hitched at the end.

"Yes. You have to send help. I think he's taking us to the Higanti."

"Hig—no! You can't let him." Strain cracked the jovial mood of Peter's tone from seconds earlier. "Get out of there, Jon. *Now!* Oh, dear God, help me think!"

"Mauk overran the island. There's nowhere else." He peeked around the palm trunk—bamboo barreled at him.

Crack!

His vision ghosted. Pain wracked his head. Warmth slithered down his face. Kimber's cries screamed into the blackness that devoured him.

CHAPTER 9

D on't move!" *With his M4 trained on her, he ignored the bead of sweat that streaked from his helmet into his eye.*

Head-to-toe gauze swayed in the hot desert wind. Dark brown eyes peeked out from the burka.

His gaze locked on the rectangular bulge beneath the light material. The fabric caught—revealing a corner. Shouts and snapped words erupted around him. The men in his unit scrambled innocents to safety behind a cement barricade.

Grip tight but not too tight, he stared down the sights. "Raise your hands! Raise your hands!" Another soldier swooped around her from the left, hollering as they kept a safe distance.

Tears poured from her eyes. She shook her head.

"Don't do it," he shouted in Pashto as he backed up. Please don't.

Screaming in her native language, she said, "I have no choice." Her hand moved toward her torso.

"No!" Max dove.

Boom!

He jolted, the memory fresh and painful of the instant his body had rammed into the barricade, breaking his arm.

Darkness drenched the night with sweat and nightmares. Wrestling with the sheet, he dragged himself off the mattress and pushed up. He stumbled to the shower and flipped the water on. Under the icy spray, he propped himself on the wall, his forehead against his arms, trying to forget the young woman who'd been forced to obliterate herself in the name of radical Islam. He pounded the wall with a guttural cry.

Why couldn't he forget her? Or the little boy who'd blown himself up after his family had been killed in a deadly engagement in the mountains of Afghanistan? Or the countless others who'd eaten his bullets? His buddies who'd lost limbs or life itself?

Two weeks in the Caribbean hadn't erased those memories. Two years wouldn't either. He'd live with this for the rest of his life.

Oh. . .God. . .help. He lowered himself to the floor and buried his head in his hands. At seventeen and stupid, he'd believed God had called him into the military, given him a gift, as it were. Some gift. Complete with everlasting repercussions. Wounds that don't heal.

"Why?" he shouted, ramming his elbow into the walls. "Why would You do this to me? Why put me in those places and rip me apart, inside out? I've lost everything—*everything* because of this job! Why? Do You enjoy tormenting me?"

Bang, bang, bang!

Max jerked himself off the shower floor and spun, as if looking through the wall to the front door. He spun the handles, snatching a towel from the shelf. Hurriedly, he dried off and stuffed himself into clean undergarments, then a pair of jeans. Hobbling as he slid his foot through the other leg, he hurried to the door. "Coming!" He zipped the jeans then raked a hand through his hair, glancing around for a shirt. No go. He swung the door open.

Cowboy tipped the rim of his Stetson back and grinned. "Am I interrupting?"

"Probably saving me from a bolt of lightning." Max waved him in and darted to the bedroom, grabbing a T-shirt. Weaving his hands into the cotton, he returned to the living room. "So, what brings you by this pit so late?"

"Visiting some old friends in the area." Cowboy handed Max a small box. "After the island, I got this for you. Might want to dig into it."

Tentative of the contents, Max considered the overgrown cowboy as he glanced at the name on the bag. "Hastings?" He wrinkled his nose. "Can't say I'd ever expect to see you at a high-end shop like that."

"The bag. . .I. . .um. . .it was the only one lying around the house. My mom shops there." He removed his hat and smoothed his hair.

Since when had the cowboy acted nervous? Max drew the box out of the bag and stilled as he glanced down at a small black Bible. The gift irritated him. Pat answers always had. "Thanks, but I think God and I are through."

"Have you asked Him about that?"

"Look, it's a nice thought, but. . ." He ran his thumb over the gold lettering of his name on the cover. Changing the subject wouldn't work. Not with Cowboy. Max just had to gut it up. Even if he did bare his soul in the process. At least he knew his venom wouldn't affect the man before him. "I joined the Navy because I thought. . .I thought that's where God wanted me." Grief choked him. "Now look at me. An angry screwup."

The man's large hand rested on Max's shoulder. "Start reading about David." He tapped the Bible. "The king faced battles, enemies who tried to kill him. Check out his story. I think you'll find out you're not alone." Cowboy squeezed. "No, I *know* you're not alone."

The gold-edged pages gleamed at him. "I don't know, man. Not really up for a guilt trip."

As he reached for the knob, Cowboy chuckled. "Who is? But if you want to salvage your life—and I'll say it again: your marriage is *not* lost—then this is where you start. Fight for something that's worth it, Max."

Alone once again, Max fanned through the pages, the burst of cool air thick with new-paper smell. A million black words whizzed past. Handwriting scrawled over the thin paper caught his attention. He flipped to the dedication page. Sentimental Cowboy had inscribed it with the To, From, Date, and a scripture reference. Maybe the cowboy was right.

Right, how? It wasn't like reading a book could fix his problems. Or blot out the gruesome images that haunted his waking and sleeping.

Could it?

He shook his head. How many times had he felt guilty hearing all the sermons about what he should be doing? What good did it all do?

Max slid the Bible onto the kitchen counter, grabbed a bottled water from the fridge, and went to his weight bench. Seated on the inclined bench, he turned on the TV then eased himself back and lifted the bar from the braces. Pumping iron, running, and baseball had always been his outlets. Tonight it just didn't seem to faze him or take the edge off his burning agitation.

The monotonous drone of a twenty-four-hour news channel blended into his puffs and grunts as he worked his muscle groups and toned his body. It was one thing Sydney *did* like about him.

He paused, hands on the bar overhead, remembering her warm fingers smoothing over his chest and abs. Longing for her touch ate at him. Max sat up and stole a peek at the Bible. Maybe. . . for her.

Won't work.

The news anchor's voice snagged Max's attention with talk of a possible bombing. *"A small community has been literally rocked during a late night explosion."*

"That's right, Alfred. Tonight the small community of Harvard

Oaks is reeling from a devastating explosion that has leveled one home and damaged two others."

Max pushed to his feet, staring at the screen. Harvard Oaks. That's where their house was, the one he and Sydney built.

"Three fire departments have responded and are battling this incredible blaze. As you can see behind me," she reported as the camera panned, *"little is left of this once-beautiful home. With me, I have a neighbor."* The reporter shifted and the camera turned.

Max grabbed the sides of the TV, staring. . . . That. Was it his home? It was! No, this couldn't be possible.

"What is your name, sir?"

"Mike Brookshire." His neighbor!

"What can you tell us, Mr. Brookshire, about this home and the people who live there?"

Disbelief froze Max. His home, the one he'd shared with Sydney, lay in ruins. He sprinted to his room and grabbed his keys and jacket, his heart jack-hammering. Ripping across town on his Hayabusa, he pushed 120. Couldn't get there fast enough. Was she dead? Had the explosion killed her?

The bike wobbled. Front tire skidded, but he pulled it straight.

God, if You're still listening. . .just let her be alive.

A hard right brought him onto the street. Emergency personnel blocked the road, redirecting traffic and ordering onlookers to stay at a safe distance.

"Sorry, you'll have to turn back," an officer told Max.

"I live here," Max said. "I think it's my house."

"What address?"

"Seven-hundred Morning Sun."

The cop's face paled. "Go ahead, but stay out of the way."

Max's stomach churned. A thick plume of smoke billowed down the street, snaking over homes and yards. As he neared, he spotted a red F-250 and guided his bike to the curb. Bryce. He should've known her brother would be here already. Why hadn't anyone called him?

Because you're not part of the family now.

But by law, she was still his wife. Max hoofed it the last fifty yards. Four fire trucks crammed into the tiny curve in the street where the house sat. A black body bag sat on the sidewalk, two techs bent over it.

His knees buckled. *God, no!*

"Come over this way. There's not as much smoke, Mrs. Jacobs."

Max jerked up, spotting a swarm of emergency workers around a woman—Sydney. A large fire jacket hung on her narrow shoulders, devouring her. Cheeks marred from the ash, she slumped into her brother's arms. Rivulets of tears marked their path with stunning clarity against the gray smudges.

"I'm terribly sorry about your mother," a woman crooned as she brushed Sydney's hair back.

Her mom? Only then did he see the white Chrysler 300 sitting in the drive, mangled and blackened. What happened?

Without hesitation, he darted toward her. "Sydney!"

She shoved to her feet, face awash with—could it be? She looked relieved to see him.

He reached for her, surprised when she came into his arms willingly. "Are you okay?" He pressed a kiss to the top of her smoky-smelling hair.

She clung to him. "She's gone. My mom is dead." Even in his arms, she struggled to remain on her feet, so he eased her down to the back of the ambulance. "It should've been me; it should've been me."

"Don't say that," Max urged, kneeling before her.

"The investigators said it looked like an accident, Syd," Bryce added, his heated glare never leaving Max.

Said it looked like an accident. Max studied his brother-in-law for a moment. Bryce the Detective knew something, something he didn't want to voice in front of Sydney.

"You shouldn't be here," Bryce finally grumbled.

Max had expected as much. The man was right—the protective order. Turning his attention to Sydney, Max stilled. He didn't want to leave her, not like this with their home burning—the last symbol of their marriage.

"You should leave," she mumbled, more tears spilling as she gripped his hand. "I don't want another fight."

"A fight?" Did she really think he'd start one here? Now? With all this?

"You heard her." Bryce moved closer.

Max tensed, his muscles flexing.

Sydney reached out, her hand touching his cheek. "I. . ." She looked down at her lap, then brought her tormented gaze to his.

"Syd." He swept her face, aching.

"Leave now," Bryce said, shouldering his way into the moment, "and I won't have you arrested or file a complaint."

Max hung his head, the volley of fury barreling up his chest.

"Please, go." She sniffled then stood and walked away.

An IED wouldn't have done more damage.

He couldn't just let her go. Inclined to follow, he started forward, but Bryce cut into his path. Max took a step back and watched as a paramedic handed Sydney an oxygen mask.

"You never did know when to leave well enough alone," Bryce said.

"What's going on?" Max glanced around the scene. "Why did she say it was supposed to be her?"

Bryce stared at him for several long seconds, the whirring of engines and sirens deafening, but distant to the chaos engulfing Max now. "A gas leak."

Max's eyes darted to the house, where the crumbling fireplace stood lonely, a smoking sentry amid fallen comrades. "Some leak."

A nod. "They've called an arson investigator."

He watched Sydney being tended in the back of an emergency vehicle. "Is she hurt?"

"Shock." Bryce took a step back. "Stay away, Max. She's putting her life back together. I won't let you hurt her again."

"It's not your decision."

"Oh yeah, it is." Bryce's chest rose, the threat obvious. "She gave you everything and every chance, and you threw it away. You didn't deserve her six years ago, and you don't deserve them now."

Nothing on earth compared to being in his arms. The burst of comfort and relief when Max had taken her into his embrace had been sudden and unexpected, so natural, that Sydney couldn't hold back. Warmth bathed her fears and grief. He smelled so good, felt so strong.

"I think you should let them take you to the hospital," Bryce said as he returned.

Hadn't he been talking to Max? Sydney's gaze roamed the chaotic scene for the black leather jacket. There. By his bike across the street, watching and probably listening. He was close enough. But could he hear with the chaos simmering around them?

Her stomach knotted when Max met her gaze. "No, I'm not ready to leave. I want to know what happened."

"Syd—"

"No." She whipped around. "Someone threatened me. Told me it was my only warning. Now our mom is dead. I want to know if someone murdered her."

"A threat?" A cop stepped forward, the fire from the neighbor's house dancing off his gold badge and the buttons on his shirt. "What kind of threat?"

Sydney let out a huff. "A phone call earlier today. It was a man.

He said, 'First and only warning. Leave it alone.'"

The cop glanced at another man dressed in a blue suit. "And what was he asking you to leave alone?"

"He didn't say," Sydney said, praying they wouldn't ask her to elaborate. If she did, if she was right about this, no doubt Bryce and a million others would order her to leave the "For Human Sake" story alone. But she couldn't.

"But you know what it is." The suit slid his hands into his pockets, acting far too casual. "Is that right, Mrs. Jacobs?"

"I have a suspicion."

"And?"

She let go of the idea that she wouldn't have to tell them. "I'm working on a story for the *Virginia Independent*. I think it might be related to that." Sydney scratched her stomach beneath the fire jacket that still kept the chill at bay.

"Why are you being evasive?"

She flashed her eyes to the man. "First, I don't know who you are. Second, it's my story, and I don't want you, or anyone else, telling me to back off when it's so important someone is killing people over it."

Bryce touched her shoulder. "Sydney, it's not worth your life."

"What if it is?" The hot, fire-driven wind tossed her hair in her face. She batted it away, tasting the grit of the ash raining down. "What if this story means someone else stays alive? Or an entire village?"

"I don't understand." The suit still hadn't volunteered his identity.

"It's a human interest story. I interviewed a refugee woman from Namibia. She said a group of elite soldiers stopped Janjaweed troops from terrorizing and destroying her village." Her breath caught, realizing how much of her story she'd just divulged. She had to turn this away from the details. "When I started digging, it upset a lot of people."

Bryce glowered. "Define upset."

She cast a guilty look at her brother. "My boss got chewed out by the Pentagon, who accused me of harassing their employees."

"Were you?"

Sydney itched to slap the smug look off the suit's face. "No. I wanted answers. They weren't willing to give them." Her gaze flicked to movement nearby. She frowned when she realized it was Max. He'd apparently sneaked closer but now jogged down the street. Why was he in such a hurry?

"So, you think your little column in the paper has brought out an assassin?"

She snapped her eyes to the suit. "Mock me, whoever-you-are, but the pieces seem to fit. Tonight I'd been to the home of a woman who survived the Mozambique raid. She was terrified of something, wouldn't talk to me. Her aunt insisted I had the wrong information."

"Maybe you did."

Her pulse quickened. "Maybe I didn't. I saw a picture her son drew. It looked just like a symbol the first woman said the soldiers wore. By the time I get home, my mom is dead, my house is in ruins, and you have nothing better to do than to call me a liar."

The cop stepped forward and motioned her toward the EMT. "Why don't you let us take you to the hospital?"

She jerked out of his hold. "I'm fine."

"Syd, let them check you out," Bryce said in a low voice. "At least to make sure the baby's okay. You've had a bad shock."

Yes, it wasn't every day you come home to find firefighters dragging your mother's crispy body out of your burning home. Tears sprang to her eyes almost instantly, her heart thundering. "Mom won't get to see my baby."

A sob rattled through her as Bryce took her into his arms, leading her into the ambulance and onto the white mattress. She stared out the back window as her entire existence smoldered in a heap of ash and charred wood, only remotely aware of the two techs checking her vitals.

Was there anything left for God to destroy? Her hand automatically went to her belly. *Please, no.*

And for the first time, Sydney yearned for this new life, new beginning.

"Get me Olin."

"It doesn't work that way," Legend said, his words sluggish and terse. Had Max woken him?

"I don't care. Someone just tried to kill my wife."

"Now hold up."

"Give me Olin, or I'll find him, and I guarantee there won't be much left."

"I'll page him to your number."

Max slammed the phone against his bike. Sick and nauseated that Sydney had been tracing the team responsible for Namibia and Mozambique, he tried to grapple with the reality that she'd been hunting Nightshade. *Me.*

Lambert vowed that he was the only one who knew their identities. Which meant the only person who could've called in an asset against Sydney was Olin Lambert.

And Max would kill him.

DAY FOUR

Shouts crawled through the muddled space of Jonathan's mind. A needling sensation worked into his wrist. Exhaustion pressed down on him, willing him back to sleep. In the hopes of ridding himself of the prickling, he flicked his hand. Tiny daggers of fire knifed through his arm.

His eyes shot open.

Blinding light stabbed his corneas. He snapped his eyes shut, squeezing them tight against the sun-bleached landscape. *Where am I? What happened?*

Slowly, he opened his eyes again. Dirt spread out before him. Soft puffs bursting before his face with each labored breath. A large shape stood nearby, but he couldn't make it out with his vision waxing soft.

To push himself up off the ground, he dragged his arms. A hollow metal clanking ensued. Vision blurring, he spied black and red wrapping around his wrist. He pulled his arm closer—

Pain chomped through his arm and shoulder. With a howl, he slumped to the ground. His head thudded against the hard earth, reverberating with shouts that erupted around him. The nearby object moved—a boot! As fire slithered through his neck and shoulders, immobilizing him for a second, he watched a man running away from him, shouting.

Where am I? Jon shook his head, trying to clear his vision. The movement felt like an anvil had attached itself to his neck. Still, his sight slowly focused. He looked around, surprised to find a dozen camouflaged huts around him—outside a wire fence. With a groan, he shifted on his side and cupped his arm. At that moment, he felt the thick stickiness. He narrowed his eyes as he looked at his arm. Swollen nearly twice its size, a portion stuck out. Stomach heaving, he lurched as his body unloaded the contents of his stomach—bile and foam.

How long had he been out? Where was he?

He groped for a connection to the pain, the disorientation. The village. He closed his eyes and wracked his brain. What. . .? Warmth crept in amid his thoughts. And like the floods during rainy season, it came rushing back to him. Datu, the hike to. . .

Higanti.

Jon looked up, still cradling his arm. The perimeter fence was not a fence. He was imprisoned! Beyond the cage, several dwellings were built into the jungle, hidden and yet in plain sight. His gaze raked the canopy. No aerial photos or satellite images would capture the truth of what went on under the palms and other trees.

He'd been right. Datu had walked them straight into the Higanti. Where were his wife and daughter? What had happened to them?

Hope sagged like a wilting date palm. Sweat dribbled down his temples as the pain radiated throughout his body.

Kimber! He plunged forward, frantically searching what lay beyond the tangled wire for any sign of her. "Kimber!" He gripped the metal with his good arm and rattled, sending shards of pain ringing through his body. Electrified!

He stepped back, his fingers tingling. He swallowed, his tongue feeling dry and metallic. Pushing past the stinging sensation, he focused on searching for his family. "Kimber, can you hear me?" His shouts echoed and bounced back to him.

Fear tormented him, knowing all too well what could happen to his wife and daughter. He'd seen the results firsthand with Kezia. The poor girl!

God! Father of all that is merciful and good—protect them!

Jon dropped to the ground. Rocks and dirt dug into his knees. Defeat clung to him like a rotting corpse. He tossed his head back, face to the heavens. *"Kimmmbberrr!"*

CHAPTER 10

The darkened interior shifted as the door opened; then the young man in black slumped against the leather seat across from him.

"This is most unusual, Mr. Jacobs." Olin quickly noted the balled fists. Trembling signaled the fury bubbling under the frayed edges of the man's control. A wrong word would ignite the highly volatile chemical mixture churning in the man's gut.

Heat blazed from the dark eyes, shadowed by anger and sleepless nights. "So's trying to kill my wife."

Max lunged.

Olin held up a hand. "I did not try to kill your wife." He gauged the former Navy SEAL. "Tell me what you know."

"You've been good to me, so I'll play your game." Max scooted to the edge of his seat, stabbing a finger at Olin. "Someone threatened her. Told her she had one warning. Less than twenty-four hours later, my home is blasted to hell, and my mother-in-law is dead." He inched closer, his arms on his knees. "So cut it straight, or I'll shove those platitudes down your throat."

Olin studied the young man. He wouldn't come half-cocked, even with his penchant for rage. And Olin wouldn't have met with him if this very scenario weren't plausible.

Apparently, the Joint Chiefs chairman hadn't kept his agreement. Since Olin was the only higher up who knew the identities of the Nightshade team, that meant the chairman had no idea he'd just tried to eliminate the wife of a team member.

"You said you were the only person who knew who we were. So tell me how someone tracked down my wife."

Olin raised his hands, his gut coiling tight. "You are my team, my men, my *sons*." He tried to temper the indignation, reminding himself he'd feel the same way were their roles reversed. "I will find out who did this."

"No good. I think you already know who did it. I want his name."

"You and I both know I don't work that way. I protect you, and I protect my sources. If I betray them, you'd never trust me again."

The jaw muscle flexed. "That's already a problem."

Olin knocked on the window. "Rest assured, I will take care of this."

"If you don't, I will. And I'll make sure they *never* hurt anyone again."

"You doing okay?" Lane eased into the patio seat and handed her a bottled water.

Sydney blinked, dragging her thoughts from the graveside service that had ended an hour ago. Church friends had gathered at her mom's home, bringing a truckload of food. Thankfully, the guests remained inside, giving Sydney some quiet.

"It's so hard to believe she's actually gone," Sydney said, twisting the lid off. Tears pricked her eyes again. "I keep expecting her to walk out the french doors and ask if I want some fruit." A sad smile pulled at her failing spirits.

A chill seeped through the thin fabric of her gray wool dress.

She shivered and swiped the sweat beads off the bottle so they didn't splotch her clothes. Gray dress. Gray clouds. Gray mood. It all fit. As if the world itself mourned Moira Kennedy's passing.

Sipping the water, she found herself drifting back to when her mother was alive. Times she'd come around the corner, a smile immediately filling her pretty face when she saw Sydney. Welcome arms always ready with a loving hug. It took the last of Sydney's reserves to remain composed, to not think about the fact that this was her mother's home, decorated by her mother and adorned with love and knickknacks by her mother. The impeccable garden flourishing because of her mother's penchant for nurturing all things living. Unlike Sydney's.

"You're shivering like a wet cat. Wanna go inside?"

With a one-shoulder shrug, she said, "Not really. I'm not up to entertaining or listening to stories, and I don't want to hear one more person say my mom's in a better place. I know that. But I miss her!"

"Yeah." Lane sat back and crossed his legs.

Something about the way he sat there irritated her. She couldn't put her finger on it, but...

She groaned, realization dawning. He wasn't Max. She was used to Max, the way he'd lean forward with one elbow propped on his knee, a hand on the other knee, looking tough and macho. Lane, on the other hand, was not macho. Or tough. Handsome and kind—she'd give him that. But he wasn't Max.

"We can go sit by the fire in the den. The girls were in there with their coloring books."

She didn't really want to be around her bubbly nieces, wreathed in innocence and naïveté, who had no idea what had taken place today. But her fingers and knees were starting to ache from the cold.

Lane tried to chuckle as he stood and held out a hand. "Let's go sit by the fire."

Ignoring his offered assistance, she dragged herself up and reluctantly stepped back into the house. Her nerves buzzed at the gospel music filling the house and at the soft chatter and laughter of the guests in the formal living room. She spied one of her mom's friends signing the guest book on the table near the door.

Grief assailed her anew, and she aimed herself toward the den. On the overstuffed sofa snuggled next to the fireplace, she settled on the suede cushions. Yet as soon as she drew the plaid blanket around her shoulders, she could almost see her mother carrying in a small plate of fruit and tea as she took up the Queen Anne chair across the room. Throat raw, Sydney pushed her mind and gaze to the crackling fire.

The cushion beside her shifted. "How you holding up?" Bryce settled an arm around her.

She bobbed her head and shrugged. "I'll make it."

He rubbed her shoulder. "We'll be here another week tying up loose ends, but when I get back home, I'm going to put in for a transfer. We should be together. You know, family and all."

Although she wanted to argue, to tell him it wasn't necessary, she didn't have the battle in her. She worried the shriveled tissue between her fingers.

"Vic said she and the girls could stay, so you won't be alone."

"No." She plastered a smile against her face and sniffled. The last thing she needed was Bryce's perfect wife with her perfect children and life as a glaring reminder of her wrecked life. "Really, I'll be okay. You need your family, Bryce. And I'm working now, so it's not like she'll have anyone to comfort or nurse."

"She feels bad; she wants to help."

Patting his hand, she sighed. "I know. You've got a gem there. Don't leave her here on my account." Knowing he'd argue to kingdom come, she scooted off the sofa. "I think I'm going to lie down for a while."

Amid sympathetic glances and somber condolences about

her mother's passing, Sydney made her way down the hall. In the guest bedroom, she leaned back against the door, her palms pressed against the slick veneer. The quaint room screamed her mother's presence—wedding-ring quilt on the full bed, lace curtains, antique dresser and mirror. The silly white shag carpet nestled against the trunk full of old family photos. Her mother was everywhere in this home. Yet she was gone.

Sorrow hung a tight cord around Sydney's neck. She moved into the room and unzipped the dark gray dress, her mind wandering back to the graveside service. She'd seen Max across the pristine lawns, standing amid the marble headstones and mausoleums. He looked so strong, so confident. So handsome in his leather jacket and slacks—when was the last time she'd seen him in anything but jeans? A soft smile filled her as she ached, remembering the supple leather against her cheek as she stepped into his embrace. He'd defied the protective order the night the house burned. Bryce had threatened to have him arrested, but she'd never been so grateful for his rebelliousness.

She lowered herself to the edge of the bed, one shoulder of the dress down, as she relived the total comfort and security she felt that night in his arms. That's where she belonged. In his arms. With him.

Remember, he's the one who refused to get help.

And she was the one who had filed the protective order. Something she never would've done if he hadn't hit her, left her scared and frightened of angering him. All those endless nights arguing and him trumpeting his tough, macho career and how important it was.

Sydney yanked off her black high heels and flung them across the room. Curse that man! She needed him now more than ever—and where was he? A safe, court-ordered fifty feet away, thanks to his thick skull. Pushing off the bed, she resolved not to pine after him anymore.

In her slip, she plodded to the bathroom, washed her face, then ran a brush through her hair. She paused as she set the brush on the marble counter, noticing the ever-so-slight bulge in her tummy. With a trembling chin, she ran her hand over the small roundness. Her mother wouldn't get to see this. A tear slipped over her stiff wall of composure. So much lost. In death, not only did the person die, so did dreams.

Back on the bed, she lay against the stack of pillows and gazed at the windows, the afternoon sun spilling through the gauzy, thin material. Despite the sun and warmth radiating into the room, a chill pervaded her. She toed a blanket from the end of the bed up and pulled it over her shoulders. Once again, she longed for Max to be here, to hold her as he had the other night.

"But he's not. So stop it," she chided herself.

Now that her mom lay buried, Sydney could not help but notice the emptiness and eerie void of her mother's presence. Bryce and Victoria would return to Maryland within the week—Sydney would make sure of that. She didn't need a woman whose life had taken the near-perfect route hanging around and telling her everything would be fine. And Max was gone.

I'm alone. Utterly and completely alone.

She blinked back more tears and stared up at the ceiling. An almost indiscernible flutter raced through her stomach. What had she eaten that gave her gas? She rested her hand on her belly and considered taking a tablet.

The tickle returned.

Sydney froze. That wasn't gas! She pressed both hands over her belly, her heart racing. *My baby!* Peering down at the protrusion sent more tears dashing down her cheeks. She blinked through the blur. A nervous bubble of laughter trickled up her throat.

"Oh, you're there. You're really real!" She laughed. Cried. All these months of thinking of this baby, she'd felt so distanced, as if it wasn't real. Even though it was. But having this sign, this tickle of reality, sent her heart soaring.

Had to tell someone. "Mom!" She lunged off the bed—and stopped cold. Reality slapped her hard. *Mom's dead.* She dropped against the soft mattress, burying her face in her hands.

Why had God torn her life apart? What had she done wrong? Hadn't she lived to honor Him? And this is what she got? An existence riddled with failure and heartbreak?

And now! An incredible miracle was happening inside her, and she had nobody to share it with. Bryce would just frown, his thoughts no doubt carrying out the brutal assault against Max he fantasized. Too caught up in her own selfish grief, she'd inadvertently deprived her mother of that pleasure. And herself. Now they'd never get to shop together for maternity clothes or for the baby.

Her baby! She'd felt the first whisper of life, tiny little legs swimming through her. How wondrous! Was it a boy or girl? The son or daughter she and Ma—

The warm fuzzies ground to a halt.

She ripped a pillow from the stack and flung it at the window. "I hate you!" she screamed at Max. The man who should be lying at her side, reveling in this awesome gift. But he wasn't. He was out somewhere living his life and pretending everything was fine.

Well, it wasn't! His son or daughter would be born and raised without him. "Why did you leave me?" she screamed through her tears, hating her rational left brain that said she wasn't being logical. "Why couldn't you fight for *us*?"

Carrying the lily, Max slunk across the near-perfect lawn. A mere hour had passed, but already the tent had been dismantled, the chairs and green carpet removed, and the casket lowered six feet under. Two workers slung dirt onto the hole. *Thump. Thump.*

He stilled, somber over the realization that it could've been Syd in that oak vault. He ground his teeth and gripped the white flower tighter. Olin had promised he'd take care of things. Had the thugs gotten the message? If not, Max would deliver it. Personally.

The men working the grave glanced at him then stopped and moved away from the semi-filled plot. Heart in his throat, he trudged closer and crouched next to the gaping hole. For several long, quiet minutes, he stared at the upturned dirt, so symbolic of his life that had been churned and shredded. The woman in the steel coffin didn't deserve this, a brutally cruel death. Sure, she'd been hard on him throughout the years he'd known her, but he'd deserved it. Truth be told, Mrs. K was the closest thing to a mother he'd had. Maybe that's why he rebelled against her. Didn't want to own up to the inscrutable feelings.

"I screwed up, Mrs. K." He shifted, feeling like a schoolboy. "I know that now, and I'm sorry." He ran his thumb along the waxy, green stem, knowing that if the tough Irishwoman were still here, she'd be giving him an earful.

Man, if he felt this massive hollowness at her passing, what must Sydney be feeling? He couldn't imagine. Oddly, he had this sudden urge to reassure the dead that he'd make it right, fix things, anything.

But could he? Could he pull himself together and get it right? How many empty promises cemented the gap between him and Syd? He couldn't even count the number of times he had apologized to the only woman who could tolerate him. Maybe he should try—

He'd just fail. Again.

"I don't think I can do it, Mrs. K. It's too late." He looked at the flower and heaved a sigh. "But I'm going to make sure she doesn't end up down there, too. Right now, that's the only promise I can make."

A thought dragged out the only smile he had left. "If you have it in good with the Big Guy up there, tell Him I could use some help." He stood and held the flower out over the chasm. "I'm sorry." Releasing the flower, he watched it tumble end over end until it landed softly on the dirt. "I'll look out for her. Adios, Mrs. K."

And he'd start by making sure the contract on his wife wasn't fulfilled.

Late into the night, Max tugged back the Velcro band on his watch and glanced at the glowing numbers. Syd's bedroom light had gone out thirty minutes ago. He leaned against the bark of the tree with an energy bar and his camelbak. Someone might think he was crazy or that this stakeout was futile, but if whoever blew the house figured out it was his mother-in-law, and not Sydney, who had died, they'd come back to finish the job.

Max chomped into the vitamin-compressed bar and chewed slowly. The look on her face at the graveside service had gouged a long, deep crevice through his heart. It said everything he already knew. He might not be a part of her life anymore, but that didn't mean he'd let someone hurt her. He'd dealt with enough power-houses to know how these types operated. Which meant leaving her unprotected wasn't an option.

Around ten o'clock a police cruiser slid down the street. Max pulled himself into the shadows, hoping the moon didn't reflect off his bike and draw attention. When the car disappeared around the next corner, he let out a shallow breath.

He hauled himself up into the tree and wedged himself against a couple of branches. Using his NVGs, he scanned the quiet neighborhood through a sea of green illumination. A cat's wicked eyes glowed back at him, followed by a meaty hiss.

Max sneezed as the fur ball scooted backward. *Stupid cat.*

The throaty rumble of a diesel engine roared through the night. A minute later a door opened then closed. Max swung the goggles around—and nearly cursed.

"You realize this is considered stalking?" Cowboy taunted him.

"How did you"—Max sneezed again—"find me?"

"Having a little feline trouble?" Cowboy waved him down. "Let's talk."

"I'm not leaving, if that's what you're here to tell me." Landing with a soft thump, Max considered his friend. "I'm sticking around to make sure whoever did this doesn't finish her off."

"I'm here to relieve you."

Max looked at his friend, stunned. "Seriously?"

Cowboy tilted his hat back a bit. "How are you? I mean, with the funeral and everything. Did you talk to her?"

"I obeyed the court order and remained fifty feet away." He pursed his lips and tried to laugh it off. "Wish someone would tell grief about that order so it'd keep its distance."

"Yeah, it's kinda selfish that way." Cowboy glanced at the house. "What room's she in?"

Max pivoted toward the colonial-style home with immaculately manicured lawns. "Her room has always been the front right corner. I'm guessing her brother and sister-in-law are using the master suite, and the girls are in the back bedroom."

"All right."

"What about your Remington?"

Cowboy grinned. "Never leave home without it."

Max nodded, appreciating that morsel of reassurance.

"Go on," Cowboy said. "Run home, shower up, grab some real food, and get some rest. Griff volunteered for early morning, so you're not back on duty until noon." Cowboy started back to his truck, his black Stetson pouring deep shadows over the man's face.

Max stared after him. "Why are you all doing this?"

Cowboy spun and walked backward. "We're a team. It's what we do."

Disbelief shrouded him. Nobody had ever done something like this for him. What made Cowboy do it?

The Bible.

Max shook his head. For several seconds he stood watching his mother-in-law's home then Cowboy's big black truck. At least Cowboy had his Remington 700. The cowboy could nail a guy nearly a mile away with his sniper skills. The thought pushed a smile into Max's face. This would be a good, *real* good time for the bad guy to show up.

DAY EIGHT

Throat raw, spirit and arm shattered, Jon lay staring up through the palm fronds as they waved overhead. They arched over him like guardians. If only they'd actually guarded. His screams for Kimber and subsequent shouts for anyone only introduced him to the butt of an AK-47 and knocked him out cold. At least he had slept, which was more than he could say now.

Unable to move without his head pounding, he lay as still as possible. Stars peeked through the canopy and winked at him. Night settled in around him like a plague, bringing with it every nocturnal critter possible. His skin crawled at the sound of their tiny legs pecking over the dirt and leaves.

"Get up!"

Something rammed into Jon's ribs as he lay on his side on the ground. He curled in on himself, trembling from a fever that devoured him.

"Get up!"

He opened his eyes just in time to see a boot swing toward his stomach—and braced for the blunt force. *Oof!* Jon doubled—and snatched the man's leg and jerked hard.

The soldier flipped onto his back. Just as quick, the man pulled himself up and lunged. He pinned Jon to the ground and rammed a fist into his face. Without a shred of mercy, the guy stood and stomped on Jon's broken arm.

Volcanic fire lit through every cell of his body.

His world spun—and went black.

Water. Cool. Refreshing. *Too much!* He couldn't breathe. Jon writhed. He was drowning! He yanked forward, gagging and coughing. Just as fast, his awareness hit on his grim environment. The soldier who'd pummeled him towered over him, laughing as he tossed a bucket to the side.

Head swimming, Jon tried to steady his body's volatile reactions. Propping up with one hand only served to make his stomach churn. His arm oozed blood and puss with each pump of his heart. He winced as he studied the distorted shape his arm hung at—it'd most likely have to be rebroken and reset when they returned to the States. His stomach roiled at the thought. And what ribs weren't broken protested the swelling and movement of any muscle. He squinted, wondering why his calf muscle seemed to stretch tight the fabric of his khaki pants.

"Leave him. We'll have fun with the others."

Jon's ears burned. He tried to watch where they headed, but when he turned his head, his elbow gave out. He fell hard against the earth—and his trembling body thanked him. Huffing against the exertion, he reminded himself he wasn't alone in this. Somewhere these dogs were holding his wife, daughter, and Kezia. And where was Datu?

On the thick, humid wind, a noise snagged his attention. He rolled his head around, searching the empty distance between his cage and the meticulously concealed huts. What had he heard?

A baby's wail pierced the early night.

"Maecel!" Jon dragged his body around, faced the direction. Every muscle trembled. Still, he strained and hauled himself to his feet. He stumbled to a pole that held the fence and propped himself up. "Kimber," he called, his voice cracking and bottoming out. Fresh pains scalded his raw throat.

Another cry from his infant daughter whispered through the thickening night.

"Maecel!" His shout was lost amid a rumble in the skies. He glanced up through the trees—nothing but black. Thunder cracked.

A scream blasted into him.

Jon frantically searched the village. "Kimber!" He'd not seen a single soul in the days he'd been here, save the men who'd beaten him. How could there be so many huts draped with branches and trees, bushes heavily planted around them for concealment, and no people?

"Kimber!" His veins pulsed furiously as he howled her name.

He had no sooner heard footsteps to the side and looked—than he met with the hard plastic end of a fully automatic weapon.

Jon dropped like a rock on his left side. Pain spiked through his arm.

The hulking mass stood over him and again drove the butt of the weapon into him.

"Stop! We need him alive."

The man hovering shuffled his feet closer to Jon's head. He mumbled a curse, struck Jon's head with the steel-toed boot, then left. Jon pushed himself onto his back and lay staring up at the sky, crying. A drop plopped onto his cheek, cold and wet. Rain.

Of course. He chuckled. Rainy season. Why not? Everything else had gone wrong.

Within seconds, a deluge washed over him. He lay with his eyes closed, rain pelting his body and drenching his clothes, his very soul. Lightning splintered the darkness. A storm raged around him and in him. Invaded his life. A half snort worked its way up his throat. Hadn't he just a day ago—or was it more?—whined about being yanked from the island, afraid his purpose hadn't been fulfilled? Was this his purpose? After all their hard work, was it his fate to be a martyr?

Be a missionary, save a tribe, see children clothed, fed, and educated. Being here, being a hand, a physical extension of Christ's love, had given him pleasure. He could almost say it fulfilled him. Now, was he to die for the cause? A martyr. Odd. He'd never seen his life going that way.

Temptation dripped into his soul to just let himself go. Just let the elements and injuries have their way. Already, he could feel the cold rain numbing his extremities. The ground beneath him sluiced, and he sank lower. He was being taken from the Tagalog anyway. Did it matter?

What would happen to Kimber and Maecel? If they survived.

His eyes popped open. Survive? A beautiful, white, Christian woman? She'd have no chance. They'd brutally rape, beat, and hack her up for speaking up for her faith, which she would. Oh, she definitely would. How many times had he longed for just a half ounce of her die-hard determination? If she wasn't already dead, she would be. And he couldn't do a single thing about it.

And Maecel. Her chubby, round face of innocence. Every semblance of that which Mauk and the Higanti hated.

He had to get himself together. If he wasn't dead yet, then maybe God wasn't finished with him. And if Maecel was still out there crying, then no way would Jon Harris lie down like a dog, lick his wounds, and die. He had to fight. Had to save them!

He tried to pull himself up, but the muddy ground formed a suction, resisting his efforts. Finally, with a slurping noise, he broke free from the hold of the earth. He pushed and dragged himself to his feet. Shuffling back to the pole, he weighed his options. Shouting in this storm would do no good. Nobody would hear him, let alone care.

He sighed and did the thing he should've done first. Prayed. "God," he began, emotion clogging his throat. Head tucked, he peered through the rain in the same direction he'd heard his baby girl. "They're out there. I don't believe You brought us this far to have us slaughtered." At least, he seriously hoped not. "Help me stand firm. . . . Just. . .help me."

White lit the night. Jon waited for the rumble of thunder sure to follow. Would they have a chance to escape? Slipping and sliding down the hilly terrain could prove deadly. Jon looked up to gauge how hard or long the storm would last, but he couldn't see anything.

Can't see.

A smile dug into his face. He might not be able to see, but Someone else could. And maybe, just maybe, that Someone could open someone else's "eyes"—the military used heat-seeking satellites, right? Maybe if Jordan got a message to someone, they could track Jon's sat phone to the area, then use thermal imaging.

Was it hoping for too much?

What did he have to lose?

His wife and daughter.

CHAPTER 11

Suspicious? How?"

"Bryce, grow a brain!" Sydney worked hard to control her irritation, still exhausted from yesterday's funeral and the exhilarating first flutter of life within. "I don't believe it's a coincidence that my house explodes and kills our mother on the same day I got threatened."

He held out his hands. "I can see why you might come to that conclusion, but there's no evidence, and until the investigation report comes back, we can't do anything."

She wanted to claw the reasonable, rational mentality from his skull. He'd been a detective too long. "So we just sit around while Mom's killer runs free? What if they come back?"

Bryce scowled. "Sydney." He looked toward the living room where Victoria was herding the girls for bedtime. "Let's just take things one fact at a time. Okay?"

"Fact? You want facts? First—"

The shrill tweedle of the phone cut her off. She glared at him and snatched the phone. A glance at the caller ID warned her to take this call privately. "Excuse me," she said and slunk away to answer. "Hello?"

"Hey, how're you?" Concern oozed through Lane's voice. "Can you talk?"

Sydney sighed and slipped down the hall to talk with Lane in private. "Anxious to get back to work, and yes, I can talk."

"Buck would shove me face first through the window if he knew I was calling."

She closed her bedroom door. "What's going on?"

"Well, I wanted to see if you'd share your notes on the incidents with me."

She straightened, feeling an innate possessiveness regarding her stories. "Why? Those are mine. I've worked them front to back—"

"I'm not trying to steal them. I just. . ." He huffed. "I found something I think is related."

"What?"

"I. . .Sydney, someone blew up your home. I don't think we should talk about this over the phone. Can you meet me?"

With a furtive glance to the door and knowing Bryce would have a conniption if she left this late, she hesitated. Then drew up her shoulders. Her brother wasn't going to rule her life anymore. Max had always said she was strong, but being protected by a detective brother and a spec ops husband, she'd never had to prove that strength.

No time like the present.

"Where?"

"Cassidy's at the North End. Say, in an hour?"

"I'll be there." Exhilaration swirled through her at the thought of defying her brother. Of a late-night mission about her story. In her closet, she changed into her favorite jeans, noting the waistband was fairly snug, and a black embellished T-shirt, then slipped into black flats. Armed with her messenger bag, purse, and phone, she strode into the kitchen, replaced the phone on its cradle, then started for the door. "I'll be back in a couple of hours."

"Whoa. Hold up," Bryce said, leaping over a couple of toys, his large strides carrying him quickly to her. "Where're you going?"

"Out," Sydney said, giving him a look she hoped conveyed her determination.

He paused, reaching for her. "Do you think that's a good idea? It's late, and—"

"I'm a grown woman, Bryce. I can't hide here. I can't bury my head in the sand."

"Nobody's asking you to do that, but Sydney, the baby. . . Mom."

"What about them, Bryce? Mom is gone." Her heart cinched into her throat. "I can't change that by gluing myself to her home for the rest of my life. And this baby is coming whether I'm here knitting a million outfits or meeting friends." She let out a stiff breath. "Please. Just give me room to be a person again, okay? I'm going insane here. You and Vic—" She clamped her mouth shut and looked away. She couldn't tell him how much it pained her to watch their perfect family going on without a hitch. "Don't wait up for me. I'll be fine."

Hustling down the steps to the path, she tried to calm her bouncing nerves. She'd never been so direct with him, so adamant. It wasn't that he meant to run her life or tell her what to do. Bryce had just been the man of the family for the last fifteen years, and with Mom's murder, he probably felt more burdened with the responsibility of watching over her than ever. But she wouldn't let him suffocate her.

Forty minutes later, as the adrenaline rush bottomed out, she pushed through the doors of the small pub with a massive reputation. She smiled, knowing Lane had chosen this spot not for the liquor and merriment, but for the crowds.

He spotted her and waved her to a booth in the far corner. A lone candle flickered on the table as she squeaked over the bench seat.

"Wow," he said, his grin large. "You look great, glowing."

Heat crawled up her neck and into her face. "Really?" Could

it be that the baby was already making her glow? She wondered what Lane would say about the baby. Would it temper his attraction to her, the attraction he'd never been able to hide? Or would he get all overprotective like Bryce? She shuddered.

A waitress slid a glass of water onto her table. "Something to drink?"

"I'm good. Thanks," Sydney said. Drawing the glass on the paper coaster toward her, she looked at Lane. "So, what'd you find?"

"Well, it's not so much what I *did* find as it is what I *didn't* find."

She shrugged out of her jacket and settled back against the vinyl seat. "Okay."

He leaned in, his green eyes probing the pub. "You've found two situations in which atrocities were carried out and many UN-bound countries had their hands tied."

"Right."

"Yet someone went in and silenced the problem."

As a tendril of smoke wove toward her, Sydney's irritation grew. "Lane, you're not telling me anything new. I've lined up interviews and am waiting on calls from the Pentagon."

"Exactly."

She blinked at his animated expression. "I'm not following you."

"What if the American government is connected?"

Sydney's ire ratcheted as she held up her hands in question. "Why do you think I'm trying to contact the Pentagon?"

"No," Lane said, hedging closer, his finger poking the table. "I mean, what if they're buying some favors. Classic Capitol Hill maneuver—you scratch my back, I'll scratch yours. If they're meddling in tribal uprisings—something we would never get involved in normally—it would seem they're intentionally shifting the balance of power."

"Why? And who would do something like that?"

"The payoff is greater than doing things the UN way? Someone's getting a fat pension? I bet some senator or congressman is living high off the hog for intervening, maybe the chairman of the Arms Committee? And with the threat against you, the attack, I can't believe it's random. Something is going on here that is far bigger than a human interest story."

Sydney swallowed the bitter burst of fear that glanced off her tongue. She ran her fingers through her hair, detangling the long strands as she worked the information over. "It would make sense." She nodded and smoothed back her hair. "I call the Pentagon about Namibia. They blow me off. Then I call about Moz, and they accuse me of harassment, nearly get me fired."

Lane propped an arm on the table. "Then you get the threat. And boom."

Sydney flinched.

He reached across the table and placed his hand on hers. "Syd, I'm sorry, I didn't. . . . Bad choice of words." Shifting closer, he eased into her personal space. "You okay?"

Feeling awkward at his touch, she forced a smile and burrowed back against the seat with a shaky nod. "I guess I'm not feeling so great."

"Would you like to get some air? We could walk the Strand."

After a curt nod, she strode out into the night, grateful for the early spring weather that doused her with a cool breeze. She inhaled deeply and tucked her purse over her shoulder. Burning around her lower abdomen begged for scratching, and she appeased the call, her mind drawn to the precious life inside her. Wonderful and bittersweet.

Lane emerged a minute later and joined her, his hand going to her elbow. "What was that smile for?"

"Just thinking."

They started up the sidewalk, making their way toward a well-lit street lined with shops and restaurants. "You look beautiful tonight." He tucked his hands in his pockets and hunched his shoulders.

With a shy, disconcerted smile, she thanked him and kept moving, trying not to think about all the times she'd spent on this very street at the little Italian eatery. Giuseppe's. Max's favorite spot. He always called ahead and arranged to sit at the table next to the pier. Max and water were like her with chocolate and peanut butter. Never enough.

"You seem distracted."

"Huh?"

"I've asked you twice now if you were hungry."

"Why would you ask that?"

"Because you're staring at a couple eating dinner."

Sydney jolted into the present, a blush heating her face. "I'm sorry. It's hard to let some things go." Once again walking, she steered her wayward thoughts back to the reason for meeting with Lane. "So what can I do? I mean, I'm not ready to let the stories go. I've hit a nerve." The salty breeze tousled her hair into her face, and she plucked the strands free. "I want to know what nerve that was."

"Me, too. I've never seen such a strong reaction. It has to mean something."

"Yeah, but can we prove it?" Would it be too dangerous to prove it? And how on earth had she ended up threatened by something that seemed so innocuous?

"The bigger question is, will we live if we do?"

She stopped short and looked up at him. They'd already killed her mother, so why wouldn't they come after her? Especially if. . .

She gasped.

Lane frowned. "Syd, what's wrong?"

"What if they hit my mom's house, and it kills Bryce and the girls?" Trembling at the thought, she felt her stomach heave. "What if they all die because of me?"

His arms came around her. "Shh, it'll be okay."

She pushed out of his arms and turned around. "I'm going home. Convince him to return to Maryland. At least then I won't have to worry about them." Half jogging, she hurried back to her car with an urgency she'd not felt in years.

"Syd, wait. There's no guarantee—"

"I have to try." She stepped off the curb and wove through traffic as she made her way to her silver Lexus. As she neared it, she slowed. What was that? Something flickered from under her windshield wiper. Stupid sales flyer. She reached for it—and froze. Her blood ran cold.

Not sales flyers. Two photos sat cockeyed under the blade. A photo of her and Lane in the pub. Another of them as they stood outside Giuseppe's.

Scrawled in red, three words glared at her: STOP OR DIE!

Hurtling over a motorcycle, Max ignored the screams erupting around him. He hit the ground and rocketed down an alley lit only by a corner lamp on the side of a building. Scattered light made specters out of every crate and trash can. But his focus remained locked on the man sprinting ahead of him. The man who'd stuffed something under Sydney's windshield wiper.

Max had almost missed the drop, he'd been so ticked to find his wife and her coworker taking a cozy stroll down the Strand. Once he saw the threat scribbled over the grainy photographs, he burst into action.

"If you want to live, stop!" Max shouted as he barreled around a corner.

A shop door sprung open.

Max spun around the obstacle and resumed the chase. When the man tried to scale a wall, Max caught up. He threw himself full force into the guy's back, grabbing the black windbreaker.

They dropped backward onto the hard ground. *Oof!* Wind knocked out of him, Max rolled right as the man scrambled. Scissoring his legs, he caught the guy's long legs and made him do a face plant. Arching his back and winging his arms, Max flung himself forward, nailing the guy in the spine. He couldn't kill him. Not yet. Needed information.

Max jerked him onto his back and slammed a hard right hook into his face. "Who are you? Who do you work for?"

"Nobody." The man coughed and spit blood.

"Who do you work for?" He punched him again then boxed his ears. A thousand messages bombarded Max—the guy didn't fight like an assassin. His moves were jerky, frantic. He couldn't even defend himself. "The pictures! Why are you taking pictures of her?"

"It wasn't me. It wasn't me," the man whimpered, his cement-shredded palms waving. "Some guy paid me to put them on the Lexus. That's all I know."

Even though Max knew hesitation killed, the panicked expression on the man—no, the teenager—stayed his lethal skills. "What'd he look like?"

"I—I don't remember."

Another hard right. "Wrong answer."

"Okay, okay." Eyes wide and mouth oozing dark spittle, the guy shrugged. "Dark hair. Tall. Oh! He had a—"

Thwat! Thwat!

Max flinched at the familiar sound—instincts sending him spiraling into the darkened corner. Where had the shots come from? Spine pressed against the steel back door to a shop, he crouched and peeked around the alley. Since he wasn't getting peppered with cement or bullets, he guessed the shooter didn't have a clear line of sight. Or he'd left. But the latter was a risk Max wouldn't take yet.

He eyed the kid, wanting to drag him to safety. No movement.

They'd killed their own messenger? His gut roiled. Max eased the Ruger from his holster and pushed up onto his feet, his back hugging the brick wall behind him. Checking around the corner—

Plaster spat at him.

He jerked back. If he went down, he didn't want someone framing him for the kid's murder. He tugged his phone from his pocket and punched in the code. "Bravo One. Tango engaged. Sending coordinates," he said into the coded program that would relay the information to the Nightshade team. They'd never get here in time, but at least he had covered his tail.

Eerie silence strangled the vibrancy of the once-busy area. With his shoulder forward and his focus streaking past the sights on his weapon, he slowly stepped from the shadows, inching along the walls. Processing every little shift in light, wind, and odor. He took a second to double-check the kid. The moon's glow glared off the blood pooling on the messenger's chest, mirroring the faint rise and fall of each breath.

Max stilled. The kid wasn't dead. Could he get to the kid in time? He searched the alley. If he went into the open, he could end up on the cold slab right next to the kid.

This wasn't Afghanistan or Iraq. And he couldn't leave an innocent teenager to die. Clear the alley fast. Get back to the kid. Plan in place, he quickened his pace, side-stepping down the alley. He cleared each shop alcove. As he eased around the corner— something big and woody barreled at him.

He swung hard to deflect. . .too late!

Pain shot through his head and neck. Blackness descended.

DAY NINE

Hours. He'd stayed up all night in the wind and rain, praying there was enough of his body heat to register on a thermal scan. But now, limbs aching and chilled to the bone, he watched the approach of dawn. With it came an oppressive sense of hopelessness.

Who was he kidding? The chances were bleak that the events could be lined up to bring a rescue. They were lost. They all were lost.

No. God is a God of miracles. All things are possible with Him.

All things were possible, but would they be rescued? What if God had other plans? What if God received more glory from Jon's death than his life? The thought twisted his gut.

Surely God wouldn't lead them here only to have Kimber and his sweet daughter butchered by men roused by violence and bloodshed.

Jon moaned. Longed for Kimber, to hear her calm voice, her ability to remain at peace in the midst of the storm. A strange feeling filled his chest—and yanked a hard cough out of him. On his side, he struggled through a coughing fit.

Dawn chased away the rain. At least for now. Jon had been on the island long enough to know once the season began, it would unleash its fury for weeks to come. He endured the harsh elements for two more days, each night lying out in the open, stretching his legs back and forth making mad angels. Ones he hoped could fly into the heavens and tap the shoulder of a U.S. satellite. It was his only hope.

Please, God. Just this one small miracle.

A third night descended with another deluge of rain and cold. Jon curled into a fetal position, his arm receiving a good cleansing. He prayed it'd rinse out the infection, since these goons weren't going to give him medical attention. A hacking cough seized control of his body. He coughed. And coughed. Struggled for air. Beat his own chest, trying to free the muscles that had clenched. But they wouldn't release.

His vision closed in, fading from gray to black.

CHAPTER 12

Awarbled sound bit through his brain. Max groaned.

"Hey, Frogman, time to rise and shine."

Pulling himself up, Max winced under the thunderous roar that surged through his head and shoulders. "What. . .?" He squinted at the brilliant light pervading the alley. Only. . .he wasn't in the alley. "Where am I?"

Legend loomed in front of him. "At the Shack."

Max swung his legs over the edge of the bed and hung his head. How'd he get back to the warehouse? "What happened?"

"Don't know." Legend joined him on the mattress. "When I showed up, you were out cold and some kid was dead."

Max stiffened, shards of pain stabbing his spine. He'd failed the kid. Failed! Again!

"So, Mr. Jacobs, what happened?"

Trying to find a position in which he could look up at Lambert without feeling like someone was sawing him off at the neck, Max grunted. "The kid. . ." His head pulsed with each syllable. "He planted some threatening photos on Syd's car. I chased him down. We fought, and that's when someone took him out."

General Lambert sighed. Paced, his slick shoes scratching over the cement floor. "I've managed to put a tight lid on this incident."

"Yeah," Max grunted, staring down at the dried blood on his knuckles. "That anything like your assurance that you'd make sure the source backed off, leave my wife alone?" He glowered at the general in the doorway.

"Point taken, Mr. Jacobs. While my words may feel like platitudes, I've taken extreme measures to put an end to this."

Max pried his gaze from the man. "I doubt your extreme measure and mine are the same."

Olin chuckled. "I would agree. The source is not dead."

"If he makes one more attempt on my wife, he will be."

"Give us a moment alone, please."

Max accepted the ice pack Legend stuffed toward him before he left. Applying the pack proved almost as painful as taking a hammer to his head.

"Max, what has happened is reprehensible."

"We're on the same page there."

"The source is trying to protect the team."

"Bull!" He cringed and let out a breathy groan. "He's covering his own backside."

Olin paused, tension lining his aged face. "Agreed." He finally lowered his gaze. "Remember, the only person who knows the identities of Nightshade team is me. The source has no idea he attacked the very hand he's feeding."

Max grunted as realization burrowed past the thunder in his ears. "And you can't tell him." Because if he did, the team would be exposed.

"I'm afraid not. I have, however, guaranteed your wife will be heavily compensated for what has happened."

He considered the general, a mixture of relief and outrage coursing through his veins. Compensation usually meant a bribe, a way to keep people quiet. Max wouldn't stay quiet if this happened again. But knowing that Sydney was being looked after felt like a salve. "While I don't like you buying my silence, and this in no way makes compensation for my mother-in-law's death, I'm grateful you're taking care of Sydney."

"She's important to you, so she's important to me."

Good. Because if not, he was gone.

"Reporting live from the Philippines, I'm Rorie Mills. Back to you, Alfred."

"So tell us, Rorie, how is Kezia doing now?"

"Hey, look, it's her!" Marshall grabbed the remote as he hushed the rest of the team gathered around the pool table. "Have you seen this reporter? She's hot!"

"Kezia is recovering with her family. Right now, she has twenty-four-hour guards as they protect this girl so she can bear witness against the atrocities of the local radicals who have slaughtered hundreds, possibly thousands, across this tiny island. As you know, this area is a hotbed for radical Muslims, who believe the only true religion is Islam, and they will kill those who disagree, including innocent girls like Kezia."

"And you say she's being guarded?"

"That's right. Her identity and location are a profound secret. When we inquired about her and requested this interview, we were blindfolded and driven to a remote area. While we were allowed to ask the questions, we were not allowed to see her face. She remained behind a thin cloth, as you saw in the interview, the entire time."

"Turn it down," Max grumbled from the corner, a fresh ice pack propped on his head as he slumped in the chair.

"Check her out, man." Marshall laughed. "I mean, not that you would have an interest. You're married, sort of." The Kid shuffled backward, his expression filled with uncertainty and outright fear, as if he expected Max to spring at him again.

"Don't worry, Kid, he's not up to a fight today," Legend taunted as he leaned over the pool table and smacked the cue ball.

"Probably the one day you can take your best shot—and actually place it!"

Laughter rumbled through the open room.

"Nah, Marshall is *vain*. He knows Max will take it out of his face later. Wouldn't wanna mess up that pretty mug," Fix said.

"My name's pronounced *Vaughn*, not *vain*. And pretty? My eyes are still yellow from his last temper tantrum. Trust me, if he's that foul without a knot on his head, I'm not going to mess with him now." Marshall walked out mumbling something about another broken nose and ribs. Then over his shoulder, he shot, "He'd probably whip out that Ruger."

Max held up his hands.

Fix and Midas laughed, the taunt half aimed at Max, but the rest at the inexperienced Kid. The camaraderie of the team made Max smile. And they were right. No way would he engage Marshall tonight. Not with the team heading out at oh-dark-thirty and him still recovering from the golf ball growing out of his thick skull. He dragged himself off the chair and trudged back to the bunks to get some shut-eye. On the cot, he positioned his pillow and laid back—and tensed at the pain prickling his nerves. He closed his eyes and shifted to the side.

His mind raced over the last week, returning from a vacation that felt more like a nightmare, finding the home he'd built with Sydney blown up, and then discovering his mother-in-law had been murdered. Would her death be avenged? He ground his teeth, knowing nothing would be done. The man responsible was buried in anonymity. Just like Nightshade. And tonight, running down an innocent kid, practically holding him down so the bad guy could silence him.

Would any of it ever make sense? Would he ever feel like what he was doing had a point, served a purpose?

"You read that book yet?"

A slow smile slid into Max's face, listening as Cowboy settled on a nearby bunk. "Vision's blurry."

Cowboy chuckled. "You could've read it last night."

"Busy. Sleeping."

Another chuckle. "Fair enough. When you're ready for change, the Word will be there."

The only thing confronting his anger or facing the pain did was make him angrier. And nobody needed *that*. "You always this pushy?"

"Call it a gentle prodding."

"You mean like a cattle prod?"

Cowboy broke into a fit of coughs. Pounding drew Max's attention to the fact the guy had a bottle of water. Tears pooled in his eyes. He thumped his chest then cleared his throat. "Shouldn't do that while a guy's drinking."

"Better be water. You wouldn't let me have any liquor." Settled back against the mattress, he closed his eyes and concentrated on loosening every muscle in the hopes of ridding himself of the bass drum booming in his head.

Cowboy's movements might as well have been a jackhammer for the way they rattled Max's nerves. But he remained still and quiet, knowing his body would thank him for it. Besides, the chopper would make ground meat out of his gray matter if he didn't.

"You talk to her yet?"

That pried open an eye.

Cowboy nodded. "Figured as much."

"She's already replaced me." He tried not to let the emotion thicken his voice. Tried not to remember the way she didn't pull away when Lane embraced her. So he'd been right to be jealous four months ago when he'd reset the guy's jaw.

"How's that?"

Painfully, he recounted the events. "She just stood there while he has his arm around her shoulder. Then they walked the Strand like star-struck lovers." His chest tightened. Had he really driven her that far away so fast? Heat worked its way up his vertebrae into his neck as he remembered when she'd stopped in front of Giuseppe's. Probably would've throttled Lane if he'd taken Syd in there. That was *their* spot. At least, it used to be.

"Do you really think Sydney was interested in him?"

That very question niggled at him, plucking his own doubts to the front of his mind. "Maybe she's better off with him." Yet it irked him. Sydney and that long-legged preppie. The images didn't click.

"You're full of it if you expect me to believe that."

Max rolled onto his stomach and reached down into his ruck-sack for some ibuprofen. Anything to chip the edge off this killer headache. So what if the cowboy didn't believe it? He hadn't been there when fury overrode common sense, when control was the furthest thing from Max's mind. Or when his fist accidentally collided with Sydney's sweet, round face instead of Lane's.

Like he said. Didn't want to think about it. It only made him angrier.

He grabbed the tablets and stuffed them in his mouth and swallowed as he gingerly pushed off the mattress. "Going to shower up." Anything to get away from the cowboy with the answers. Anything to get away from himself.

In the locker room, he flipped the knobs and set out his soap and shampoo. While the furnace took all year to heat the water, he sat on a nearby bench. Escape from the headache wasn't possible no matter what he did. Funny, same thing with the other pain. The one that disabled his ability to be the man his wife needed.

Grief strangled him. He bent, elbows on his knees, as he stared at the scabs on his knuckles. How many faces had rammed into his hands? Too many. He flexed his hand and stilled, the gold of his wedding band glinting under the harsh tease of the fluorescents.

He turned his hand over and twisted the ring around his finger, thinking of the day they'd exchanged vows. She'd looked fabulous in her Vera Wang gown. Although Sydney wasn't obsessed with fashion, she'd always wanted a Vera wedding gown. And she'd bowled him over, walking down the aisle on Imperial Beach. He grinned, remembering the incredible and daunting second he realized she was his responsibility. Maybe he'd known even then he couldn't cut it.

He eased the ring off and set it in his palm. Wouldn't need it in a few months. A complete circle not meant to be broken. But Max had broken it.

I serve with honor on and off the battlefield. The ability to control my emotions and my actions, regardless of circumstance, sets me apart from other men. Uncompromising integrity is my standard. My character and honor are steadfast. My word is my bond.

Haunted by the creed he'd failed, Max stuffed the ring back on, flipped off the shower, and strode toward the weight room.

Ability to control my temper. And yet he couldn't.

Or wouldn't.

He'd shower later. . .after a workout. A hard one.

Boxing gloves on, he trounced around the bulbous bag and beat the thing. Although he dripped sweat, the workout wasn't helping. His head howled. But that was good. Kept his mind busy or numbed. He didn't care which, as long as he didn't have to think about *her*.

At the bench press, he lay back and stared up at the mirrored ceiling, ignoring the pinch of pain from the knot. Next week was her birthday. His mind scrambled back to the pendant in his bag. He'd never given it to her for Christmas. Maybe. . .

He glanced at his watch.

Max jogged to the bunk room and found Cowboy where he'd left him. On the bunk and reading from a small black book, the cowboy sat with his eyes closed and head down.

He patted the guy's leg. "Cowboy, you praying or sleeping?"

Cowboy flinched but didn't open his eyes. "Resting my eyes," he murmured with a soft laugh before yawning.

"Do me a favor?"

DAY TWELVE

Sniffles drifted in and out of the darkness, strangled by a screeching noise.

Jon shifted and moaned. Heaviness soaked his muscles.

"Jon, please don't die on me."

Kimber.

He struggled to force his eyes open. Nothing. His body wasn't cooperating.

A coolness settled over his hand. "Jon, can you hear me? Please. . .we need you." Another dose of the screeching—wait! That wasn't a noise. It was Maecel's crying. His heart stirred and raced, speeding blood through his veins.

"Ki. . .m," he breathed.

The cold feeling on his hand tightened—she was holding his hand! "Yes, it's me." His arm lifted, and soon he felt her wet tears against his hand. *Merciful God, help me!* He concentrated everything he had in him. Slowly, his eyes fluttered. In that brief second, he saw the worry smothering his bride's peace.

He again focused his attention and opened his eyes, rolling his head in her direction.

Relief washed through her features. "Hey, you." She scooted closer.

Although he tried to take in their surroundings, it was too dark. A shaky breath escaped him, and he met his wife's gaze. "What happened?"

"A doctor has been tending you for more than a week." She sniffled and shifted, drawing Maecel into her arms. Kimber's large dark eyes speared his. "We didn't think you were going to make it."

A hollow chill raked through him, drawing his muscles into a knot. The cough worked its way up his throat, unleashing its vengeance as he broke into a series of fits. Exhaustion seized his muscles, and he slumped backward.

His wife smiled down at him—and only then did he notice the welt on her face. She smiled and shook her head. "Don't worry about me. I'm fine."

"You—" His voice cracked and vanished with a rasp. Jon cleared his throat, just then realizing his right arm was pinned and strapped to his side. He dragged his attention back to his wife. "You don't look fine." The dark circles under her eyes worried him and cinched the existing tightness in his chest.

"You're alive, and Maecel. I *am* fine."

No. There was something in her expression, something that made his mind do flips and flop like a beached whale. What had happened to her?

Oh Lord, please. His mind ventured to places best not explored. *Please, God.* He shook his head, feeling every inch a failure.

"You made the call," she said, a smile pinching the dimple in her cheek as she cast a furtive glance to the side. "Did you talk to him?"

Jon raised his head and glanced back over his shoulder. A guard with a weapon slung over his shoulder leaned against the door. So, no escape. At least not without bloodshed.

"Yeah." He sighed and looked up at the thatched roof. "Let's hope it was enough." Enough to get them found and out of there. "Before something happens to us."

Something ghostlike flickered in her eyes, startling him.

His hackles rose. What was that about?

Kimber curled into his side, Maecel perched between them. Only then did he feel the thinness of her frame. They must've been captive longer than he realized. How could his wife and child go from healthy and vibrant to gaunt and thin so quickly? Unless. . .unless he'd been unconscious for longer than he thought. Then again, the days did bleed into weeks.

"Somehow," he mumbled, already feeling the weight of sleep pushing against his mind. "Somehow, we'll get out of here. I promise." With the last measure of his strength, he squeezed her shoulder.

"Yeah. Please."

He craned his neck back, peering down at her. Only she burrowed farther into his arms. Soft tears bled into his tattered and stained shirt. His heart raced. Kimber. Something had happened to her.

Any idiot knew what.

CHAPTER 13

Full and immediate compensation has been approved.'" Sydney stared at Lane, who sat at the kitchen table in her mother's house, the laptop casting light on his lean features. She tugged another piece of paper from the envelope and gasped. "A check for five hundred thousand dollars!"

"Let me see that," Lane said, his chair screeching on the tiled floor as he shoved it back and stood. He read over the letter, shaking his head. "This makes no sense. It hasn't even been a month since the fire. I thought you said the arson investigator hadn't filed his report."

"No, I said I hadn't received a copy yet."

He frowned. "Insurance companies don't move this fast." He took the envelope and studied it.

Sydney chuckled. "Well, apparently they do."

"Stamp's normal. Address is preprinted. Why didn't they send a copy of the report with the check? You'd think they'd want all that here. I don't get it. I've never seen a turnaround like this, and certainly not full compensation."

"Hey, party pooper, don't rain on my parade. This is the first good news I've had in a very long time. With this, I can start over, get a nice home, and be settled before—" Sydney choked off the words. Right now she wasn't ready for anyone else to know about the baby. She'd have to tell Lane eventually, but not tonight. "Before I go out of my mind here. Besides, the timing couldn't be more perfect. Bryce starts his job with the sheriff's department at the first of the summer. He and Victoria can have this house, and I'll have my own."

"I'm not trying to rain on your parade; it just seems fishy."

"Fishy?" She quirked an eyebrow at him. "What? You think the bad guys felt bad, forged the insurance company's letterhead, and sent me a check for five hundred grand?"

The absurdity made her laugh. Then again, was it possible someone was trying to buy her silence? Yeah, and she was Jane, Jane Bond. With a snicker, she stuffed the check in her purse. After grabbing a glass of water and some crackers, she returned to the mess strewn over the table. "So, where are we?"

"No closer than before. But I have to get going. I'll call my military sources tomorrow and see if we can make any headway."

"And I'll contact CougarNews. I met Holden Crane at the journalism conference last year. Maybe he can give me some leads."

"Great idea. See? You're a natural at this," he said with a wink, working his laptop into his bag. He placed his empty tea glass in the sink and hoisted his bag onto his shoulder. "This series is perfect for you, Syd. You have the heart and tenacity."

Following him to the front door, she found herself yawning despite being buoyed by his praise. She stretched. Being pregnant drained her energy but not her mind. She never felt more determined to make her own way.

"Hey," Lane said, holding the door knob. "Wanna meet me at Giuseppe's tomorrow?"

Her heart hiccupped. Giuseppe's was Max's place. At least she had a legitimate excuse this time. "I'm sorry, but Pastor Robertson invited me to a meeting at the church. Some of the ladies from

Mom's Bible study are having a memorial service celebration thingie."

Disappointment flooded his eyes. "Okay, sure. Maybe Friday?"

"Maybe," she said, forcing a smile. Would he ever understand?

After seeing him out, she prepared some tension-taming tea, grabbed the crackers from the table, and moved to the sofa in the living room. With the TV clicked on for white noise, she tucked her legs up under her and rifled through the rest of the day's mail. It'd been really nice to get that insurance check. Why'd Lane have to act like the check was fraudulent?

A catalog stilled her. A *Cradle of Love* catalog. She vaguely remembered Victoria saying she'd ordered one for her.

It was odd, but somehow, flipping through the pages gave credence to the life inside her. Giant stuffed, floppy elephants. Cribs. Dressers. Princesses. Race cars. Blocks. Ballerinas. Surreal, yet very real. This baby was real, not some glob that bloated her stomach.

The lone side-table lamp glowed softly against the matte pages. While she liked the round crib that dripped with lace and luxury, the convertible crib-toddler-twin bed piqued her interest. The only thing she knew with resolve was that she wanted dark wood in the nursery. She sighed as she turned another page and saw pink gingham material seemingly fluttering on the page.

A girl. Wouldn't that be something? Next week she'd find out the sex of her baby. She set the catalog aside and smoothed her hands over her belly, stretching the black T-shirt so her baby bump was noticeable. "So I guess I'll have to find a name for you." A familiar ache wove through her chest, filling her with longing for a complete family. But she wouldn't fixate on the fact that she would name the baby alone. "Of course, it will help once I know what you are."

For a moment, she closed her eyes, trying to imagine a baby girl. Sweet rosy cheeks, thick head of hair. Maybe dark eyes like

Max. Would she be a girlie girl? Or a tomboy? The thought forced a grin into her face.

What if it was a boy? He'd be adorable, of course. Probably have dark hair, but she could only hope whatever sex this baby was, he or she would have Max's passion. She'd always admired him for that. No matter what he did, no matter what he got involved in, he gave it everything he had. Full throttle.

A gentle knock snapped Sydney out of her musings. She glanced at the foyer, wondering who could be here at this late hour. Heart in her throat, she plodded to the door, loosening the shirt around her belly. Pausing, she considered not answering, given how late it was and the fact that her mother had been killed in a suspicious fire.

She tiptoed to the far corner of the living room and peered through the thin slots of the plantation shutters. A large black truck sat parked at the curb. She'd seen that vehicle before. Back at the door, she hesitated. "Who is it?"

"Pardon the intrusion, ma'am, but your husband, Max, asked me to deliver something."

Opening the door a crack, Sydney's heart skipped a beat. The man from the hearing stood on her stoop. She eased the door open more. "He sent you?"

Kind blue eyes sparkled under the strain of the porch light. "Yes, ma'am." He held his large black Stetson, turning it nervously in circles. "Sorry for it being so late and all, but Max said this couldn't wait." With a half smile, he extended a hand—and a small black box.

A gift. Obviously jewelry.

Her breath backed up into her throat. This wasn't fair. "I can't. . .won't." Seedlings of anger sprouted. "Tell Max this is low. He shouldn't be sending me gifts. I don't want gifts." *I want my marriage back.*

He pursed his lips and looked down before bringing his rugged face back to hers. "I understand." Donning his hat, he gave her a curt nod. "Night, ma'am."

"Wait." She stepped onto the porch. "You were with him at the MSA meeting. Why? I mean, I've never met you before. Have you known him long?"

"'Bout five months." With one foot on a higher step than the other, he turned toward her. "I reckon you could call it moral support."

"Support? Or restraint?"

The cowboy grinned—and the man could knock a woman off her feet with those pearly whites. "Well, ma'am, not really my place to say." He started down the steps again.

"Why would you venture out in the middle of the night to deliver something to a coworker's wife whom he's separated from?"

Hat on, he faced her again. "Max is a friend. He's never asked for anything in the months I've known him. All-sufficient, if you know what I mean."

"Definitely," Sydney said with a laugh.

"So, I couldn't refuse when he asked." He stared at the box, popped it up in the air a few times, then shrugged. "I'm sure he had his reasons, but I didn't ask." He touched the brim of his hat and said, " 'Night."

Why did the thought of him leaving with that box send her into a panic? She *did* want that gift. She wanted the minuscule hope that things might work out, that this baby she carried would be raised by a mother *and* a father.

Was it a fool's fancy?

"Wait." Sydney tentatively moved down the steps and joined him on the sidewalk. "What's your name?"

He tipped his hat. "Colton Neeley, ma'am."

"Well, Colton," she said, steeling herself and uncertain she wanted to do this, "my husband is a very deliberate man. Intense.

Passionate." Tears pricked her eyes. "It's one of the things I love about him." She drew in a quick breath. "So like you said, when he does something, he usually has a reason, even if I can't understand it."

A faint nod.

She held out her hand. "May I have the box?"

Slowly, he set the gift in her hand and left without another word. Sydney watched as the lights of his truck faded into the black void of the warm Virginia night. Back inside, she flipped the dead bolt and returned to the sofa. Cuddling a pillow close, she inhaled deeply then braved the contents of the box.

A solid gold anchor with a row of diamonds swirling around the post like sparkling ropes gleamed up at her. Tears flooded as words Max had once uttered rushed to the front of her mind.

You'll always be my anchor, Syd.

DAY SIXTEEN

Bitterness sprouted long ugly roots. Though Jon tried to rip the tangled threads from his heart, he only ended up watering them, waiting as he recovered for the strength to effect an escape plan, watching the way his wife and daughter went white like flour at any sign of their captors. His thirst for freedom—or was it vengeance?—served as a heaping dose of fertilizer on the gnarly roots.

If God wasn't going to act. . .

Kimber nuzzled into his arms, night descending deep and thick. The heavy rains pecked out a soothing rhythm on the roof and seeped gently into the hut, dribbling on them. Despite the cooling rain, heat radiated to Jon. An hour earlier, they'd tucked Maecel under a blanket and made a pallet high enough off the ground that she could sleep in relative warmth.

"God's going to rescue us, Jon." Kimber's words came faint and breathless.

Was that a question? He hoped not, because his faith was seriously lacking. And in the last few days, he'd seen even Kimber's rock-solid faith begin to wane. He wanted to tell her that they just needed to trust God. But isn't that what so many before him had done? And how many of those had come home in a pine box?

Sure, yeah. Jon was willing to make sacrifices when it came to fighting for the cause. And he didn't want to limit God—but *this*? Waiting for a group of radicals to hand him and his family off to a group of ultraradicals, who would take great pleasure in dragging their naked bodies through the streets as a sign of what they did to the infidels of the Great Satan?

Who knew what they'd already done to Kimber? Over the last several days since he'd awoken from the coma, she'd been vague and downright evasive about what had happened to her during those days of unconsciousness.

"Kimber, what did they do to you?" He finally whispered the question, letting it hang as thick as the deluge pelting the shelter.

She tightened her arms around his waist. "It doesn't matter." Her body trembled, radiating firelike heat.

He clenched his jaw. "It *does* matter."

Raised up on her elbow, she stared down at him. "Why? Why does it matter?"

How could she even ask that? "Because you're my wife. I'm supposed to protect you."

"And what would you do?" Kimber traced his bearded jaw, smoothing the wiry hairs. "Jon, the only reason you want to know is to fuel that anger I already see burning in your eyes. To fan the flames of your pride. Let it go."

"How can you—"

"Because, this," she said, motioning around them and up and down her body, "is all temporal. But our witness, our God, is eternal."

He pushed off the cot, his legs nearly buckling—which made his feet slip on the mucky earthen floor. Steadied, he trudged to a small chair on the opposite side of the room. "We have to do something."

She came to his side, her clothes all but hanging on her after the weeks in captivity. "We pray. That's all we can do. Besides,

Kezia is still here." Kneeling before him, she peered up with those dark eyes that had stilled more than one storm in him. "I have hope that they will release her to us."

"Kezia?" Jon pushed himself out of the chair and raked a hand through his hair, his fingers catching on the muddied, bloodied, tangled kinks. "Kezia! You're worrying about her, but what about you? And Maecel?"

She smiled. "God will provide, Jon. You're always telling me that. Besides, Kezia is the reason we're here. I'm positive. I've seen it in my dreams. She's going to be an amazing woman." Kimber crossed the gap between them and placed a hand on his arm. "God *will* provide a way."

Yeah.

But did he believe it? How many times had he uttered that axiom? They'd been tested before. But never like this. Never truly, brutally tested. Would this time be different? Would they, like Abraham, need a sacrificial ram to take their places? Jon wasn't sure he could do something like that, offer his own daughter to God. His gaze drifted to the sleeping form of Maecel, and everything in him bunched up into a million knots. *He* would be the ram if it meant Kimber and Maecel lived and were freed.

God, take me. Not them. Me.

Agitation writhed through him, wresting him of the ability to stand still, to hold Kimber. He nudged her aside. "I can't do this. I'm going insane." He paced the length of the hut, his mind racing through the options. Each one came up empty, defeated. With all of them dead.

He roughed a hand over his face, hating the patch of wilderness growing on his chin. Hating the grime clinging to his skin. Hating the sores under the beard and rat's nest of a hairdo. His arm still ached from the makeshift surgery, and he wondered more than once if the doctor had been licensed for humans or animals. Or did the man even have a license?

She came to him again, wrapping her arms around him. Hugging him.

But once more the desire to be free of this confining place, to find a solution that guaranteed that nobody—*nobody*—ever touched Kimber again, ignited more frustration. He pushed around her and went to the opposite side. Huffed. Turned and walked back. Shook his head.

"Jon?"

He paused in the path he was pounding into the earthen floor.

"What if God's plan *is* for us to be the lamb?"

He spun, shaking a finger at her. "Don't *ever* say that again. Ever!" Anger flashed through his mind and chest, burning. Raging. Because—

His shoulders sagged. Because he'd wondered that himself. And he didn't want to think of the unimaginable ways they could die at the hands of the Higanti or the Abu Sayyaf or the other groups razing the land. He wasn't sure which was worse. All too well, he remembered the American sailors strung up on the beach like a fish fry. Or the leader of a local Christian church left hanging from a tree the night a monsoon hit. His body had never been found.

Was that what God had for them? Was that their *purpose?* The sneer smearing into his face set off a warning in his gut, but he ignored it. "What would that prove?" He fisted his hands, rubbing his knuckles. "Who would profit from *that?*"

"Jon—"

"No." He flung around, glaring at her, his chest rising and falling hard. Too hard—a cough rumbled into his throat and seized him, nearly bringing him to his knees. In his periphery, he saw Kimber coming toward him. He held out his hand. "No!" He dragged himself upright and propped his body against the thatched wall. He shook his head and hacked up phlegm. He spit.

"No. I'm not buying it. No way God has brought us all around the world to let those goons slaughter us."

Peace and tranquility washed over her features, sympathy and empathy rolled into a beautiful package called Kimber. And merciful heavens—she looked like an angel, even with the hollows of her eyes darkened and her skin. . .pasty. Her bones protruding—the paleness. The fever. Her chills.

Oh God, help me! The air whooshed from his lungs as he reached for her, his eyes wide and hands trembling. *Dengue fever.*

CHAPTER 14

Fragile china clinked and glinted under the gentle massage of warm candle lighting. White linen tablecloths draped over tables, spanning the short distance between couples and business associates. Supple red leather cradled Olin as he carved out a small chunk of his T-bone steak, dipped it in the signature sauce, and lifted it to his lips.

His taste buds exploded with the spiced, savory mixture. Eyes closed, he relished the flavor, thankful for this exquisite restaurant near the wharf. "Mm, blissful."

Diamonds sparkled against the short crop of pearl-colored hair. Blue eyes glittered at him, adoring and sweet. His precious wife smiled. "Perhaps if it were your first time here, I might agree. But we've been here every Saturday night for eighteen years, and you always have the same meal."

He winked at her and her taunting tone before he slid another piece into his mouth. Slowly, he chewed. Slowly, he savored. And swallowed. "If it's not broke. . ."

She laughed and speared another piece of her salad. "Yes, yes. Really, Olin, you must find—"

"You have to help me!"

The shout jerked Olin from his tranquil dinner, nerves

186

thrumming. He glanced to his right where a bedraggled man, arms hooked between two security officers, struggled for his footing. His eyes were locked on Olin.

A police officer rushed into the once-quiet restaurant, gaze intent on the rowdy man.

"Please, General! Please let me talk to you." His wild eyes screamed at Olin, begged for the very help he shouted for.

"Get him out of here! He's disturbing the guests." A man in an Armani suit shooed the wrestlers away. "Out. Out!"

"General Lambert, I beg you," the man howled, his face red. "I know you can help me. No one else can. I know about *them*. Please!"

Appetite vanished, Olin tossed down his burgundy linen napkin just as the maître'd rushed toward him. "I am deeply sorry for this interruption, General. Please. There is no cost for your meal. We are most apologetic for this disruption. We will most certainly press charges—"

"No." Olin nodded to his wife, who received the signal and slid from her chair, smoothing her perfectly coiffed hair. "Thank you, Jorge."

His gut churned as the scene replayed in his mind. Surely the man couldn't be talking about the one secret nobody knew about. Because if he was, then, well. . .someone knew. And that would have to be remedied. The invisible threads that connected the team seemed to have found visibility.

He shuttled his wife to the car where their driver waited. Over the hood of the car, he saw the police officer, now joined by three other units, wrangling the still-screaming man into the back of a cruiser. "I'll be right back."

"Olin," she said, catching his hand before he could shut the door. "Please hurry. The opera starts soon."

It wasn't the opera or the time that was on her mind. Charlotte knew enough about his job to know she couldn't speak freely. The opera, in their private, coded language, warned him to be careful. Careful but compassionate.

Smoothing his Italian suit as he strode toward the chaos ensuing across the parking lot, he drew up his courage. "Excuse me, officers."

The scene fell ominously quiet as all struggle ceased.

When the wild man's gaze hit Olin, he started rambling again. "I called your office, but they wouldn't listen. They told me to leave a message. And I did. Twelve! Then when I demanded to speak to you, they hung up. And when I tried your home, the phone just rang."

Olin smiled, admiring the tenacity of spirit. "It is a *private* residence."

The man swallowed hard. Straightened, he darted a gaze to the cops. "Please, General Lambert, will you just speak with me?" He waggled his hands, locked in plastic rings behind his back. "You can see I can't hurt you. I just. . ." Suddenly, he seemed reticent to speak—perhaps because there were witnesses. "Just a few minutes of your time."

Olin studied the man. How much did he really know? "You realize, I am in no position to give orders."

The man seemed to calm. "I do."

"And you realize that my role with the Joint Chiefs prevents me from affording favors or taking them."

Wild eyes again surfed the sea of officers before he licked his lips and nodded.

"Then what do you think I can do for you?"

"In all things prepared."

One of the officers clucked his tongue and stepped in. "I think he's had one too many, General." With his hand on the man's head, the officer aimed him into the cruiser. "Come on, you. Let's get you dried out."

At the words the man had spoken, Olin's heart chugged to a

stop. Then reengaged. "What is your name?"

The man froze and stared at him. "Peter Jordan."

With that, Olin returned to his wife and their evening. By midnight, he stood in an empty bunker, the man stuffed onto a steel chair and guarded by two well-armed men. Olin gave the signal and the men removed the hood.

Fear etched into Jordan's face flashed into relief. "General Lambert." His shoulders slumped. "You believed me."

"That remains to be seen." Olin knew better than to give away information. "Tell me what you know." Let them play the knowledge cards, show their hands.

Over the next hour, the man explained the chaos ravaging a small island, about their missionaries and a young girl.

"And what did you mean by saying, '*In all things prepared*'?"

The man's gaze dusted the cement floor. "I've heard there's a team of men who can help in places and situations nobody else is willing to interfere in."

"Would that it were so. Imagine the problems we could solve. Where on earth did you hear of such a thing?"

Jordan's face paled. "I can't say."

"Then neither can I help you." Olin turned and started for the door.

"Wait!" A half-choked sob snapped through the cold morning. "Wait, please." He swallowed. "I got a note."

"Go on."

"It just had your name, the words I told you about, and said to tell you that I knew about them." Jordan shook his head. Shoulders sagging, he hung his head. "It was my last hope. Jon's my best friend. . . ."

Thick and hazy, an early spring mist coated the windshield. Sydney flipped the wipers, hoping the blades didn't snag attention.

She burrowed into the leather of her SUV and shrank, rethinking her plan to sit near the streetlight. Shadows scampered over the hood of the car, sending pinpricks of dread spidering across her shoulders.

Her gaze darted down the lonely, darkened street. Maybe this wasn't her smartest move, but she had to get answers. Stonewalling was about the only thing the government sources had provided. Someone had added a deadly slant to this innocent human interest story. They'd killed her mother and stolen the only bit of sanity in her life. And she was going to find out why.

Scritch. Scritch.

Warmth puddled in her stomach as she darted her gaze to the side-view mirror. A man shuffled up the sidewalk wearing a long trench coat and hat. Over his shoulder he carried a large duffel bag. She could only hope he was just a vagrant who didn't want trouble, only a good meal. Maybe he was heading to the nearest shelter for breakfast. All the same, she nonchalantly double-checked the door locks. A fleeting and minuscule source of comfort.

Bright light broke the dimness of the early morning, yanking her attention back to the building across the street. A woman emerged, pulling a coat tighter around her as she stepped onto the stoop, locked the door, then hustled down the stairs.

Heart ricocheting through her chest, Sydney crouched a little lower as the woman crossed the street and slowly melted into the darkness.

Sydney started her vehicle and pulled along the curb in front of the townhome. Armed with her purse, voice recorder, and folder, she hurried to the apartment door. Hand poised to knock, she remembered the little boy whose drawing had convinced her Anisia knew something. The boy was probably sound asleep at this early hour, so she knocked lightly.

Hugging herself, she kept watch on her surroundings. When

another man strode up the sidewalk toward the building, she knocked a little harder. A chill settled into her bones, but she wasn't sure if it came from the weather or what she was doing.

She raised her hand for another rap on the wood, when light seeped out from the threshold. Sydney took a step back, listening. Waiting.

"Hello?" A faint, accented voice called through the thick wood.

"Anisia?" Sydney fumbled with her purse and folder, searching for a small light to read the prompts she'd printed to help her through this interview. She aimed the light at the page and read, asking in the woman's South African language to please talk with her.

When only silence met her plea, Sydney wondered if she'd made a mistake. Had she pronounced it wrong? Or maybe she shouldn't have come. "Anisia, please," she said again.

Finally, the lock clicked. Slowly, light splintered the darkened porch. Ebony eyes peered at her. "They say I not talk you."

"I know." Well, she hadn't for certain, but she expected as much. "Who? Who said this?"

Anisia shook her head. "I not know."

Glancing at her notes again, Sydney repeated the phrase that promised she didn't want anything but to talk. Obviously, she couldn't tell the poor woman that she feared that the people who told Anisia not to talk had killed her mother. Then Anisia wouldn't talk to her for sure.

A dingy white sweater hung large and loose on the woman's thin frame as she stepped out of the way and let her in.

"Thank you." Once inside, Sydney followed her down the hall and into the kitchen, where a kettle let out a soft whistle. Anisia rushed toward it and set it to the side, turning off the burner.

Having studied up on the customs of Anisia's people, Sydney hung back until the woman motioned for her to sit; then she took the chair and mumbled her thanks.

As Anisia poured a cup and set it before Sydney, she met her gaze. "I speak English." A shy smile softened the woman's features but also strained the color around a scar along her cheek. "A little."

"I speak Tsonga—a little." They both laughed, easing Sydney into the conversation. "I only have a few questions." She added cream and sugar to the mug of coffee. Despite the fact she normally wouldn't drink caffeine, she also wouldn't refuse this woman's hospitality. But coffee wasn't what she'd come here for. Best to just get on with it. She set down the cup and peered at the woman. "Can you tell me what happened?"

Anisia gave a faint nod then drew in a long, staggering breath before she let it out. "They come at night when everyone sleep. I not sleep. My son sick. I hear strange...uh...noise. See men dress like trees come. Bad soldiers no see them."

"Soldiers—who are they?"

"They take us from villages, force us to work fields and do things. They. . ." She hung her head. Then her gaze drifted past Sydney to another room and lingered there for so long it eventually drew Sydney's attention round.

Through a narrow door, Sydney saw the boy asleep on the sofa.

"They rape."

The words backed up Sydney's breath and thoughts. The boy was the product of a rape? Is that what she was saying? Suddenly, she found it hard to look at the woman. Licking her lips, she turned back.

Anisia shrugged. "He good boy." She sipped her coffee. "Here, he have chance be good. Strong. Not like them."

Only then did Sydney notice what she had mistaken for age was in fact a maturity forced upon this sweet woman by years of hardship, brutality, and unimaginable terror. "Yes, he has a chance for a good future here. He's a sweet boy."

The smile filled Anisia's face; then she rose. "I be back."

Sydney shifted and watched the tall, lithe woman glide into the front room and kneel next to her son. Anisia brushed a hand over his face then stood again. When she returned, she laid several papers on the table, bringing with her a swirl of heady spices. "He draw those. The men who save us." She patted her shoulder. "They wear."

Sydney frowned but looked at the small stack of drawings. The star with the odd center and sword. Lightning bolts.

Another drawing had a half dozen men, each depicted differently. She glanced at the beautiful, dark-skinned woman. "Six men?"

Anisia nodded.

Sydney used her phone and took a photo of the star symbol—and noticed that sketched onto one man was a very crude rendering of the American flag. She pointed to the star and shot the woman a questioning glance. "Did you see this?"

She shook her head. "No. My son draw that after we come here." She patted her forearm. "The star? He have there, but hide when we see. All very good fighters. Fast." Tapping her head, she smiled. "Smart. They trick soldiers. Make them sleep."

"I'm sorry? What do you mean they made them sleep?"

Another smile lit the woman's face. She held her hand like a cup and tipped it toward her face. "Drink. Janjaweed not know."

"Did they drug you and your people?"

Anisia laughed. "No. We not allowed water at night. Little in morning and after work." Arms folded, she leaned back with an expression that betrayed her pleasure at what happened. "Soldiers always celebrate weekend. Men this know and drug them. We escape. But some wake, and they shoot. Star men not hurt, but Janjaweed lose many."

What must it have been like for this young woman to see all this, to endure such atrocities? And being so young, yet she seemed so content. "How old are you?"

"Twenty."

Sydney tried not to let her shock show. This woman had borne a child at the raw age of fifteen—a pregnancy forced on her by a brutal, fierce soldier. A man who murdered her loved ones and raped her. Sydney's hand went to her rounding belly. Her baby had been conceived in love. How great the irony. Anisia's baby was conceived in hatred and violence but now had a better life. Sydney's baby was conceived in love and the bond of matrimony but now would be raised by only one parent.

"You baby?" Anisia smiled and nodded toward Sydney's hand and belly.

The heat crawling into her cheeks must surely have given her away. "Yes."

"Your baby have good mom. And father." She reached across the table and touched the wedding ring on Sydney's finger.

Tears blurred her vision, but Sydney blinked them away. How could she explain to a woman who'd been through such an unspeakable existence that this was a point in her life where she questioned God. "No. My husband. . .is gone."

Anisia's face fell. "He die?"

Sydney swallowed the tears. "No, he's just a very angry man."

"He beat you?"

Sydney shook her head. "No." Why did her pain sound trivial? It wasn't. Max refused help. Refused to work on their marriage. "I should go." She gathered her things. "Thank you so much for talking to me, Anisia. I am very grateful."

Dark fingers wrapped around Sydney's arm. "Pain come in many colors." She smiled sweetly.

Sydney sniffled. "Yes. Yes, it does."

"You baby have good mother. I pray God take good care. Maybe even bring back you husband."

Words failed. Her brain wouldn't cooperate. She hugged Anisia and quickly left. As she drove home, tears flowed unchecked. *Stupid hormones.* If only that was all it was. The pain remained despite the months that stretched the separation closer to the actual divorce. She banged her hand on the steering wheel. "I won't do this. I won't cry anymore." Phone in hand, she called Lane. "Hey, I've got the proof we need."

The line went silent.

"Lane?" Her heart skipped a beat, remembering when the line died—and so had her mother. "Lane!"

"Sorry. I'm. . .what did you do, Sydney?" Concern and hesitancy laced his words.

Why did he sound so irritated? "I spoke with Anisia. I'm certain the men we're after are Americans."

"Sydney, I hate to break it to you—"

She frowned. "What? What's happened?"

"Buck's looking for you."

"Looking for me?" She glanced at the digital clock on the dashboard. "It's only six in the morning."

"He called me an hour ago."

Sydney tried to steady her racing pulse.

"We're off the story."

"No! Why? He can't do this."

"Well," Lane said. "He can and did. And vowed to have you arrested if you tried to contact anyone again."

Laughter permeated the country home filled with the thick scent of pine and simmering cinnamon spices. Max shrugged out of his leather jacket and set it on a chair as they passed through the dining room into the large, open living area.

He couldn't stand the suspense anymore. "So, what'd she say?"

Cowboy grinned as he lowered himself into a thick gold chair. "Who?"

Perched on the edge of the sofa that divided the dining and living areas, Max narrowed his eyes. "You know full well who I'm talking about. Did you give her the box?"

"I did." Cowboy smoothed a hand down the leg of his blue jeans.

"And?" The suspense was killing him.

"She wouldn't take it."

His heart hitched, disappointed. "You're kidding?"

"At first." Cowboy chuckled.

Max landed a fake punch on the guy's shoulder.

"She knew you would have a good reason, so she took it and went back in the house. I honestly don't know if she loved it or hated it."

A small child with white blond hair darted across the room and leaped into Cowboy's lap. "Daddy, Nana said dinner would be ready in fifty minutes."

"Thirty," a woman called from the kitchen.

"That right?" Cowboy grinned, scooting forward as the girl straddled his leg like a sawhorse. "Max, this is McKenna." He looked into his daughter's eyes. "Mickey, this is my friend Max."

"I know who he is, Daddy." She swiped at the blond hair that fell in her face, swinging her legs and bright red boots back and forth.

"You do?"

"Uh-huh. Nana said you were shooting pool with him late one night." McKenna bolted back to the living room, her knee-high boots clomping over the wood.

"You're in trouble," Max taunted his friend.

Cowboy slumped against the seat. "You have no idea." Then he pulled himself up and slapped Max's leg. "Come here; let me show you something."

They headed to the back of the house, but instead of climbing the stairs, Cowboy opened what looked like a closet door, flipped on a switch, then disappeared inside. "You coming?" His voice carried from a distance.

Max peeked around the corner, surprised to find a set of stairs leading down under the house. He hustled down the steps, surprised at the cement walls. "What is this, a bunker?"

Cowboy clicked on another light and shrugged. "You could call it that." He punched a code into an access panel, and the wall in front of him slid back. "We had one in Texas. Ya know—with the tornadoes and all. So, out here on seventy acres, I figured it couldn't hurt."

Inside, Max stopped. The guy had a small arsenal racked on the wall. "What is this?"

"I'm a collector." Cowboy folded his arms over his chest, fingers tucked under his armpits. "Most of what you see is antique."

Max ran a hand along a long rifle. "They look pristine."

"Yep. Had 'em restored. Some I outright paid a small fortune for, like that early nickel Remington Model 1875, single action Army revolver." He pointed to a shiny silver-barreled gun gleaming under a tinkling fluorescent light. "Look at 'er. All original, excellent metal and markings, including the barrel address and number 44 on the frame."

With a low whistle, Max stepped back. "I'm impressed."

"Kinda used to be an obsession, ya know?" Cowboy shrugged. "Not so much anymore, but it's a way me and my dad would connect. Go to gun shows, plan our next purchase. He bought some of these, but his hands don't work so good anymore, so he passed 'em on to me."

Dad. What would it have been like to have a dad who actually wanted to connect rather than beat the fastest path out of his life?

"Colton!" a semishrill voice carried down into the cellar. "Dinner's almost ready. Why don't y'all wash up?"

The cowboy pinched the bridge of his nose. With a sigh, he shook his head. "I am grateful for their help with Mickey, but some days I'd be glad for the privacy." He patted Max's gut. "Ready for some chow?"

Upstairs they headed into Cowboy's "apartment" to wash up. As he waited for the cowboy, Max noticed the brown, oversized bag sitting on the bed. Hastings. Max tilted his head, remembering the bag Cowboy had delivered the Bible in.

"Go ahead," Cowboy said, stepping from the bathroom.

Max pointed to the bag. "I thought you didn't shop there."

Cowboy looked at the bag then quickly wiped his hands on a towel. "I. . .it's. . .old."

Was the guy's face turning red? Oh, Max couldn't let this go. "Come on, Cowboy, cough it up. I've bared my soul. Time for some of yours."

Blue eyes flashed at him. "I don't like being cornered, but you're right. Friends cut it straight." He huffed. "But this stays between you and me, got it?"

A grin pulled Max's lips apart. This was going to be good. "Okay."

Cowboy scratched the back of his head. "There's this. . .*person* at the store." He glanced at Max, looking guilty and embarrassed. "I guess you could say I've been reconnoitering."

"*Recon*? On a Hastings employee?" Max held a fisted hand to his mouth to cover the laugh seeping into his throat. "What does she look like?"

Rivaling songs belted into the room. Max gripped his phone. Cowboy did the same. They both glanced at their screens. The Nightshade signal.

"Looks like we're going to miss dinner."

DAY TWENTY-FOUR

It was true. With each day that Jon's strength returned, that his limbs firmed and the cough subsided, Kimber weakened. What alarmed him was that the woman who never complained, not even in childbirth, now moaned about the ache tightening her back that made it difficult to move. Neither of them voiced what was quickly becoming obvious. At any other time, the fever could be treated medically and the patient would recover. But here? Where their captors seemed to be waiting for the end of the world, hope faded with each sunset.

He gazed out the thin gaps in the thatched hut, peering up at the light that snuck past the thick canopy of leaves. Light. Of what day? How long had it been? He wrapped his fingers tightly around the wood spindles and squeezed. According to Kimber, he'd lost nearly a week to the fever that—

Jon froze. Had he given his wife the sickness that now ravaged her body? He shifted back and peered over his shoulder. She lay on the small cot, curled on her side, pale. So very pale. He turned back to the bars and hung his head. How long would God leave them here? Why hadn't Peter gotten them out yet? The insanity was the fact that he and Kimber had left the civilized world to come out here, be a light to the darkened world, and bring hope, and yet he had no hope.

I am your hope.

Clenching shut his eyes, Jon gritted his teeth. He wanted to believe the soft whisper truly came from the Divine, but after all this time, all these weeks. . .

Then again, the Higanti had kept them here much longer than he'd anticipated, apparently unable to reach an agreement with the radicals. No surprise there. At least they were still alive. But it also made him realize their chances of a rescue were all but a fantasy.

A gentle touch against his leg snapped him out of his morose thoughts. He glanced to the side—and down. White blond hair, though dirty, gleamed like a halo against the dank backdrop. Soft blue eyes glittered up at him. Maecel held both hands toward him. "Up, Daddy."

With a smile, he hoisted his daughter into his arms. She nuzzled into him, her no-longer chubby hand patting his shoulder. Jon rubbed her back, noting the rank odor emanating from her. And this time, it wasn't dirty diapers. They'd been unable to bathe her—for that matter, nobody had showered. He missed the sweet smell of mango soap Kimber had made that normally clung to Maecel's shoulder-length hair and skin.

He tightened his hold on her, nudging her to rest against him. "Soon, baby. Soon we'll be home."

She lifted her head and smiled at him. "Go?" She nodded, innocence supreme. "See Imee."

Imee. He hadn't thought of the woman since they'd been captured. Guilt wove a thick band around Jon's chest. He didn't know where Imee and the others were. Was she even alive? Would he ever see his parents again? If he did, his dad would probably take him up into the mountains for a long walk and talk. His mother would scoop Maecel into her arms and not let go for a week. He would get away to a lodge with Kimber for the weekend, leaving their daughter in the protective care of her grandparents. He ached to stretch what little morsel of hope remained and believe that a rescue could happen.

Rescue. Right. The Higanti were holding them just long enough to hand them off to the radicals. Which meant being moved. Eventually. Surely it didn't take this long to put together a team and come save the day, did it? What hope was there?

I am your hope.

In that moment Jon realized that maybe, just maybe, they did have hope. Assemble a team, get them out. It could be done, and stealthily.

No. Hope should not be based in anything temporal. Like Kimber said, they would be gone one day. Only God was eternal. If Jon transferred his hope to God and *only* God, then he couldn't be disappointed.

As he rubbed Maecel's back, he lowered himself to the chair, watching as she drifted off to sleep. Light as a feather, she gave a soft shudder as Jon lowered her into his arm and cradled her. He stared down at the little angel who'd overtaken his heart and life. Love found new meaning and depth the moment she was born, grunting and offering her first protest at the world.

Movement to the side startled him. Kimber knelt next to him, brushing Maecel's hair from her face. "To have the peace of a child. . ." Dark patches encircled her eyes.

"You should be resting," he whispered.

Soft and slow, a smile came to her lips. "I feel fine." She leaned into him, resting her head on his shoulder. "I had another dream."

"Yeah?" He lowered Maecel onto the cot and turned to his wife—and stilled. Even with the circles and the gauntness, even more than that, she looked haunted. "What's wrong?"

Her lip quivered, forcing tiny dimples into her chin. She shook her head. "A rescue team is coming." A tear slipped free, mingling with the dirt on her face and forming a dark streak down her cheek.

He started. "A rescue?" Jon clasped her shoulders. "You're certain?" Only then as he held her and light streamed through the slats of the hut did he see it. Yellow tinged her skin. Jaundice. His stomach clenched. A fatal phase of the dengue fever.

Shouts outside jerked them both rigid. Jon rushed to the wall and peeked through the wood. More than a dozen Higanti swarmed toward them, yelling and shouting. Faces streaked with red and white, they bore the blue cross that smeared from chest to belly. Two rushed forward. Several others seemed to be wrangling someone.

"Get back," Jon hissed, snatching Maecel from the bed, startling her awake. "Stay in the corner." Even as he talked, he nudged them into the space between the wall and the foot of the cot. "Down." He pushed on Kimber's head just seconds before light burst into the hut.

He spun—only to see the two warriors lunging at him with their sticks. "Back!" they demanded in a foreign tongue. "On the ground. Don't look."

Jon complied, turning his face toward his wife and daughter. Despite Kimber's gentle words and bouncing, Maecel shrieked.

One guard started for them, but Jon leaped in between. Pain stabbed through his back. He grunted but withstood it, huddling with Kimber and Maecel.

Seconds later the chaos ended. The hut darkened. Jon braved a glance to the side, verifying that the door was locked. "Okay," he mumbled.

"Are you okay?" Kimber asked as they both stood, hugging each other.

"Fine." The sting in his back would go away eventually.

"They hit you," she mumbled, her eyes glossing.

Jon cupped her face. "I'm fine. Okay?"

Behind him, he heard a soft crunch.

He whipped around—and froze.

Cowering in the corner, arms wrapped around her, was a young girl. Her face was badly beaten and swollen. But the eyes. . .he remembered the eyes.

"Kezia?"

CHAPTER 15

Y ou ready to see your baby, Mrs. Jacobs?"

Flat on her back, Sydney stared up at the ceiling, wishing the doctor would say that a little more quietly. Having grown up in Richmond, she knew just about every woman in the office. And what if a friend sat on the other side of the wall?

"Yes." No. Yes. This baby she'd never planned. . .but wanted. Yet didn't want. Guilt hung low and wide over her for even thinking that. Cutting ties with Max wouldn't be as clean now that they'd have a child together.

The OB squirted what felt like ice-cold gel on her belly, making her gasp. "Sorry. I guess the warmer isn't working."

Taking the bottle of goo from the doctor, the nurse smiled down at Sydney. "So are you hoping for a boy or a girl?"

"A healthy baby."

The Doppler glided over her slight protrusion as the doctor worked a keyboard. "I'm going to take measurements, check the fetus's health; then we'll get to the fun part." The doctor worked quietly for several minutes, clicking, angling, and measuring, then typing.

Mesmerized by the color 2-D imaging, Sydney stared at the monitor. *There you are.* Something deep and maternal welled up within her as she stared at her baby. A real, live growing and developing baby. *Her* baby. Tears pricked her eyes as she watched an arm swimming across the screen. A foot dashed out.

She felt a kick against her belly.

The doctor chuckled. "A feisty one. Doesn't like me poking around."

Sydney laughed at the personality already budding in her womb. She wished for her mother's hand while she caught the first glimpse of the child stirring up chaos in her life. *Already like Max.* Familiar longing slithered through her, aching for Max to be a part of this. But he wasn't. And wouldn't be. She just had to draw up her chin and survive as she'd always done.

"Well, everything looks good. I see no abnormalities. The heartbeat is strong and steady."

Oh, thank You, Jesus. Sydney tried to stem the tears that slipped over her composure.

"And," the doctor said, angling the Doppler to the side, "there. Can you tell what it is?"

It was difficult enough to make out the arms. Sydney wouldn't even attempt a guess at the baby's sex. "I haven't a clue."

"It's a boy. And according to the measurements, you're right on target with the projected due date of June 1, which means you've got just a little less than four months left. You're carrying small, but that won't last much longer." He chuckled.

A son. Tears streamed down her face. Max would have a son. A new pain embedded itself in her heart. She and Bryce had grown up without a father, and she knew how much that had affected her brother. Even though Max had never told her exactly what had happened with his father, he detested being associated with the man.

God, I want my son to know his father. He was a good man, honorable and strong. When he found out about this baby—his son—he'd demand to be a part of the child's life, wanting to do the right thing. Sydney just wanted her husband and his love back.

A soft touch to her shoulder reminded her she lay on a table with goo all over her belly and was flanked by a white-jacketed doctor and his nurse. "You okay, Mrs. Jacobs?"

"Yes," she mumbled, wiping her tears as the nurse cleaned her belly and lowered Sydney's shirt so she could sit up. "Just overwhelmed."

"Do you have a name picked out?" the nurse asked, washing her hands.

Shaking her head, Sydney realized that she had not fully accepted her child's existence until this moment. "Not yet."

The doctor laughed. "Well, I've seen couples nearly end their marriage because they couldn't agree on a name, so take your time with it."

An hour later and feeling borderline euphoric armed with her single snapshot and video disc of the baby, Sydney walked the aisles of a supercenter for groceries. She had no idea if she bought what she was supposed to buy, because every few minutes she tugged out the photo and stared at the two-dimensional image of her baby. Her son. She sighed—and froze as her gaze hit the infant section. Glancing down at the carpet that divided the infant department from the aisle, she felt that if she crossed that, it was like. . .no going back.

Insane.

She couldn't back out now anyway. She pushed herself and the cart onto the carpeted area and browsed. Rounding one corner, she spotted a man and woman huddling over a portable scanner. He bent and kissed her, and she wrapped her arms around him.

Throat raw, Sydney hurried past them, past the painful reminder that she was alone. Would she ever stop thinking in those terms? Would she ever feel whole again?

A book of baby names caught her attention and stopped her. Flipping through a few pages only had her wrinkling her nose.

None of them appealed to her. What would Max think of the name Devin? He'd probably call it too uppity. Smiling, she laid the book in her cart and started on—only to stop again. A small onesie seemed to dance under the tease of the air conditioning. Camo. BORN IN THE USA scrawled in red, white, and blue across the front. Sydney lifted the ultrasoft garment from the rack, rubbing the material between her fingers.

Her phone rang, snatching her out of the moment. She laid the onesie on the book and answered the call. "This is Sydney."

"Sydney, you're not going to believe this."

At the sound of Lane's voice, she pushed her cart toward the front of the store. "What now? Is Buck threatening to fire me because I'm not in the office?"

"No, but listen. You need to come first thing in the morning."

"He ordered me to take a week off after he yanked me from the story. I have two more days left." And she was going to take them.

"I have one name for you."

Sydney wheeled up to the register and started unloading the groceries, silently daring him to make a difference in her obstinate decision to wait out Buck's grumpiness. "Okay."

"Holden Crane."

"I'll be there at eight."

A scream shattered the quiet beach.

Max spun, squinting against the sun-drenched Filipino shoreline. A dozen feet away, the Kid, dressed in nice slacks and an expensive button-down, writhed against the two hulking giants carrying him down the dock. He screamed like a little girl. "Put me down!"

"Say that again," Legend boomed as he and Cowboy—one holding the Kid's ankles, the other his arms—swung him back and forth toward the churning waters. "Say, 'Marines are wimps,' again." Each swing gave them more momentum.

"I take it back! I take it baaacckkk." He was hurled up into the air, flipping like a fish out of water.

Splash!

Cowboy and Legend high-fived.

Max laughed as the Kid burst up out of the water, shouting and vowing revenge. Dressed up for a night on the town, the team waited as Marshall dragged himself to dry ground. He glared up through thick black hair plastered to his face. "That was un-called for."

"What you said was uncalled for," Legend corrected. "Look around you, Kid. We are the best, the elite of the elite. Each of us deserves respect."

Marshall pushed his hair out of his face, panting. "I have to go and change."

"We'll wait," Cowboy said, the laughter clinging to his words.

The sparkle of the water glistening under the bright glow of a full moon, beauty unparalleled, stretched around Max. In the hills of the island. Over the surging ocean. Serene and peace-ful. Reminded him of his honeymoon in Maui. Watching Sydney trudge through the waves back to their rented beach house, know-ing that she was his, forever and always.

Only forever wasn't forever. And always was only a memory.

"Sure is beautiful."

Max eyed the cowboy, the only member of the team in jeans. Granted, the jeans were crisp and dark, making him look just as dressed up as the rest. Finally, he turned his attention back to the waters. "Ever notice how peaceful it is, how calming? One of the reasons I became a SEAL. I run and swim to work off tension."

"Then you've been swimming for what, three years straight?" Cowboy's tease morphed into a laugh. "It's a good way to work it off, Frogman. But what do you do when you can't swim or run?"

Explode.

"That's where God makes the difference," Cowboy said. "Did you do that reading yet?"

Max shook his head. "Can't be that easy."

Cowboy chuckled. "That's the exact thought that keeps you from God. It's part of our sin nature to believe more in our own mortality and inept power than in God's sovereignty and majesty." He pointed to the waters. "Look at it, Max. All this was an accidental explosion of atoms? I don't think so. Neither are you. God made you just as you are, but something broke down on the way to here. Only God can show you the blueprints and how things should work. Open up. Let Him. I think you'll be surprised—and maybe, just maybe, if you get 'er done, that beautiful wife of yours will still be available. And waiting."

The words speared Max's soul. Like little piranhas, the thought of Sydney with another man, the thought of her going on with her life, the memories of all they'd shared in the six years they'd known each other, ate at him. Pecked and chewed his courage. He'd failed her so completely and utterly. She was the one person he was willing to be real with, give 100 percent to—outside the SEALs—and he'd failed.

"I can see how much you still love her, Max. Part of God's plan for you was Sydney. Your pride got in the way. Don't you think it's time to let go of that and reach for her, for God?" Cowboy slapped Max's shoulder. "We're going to check on the Kid. See if he needs more saltwater to wash his mouth out."

Sand crunched gently under Cowboy's feet as he plodded up the sand bank to the strip of hotels and tourist traps lining the street. With one last glance at the waters and the past, Max headed back to his room at one of the four hotels the team had holed up in.

You're running again.

He stretched his neck, ignoring the conviction that penetrated deeper than he'd admit. Never had liked thinking, sitting around bemoaning choices and events. Life was cruel and unforgiving. He'd learned to accept that when his father had walked out on him and his mother on Max's thirteenth birthday. He doubted his absentee father had even known it was his birthday—he'd had that other woman to distract him. Then his mother disappeared, leaving Max to be raised by his grandmother, a wonderful woman who'd tried her best to raise an angry teen.

Max marveled—why hadn't he thought of Grandma Lollie in years? She was a good woman. But Max ran over her like a quad over dunes—behavior he profoundly regretted.

Just like with Sydney.

He let himself into the room and locked the dead bolt. Collapsed on the bed, he stared at the cracked and brown-stained ceiling. What was with his treatment of Lollie and Sydney? How did he never see the parallel until tonight? Two women who'd loved him completely and always given him the benefit of the doubt, and he'd torched their efforts. Torched their attempts to attach roots to his heart.

Pulling himself up, he rubbed a hand over his chin. He bent forward and rested his arms on his knees. Lollie had died shortly after Max left for the military. She'd probably believed he hated her, resented her. Truthfully, he'd been so humiliated by his parents and so convinced that he must've been the cause for their hasty departures that he had pushed her away, not wanting to hurt her or be hurt by her when she realized the trouble he was.

But Sydney. . .

He felt like an animal. An angry, violent animal. He hated the way he dealt with things—or in more cases than one, didn't deal with them. Yet everything in her, everything she'd given and shared with him, left him aching for more. Left him wanting her to see that he wasn't a screwup.

But I am.

God made you just as you are. Cowboy's words seeped past the condemnation. So, had God made a screwup?

A nagging desire wormed through his chest to read up on King David like the cowboy had told him to. He had nothing to lose. Max huffed and lifted his almost indestructible laptop from the bag and powered it up. He searched for an online Bible then stared at the books of the Bible listed on the page and paused. Where was the story of David? What had Cowboy said?

Irritated that he couldn't remember, he went back to a search engine and typed in "King David." Dozens of pages of results popped up. He picked one randomly. Over the next few hours, he read details of the famous king's life, of his riches, his wise and incredibly wealthy son Solomon, and…of David's failings. Killing a soldier under his command so he could take the man's wife, whom he'd impregnated. Then the punishment for that mistake as he pleaded with God for the life of his son.

Yet when God did not grant that request and the boy died, David stood up and went on with his life. Max clicked on the commentary link, which explained that David had realized that he had been seeking his way instead of God's way. As a result, his son had died.

Reading more, he saw a dichotomy. God called David a man after his own heart, yet He refused David the privilege of building the temple, saying David had been a warrior and bore too much blood on his hands.

Max looked at his own hands. He curled his fingers inward and clenched them. He'd killed. Many. As a soldier, it was part and parcel of the package. A grim reality he never liked. Yet the adrenaline rush left him wanting more.

He shoved away from the laptop and stalked to the barred window overlooking the small bay. Night-blackened water stretched toward the shore, kissing it and then sneaking away into the night. His gaze wandered to the twinkling stars in the sky, and he sighed.

"God..."

Everything in him closed up.

He couldn't do this, couldn't face the deep well of burning fury that choked him, made him—

"No." He braced his hands against the windowsill. "I have to do this." Every muscle tensed, he pushed his eyes to the heavens. "God, I—"

Bang! Bang!

"Open up." Legend's voice stomped through the air.

Defeat leeched his strength as he crossed the room, unlocked the door, and yanked it back.

"Intel's in. Time to go."

CHAPTER 16

Could you repeat that, please?"

The man in the blazer and jeans smiled at her, looking and apparently feeling pretty cocky. "CougarNews will fund the trip to London, arrange the meeting with a contact who has the information you need, and we will grant first rights to print."

Sydney eyed him, hesitant and wary. Max had always said if it looked or sounded too good to be true, you could bet it was—and to shoot before you ended up dead. "And what do you get again?"

Holden Crane chuckled. "First broadcast rights."

What was she missing? "I'm not getting it. Why don't you just take my story and run? Isn't that the way things work in this dog-eat-dog industry?"

A red hue tinged his face. Holden rubbed his eyes then let out a big sigh. "There is information here that I need, and it's going to work against both of us if we don't cut to the chase." He gestured with his hand and smiled. "Look, I'm not here to screw you out of a story. I've seen what you've worked up, and I believe you're on to something big. Very big."

Speechless, she stared at the man's business card. Holden Crane, correspondent with CougarNews, the largest conservative syndicated news agency in the civilized world. "You didn't return my calls." Yet here he stood.

"I know," he said. "I had to take time to do some research on you and on this supposed story. When I heard about the response you got from the Pentagon, I knew you'd hit a hot spot."

She licked her lips and came out of her chair, heart and mind thundering. "Would you do me a favor?" Sydney wrapped her jacket a bit tighter around her. "Tell that to my boss. He's been less than pleased with what my stories have unleashed."

He held up his hand. "Buck and I have already spoken."

Disbelief doused her. "And he agreed?" Her gaze shot out the window and across the cubicle maze to Buck's office. To her surprise, he stood there with his typical unlit cigar, staring back. He scratched and shook his head then returned to his desk.

"Well, he wasn't happy about it, but he said you could have one week." Holden leaned against the table, crossing his legs at the ankles. "Think about it, Sydney. Do you really think you would've gotten the reaction you did from the government if the story had no validity or value? They want this kept quiet. And like you, I want to know why."

He wasn't really telling her anything new, yet her mind reeled. She marveled at how things had come full circle in just a matter of days. After Lane delivered the brutal news about being yanked off the story, she'd been ordered to take a week off and get herself together. About the only thing she'd accomplished was a quick trip to the supercenter for a pint of Chocolate Delirium ice cream then that journey through the baby section.

Baby. Safety. Her mind worried the details of the trip. But she shrugged the concern aside. A week in London meeting a source would be fine. After all, it wasn't like going into a firefight in the middle of a jungle. They would investigate events that had already taken place in locations already quieted.

Holden folded his arms over his chest, looking completely

comfortable and in his element as he explained all the details. "Do you have your passport?"

"Yes."

Holden's blue eyes twinkled. "Good, good. Mr. Kramer insisted you take someone with you and suggested Lane Bowen."

"Oh." Why that bothered her, she didn't know. Not only had Lane helped her get the For Human Sake column, but he'd been thrilled. Maybe it was his growing attachment and attentiveness that wore on her, his feelings more obvious with each day.

Holden tilted his head, considering her. "Is that a problem?"

"No, he's a friend. Good guy."

"You don't sound convinced."

She faked a smile. "It'll be fine. Lane's a good reporter."

He quietly looked at her then to her stomach. "And what about your con—"

"Syd!" Lane burst into the room and rushed to her. "Isn't it great? You're going to get your story." Grasping her shoulders, he gave her a quick hug.

Gulping back the threat of being discovered—did Holden really know she was pregnant?—she smiled and eased herself from Lane, noting Holden quirked an eyebrow at the embrace. She could almost hear his unvoiced question, *Just a friend?*

"It's wonderful. I'm still shocked." Before Holden had the opportunity to repeat his question, she stuffed her hands in the pockets of her jacket, effectively covering her belly. She drew in a breath and let it out. "When do we leave?"

"I've secured three seats on the next flight out. It leaves at six." He handed them each a piece of paper. "We'll fly out of Reagan National, catch a red-eye out of JFK International, and land at London-Heathrow shortly after four tomorrow."

Sydney stared at the paper, the word ITINERARY stamped in bold letters under the CougarNews header, and felt a zip of giddiness rush through her. She was officially working with *the* Holden

Crane from CougarNews.

But the thrill faded, realizing she would essentially lose an entire day traveling, what with the flight time and the actual time difference. They'd arrive in London tomorrow, meet with one of Holden's contacts for dinner. But their return flight to the States wasn't for another six days after that. "Why the delay in coming back?"

"Always allow for contingencies, for following up on leads that might surface. The man we're meeting is an intermediary. If he decides we can be trusted, he will arrange an introduction to his source, who will give you what you are looking for."

"Or won't." They both looked at Lane, who seemed defensive and irritated. "Sorry, it's a long trip, and I'm just a little peeved that we're heading there with no guarantee that Syd will get anything but a backache."

Sydney rolled her eyes. "I'll be fine." She didn't want him using her as an excuse not to go. "It's worth it, even if we come back empty-handed. If they don't talk, that in and of itself is a story that I can capitalize on."

Pushing off the table, Holden stood closer to her, grinning. "You have the right attitude to make it in this business, Sydney. When this is over, if you want a job in broadcast, let me know."

Wow. The thought sped through her, tingling. "I've never really considered that."

"Well, you should. You're intelligent, attractive, and you know how to nose out the story." Back at the conference table, he snapped shut his briefcase and lifted it. "It's getting late, and I imagine you both have some packing to do. So I'll see you in a few hours at the airport. If you need anything, you have my card. Give me a ring."

Sydney walked him to the elevator, still soaring from his praise. "You really think I can make it?" *Attractive and intelligent.*

Why did she feel starved for the attention? Then again, how long had it been since someone had complimented her so openly? Or just on the fact that she had value outside of being a warm body filling a chair?

"Absolutely," Mr. Crane said, holding the elevator door open. "I've already spoken to my supervisor about you."

Sydney gaped. "You're kidding."

"Of course he did," Lane snapped. "He had to get approval for this trip."

Holden snickered. "No, actually, that's not true. CougarNews trusts me. I don't need to be babysat." He dragged his attention back to Sydney. "No, I told them Sydney Jacobs was a reporter to watch, one who could be an asset to CougarNews." With that, he stepped back and let the steel doors sever the conversation.

"I don't like him."

Sydney flinched. "What don't you like about him? He's paying our way to London for a story that I unearthed, and he's footing the bill for the hotel and everything." She returned to her cubicle and slung her purse over her shoulder. "And beyond that, he carried enough clout to force Buck Kramer to give me back the story."

"That's not what bothers me."

"Yeah, what is?"

"He was too slick, too sweet-talking."

Defenses, strong and resilient, slammed up. "Why? Because he complimented me?"

"It wasn't just that he complimented you, but how he complimented you."

She rolled her eyes again. "Is it too hard to believe that someone besides you sees my work as professional and worthwhile?" She walked from her desk. He was starting to sound just like Max. Overprotective and overbearing. "I have to jet and get packed. I'll meet you at the airport."

Jetlag had nothing on the nausea swirling through her though once they'd landed. Sydney asked—no, begged—God to calm down her stomach. She hadn't experienced morning sickness, but the flight over unseated all her nerves. Armed with a package of stem ginger biscuits and a bottle of water, she followed Holden and Lane through Heathrow, navigating the tangled mob. Dragging her overnight bag behind her proved challenging, but no way could she let go of the cookies. They'd been the only thing that seemed to quell the acidic taste rising in her throat, and the only palatable thing she'd spotted after landing and clearing customs.

In the somber haze of the late afternoon sun, they piled their luggage into the trunk of Holden's rental car. Lane took the backseat of the sedan, affording her the front passenger seat. She'd never been so grateful for his consideration and gentlemanly manners, because sitting in the rear would jostle the contents of her stomach right onto the fine leather.

As she folded herself into the car, she thanked God neither of the men had noticed how sick she felt. Besides, this nausea wasn't anything serious, just the upheaval of taking off and landing then doing it again. Now that her body was out of sync, Baby Jacobs protested.

Glancing at his watch, Holden grunted as they hit a red light. "We're cutting it close. Let's hope we don't run into any traffic."

"Why?" Lane pulled on Sydney's seat as he leaned forward.

"The contact, a man by the name of Jerome, will take that as a sign that we're unreliable and untrustworthy."

With another cookie in hand, Sydney gripped the dash, momentarily disoriented with the wrong-side-of-the-road driving. She glanced at the driver, still harboring a tremor of disbelief she was with Holden Crane. "Meaning we're one point behind before we even get there?"

"No, meaning he won't wait."

After the nearly seven-hour flight from New York and less-than-stellar first-class airline food, she wasn't coming all this way to go back empty-handed because they were late. Sydney whispered a prayer for mercy and protection as they whipped through the clogged London streets, winding around one turnabout after another. Mentally, she applied pressure to Holden's foot on the gas pedal. *Hurry!* Something brilliant waited at the end of this story, she was certain.

A song pelted the stale interior of the sedan. Sydney rummaged through her purse for the smart phone. She checked the screen. "It was Buck. He must've called while we were in flight." A *bleep-bleep* signaled a voice mail.

"He told me he wanted hourly updates," Lane said.

Sydney pushed the voice mail autodial button, but nothing happened.

"Your cell phone won't work here," Holden said, handing over his phone. "Use mine. It's a world phone."

She dialed her cell phone voice box and retrieved the message—only to hear Buck ranting about wanting an update just as the car slowed rapidly. Jerking her gaze to the road, she groaned. Stretching for miles ahead, a steady stream of traffic pointed to the horizon. "No no no!"

Holden checked his watch again, tapping the wheel. "Okay, we need to find a way out of this mess." He reached behind his seat and rifled through his portfolio. A second later, he lifted out a square device and mounted it on the dash. After punching a few buttons, a map came up. "We'll take the next—"

The car veered right sharply.

A horn blasted behind them.

Sydney white-knuckled the roll bar, willing her stomach not to heave at the maniac driving, the way-too-narrow lanes, and the whole left-side driving thing. Bumbling down the skinny alley, the car careened toward what looked like a dead end. Sydney leaned away from the door, afraid she'd scrape her shoulder against the wall that seemed hungry enough to slice off a piece of them for dinner.

Bobbing around and through more alleys, Holden delivered them to an unclogged street and barreled down it. "We're almost there." He whipped the car around and stopped at the curb in front of a sidewalk café. Several patrons gasped and yelped then glared at them.

Holden reached across the compact sedan and flung open her door. "I can't park here. Go in and meet the contact. Third table on the right, in front of the window. You're the one he's expecting. Watch what you say. Don't let him manipulate you. Above all else, do not agree to go anywhere with him."

Mouth dry at his last words, she mutely nodded and climbed out of the car. Don't go anywhere with him? Why did that unseat her last nerve? She pushed herself around the black, wrought-iron, waist-high fence guarding the sidewalk café and its patrons. *Jingle-jingle.* Quiet bathed her as she stepped into the quaint restaurant. A slight burning stretched across her lower abdomen as she searched out the table Holden had told her about. She rubbed her belly, feeling drained and apprehensive. Her overactive imagination lurched to vivid, startling encounters. *This is insane. I'm not a spy. I don't know what I'm doing.*

She located the table. The *empty* table. Her stomach plummeted. She slumped her shoulders just as a tall man stomped toward the exit. He brushed past her, nudging her shoulder as he made his way outside. He sure seemed in a hurry.

That's him.

Sydney spun. Watched the way he strode down the sidewalk, determined. When her brain caught up with her feet, she was hot on his tail. "Excuse me." She skipped a step to stay up with him, despite his ignoring her. "Excuse me!" She caught his arm.

He whirled toward her, scowling.

"Syd, no!" Holden's voice carried down the street at the same time she registered what a stupid thing it was to chase and stop this contact. She'd probably just ruined everything. He'd never tell her anything, and this trip would be for nothing.

No, she couldn't accept that. She took a step back, feeling the presence of Holden and Lane behind her. "I'm sorry," she said to the man. "I'm looking for a friend, someone to help me."

He glanced down, and only then did she realize she was again holding her baby bump. Unnerved, she slowly slid her hand away and held his gaze.

"You're late," he growled.

It was a good thing he was talking—and not shooting or strangling her, right? "I'm here now."

Again, he looked at her belly, and she wished she could crawl into a hole. "This must be very important to you if you're willing to risk your unborn child."

Heat flared up her shoulders and neck, straight into her cheeks. "Risk?" She tried to steady the crack in her voice. "I thought you could be trusted."

Like the ebbing tide, his foul mood bled away, and he smiled. "Two days. Ashburn Hotel. Dawn. Come alone." With that, he was gone.

With puffed cheeks, she blew out a long, exhausting breath.

"Sydney?"

She smiled and glanced over her shoulder at Lane and Holden. "We did it."

Holden patted her shoulder. "No, you did it. And you were awesome. Who'd have thought your pregnancy would save us."

"Pregnancy? Is it true? The man asked about your unborn child." Sandy blond brows dug toward Lane's eyes. "How. . .why didn't you tell me?"

Holden chortled. "You're going to tell me you didn't know?"

Lane's shoulders drooped. "I–I'd noticed she'd put on weight, but. . ." Lane's shock shifted, darkening his face with anger. "No, I didn't know. How was I supposed to know? Why did you tell him?"

Irritation skidded up her spine. "I didn't tell anyone, Lane."

He pointed to Holden. "How did he know?"

"For cryin' out loud. How could you *not* know? You're around her every day."

Red colored Lane's cheeks. He balled his fists. "We're going back on the next plane."

Sydney stopped cold. "Excuse me?"

"You're pregnant!"

"Yes, pregnant, not paralyzed."

"What if something happens to you? What if you get hurt? Max would kill you—no, he'd kill *me* because I was here with you."

"Max is living his own life, okay?" Tears welled, threatening her composure. "And what I'm doing here is important. I won't walk away just because things get a little tough. And in case you didn't notice, that man just gave us a green light *because* of my baby."

He shoved his hands in the pockets of his overcoat, his gaze bouncing to the street. Slowly, those green eyes came back to her, wounded. "Syd, why didn't you tell me?"

"I think your feelings for *Mrs.* Jacobs clouded your perception." Holden directed them to his car. "We need to get back to the hotel and find out where the Ashburn is."

And she could only hope her baby's role in this meant *good* things. Not danger. Or death.

CHAPTER 17

"What is that smell?" Max stopped and shielded his nose.

"Durian," Midas said, pointing his machete toward a tree ten yards east. "They're all over the place. Strong odor, very potent flesh." He nudged aside tall grass and speared a fallen prickly fruit with the tip of the blade. "A very. . .unique scent."

"Disgusting is more like it."

"Oy!" Fix tied a black rag around his face.

"Because of the odor, they're banned in Singapore."

"Next mission is there." With a grunt, Max shook off the lingering stench and regained his bearings. Glancing at the blue-green screen strapped to his wrist, he scrolled the map up and monitored the progress since leaving the hotel early that morning. He sketched the tree and prickly fruit then tucked the paper and pencil into the pocket on his right leg. "Let's head northeast." A hot, sticky breeze rifled the rag he wiped over his face, and he kept moving.

Midas stopped. "That's toward the mountains."

"I know."

Fix shifted his weapon propped over his arm. "But the radicals—"

"Are up there." Max smiled at his teammate. "Don't worry,

Fix. We aren't going to get far enough for a close encounter of any kind. I want to test the terrain." Who knew? They could get locked into a firefight during the mission and have to hoof it into the mountains. He prayed it didn't come to that. It'd be like David against Goliath.

The thought smacked him hard as they wove through the dense foliage. What was the point of remembering and focusing on that—to find out how far from God's heart he really was? No thanks. He already knew he didn't measure up.

Another hour bathed in thick humidity and mosquitoes ate—literally—into Max. Good thing he'd had vaccines to stave off malaria. Swiping the sweat from his brow, he paused and removed the map, eyeing a crooked, twisted tree sprouting up out of the boulder. He scratched it out along with a few more landmarks then consulted the GPS. "Okay, there should be a river outlet just over that ridge."

"There's a village nearby."

Max shook his head. "Not in our intel."

"Water source. Trust me," Midas said. "There's a village nearby."

"Possibly. But nothing on the GPS or intel, so we should have a clear shot to the river." Which meant a swift exit. Max squinted up at the sun. "We're running out of daylight."

"Let's spot it and get back." Fix stretched his back. "I need a bed and at least two hours' consecutive sleep."

"Sorry, we'll be up half the night planning."

Midas laughed. "Assuming everything goes well here."

Shooting the man a glare, he stored his supplies. Canyon Metcalfe had been an enigma from day one. He kept to himself mostly but displayed an almost casual arrogance. He obviously knew the area very well. He'd been here before. When? And come to think of it, the former Green Beret had never divulged much about his past.

Max narrowed an eye. What was the guy hiding? "Let's check it out."

They scurried the last dozen yards and pressed their bodies to the earth as they peeked over the small crest. Max jerked back, hunching and curling away. A hut lay almost within an arm's reach below. Shock spiraled through him, but he eased his head forward. Through a bramble of leaves and branches, he saw a dozen or so women gathered around a fire pit. Children darted here and there. The most disturbing part was the armed men lounging around the fire opposite the women.

Midas was right. Max dragged himself out of view. Using hand signals, he motioned Midas and Fix back so they could come up around the other side and get a better vantage.

Out of earshot, he sighed. "Where did they come from?"

"My point exactly. And by the looks, there are hundreds."

Max bit the curse on his tongue. They'd have to figure out a whole new route. "I'm going to need extra time. Have to go out tonight."

"No way." Midas gaped. "If you pull an all-nighter, you'll be dead on your feet."

"Either way, that's the outcome. If I don't, there's no escape route. If I do, we have the route, but we'll be exhausted." He grinned and patted the man's shoulder. "Like a walk in the park, eh?"

A slow smile seeped into Midas's face, as if he enjoyed the brutality of their job. "If by park you mean a malaria-infested, stench-doused park, then yeah, a walk in the park." He fell into step behind Max as they trudged around the rim and dropped to all fours.

Max's heart thrummed as he yanked the cloth from his mouth. How could so many be settled without intel knowing? By the weapons, he guessed the men were expecting trouble. After quickly sketching the vast village on the map, he back-crawled to safety.

They spent the remainder of the afternoon working their way

back down to the coastal city where the team had taken up residence. He'd made voice contact with Cowboy, Legend, and the Kid, who should be crawling down from the stronghold in the mountain with their reconnaissance information.

As they came to the edge of the thick vegetation, Max scanned the beach. "We're early."

"Not by my watch," Legend's deep, familiar voice boomed. " 'Bout time you showed up."

Max tensed, watching as Legend, Cowboy, and the Kid emerged from a thick banana grove. He loved the way they seemed to bleed from the jungle itself, their stealth and reconnaissance skills unrivaled. "You always sit around and let others do all the work?"

"Whenever possible, my friend," Legend taunted. "Whenever possible."

"Anything interesting?" Cowboy motioned them onto the beach.

"Like a village full of women and children and well-armed tangos right on the river?" Max shrugged his pack off and let it drop to the sand.

Cowboy and Legend's faces bore the gravity of the situation. They stood in a semicircle, no one speaking. Legend rubbed his jaw then nodded. "Go on."

Camped out on the sandy stretch of coast, Max flattened his map over his leg and explained the route he'd chosen and the roadblock. "I'll head out when the moon's at its zenith and scout another path. We'll meet up here." He pointed to a grove of trees he'd drawn and looked at Cowboy. "How long will it take you and Griff to get in position?"

"To clear that and remain invisible? Two days."

Max nodded. "Midas, Fix, and I will figure out the route, and we'll move into position on the north side of the encampment so we can slide in and out." He glanced up at the Marine buddies.

"Did you actually see the targets?"

"Yeah," Cowboy said. "Our objectives are exactly where we were told, and if I assessed the situation right, the girl we're here for is with them. A third heat signature registered with the family, and I'm sure she's holed up with them."

"Good."

Frowning, Cowboy drew in a long breath and slowly let it out. "There's a problem." He pointed to a spot on the map. "They went to high ground—which essentially surrounded them by radicals."

Max whistled. "That means hiking up the mountain will be brutal, but. . ."

Midas leaned in. "Getting back down will be deadly."

"Especially with three more people—people who aren't trained."

"Actually, there's four." Legend pursed his lips then smiled. "The missionaries have a small child, one or two years old."

Fix groaned. "We'll have to sedate the kid. No way we can trust him to keep quiet."

"It gets better," Legend groused. "It seems our missionaries are being held by a group known as the Higanti."

Midas jerked visibly. "Are you sure? The Higanti? Did you confirm that?"

The team fell silent, watching the shock ripple through the former Green Beret.

"One hundred percent," Legend said, pride thickening his words. "Why? You know something about them?"

Midas grunted. "They are hell-bent on reclaiming their island, running out any and every *unpure* culture. You think radical Muslims hate Americans? You haven't seen anything. But there's only one thing the Higanti hate more. Christians."

"So," Max asked, looking between Cowboy and Legend. "Why aren't our objectives dead?"

"Our guess is that they're planning an exchange."

"For what?"

Legend looked at his partner. "Our theory is that the islanders foolishly believe if they hand over the missionaries, Abu Sayyaf will leave them alone."

Cowboy agreed. "This is just making it very clear that it'll be like walking over glass—every step, every move will alert someone somewhere."

"Right," Legend said. "There are at least a dozen radical camps dotting the paths up the mountain. And they've got more ammo than a group like that needs. They're heavily guarded, and we're not talking drug-runner armed. They're serious, and the cache is large. Not afraid to use whatever they can get their hands on."

Max's gut churned. If the radicals were this well outfitted, that meant one thing. He gritted his teeth, glaring up through his brows at the others. "We'll need a distraction."

"Why's that?" the Kid asked.

"Because they know we're coming."

Gentle rocking lulled Sydney's senses until she rested her forehead against the window and closed her eyes. She hadn't meant for Lane to find out about the baby, not that way. He hadn't spoken to her since they left the ticket station and boarded the train bound for the West Yorkshire town of Keighley, the only town with a hotel named Ashburn. It fascinated her to watch Holden whip into action and get them on the train within the hour. Thankfully, his connections and full-steam-ahead mentality kept her mind busy enough not to get upset or depressed over the way things had gone down.

Movement snatched her attention back to the cabin of the Quiet Car. Holden eased into the seat closest to the aisle, leaving a seat between them.

"Where's Lane?" she asked as he handed her a bottle of apple juice.

"On a phone call, so he stayed in the restaurant. Mentioned something about a big fat piece of cheesecake." Holden crossed his leg over his knee and wiggled into the seat more. "How're you holding up?"

"I'm good." She opened the drink and took a sip. "You think it'll be okay for you and Lane to be there at the hotel?"

He nodded, swallowing a gulp of his soda. "Keighley's only other hotel is booked solid. And Jerome knows we won't leave you alone. You'll be there to meet the contact, but we won't be far away." For a moment he paused and studied her. "Are you scared?"

She wanted to be brave, to be an investigative reporter like him, make him proud of her and her skills, but she couldn't fool anyone, not even herself. "I wish I could say no. I keep hoping that being pregnant is a guarantee of safety."

A soft laugh rumbled in Holden's chest. "Well, I wouldn't go that far. But I think you're right. For some reason, your pregnancy changed his mind."

"I noticed." Sydney bobbed her head. "Lane and I had looked at a political map of sorts, and determined that, considering recent uprisings, activity, etcetera, the most likely destination for our mystery team is Afghanistan or the Philippines."

"I agree. There's a lot happening in Afghanistan right now that could probably be equalized if we just got a few good men in place." Holden grinned. "But our first focus is Jerome. If this man can't get us connected, we may be at the end of the road."

"I won't accept that," Sydney said, railing at the thought of giving up so soon. A burning on her belly made her rub her side, and she noticed how much bigger her belly seemed. She'd managed to conceal the bump with loose-fitting clothes and excuses of loving food and too much ice cream, but still. . . . "I bet Lane's still mad about the baby. It's kind of hard to miss, huh?"

Holden chuckled. "Like I said, I don't think he wanted to notice. Obviously, he was trying to woo you." He reclined against the vinyl seat and nursed his soda. "So, I haven't heard you talk about your husband. Lane mentioned Max. Is that your husband?"

She shouldn't be surprised he'd noticed. He was a hard-hitting reporter with a nose for dropped lines and inferences. "Yes, Max and I are separated." After a few sips of the juice, she screwed the lid back on and looked out the window, watching as a lone light smeared into a streak that whizzed out of sight in the darkness

"So how does Max feel about the baby and being separated?"

Sydney glanced down at her growing womb. "I didn't find out until after I filed for the separation." She met his sympathetic gaze and shrugged. "He doesn't know." She really didn't want to open all this up, explain about her husband and how their marriage fell apart. That she hadn't even told Max. And for some reason, that really rankled her now that Lane knew. With her pregnancy apparent, she felt devious and guilty for keeping this secret from the father of her child, from the man she loved.

"I didn't mean to pry, Sydney. The whole thing just got me curious when Lane mentioned how angry Max would be."

"Max is easily angered," she whispered. "He's a former Navy SEAL. Saw things, probably did things that changed him—for the worse."

He leaned forward and rubbed his hands together. "Have you heard about the ministry to soldiers based in DC?"

A ministry? She eyed him, curious as to whether he was a Christian. "No."

An intensity darkened his brow, bringing with it a startling determination and vehemence. "Did you know that only in recent years has war-related PTSD become its own diagnosis? Our doctors and psychologists are just beginning to know how to properly treat"—he hooked his fingers in the air, making quotation marks—"these soldiers who've seen and carried out gruesome acts." He huffed and sat up straight. "Anyway, there's an organization that helps men like your husband who return from war. It teaches them the different phases of reintegration into society. Helps them find jobs, and there's even a hotline number."

She studied the man opposite her. Handsome and kind, he had a maturity that almost belied his age. "How do you know about this ministry?"

A sad smile crossed his lips. "My brother was a decorated war veteran. He tried to commit suicide when he came back but failed." He snorted. "I'll never forget how mad he was when he woke up in the hospital with a cop and an IV. So being the reporter I am, while I sat with him those first few nights, I used my laptop and researched ways to help him. That's how I found the group. Steve now works with this ministry, helping other grunts like him. He got married last month."

Wow. What she wouldn't do for a happily-ever-after ending. But that was a fantasy. The brutal truth was that most soldiers just buried it, gutted it up, as Max said. Only the pain within became the fire outside, the rage that destroyed anything in its wake. Besides, Max would never agree to something like that. "For that to work, the soldier—or sailor—has to want the help."

"True," Holden said, nodding. "I think they all want to be better, to fit in, to be normal. But facing those demons, those ghouls that have plagued their minds and dreams, isn't easy."

Ghouls? Demons? She knew Max had bad dreams, but he'd always shaken them off, said it was nothing. Maybe even she had bought into his belief that what he'd experienced wasn't so bad. Had she even become convinced that anger and isolation were who Max was, the way he'd always claimed?

"Ya know, I always knew the guys had it bad, that they saw cruel things, but until I did my stint as an embedded reporter two years ago, I didn't have a clue."

Sydney turned toward him, again surprised. "You were embedded?"

With a lengthy exhale, he slumped against the leather, his arm over the back of the seat. "I wasn't there two hours when our convoy got hit by an IED. The Marines were amazing, but it really jerked the slack out of my attitude. I now have a very heightened awareness of what they face and battle every day. It's easy to become inoculated against the pain when you're sitting at home reading or watching one-sided, liberal media reports. It's another thing to live and breathe the dust after a car bomb explodes and kills fifteen men you just had dinner with."

Two years ago. . . . She ticked back her mental counter to the stories he'd done. She widened her eyes. "That's when your stories started getting national acclaim."

He laughed. "Yeah, my stories finally had a message. In my time in Iraq, I learned how to dig until I found the heart of a story, learned how to make the reader care. It's so easy sitting in recliners, feet propped up and watching the news, to spout off about how terrible war is, how it only breeds violence and monsters. But out there, in the thick of an RPG attack, you find out real quick you're battling a very mean evil, one bent on your destruction."

Chills trickled down Sydney's spine. She'd never thought about it this way. Is that what Max had encountered for all those years?

Holden patted her leg. "Well, you should probably get some rest. Dawn comes early, and we aren't going to be there in time for you to get any decent sleep." He dug his laptop out and powered up.

Sydney burrowed into the seat, yawning even at the thought of getting rest. But there was no way she could sleep—not given the way Holden's war stories had spiked her with a realization that Max may have had a good reason for this behavior. Had she been too quick to step away? Although she believed God would understand her seeking protection for her and the baby, she knew in her heart that she'd given up too soon.

With a sigh, she twisted and yawned. This would make her second sleepless night in a row. Maybe they could stay in Keighley for an extra day so she could get caught up on rest. Being pregnant really sapped the last of her energy reserves.

When sleep finally lowered its defenses, it only brought frightening images of men dressed in weird costumes chasing them down narrow alleys and launching grenades. Explosions, screams, and shrieks echoed in her ears as she jolted awake.

Heart palpitating, she glanced at Holden, whose face held a glow from the laptop monitor. Apparently his information about his term as an embedded reporter had had a bigger impact on her than she'd thought.

Where was Max now? What was he doing? At least she could breathe easier, knowing he'd resigned his commission and was back home, safe and out of danger.

CHAPTER 18

Night hung thick with humidity and needling mosquitoes. Palms swayed overhead like giant shadow soldiers guarding the small island. Trudging through the dense, tropical vegetation kept Max on guard enough against nocturnal predators that he didn't want to consider the human predators lying in wait. But he had to. Or he'd end up dead.

"Another twenty meters, there should be a river." Midas hacked his way through a mess of vines.

"We can verify and follow that route, then meet back up with the team." Max glanced up and smiled at the moon peeking through the light cover of palm branches. Something about the ominous glow against the ebony void of space soothed him. Maybe it was the fact that it was open, not crowded.

Ahead, a flurry of low-voiced curses and frantic movement stopped Max. Shifting his M4 into a better grip, he met Fix's confused glance. They inched forward until they met up with Midas.

He grumbled and stomped hard several times. Glared at them. "Keep your head low."

"Why?" Max asked, his gaze skating the foliage.

"Tarsiers."

"That a country?" Fix asked, sarcastically.

"World's smallest monkey—looks like a cross between a rodent and a lemur. Large, bulging eyes make them perfect night hunters." Midas sighed. "Stupid thing jumped on my head."

Max couldn't help the chuckle. "Okay, we're just around the ridge from the river." A dull green glow emanated around Max as he consulted a GPS device. "We'll take it low and slow." The last time he'd approached a water source, he'd nearly stumbled into the middle of a village, which would've exposed not only him, but the team.

Then again, weren't they already exposed if the radicals expected them?

The three men lowered into a crouch and shifted around the bend in the dirt path. Even as he inched closer, Max could hear the tumbling river nearby. They really needed this break, needed to find the most direct path down the coastline for the extraction. That was the tricky leg of the trip.

The nearby churning water called to him like a siren. He'd love to ditch the gear and immerse himself in the cool liquid. Anything to abate this putrid humidity that had his clothes sticking to him like a second skin.

At the edge of the tropical forestation, he scanned the outlying area with his night vision goggles, searching for predators of the two- and four-legged kinds. "Clear," he hissed over his shoulder to Midas, who had his back to Max and was watching the jungle.

"Roger. Here, too."

"And here," Fix said from a few feet off the path.

With a deep exhale, Max stood and removed the NVGs. For several minutes he worked sketching the new path into the plan. He pursed his lips, realizing it'd add just under two hours to the route. Since they only afforded themselves a three-hour window, this detour would cost them dearly. They wouldn't be able to incur any mishaps.

Like that was possible.

"Okay, let's get the equipment stowed." Max slid the pack from his shoulders and unloaded the inflatable raft from the gear. Behind him he heard the *skritch-thump* of Midas's hole-digging. Fix scoured the area for vegetation to cover the dig site. To keep them supplied on the last leg of the journey, Max retrieved a few energy bars and water bottles, just in case it took longer to get there than expected. At least they'd have food.

Once they dropped the raft and supplies into the hole, they quickly covered them with the dirt. He smiled, watching as Midas meticulously uprooted a small shrub and replanted it directly over their goods.

"Nice job," Max said. "I have a feeling this isn't the first time you've been here."

Midas tamped down the edges and glanced at him, the moon casting an eerie glow on his face.

"The tarsier, knowing about those radicals, your knowledge of that rotten fruit."

"It's actually ripe, not rotten."

And the man avoided his question. They all had parts of their lives they weren't willing to share, and as long as it didn't interfere with the functioning of the team, Max wouldn't press the issue, no matter how much his curiosity nagged him.

Studying the map with a small flashlight, he traced the line around two villages. It'd be tricky going, especially with four extra bodies—including a child. If they rigged some type of sling or carrier, they could make the hike without tying their hands.

"What're you thinking?"

"Huh?" He looked up, his mind reengaging. "It's the kid with the missionaries. This section of the route is laden with radicals, villagers, and rushing water. It'll be something else to get the team through there on our own, but with extras and the kid. . ." He pointed to another point—the clifflike pass where they'd had to hug earth to get by. "Imagine trying to get unskilled people to negotiate that pass with a kid in tow."

Midas slapped his shoulder. "Don't borrow trouble. We'll work it out when we get there." He squatted and dug through his rucksack. He pulled out an energy bar, peeled back the wrapper, and bit into it. "Besides," he said, standing and threading his pack over his arm, "these missionaries have been here a few years. They know what they're getting into—or should I say out of?"

Off to the side, Fix sat digging an energy bar out of the pocket on his black tactical duds.

True. "That's the thing—they know the land well enough to know it's too dangerous to be here. Yet they stay." Max reached back and grabbed a bar for himself from the side pocket. "Then it takes a team like us to come in and save their hides. Is converting people to their beliefs that important?" He glanced back at the Latino, who watched casually. "Fix, keep up."

"I'm cool, ese." He grinned and came to his feet, lifting his weapon to the side.

Midas started walking along the bank, following their exit strategy. "I'm not sure it's that so much as it is falling in love with the people and being determined to show them God's love. You know, the verse, 'Greater love hath no man....'" Moonlight glinted off Midas's grease-painted face as he chewed.

"Sounds personal."

Midas shrugged. "Stranger things have happened."

Was that an admission of his faith? What was with the enigmatic questions? Considering the man with him, Max realized a few things. First, Midas had the Christian talk down to a science. He spoke it so easily and casually, it seemed like second nature. Sort of the way Cowboy spoke. But something was different in the two men, and he couldn't quite figure it out.

Second, Midas knew this terrain too well. Sure, in special ops, no matter the branch of military, a soldier was trained to recon, to know the landscape and vegetation, as well as the political and religious landscape. But to know about indigenous life and to know it without skipping a beat—like that obnoxious fruit. . .

And last—the part that concerned him most—how did Midas know the missionaries had lived here a few years? The information relayed to the team was scant at best. Location, identities, photos, extraction point, and drop-off point. Of course, with their names, it wasn't real hard to figure out they were Caucasian. And a little back-channel research helped him dig up the group they were with—someone really should show them how to hide their tracks a little better. If Max had really wanted to hack, he could probably track down their contacts, family members, and even "incriminating" letters or e-mails—maybe even illegal literature.

"So tell me." Max feigned indifference as they trudged along the river snaking through the small island, eventually dumping into a main tributary that carried out to the Indian Ocean.

"Tell you what?"

"You said stranger things have happened."

"Tss." Midas shook his head. "It's a figure of speech, Frogman."

Max kept moving. The former SF soldier didn't want to talk. He'd find a way to get the guy to open up. "I don't get it. Two groups fighting over this girl. That seem right to you, Midas?"

"I just go where they send me."

Cryptic again. Tension crept into Max's shoulders and neck. What was the soldier hiding? Surely he wasn't a Hanoi Jane. That wouldn't make sense—they'd done a half dozen missions together already. But then again, what did he really know about the man working this island with him? Almost nothing, come to think of it. Family? Prior service—besides being a part of the proud U.S. Army Special Forces and a darn good soldier, Midas hadn't said anything. He dressed nice and drove a nice car. So being a retired serviceman, where did he get money for slick clothes and cars?

Thoughts of hog-tying the guy slithered through Max's mind like the river monitor rippling through the water. "You must've served a long while with the Green Berets to be as fluid in your job as you are now."

Midas stopped, turned to Max, and shouldered his way closer, his clear eyes sparkling as the moonlight glanced off the river. "If you want to know, just ask."

"All right," Max said, his fists balled. "How do you—"

A shrill scream pierced the night.

Max dove into the shrubs, hearing two similar movements from his men. He rolled and came up, crouched, his M4 at the ready. "Anything?"

"Negative," Midas whispered back.

"Clear," Fix said from less than two feet away.

They side-stepped along the path. Soon more screams filtered into the darkness. Haunting and foreboding, the cries lured Max closer. He eased his NVGs back on and scissor-stepped through the shrubs and under low-lying branches. A pair of wide, bulging eyes popped into his field of vision. The miniature monkey nearly sidetracked him.

A whimper whipped out at him.

He moved quicker. Whatever—*whoever* it was, they were down. A faint outline showed through the camouflage of tall grass and shrubs. The body was small. He hurried, his stomach catching in his throat.

Within seconds, he towered over a young girl, her clothes ripped and hanging in shreds on her thin form as she lay curled up like a baby. Max slowly lowered himself to a knee, watching as Midas moved stealthily into the jungle, sweeping back and forth for tangos.

He winced when she hugged herself tighter and whimpered, apparently afraid of him. "Shh," Max said to the girl. He could see blood staining what little clothes were left on her body.

Branches swished, followed closely by an ever-so-light snapping. A second later, Midas emerged ten feet to the left, his M4 held close but down. "It's clear," he whispered as he glanced over his shoulder at the girl.

Anger clawed up Max's spine as he assessed her. "They beat her, probably raped her." What kind of animals assaulted a girl who couldn't be more than twelve? The thought sickened him. He touched her hair, trying to brush the strands back—but she jerked visibly and yelped. "Tell her it's okay."

Midas stilled.

Max pushed his gaze to his teammate's. "Tell her it's okay," he ordered. "That we're not going to hurt her—we're friends." When the man didn't move, Max growled, "Tell her!"

Without taking his eyes off Max, Midas squatted beside them, his weapon aimed at the trees. Slowly, he bent toward the girl, and finally diverting his attention to the battered child, a stream of foreign words flew off his tongue, soft and caring.

The crying stemmed, shudders wracked her body.

Midas whispered more words to the girl as Fix knelt beside them and probed her injuries. "Nothing too serious, but we need to get her out of here."

"We can't. This will directly compromise the mission."

"They've left her to die. If we don't take her, she'll be eaten alive."

"And if we take her, they'll know exactly where. . .we are." A grin pulled Max's lips apart. "Perfect. Just the distraction we need."

An eager expression overtook Midas's consternation. "If they think we're here, they'll call in backup, which will take attention off the Higanti settlement."

"And we can get the missionaries out."

Greedy and foreboding darkness swooned around Sydney. Forcing iron courage into her spine, she stood straight, listening to every chirrup and rustle that snuck into the dead of night. Blue barely peeked through the skyline, warning of dawn's approach.

Still stuffed from the full English breakfast the hotel owner had prepared—why did they insist on that nauseating black pudding?—she rubbed her belly and glanced around the narrow road. Since the British drove on the wrong side of the road, should she be waiting on the opposite side?

She wiggled her jaw, hating the tracking device/transmitter Holden had tucked into her ear. Despite it feeling as if she had a tennis ball sticking out of her head, he'd promised it wasn't noticeable.

"We can hear everything, Syd. The tracer is showing bright and green. Just relax." Holden's voice carried through the tickling device.

Crunch. Crunch. Crunch.

The steady approach of footsteps over the crushed-gravel side road sent waves of chills and jitters over her. From the empty void of night, a large figure loomed, growing larger with each step. A man. Jerome.

Could Lane and Holden hear him coming? "I'm here," she said to the contact.

He continued straight toward her without speaking. A scowl marred his features as he walked right up to her and reached toward her face. Cringing, she sucked in a breath and stumbled back, panic beating a rapid rhythm in her breast.

He gripped the nape of her neck with one hand, swept her long hair aside, and deftly removed the bug with the other. Then he handed her a cloth. "Put this over your head."

Sydney hesitated for only a second, thinking it was a bag. Instead, a long, silky length of fabric draped over her head and shoulders. A scarf!

"Let's go," Jerome said, hooking her elbow and starting down the road. A block away, he stuffed her into a car and pulled onto the road.

Scrambling to secure her seat belt, Sydney's stomach churned as they roared past the hotel—just as Lane and Holden burst through the front door, light from the interior spilling out after them. She clung to the sides of the seat as he barreled down the pothole-riddled road.

"Where are you taking me?"

"No questions!"

They drove for an hour, the silence excruciating and frightening. *You're an idiot, Sydney Moira.* She placed a hand over her belly, over her son, and quietly prayed that her exuberance for the story wouldn't kill her baby. Peace settled into the inner recesses of her heart and calmed her fears.

Finally, he pulled off the two-lane road onto a narrower road, if one could call it that. With barely enough room for one car to navigate, the road wound up into a hilly area, thick with trees and waist-high flowers.

Serenity bathed the West Yorkshire landscape, revealing the beauty and splendor of the hillside for the first time. But ahead, the road ended. Panic gripped her tighter still, squeezing against her chest as Jerome stopped the car.

"Get out," he said.

She froze, noting that he climbed out and shut his door. Her gaze combed the hills, searching for a home or road or *something* that would reassure her she wasn't about to be murdered and left for the vultures. Nothing. They were alone. And he wanted her out of the car. Why had he brought her up here, alone and at dawn? Would her body be found days from now, rotted and half eaten?

Almost as if in answer to her questions, a gentle vibration tickled her feet. Soon the deafening roar of a helicopter rattled her bones. It descended less than a hundred feet from the car like a giant bird of prey.

Jerome jerked open the door, grabbed her shirt at the shoulder, and dragged her out. The seat belt dug into her throat as she pawed at the latch. Freed, she stumbled into the open.

"Where are you taking me?" The rotors whipped her hair into her face as she shouted, but whether he hadn't heard or ignored her, he didn't answer. Instead, he hauled her to the chopper and shoved her inside.

Metal slammed into her knee as she struggled to climb into a seat. Yelping, she straightened and climbed into a seat—and froze. A gunman sat across from her, leering. She glanced back to Jerome—only the door shut tight, and the pressure of gravity pushed her down as the chopper lifted.

"You safe now," the man taunted amid a wicked laugh.

Oh God, help me! Pressed against the seat, Sydney stared at him. Breathing became a chore. She braced herself as the nose of the chopper angled down then seemed to drag forward before finally lifting upward. The hearty breakfast clawed its way back up her throat. She gulped back the acid coating her tongue.

Twenty minutes later the chopper delivered her to an airstrip hangar. Peering out the window, she spied a small jet. As the rotors of the helicopter slowed, she heard the deep thrum of the airplane's engines. What were they planning to do? Or better yet—where were they planning to take her? This didn't make any sense. If they were going to kill her. . .

The gunman hopped out and waved her onto the tarmac. If she got out, they'd put her on the small jet sitting a hundred feet away, and who knew what would happen after that. Mustering every last bit of courage, she refused.

He reached in and tried to grab her arm, but she kicked his claws away.

A fresh burst of air slapped her hair into her face, concealing her view. Something caught her from behind—and she felt herself falling—right onto the tarmac and into the arms of a burly man. She screamed and struggled to free herself, but between him and the leering man, she had no hope. Each man held an arm as they hustled her up the steel steps to the jet.

Stale and mechanized, the air in the cabin enveloped her as they pushed her into a leather seat. Almost immediately the plane began to taxi down the runway.

As gravity again worked against her, pressing her spine into the cream leather, she lashed out—tears spilling over her cheeks. This was it. She would never be seen again, except maybe when Holden reported on her death via a live feed from Keighley.

Through the tiny portal to her right, she grieved the disappearing lush hillside. It meant her doom. *Don't be so morose!* But it was true. Burying her face in her hands, she surrendered to the fear that strangled her. It wasn't supposed to happen this way. A simple meeting with someone who knew about a group of men saving the world. She just had to push, had to insist on tracking down the story. Even the American government had tried to warn her through its silence that this was far more dangerous than she knew. And Lane wanted her to go home and not find the Ashburn Hotel. Why hadn't she listened?

As the plane leveled off, Sydney stared at the white cottony sky, resigned to her fate. Now she was on her way to only-God-knew-where, and she wasn't sure she'd live to give birth to her baby. Tears still streamed as she wished she'd told Max about the baby. Wished she hadn't listened to Bryce. Wished she'd had a backbone and been stronger.

"I am sorry to frighten you with such extreme measures."

The soft words jerked Sydney's gaze to the right. As she wiped her tears, her vision slowly focused on a woman seated across from her dressed in a beautiful teal-colored dress, the apron heavily beaded and sparkling. Sheer material draped around her face added an air of mystery and Scheherazade-ness to the woman, who smiled. Sad eyes drifted down to Sydney's belly. "You carry a child?"

Hand on her stomach, Sydney couldn't bring herself to speak.

The woman smoothed out the material over her own well-rounded abdomen. "We have much in common, yes?"

"Wh—what do you want with me?"

"My name is Raisa." She looked around the cabin and waved someone Sydney couldn't see out of the way. "Again, I am sorry for the way you were brought here, but it is necessary for my safety. I swear you will not be harmed."

Why weren't the words comforting? Maybe because they were thirty thousand feet over nothing that could guarantee Sydney a safe return.

"I am told you are looking for a group of soldiers."

That piqued Sydney's interest. She shifted and straightened. "You're the source?"

"I stay hidden. They guard me because if I am found, then my child will be cut from me to make sure he dies."

The gruesome mental image shook Sydney. "Who?"

"The men the soldiers saved me and my family from. You see, my husband—the father of my baby—led a rebellion against those who would deny freedom to all who desire it. Freedom for women; freedom to worship whatever god one wills. I hold to Allah, but it does not mean all should. Yes?"

"So you saw the men who saved you?"

Even behind the veil, her smile shone. "They delivered me to a safe place, and now I live on this plane. But I am not safe. I will not be, nor will my son. They murdered my husband, but we still have a voice. Once the men who butchered so many are caught, I will testify against them, and they will go to prison or be executed. Then my son and I will disappear and begin a new life."

"Can you tell me about the men who came to your city?"

The woman shrugged, motioning toward an open doorway. "They wore the color of night. No flags. No names. I think they did not want to be recognized."

"Yes, but I have been trying to find them. They saved another woman, and she wants to thank them publicly."

Garbed in similar attire to Raisa, several female servants shuffled in with silver trays of tea and biscuits. They set up a table between Sydney and Raisa then discreetly served them. With a reverent bow, they backed out of the cabin, their faces still down, a sign of respect often shown to royalty.

Was Raisa royalty among her people? Shamefully, Sydney couldn't identify the woman's nationality, other than to know she was Middle Eastern.

"Is there anything you can tell me—" Silenced by Raisa's snapped-up hand, Sydney bit back the torrent of frustration.

The woman lifted a cookie between her manicured fingers and took a small bite. After she wiped her mouth, she resumed the conversation. "I am hiding, protecting myself, going through extraordinary measures to protect my unborn son. It's important, would you not agree?"

"Yes, of course. Your life is in danger. It makes sense."

Raisa smiled, her olive skin shining under the fluorescent lights in the cabin. "And so it is that I understand their desire not to be found."

"Yes, but—"

"Would you like something to eat? As a pregnant woman, I know how the little one within saps strength and vitamins from your very bones." Raisa set a plate on Sydney's side of the table and placed several treats on it, then poured her a drink.

The woman wasn't going to cooperate. Being one to seek anonymity, she wouldn't want anyone to betray her whereabouts, so she clearly wouldn't say what she knew about the men who'd saved her life.

"You dragged me to the middle of nowhere, had me transported via helicopter then on this plane to I-have-no-clue-where, only to tell me you won't tell me?" Incredulity streaked Sydney's words.

For a moment, Raisa's composure slackened, and she flashed a heated gaze toward Sydney. But then the cool facade slipped back into place. "Perhaps you do not realize who I am, and for that, I will forgive your outburst. I have my reasons for everything, and just think of this as my way of saying it's better left alone."

"Better left alone?" Indignation scampered up her vertebrae and in between her shoulders, heating her neck.

"Tell me, have these men helped others?"

"You know they have—I just told you!"

"Would you say that these men are heroic? That they have done wonderful things by helping so many?"

Sydney sighed.

"If you unveil these men, if you go before the world and destroy the anonymity that they have worked so hard to create, who is that helping, besides you?"

The accusation stung, but Sydney couldn't deny it. "It wasn't my intent to *expose* them." She wanted this story, wanted to find the men who were heroic, who swooped in and saved lives and the day. And this woman probably had the answers but wouldn't give them. There had to be a way to get her to talk.

Sydney's gaze roamed the silver trays as she munched a cookie, thinking. She sipped the cool drink. Then she saw it. The implanted stem of an orange tossed an idea into Sydney's mind.

She grabbed a napkin, exhilaration pinging through her. "If I show you a symbol, would you tell me if you've seen it before?"

Biting into a chocolate biscuit, Raisa's dark, expressive eyes came to hers. Licking her lips, she took her time. Patted her red, full lips with a napkin. "It's senseless, this little game of yours, Mrs. Jacobs."

Sydney asked for a pen then drew the symbol Mangeni's son had depicted. She slid it across the table.

Recognition flickered through Raisa's eyes, but she cooled her reaction. "I have not seen it." Chin lifted, she looked away.

Sydney could see the lie written over the woman's beautiful face. "I don't believe you."

Raisa rose sharply. "Allah has gifted these men. Allows them to do what he has willed. *Insh'Allah.*" Then she softened ever so slightly. "Besides, it is too late."

"What do you mean?"

"For you." Raisa almost sneered, glancing at the cookies and drink. "You will be able to sleep now, no doubt."

With a hard swallow, Sydney noticed the tiny grains filling her vision. The edges smudged into a gray nothingness that slowly devoured her entire sight. She gasped, gripping the chair. "What did you do to me?"

"Insh'Allah."

# CHAPTER 19

Cheek pressed to his M4, Max ignored the sweat rolling into his eyes. Dawn teased the village as he sidestepped closer to it, the soft sounds of Midas's movements behind him. Fix had his flank. Raspy breathing, uneven and almost gurgling, trickled through the humid air from the girl now unconscious in Midas's arms. They'd hiked more than a mile to reach the only village where he felt confident the natives would ask questions first, shoot later.

But he wasn't taking chances. Slowly, he swept the sight across the huts, searching for danger.

Midas grunted. "If they see your weapon—"

A man stepped from the shadows beside a hut, stared at them for a second, then shouted over his shoulder.

Hustling forward, Midas angled his body to show the girl, talking in Tagalog to the man. Each word grew louder until a half dozen men with spears stood blocking the path.

Max pinned his sights on the man who'd signaled the alarm. He wanted to ask what his teammate was saying, but he'd keep his peace and wait. Midas would let him know when things were clear or if he needed to do something. Still, tension balled at the base of his neck.

"Lower the weapon," Midas whispered to the side.

Stealthily, he rolled his shoulder, hoping this wasn't a bad idea. He had good reflexes and knew a few jujitsu moves, but if one of those spears spiraled through the air. . .

Max eased his face away from the weapon, monitoring the villagers' reaction. When two of them echoed his actions by lowering their spears, he propped the M4 on his other arm with the muzzle down and nodded for Fix to do the same. Prepped and only seconds from the ready.

"Why you come?" A short man, a blue stripe painted across his forehead, strutted to the front of his men.

"We need shelter for this girl," Midas said and motioned toward the girl. "He's a doctor. We must help her; she's dying."

Without taking his eyes off them, the elder spoke to the others in Tagalog. Finally, he nodded. "You come."

Weapon to the side, Max followed Midas and Fix into a hut, where the elder cleared a small mat and motioned to it. "Here."

Max stood watching the door, feeling distrustful and anxious. Intel might state this village behaved friendly to outsiders, but the reception they'd received was anything but friendly. He positioned himself at a small window and stood guard, hoping this diversion worked, that the soldiers lying in wait for Nightshade would be distracted by a call to this village where two American soldiers brought a wounded girl.

A half hour later as Fix ministered to the girl, Max lowered himself to a crouch, attention on the group gathered outside, and Midas watched from the door. At least the villagers hadn't asked who they were—then again, that worried him. He tugged jerky from his pocket.

"He's not a doctor," he mumbled.

Midas grunted. "Technically, no. But you try explaining to them that he's a PJ with enough medical skills to do more damage than a licensed doctor."

Needle and thread worked together to stitch up the girl's side.

"Not sure she'll make it, but we got their attention." Bent over the girl, Fix tied off the thread and assessed his work. "I think. . .I think that's it."

"No," Midas mumbled as he moved toward the dais where the girl lay outstretched. "That's too much blood for—" He lunged and clamped a hand over her side. "Look! She's been shot."

"No way—" Fix gasped. "*Dios mio!* I never saw it." He flew into action with Midas at his side.

Max considered the men, once again disconcerted over Midas. The guy knew the island, knew. . .medical stuff? How was that possible?

A flurry of raised voices and shouting drew Max back to the window. He eyed the villagers in the early morning light. "They didn't ask who we were or why we were here."

"Figured that out, did ya?" Midas resumed his position by the door as Fix finished the small operation to remove the bullet.

Fix dabbed antiseptic over the wound then began applying gauze.

"Means our time is short."

"No." Midas glanced back at the operating area, frowned, then looked outside. "It means we're already late."

Raking a hand through his hair, Max sighed. Nothing about this mission had gone right. Maybe they shouldn't have come. Maybe they should've passed on this mission. Did they even have that option? He'd have to check with Lambert when they got back. By far, this was the most detailed assignment, and the lengthiest.

"You got someone to go home to, Midas?" Fix asked.

"Nope."

Fix stood and dumped water over his bloodied hands then used a cleanser to scrub them clean. "What's the point, ese?" He clicked his tongue. "I mean, you're out here so long, life back there seems like fairyland."

"Yeah, everything's screwed up; everything goes wrong no matter how hard you try. And she only gets mad and wants you to leave." Max swallowed the thick swell of emotion, only then realizing how much he'd revealed. Unsettled, he shifted and glanced at his teammate.

Covering the girl, Midas swept a strand of hair from her young face. Max grunted. She couldn't be more than twelve. And now she had psychological bruises for the rest of her life. It was wrong in all kinds of ways.

"I've done all I can do," Fix muttered.

"Then let's clear out."

Midas stood and shouldered his supplies then glanced at his watch. "I don't imagine we have much—"

Throaty and loud, the rattle of a diesel rumbled through the morning.

Max jerked up his weapon, peered outside the hut, and bolted toward the trees. He heard Midas and Fix behind him warning him not to stop until they couldn't go any farther. Branches whipped back under the stinging reprimand of bullets. Bark flew out at them.

Nothing like being able to predict guerilla movement.

After a solid forty-minute jog through the dense terrain, they pulled up next to a small cluster of trees. Max consulted his GPS and looked out at the skyline, assessing the dark clouds sweeping in.

"Think the team's ready?" Midas sipped from his camelbak, swished the water around his mouth, then spat it out.

"Ready or not, we're hitting tonight. These guerillas are too keyed into our movements. If we don't do it tonight, it'll be too late." He plotted the quickest route to where he'd penetrate the Higanti camp and extract the missionaries. Tugging the radio from his pocket, he drank from his water pack. "I'll notify the team, see what effect our stunt had."

Midas sat against the trunk of a tree, eyes closed and arms folded over his chest. Fix, propped up next to him, did the same. The one thing they'd all learned was the incredible benefit of power naps. Get rest at any possible point. Sleep called to Max.

He keyed his mic. "Ghost One, this is Delta One, come in."

Static hissed through the line, forcing Max to shift and stare up the hill, as if he could see where the snipers were settled into position.

"Ghost One," he spoke into the secured radio. "Repeat, this is Delta One, come in."

"Copy, Delta One," broke through his ear mic. "This is Ghost One. Over."

The kinks in Max's muscles unraveled at the sound of Cowboy's whispered words. He was probably already in place and waiting for the fireworks tonight. "Give me a sitrep."

"Tangos reduced, headed to the six." South. They were headed south.

Perfect. Max grinned. "Roger that. En route. Over."

"Over and out."

When Midas came up without a hesitation, Fix slapped his shoulder. "You realize a power nap means you actually sleep."

"Not in this life." Standing, Midas shrugged the pack farther onto his shoulder. "Let's get it moving."

The plan had worked and afforded the team a bit of time and fewer bodies to wrestle with to extract the missionaries. Why these people didn't leave when they had the chance, he'd never understand. Of course, the same could be said about him—why did he keep doing missions that threatened his very life? The thought pounded him. He'd always known he'd be a sailor; then when his grandmother had died and there was nothing left for him, he hadn't thought twice. And hadn't again, until. . .Sydney.

Silently, he thanked a God he hadn't addressed in years that she was safe in the States, probably out on a date with that puke

Lane Bowen. He'd never want her to see the cruelty of war and its gruesome effects.

Someone must've clobbered her good. Sydney moaned as she fought the haze clouding her mind. Each arm rivaled the weight of an anchor, pinning her body down. She opened her eyes and—and cringed. A gleam shot through the back of her eyeballs, the fluorescent light painfully bright. Dragging her hand to shield her face, she groaned. She squinted around the room, trying to catch her bearings. *Where am I?*

Voices rose and fell from somewhere behind her. Was she still on the plane? The concrete floor and long hall warned her she wasn't. Propped on her arm, she peered through a knitted brow to decipher the setting. White halls. To her side, she spotted someone moving.

" 'Ello, what's this? I thought you cleared the bay."

"Indeed, I did," another replied. The sound of shuffling feet soon delivered a nurse to Sydney's side, but she looked around. "There's no chart, Dr. Gallance."

Doctor? Sydney pushed herself upright—and wobbled. The woman wrapped her arms around her, and Sydney clung to her as the room spun and whirled in a dozen crazy colors. Chills pimpled her skin. She shivered.

"Whoa! Easy there, ma'am. You're going to fall off if you aren't careful." The scent of fabric softener tingled against Sydney's senses as the woman peered into her eyes, apparently assessing her. "Are you feeling okay?"

"Where am I?"

The nurse laughed. "In a hospital. But I'm not sure why."

In a flash, it all rushed back to her. Raisa unwilling to give helpful information, the airplane ride to nowhere, then some off-the-wall comment from her host about sleeping well. At least with the British accents shading the words of the medical staff here, she had good reason to believe she was still in England, but *where* in England?

"What city am I in?"

The nurse cast a furtive look to the doctor, whose shoes squeaked against the floor as she joined them. The doctor assessed her. "Get her a warm blanket." With a smile, she stood in front of the metal gurney. "I'm Dr. Charlotte Gallance. What is your name?"

"S–Sydney Jacobs," she murmured as the doctor placed two fingers on Sydney's forearm. Nervous jitters snaked through her body. The baby thumped in silent protest to her hunched position. Sydney nudged her shoulders back to afford more room. She put her hand on her belly, wanting the doctor to verify his health.

As if on cue, Dr. Gallance lifted her stethoscope and pressed it to Sydney's chest then to her swollen womb. "Well, your heartbeat is a bit slow, which could explain your chills. Do you know what happened or how you ended up here?"

"No, I don't." She would not tell this doctor or anyone else that she'd been drugged. The most important thing was getting hold of Lane and getting out of here. What if they were dead? What if Jerome had gone back and killed Holden and Lane? The thought nearly sent her into a panic. "May I make a phone call?"

Dr. Gallance considered her then nodded. "I suppose that's in order. Can you walk?"

Sydney eased herself off the gurney—and instantly Dr. Gallance reached out to steady her. "I'm still getting used to this," she said, patting her belly.

The doctor led her to a nurse's station and leaned against the counter. "Since you seem to only have what's on you, I'm going to assume you have no money to use the public phones. Keep it short."

Handset in hand, Sydney punched in Lane's number, trying

to distance herself from the station, not only to hide her conversation, but to conceal the fact that his number was an international number from here. Wherever *here* was.

"Hello?" Strain roughed up Lane's voice.

"Lane, it's me."

"Sydney! Where are you? We've been frantic. Holden called in some friends, and they've been scouring the map for you."

"Slow down, Lane." She cradled her head in her hand as she lowered herself into a chair. As she reveled in the relief of sitting, she spotted the double-door emergency entrance—and the name of the hospital. "I'm at the Tooting Hospital."

"Hospital! What on earth? How di—"

"Please, just come get me." Suddenly she felt alone and desperate.

"We're leaving now. We returned to London yesterday when you disappeared, so we're not far away."

"Hurry. Bye." She gave back the phone and thanked the receptionist before returning to the vinyl, scoop-shaped seat. Wait— Lane had said yesterday. She snapped her gaze to the receptionist. "What day is it?"

"Thursday."

Thursday! Two days? She'd been unconscious for two days? She rubbed her temple and resisted the urge to wilt. It had been her choice to come out here, her choice to press on with this story and find the truth—and it could've ended a lot worse.

A cup appeared in front of her. She peered up at Dr. Gallance, who smiled. "It's juice—it'll help your blood and sugar levels, hopefully stave off that chill and throbbing headache. Too, you're probably dehydrated."

"Thank you." She took a sip and savored the coolness rushing down her throat. The sensation trickled through her entire esophagus and into her stomach. Doing away with propriety, she guzzled the rest and let out a long, ragged sigh.

Dr. Gallance pulled another juice bottle from her pocket and handed it to her.

Sydney laughed and took that one, too.

"Are you in trouble, Sydney Jacobs? Do you need the authorities?"

Her first reaction was to snap no, but that would look and sound suspicious. "No. I can't explain what happened, but my friend will be here soon. I'll be fine."

"You're American. You've obviously been drugged—there are no apparent abrasions or cuts, but your balance is off, and your pupils are still partially dilated."

"I suppose that would explain why it seems so bright."

Dr. Gallance nodded. "It appears you're fine, but I am concerned. It is my duty as a doctor to report suspicious events to the authorities."

That pulled Sydney's gaze to the good doctor. "Please, I know you have a responsibility, but I'm fine. My friend will be here—" Just then she saw Lane's long-legged stride tearing up the sidewalk and storming through the doors. "That's him there. He's going to take me home. Everything will be fine."

"Syd!" Lane rushed down the hall toward her, Holden hot on his heels. Lane dropped to a knee beside her. He cupped her face in his hands then kissed her—right on the lips!

Sydney jerked away and flinched at his intimate behavior. She gulped back the sickening feeling of having him cross that line from friend to. . .something else.

"Is there anything we need to sign?" Holden asked, handing the woman his business card. "You can send any bills to that address."

The woman gaped.

With that, Holden turned and guided Sydney out of the hospital. Disoriented after Lane's kiss, she leaned into Holden, only then realizing how fully terrified she'd been to wake up in a strange place, having no idea where she was or how she'd gotten there.

Once inside the car and pulling away from the hospital, Sydney slumped, resisting the tears blurring her vision.

"Are you okay?" Holden asked quietly. "Have you been harmed?"

"No. No, I don't think so. I feel groggy. The doctor said my pulse was low, and I'm dehydrated, but otherwise I'm fine." Elbow on the window ledge, she held her head.

"I need you to tell me everything, Sydney. We've lost two days."

"A lot has happened in those forty-eight hours, too," Lane offered.

She glanced over her shoulder at him and saw the concern in his eyes. "What?" She looked to Holden. "What happened?"

"Two incidents—uprisings, if you will. I think, if we're going to catch this team you're after, we will need to look at those places." The skin around his knuckles whitened. "Both locations involved radical groups that won't hesitate to kill us. So I need to know exactly what happened to you to know how to proceed."

Sydney huffed. "Well, I doubt what I experienced will be much good to you. I was ferried from Keighley to a chopper then to a jet. On board I met a woman named Raisa who was pregnant like me—only further along. She mentioned that her husband was a rebel leader and that she was in hiding for her and her baby's safety."

Holden's jaw muscle bounced. "What else?"

Raising her hands in surrender and frustration, she half laughed. "That's just it. She wouldn't say anything else. Just told me to let them do their job."

"Are you sure?" Intensity darkened his face. "Anything."

"What? Do you think I'm holding back on you?"

"No." Holden braked at a roundabout then accelerated and

whipped them around the circle. "Listen, these people that this woman is a part of, they are notorious for speaking without speaking. Conveying hidden meanings in things they do." He banged the steering wheel and cursed. "If I'd known you'd be talking to them, I could've prepped you on their so-called codes. Told you how to speak that silent language." He banged the steering wheel. "What a waste!"

"Wait," Lane said, easing a hand between their seats as he spoke. "These people, this woman, knew that Sydney wouldn't know the codes, right? So maybe she left a clue or something."

"Not likely," Holden said.

Frustration coated Sydney. She felt as if she'd ruined the whole thing, lost their only real chance to get some traction on this story.

"Unless. . ." Holden shook a finger in the air. "Sydney, tell me everything that happened, right down to people on the plane, water glasses—anything!"

Scrambling, she searched her memory. Slowly, she recounted everything that had happened, from being dragged aboard by two thugs, to being stuffed in a chair, and then the woman sitting down in front of her. The beginning of the conversation edged on boredom. Then she'd ordered tea.

"Tea?" Holden straightened in his seat. "You had tea?"

Why did that excite him? "Yes."

"What does that mean?" Lane asked.

"Shh," Holden hissed. "Go on, Sydney."

"The servants—"

"How many?"

"Two women and a man."

Holden nodded, waiting.

"They. . .um. . .they brought in the silver serving tray with a carafe and cookies. There was a tiny bud vase, I remember now, that I didn't think much of."

"What kind of cookies?"

Was he serious? She blinked and told herself to answer, to trust him. "Chocolate, raspberry, and some other kind with some reddish-dark filling."

"Red?" Again his head snapped toward her. "The flowers, what did they look like?"

"Weird—really odd. There were three—two red and a pink."

"Were they bulbous looking?"

Sydney nodded, holding the dash as he yanked the car to the curb in front of their hotel.

Holden laughed a triumphant laugh as he parked and shifted to face Sydney, his brown eyes sparkling and alive, leaving her out of the excitement. "Beautiful! Okay, anything else? Other foods, drinks, anything else she said?"

With a shrug, Sydney felt like she was seriously failing her foreign correspondent crash course and letting everyone down. What if she forgot something that was vital? A key clue to the whole story? "As far as I can remember, nothing. It was after the cookies were served that she insisted I leave them alone, said it was better to leave them to their fate, that Allah had gifted them. Just before she told me I was drugged, she said they were doing God's will."

Holden's eyes widened. "Insh'Allah? Is that what she said?"

"Yes." She peeked at Lane, relieved to find he looked as confused as she felt. "What am I missing? What does it mean?"

"Let's get our bags," he said and climbed from the car. In the elevator, he bounced on his toes as the car lifted. "This is unbelievable. Do you realize you're the first American woman to ever have a conversation with Princess Raisa?"

"Princess?" Sydney's pulsed zapped. "No wonder she acted so uppity."

"She's the wife of Prince Ubai, who was murdered a few months ago. She was all over the news; then she disappeared."

"So what does the code mean?" Lane asked.

A smile filled with glee and pride spread across Holden's face. "It means we're going to Kandahar."

Sydney slumped against the mirrored walls. "Afghanistan?" She tried to keep the shriek out of her voice. "I thought they hated Americans."

"Well, in some places, and it seems Raisa was pointing you to a particular Taliban stronghold."

"Taliban?" Sydney rubbed her temple—the door to the elevator slid open, and she rushed out, her heart ramming against her chest. "Are you crazy? That's not something we can do! We'll get killed."

"I hate to agree with her, but—"

"Think about it. What other hot spot would be a perfect location for this spec ops team? I have contacts there. I can get us into Kandahar, but finding the right street or building or sect—that's the trick."

"Trick?" Sydney stuffed her hands on her hips. "I'm five-and-a-half-months pregnant. I don't do tricks!"

Holden smiled gently and came to her, clasping her shoulders. "I promise, I have this under control. It will be *tricky*, but I'm certain we can pull it off. Now, please—get your bag, and meet back down here in a half hour."

In her room, Sydney plopped against the bed and buried her face in her hands. All she wanted right now, with her energy and courage bottoming out, was to go home. She sighed, feeling grungy and exhausted. Maybe a quick shower would rejuvenate her, pelt some sense back into her. . .coming all the way across the ocean to play investigative reporter, putting her life and her baby's in jeopardy. And now—*now!*—Holden wanted to go to one of the most hostile territories in the world.

She grabbed a pair of jeans and a white top. In the bathroom, she flipped the shower knob then worked the buttons on her blouse. She caught her reflection and groaned—death warmed over. Twice. Peeling out of the grimy top, she reached for her pants—and froze.

On her swollen belly and in an odd, greenish black ink, a meticulously drawn, strange symbol stared up at her.

"I thought you were handling this."

General Olin Lambert tucked back the footrest of the recliner and pushed to his feet as he pressed the phone to his ear. "What 'this' are you referring to?"

"The reporter!"

In the kitchen, Olin drew out a glass and moved to the refrigerator. He lifted a crystal pitcher of orange juice. "I have taken care of things there."

"Have you?" A smack resounded through the line. "Then explain to me why this reporter ended up in a London hospital, drawing the attention of every authority in that country."

Glass paused in midair, Olin's stomach plummeted. He lowered the glass to the granite counter. "What are you talking about?"

"Watch the news for once in your sorry life, Olin. She's all over the news in London. She's not leaving it alone, and you promised me—*promised!*"

What was Sydney Jacobs doing in England? "Calm down—"

"Don't tell me to calm down. That team is out there in the middle of a mission that could blow all of us into the next century politically." The chairman cursed. "You take care of this, or so help me God, I'll send every spook in the EU after her."

CHAPTER 20

"Are you up to it?"

Sydney glanced down at the belly she'd bared to them as they headed to Heathrow. "I don't see that I have a choice. I tried to wash off the symbol, but it wouldn't come off. Is it permanent?"

"Henna, most likely. Fades eventually."

With a sigh, Sydney pinched the bridge of her nose. "I mean, it's almost as if she chose me; she wants me to go there."

"I definitely agree," Holden said, his excitement still evident.

"Imagine if you hadn't felt the need to shower." Lane chuckled. "Who knows how long it would've been before we would've figured it out?"

Holden lifted his world phone and pulled up a number. He pressed the phone to his ear and started rambling in a foreign language, apparently working his connections to get them on the ground and to the location—he'd insisted the symbol was one of an organization there and would most likely lead them to proof of this team. The most tangible proof they'd had yet.

Leaning against the headrest, Sydney stared out at the city blurring past. Uncertainty dogged her, warning her she should just head home right now. Forget this story. It wasn't as important as her son or her own life. Rubbing her belly reminded her of the brownish symbol beneath her hand. With all these clues, maybe they'd get in and out before anyone knew where they were. She'd go home then and never *ever* take an assignment overseas. Yes, it was thrilling, but she wasn't an adrenaline junkie like Holden. Or Max. The two were eerily similar. She had a lot of respect for both men.

"Okay, we're set. We'll get a hop into Bagram, and I have some friends who are part of the security detail at the base who'll escort us to Kandahar." Holden scrolled through and found another name.

Escort. Why did that sound so ominous? "Can you do that? Pull our soldiers from their duty?"

"Sorry. My friends are civilian contractors working with the military. They don't answer to the U.S. government when they want to leave."

Her mind reeled with images of explosions and gunfire and suicide bombers. Women walking onto buses with C-4 vests. Killing themselves and everyone else.

Oh Lord, what am I doing?

She closed her eyes, letting the motion of the vehicle lull her to sleep. She didn't want to think; she didn't want to imagine what could happen. Just get it over with. Get in. Get out. They'd have the story of a lifetime, and she'd never do it again. This just wasn't worth it. The throb in her head and the pounding in her chest said so. Not to mention the small life inside her, kicking and punching her, as if even he were telling her she wasn't thinking straight.

Would she make it back to the States to tell Max about this baby? Give him the chance to be a father to their son?

Within hours, they boarded a C-130 and were strapped into a five-point harness along with a couple dozen camo-clad men. Soldiers.

"Marine Special Operations Command—MARSOC," Holden whispered casually to her as he stowed his pack between his legs.

Sydney eyed the men. Some so young. Others weathered by age and battle. They reminded her of Max—the same intensity and determination to get a job done.

She almost laughed. Even though she could relate, she knew it was only a small inkling of what it was like to want to get it done and get home.

The flight, rocky and horrendous—nothing like their first-class flight to London five days ago—left her sick to her stomach. She forced herself to fall asleep, but dreams invaded her slumber with haunting encounters of a woman wearing a suicide vest. Sydney had tried to talk her out of it, but the woman shook her head, a tear streaking her cheek, seconds before an explosion knocked Sydney off her feet—and jolted her awake.

"We're here," Holden said, smiling.

Her eyes burned and sweat dribbled down her back. Had someone turned off the air conditioning? Yeah, right. In the middle of 115-degree heat?

Wind slammed the unrelenting heat into her as she disembarked, following Holden and Lane off the tail of the C-130. She let out a small grunt against the smothering air that already threatened to bake her into oblivion. Both men turned toward her, reaching out to assist the poor pregnant woman down the ramp.

"I can walk on my own," she groused, hating the way the soldiers watched and snickered.

Two black Suburbans tore toward the unloading plane. Tires squealing, they lurched to a stop a dozen feet away.

"Aha!" Holden pointed toward the SUV. "Here they. . .are." His words faded with her breath as they watched several men in dark suits and others in what looked like security uniforms storm toward them.

A tall, lanky man tugged off his *Men in Black* sunglasses. "Sydney Jacobs?" he asked, piercing her with a steel glare.

Holden and Lane eased closer to her.

Disquieted at the way he not only knew her name but seemed ready to take her into custody, she drew up her chin. "Yes?"

"FBI, ma'am. I'm afraid you'll have to come with us," the man said, hands on his belt.

"Have I done something?"

"Ma'am, please." The man looked around then back to her. "For your safety, come quickly."

Only then did she spot the guard towers every twenty feet or so, manned and gunned. She bit back the acidic taste in her mouth as she stepped off the platform. Two men took hold of her arms and escorted her to the first SUV. She glanced through the heavily tinted windows, watching as Lane and Holden climbed into the second. Despite the anxiety welling up within her, she breathed a sigh of relief for the cool AC.

Within minutes the Suburban steered into a hangar, and just as quickly, the large sliding door closed. The men piled out but stayed close to the vehicle.

Sydney unfolded herself, feeling every bit the fugitive on the run. "I haven't done anything wrong. I'm an American citizen." She glanced around the cavernous building. Where was the second SUV? Where were Lane and Holden? Her stomach kinked.

"Which is exactly why we have direct orders to see you onto the next plane back to the States." The man removed his sunglasses and motioned her toward the heavily fortified entrance. Steel and cement barricaded what looked like a reinforced door. Two armed soldiers stared out toward them, unmoving.

The throng of guns and suited men all but pushed her into the high security structure. Past the first layer of defense, they were met with another. The lanky man swiped a card through a reader, and the door groaned out of view to the left.

They entered a sparsely furnished room—nothing but a desk, metal chairs, and a few filing cabinets. In the center a woman sat behind a glass barrier, watching them carefully.

"Margaret, relay confirmation of receipt of the package."

The woman gave a curt nod and went to work.

"This way, Mrs. Jacobs."

She wrested her arm free from his hold. "Just who are you? How do you have the right to do this to me? I'm here on a story, and I've done nothing to warrant being treated like a criminal."

"Criminal?" He scoffed as he led her into another room. "This is first-class treatment compared to what criminals get. It's for your protection, Mrs. Jacobs. Maybe you don't understand the country you just hopped a C-130 into."

He had a point. Besides knowing that women had to wear fabric head to toe and that many special ops soldiers had worked the region, she really hadn't kept up with the minute details.

With each step, strength and courage drained from her. She turned to the man—but the door slammed shut in her face. Stunned, she couldn't move at first. Then she spun, searching for another way out.

No sooner had she spotted the steel door on the other side than Holden and Lane were shoved into the small conference room.

Lane rushed to her and embraced her. She wriggled out of his hold, and when he planted a peck on her cheek, she pushed him back. "Please. . .don't." Ignoring the hurt in his expression, she propped her hands on the metal table in the center of the room and eased onto a chair. "They're sending us back." Tears pricked her eyes. Defeat clung to her worse than the heat that still seemed to seep off her clothing. "All this work—"

"Maybe it's for the best." Holden sat next to her, his head down.

Indignation dug through her increasingly foul mood. "Best? How can you say that? We've had leads, we are right on the cusp—"

"I'm just saying," he said louder, his eyes widening as he nudged his shoulder forward and rubbed his ear, "they're just trying to protect you."

"Protect me?" She rolled her eyes. "Someone figured out what we were doing—"

"*And* they were worried about you." Holden coughed into his hand then rubbed his ear.

Rubbed his ear. Was he trying to tell her someone was listening to their conversation? "Maybe you're right."

A subtle nod and smile.

"I'm just ready to get out of this heat," Lane grumbled.

"Our flight from Heathrow leaves in the morning. Hopefully we can still catch that." Quirking an eyebrow, Holden seemed to be hinting that she should go along with this.

"It'd be good. I'd hate to have to call my brother and explain why I'm arriving later. He won't be too happy. He'd probably notify the Feds in Virginia, as protective as he is."

Holden winked. "He sounds like a big brother, all right." He seemed to be trying to convey some hidden message to her, but she was lost.

An hour later, they were hastily removed from the room and stuffed in Suburbans once again. They were shuttled across the tarmac to a waiting jetliner. Two agents escorted them onto the plane then left. Sydney, Lane, and Holden sat quietly as the plane taxied and streaked into the air.

Once airborne, Lane leaned toward Sydney. "I overheard one of the attendants talking about London. They're sending us back to the States."

Amazingly, she felt relieved to be on her way home. Shame slithered through her, taunting her lack of spine. Was she so ready to give up? Yes. Exhaustion ripped at her. Fear for her life wore down her courage and defenses.

"I think I'm going to sleep for a week," she mumbled.

Holden frowned. "Sydney, don't you get it?"

She blinked. "What?"

"When we get to Heathrow, we catch the next flight to the Philippines."

"Phil. . ." The name died on her dry, chapped lips. "Why are we going there?"

He tugged a folded piece of paper from his pocket and held it out. "It's the last place on your list."

And the last place she wanted to be heading right now.

Structure B3. Inner circle. Max peered through the night vision goggles, assessing the setup of the Higanti camp. A keen intelligence lurked behind the design, laid out like an onion. Several layers had to be peeled back before reaching the middle. In other words, two defensive barriers guarded what Nightshade wanted.

"It's going to be tight." He mentally mapped the sequence they'd plotted days earlier.

"That's for sure," Midas whispered from his right.

As he scanned the first layer, then the second, something snagged his mind. He panned back, lenses fixed on one source emanating an incredible amount of heat to be lit up like that. "We have intel about electricity?"

"No. Why?"

"Check out D1, outer perimeter."

A soft grunt came from Max's left. "I think you're right," Midas said.

"So, how does that change our options?" Fix asked.

If they had electrified gates, Nightshade could bypass them. It wasn't anything they hadn't encountered before. What bugged him was the possibility of perimeter motion sensors. Getting close enough to cut the cord. . .

Why get close when they had eyes above?

Max spoke into his ear mic, his head and voice low. "Delta One to Ghost One."

"Go ahead, Delta One." Cowboy's whisper was almost inaudible.

"Target D1, outer perimeter. Confirm presence of cables."

Bright white lit the night followed by an ear-thumping crack. A rumble sifted through the skies, warning of a storm ready to unleash its venom. Nearby, a critter scampered through the leaves away from Max and the others.

"Current confirmed. Cable sighted."

Without another second to lose, Max eased himself out of his hiding place and began the descent down the hill. "Ghost One, on my mark, take it out."

"Roger, on your mark." The simplistic and robotic nature of Cowboy's sniper voice infused Max with more confidence.

With each step, he swept his weapon right and left, listening, watching. Since the Higanti were expecting them, Nightshade could expect trouble. They snaked off the path and wound through the palm trees, shrubs, and tall grass, making their way down to the encampment. Still concealed as he knelt behind the flattened terrain and brush, Max turned his focus to the ear mic and the snipers hidden nearly a mile out.

"Take the shot."

A small spark burst out about five meters north.

With a sharp snap of his wrist toward Fix, Max sent him sprinting through the open area and covered him, searching shadows for unfriendlies. Once Fix gained his spot, he confirmed his location. Max nodded to Midas, who rushed across the field to the hut opposite Fix and crouched with his weapon at the ready. Seconds later, Max broke from the safety of the foliage and bolted for perimeter. He mentally noted the seared cable. Then he passed his men, aiming for the hut just beyond them. Hunched in the shadows of the hut, he verified the locations provided by intel.

Once he visually cleared the area, they had only one path. He zigzagged toward B2.

Within a dozen feet of the hut, Max squinted through the NVGs strapped to his head. Was that—? Oh no. Of all the. . .

He tucked his head and whispered into his mic. "It's rigged."

"Repeat."

"The hut is rigged. Explosives." The bad guys wanted them to storm in to save the day and essentially blow the missionaries and themselves straight to heaven.

"I've got it," Midas mumbled as he sneaked toward the hut.

Max scoped the shadows and perimeter.

Thud!

Behind him! Max spun—and found Fix dragging a body out of view. Heart beating a little faster, Max snapped back to Midas, who worked a few more seconds then gave a thumbs-up. "Two-minute lead."

Max rushed toward the hut, barely seeing the dark shadow that leaped out at him. Without a thought, he slammed the butt of his M4 into the tango. The guy dropped like a wet towel. Max hauled the body into the shadows.

At the hut, he eyed Fix, who nodded his readiness. Confident the explosives were cleared, he gave the signal to Midas, who cut the lock from the door, careful not to rattle the chain as he snaked it out of the way. With a nod to Max, he whipped open the door.

Max stepped into the darkened hut. Split-second recon pegged four bodies. Adrenaline surging, he confirmed these were their targets—a man, a woman, an infant, and the girl. He ignored the way his tactical clothes seemed to melt against his body in the suffocating heat of the cramped space. The air swirled a bit with Midas's entrance. Max knelt next to the man, who lay on a cot facing the door, his child cradled in his wife's arms behind him. On a mat two strides away, a young woman lay curled in the fetal position.

She stirred—and Midas lunged, clapping a hand over her mouth as he whispered to her in Tagalog.

Max held his hand over the bulb of his flashlight and twisted it on. Gently, he patted the man's shoulder, hoping to wake him quietly.

The man's eyes fluttered—then snapped open. Wide. Frightened.

Finger pressed against his lips, Max gave the man the universal *shh* signal. After the man nodded his understanding, Max flicked off the flashlight. "Wake your wife. It's time to go." With only a minute thirty left on the clock, they didn't have time to explain.

Fix joined them, a dull green glow emanating from his weapon's sight. He removed a pack strapped to his back and slid out a needle.

"Wh–what's going—"

The man hushed his wife, watching protectively as Fix massaged the baby's thigh then slid the needle into her chubby leg. Amazingly, she only grimaced and whimpered before falling right back to sleep.

The wife and husband stuffed their shoes on and gathered their baby and a bag. Max shifted and keyed his mic. "Ghost One, we have the package. Is it clear?" Hand on the door, Max waited.

Crackling shot through the ear mic. "Oh cr—"

Boom!

Max twisted and dove toward the couple. He pinned them to the ground, listening as the percussion of an explosion rippled through the small camp. Rustling and popping drew his attention upward. Red glowed back at him, red twinkled through the straw roof. Fire!

Max grabbed the woman's wrist and pulled her toward him, knowing he'd need to guide her out. "Ghost One, are we clear?"

"Roger! Go!"

With her tucked under his arm, he bolted into the open, spraying bullets as fire shattered the dark void of night. Cordite stung his nostrils as he sprinted toward the tree line. Bamboo exploded off the huts, peppering his hand and cheek.

"Ghost One and Two, we need cover!" Max shouted.

He covered the woman's head, hustling her through the camp and to the safe point in the trees. They were nearly to the outer layer when she tripped and fell. She yelped. Max hauled her to her feet and propelled her forward.

"Run and don't stop," he ordered, spinning and firing shots as the camp came alive with Higanti warriors.

CHAPTER 21

Animated shouts burst out, followed by horn blasts. Sydney snapped out of the daze that had clogged every pore of her body since she'd boarded the plane that had ferried them onto Mindanao before they were dumped at Malaybalay, the capital city. Scurrying to catch up with Lane and Holden, who'd already reached the curb, wasn't going to work. She had no scurry left. No energy. If Holden hadn't been so emphatic about this trip, she'd probably be halfway across the Atlantic by now. But no. She was in a noisy, bustling city that had more smells than people to aggravate her sensitive constitution.

As she stepped up on the curb, Holden caught her elbow. He guided her to the right, down a narrow sidewalk—well, if you could call it that. With pedicabs and bicycles pedaling toward her, she wondered if it was just a really small road.

"As soon as we check in at the hotel, go up and rest. I'm going to track down my contact and see what she knows."

"She?" Sydney looked at him.

He winked. "You'd be surprised what information women can pick up because they aren't considered a threat. Anyway, you rest, I'll contact them, and I'll put Lane on the trail of a guide."

"Shouldn't I come?" she asked as he tucked an arm around her waist and nudged her through a small glass and brass door. "This is my story."

A dozen feet and a burgundy, hand-woven, wool Oriental rug separated them from the check-in desk. Holden turned toward her and bent closer. "Sydney, you have to trust me. I'm not going to steal this from you. It *is* your story, but what good does that do you if you're about to drop from exhaustion?" Concern pinched the weathered lines around Holden's brow.

For a moment she thought she saw a flicker of something more than professional respect glimmer through his hazel eyes. Shoving aside the thought, she fought back another yawn.

"I'll get the room keys and—"

"I'm tired, yes, but I'll be fine." Bristling, wanting very much to be as good and strong a go-getter as him, she straightened.

"No." Lane joined the conversation. "I agree. You look rough."

"Excuse me?"

A warm hand cupped her face. "Sydney, trust me." Nervous jitters skated through her at the intimacy in Holden's touch and the unexpected affection in his tone. So she hadn't imagined it. Where had this come from? Maybe she'd harbored a preteen crush on the CougarNews celebrity, but the only man she wanted touching her like that wasn't here.

"Fine." Using the ruse of switching her bag to her other arm, she stepped away. "I'll rest. But I'm setting my alarm for two hours. If you guys aren't back, I'll come looking for you." Not likely, but it sounded good and feisty—even if she felt anything but.

Holden's expression darkened. "Don't make good on that promise, Sydney." He tugged out his wallet and handed her a business card. "If we're not back, you lock yourself in that room and call my office. Tell them you need help immediately." He stomped to the desk, leaving her with Lane.

"He's a bit rough around the edges," Lane said as he stepped toward her. "But he's right. It's crazy what could happen out here.

They say Mindanao is the new mecca of the terrorist world. So really, Sydney, just stay in the room until we're all together again."

His words wrapped a tight vise around her chest, reminding her of the extreme danger they were facing. How could she forget? The visit with Raisa, the FBI at the airstrip—anything could happen here in the *mecca of the terrorist world*. Maybe the exhaustion had melted her brain cells.

A moment later Holden returned and handed her a pass card. "We have one room. You can have the bed, Lane and I—"

"I'm not sharing a room with two men, neither of whom are my husband." Sydney nudged the card back to him.

"You're divorced," Lane said.

She scowled. "Separated. I want my own room."

"It'll attract less attention, and it's safer to stick together."

Arms folded, Sydney held fast. This was her reputation, and she wasn't going to leave any chance for something nasty to be said about her. Besides, it'd taken her a year to get used to sleeping with Max in the same room; she'd never get any rest with two men. "My own room."

Holden clenched his teeth, booked another room, then returned with the new key. "Your room, Princess."

Irked, she took it and spun toward the elevators. As she strolled around a support, an awareness laden with unease and fear dropped into her being. Once Lane pushed the up button, Sydney skimmed the foyer of the hotel. Several patrons mingled near the door. A young woman and her children waited in some of the overstuffed chairs to the right of the entrance. But it was the man wearing a *keffiyah* that clunked hot coals into her stomach. *I've seen him. . . .*

That was impossible.

No. It was entirely possible, especially with everything that had happened. If only she'd paid better attention, maybe she could figure out where she'd seen him.

The ding of the elevator yanked her around. She stepped into the box, and just as the doors glided shut, she darted a glance to the man—and their gazes collided. He gave a solemn nod. Molten lava spilled through her, leaving her stricken and sick. Instinctively, she pulled back.

With the ascent, she let out a nervous breath.

"What was that about?"

Her gaze pinged to Holden, who considered her suspiciously.

"I don't know."

"You recognized him."

After a moment's jitters, she gave a curt nod.

"Where from?"

"I don't remember."

"One of us should stay with her," Lane offered.

"No." Sydney brushed a knotted strand from her face. "If he wanted to harm me or one of you, he would've."

"Yeah," Holden said. "He didn't harm you because you weren't alone."

She couldn't argue. No guarantee existed of his not coming after her once Holden and Lane left.

"I'll stay," Lane said. "Once we get the details, we can trade—you can stay, and I'll find the guide."

"Not the most efficient use of time." Holden checked his watch. "I'll take care of it all. Our rooms have an adjoining door. We'll unlock it, and you can check in on her while she's sleeping." When Sydney opened her mouth to object, Holden speared her with a dark look. "It's not open to discussion. You can save all your propriety and embarrassment for another day. I'm not going to have something go wrong because you won't trust me."

"It's not—" Sydney ground her teeth. "Forget it."

After she let herself into the room and had slammed the door shut, she slapped the dead bolt into place then flipped the other lock. She might be exhausted, but she wasn't a moron.

At the sound of their voices on the other side of the wall, she snatched her bag and stepped into the bathroom. The tub looked new—tiled and clean. The thought of warm, pelting water lured her into wanting a quick shower to relax for a better nap. Even if she couldn't get the funk out of her mood, she'd wash it out of her hair and pores.

As she peeled out of her clothes, the marks drawn on her belly grabbed her attention. They'd never figured out what the symbol meant. Despite both Holden and Lane doing research on the flight there, they'd come up empty. Under the undulating water, she massaged her belly—and a strong kick rewarded her touch. She laughed and flattened her palm over the spot. Another kick thumped against her hand. Glorious! A second in time when life felt almost euphoric.

Relishing the moment, she ended the shower, ready for sleep. She pulled on the jeans, then reached for her shirt—and groaned. She'd grabbed the wrong one. Her favorite rock band's logo gleamed back at her with a large gold heart, complete with main arteries against the black background. Would it even stretch over her belly? She threaded her arms through it and pried it over the bulge consuming her midsection. Amazingly, even with the tightness, the shirt seemed to give extra support to her expanding waistline. And hey—she even looked like the movie stars who preferred skin-tight shirts to announce their offspring.

A big yawn pushed her to the bed. Hair still wrapped in a towel, she dropped onto the mattress and stretched out, promising herself she'd dry her hair once her energy reserves recharged. Her mind flittered to the way Holden had suddenly revealed he had designs on her. She'd never seen that coming. He was a solid professional, an incredible reporter. Maybe he'd decided they had enough in common that he'd give romance a shot, too. What was it with men in her life?

The realization made her ache for Max once again. She'd give anything for their marriage to be whole, for them to be expecting their son *together*. She reached into her sack and drew out the necklace he'd given her then slipped it on. She curled onto her side, staring through the slightly parted curtains and a dingy window into the clear night.

With a big yawn, she closed her eyes and began a mental checklist of what she'd need to accomplish: find the men who were real-life heroes and applaud them in a blockbuster story. Raisa had said exposing them would jeopardize the men, but Sydney would ensure their names weren't published. She'd even keep the meetings a secret and withhold identities. That'd be safe and wouldn't interrupt their stealthy movement across the globe. Most important, of course, was to find someone who'd seen them here. She felt close. Yet a thousand miles away.

A lonely chill scampered across the back of her shoulders.

Insh'Allah. Going into backwater places, saving women and their children. . .

Thud! A child's wails wafted on the warm breeze. Rustle of movement. The cries shuddered to a stop. Sydney struggled to understand—where had they come from? She squinted through the darkness. Was someone there? Behind the curtain that billowed in under the guidance of a sticky breeze?

Reality shifted. The bedspread became a stretch of partially crushed grass. She crawled on all fours over the field. Closer. A man stepped from the brush and towered over her.

She jerked back, plopping onto her bottom. As she stared up at him, a brilliant light blinded her. Shielding her face, she scrambled away.

A soft fluttering. Then something landed nearby. The light vanished.

Sydney jolted upright, her heart pounding. She blinked around the room. With a gasp, she dropped against the pillows and tried to swallow the pineapple-sized lump in her throat. "It was only a dream." A nervous laugh trickled through her.

She looked out into the crystal night. So clear. So bright. No more—

She froze. The window was open! Adrenaline whizzing through her veins, she dragged her gaze, *only* her gaze, to the door that led to Lane and Holden's room. It stood ajar.

A body sprawled across the threshold.

DAY TWENTY-SIX

Just think," Jon said, his arm around Kimber as they trudged down the slope. "This time tomorrow, we should be home, or at least on a plane home."

Kimber nodded and pressed her lips to Maecel's white blond head, rubbing her hands over the hand-assembled carry pack the commandos had constructed.

Exhilaration coursed through him, making each step feel as if he floated, one step closer to soil he was just about ready to kiss. The men who'd rescued them wore no patches identifying their country, but they spoke English. With the paint rubbed over their faces, he doubted they'd be recognizable in a lineup.

Didn't matter. He was just grateful they came when they did. Kimber didn't seem as thrilled with the rescue, but her weakness from the fevers that had ravaged her body for the last several weeks probably stunted her excitement. In a matter of hours, however, they'd get her medical help, get her fixed up, and they could recuperate at home with their families.

He wasn't sure they'd ever come back to Mindanao or to this small island. Oh sure, Kimber would insist, saying this jungle was where she belonged. And she did. She'd always seemed at home here, peaceful and content. Even now, hiking from a harrowing escape and toward the embrace of safety, her pace didn't echo someone who. . .well, someone like him. She almost seemed to linger, as if she wanted to stay here. Even Maecel slept soundly—compliments, no doubt, of the hefty drug the medic had given her. Her smooth, repetitive snoring gave him reassurance that she, too, would be fine staying here with the screeching monkeys and thick air that left him almost gasping. If the commandos would let him, he'd bolt straight to the ocean and swim home.

Yeah, and maybe the fever was infecting him. The silly thought forced a smile to his face. Felt good to smile. Been too long.

He considered Kezia, who walked silently and without looking up or around. Was it too hard for her to see these men dressed like soldiers and ordering them about? Or was she just relieved to be free of the Higanti?

But were they really free?

Ahead of him, Kimber stumbled. Jon steadied her as she scrabbled over a small mound of rocks, two of the soldiers assisting on the other side. "Let me take Maecel," Jon offered.

"No," she bit out.

Jon paused, her hand still in his. He tightened his grip, wondering at her funny tone. The darkness stopped him from seeing her face or expression, but he was sure something was wrong. Once he cleared the hurdle, he sidled up to her. "You okay?"

"Tired, that's all," she said, shifting Maecel, her hands hooked on the back of the carrier as if she were holding on for dear life.

Reminders of where they were heading—home—kept his mind alert and his aching muscles moving. Maybe it would help her, too. "What's the first thing you're going to do when we get back?"

"Sleep."

"Quiet ahead!"

The hissed command from behind silenced him. It was okay. He didn't need to talk to thank God for getting them out of here.

For the phone call that had actually worked to pluck them from the jaws of death. God was good. He'd brought them this far. He'd get them home safely, too.

CHAPTER 22

They know where we are. The thought had haunted Max since escaping the perimeter of the camp. But that couldn't be possible, because even Lambert didn't know the minute details of the mission. Autonomy all but guaranteed success. The fewer who knew where'd they be, the fewer who could interfere. But he couldn't shake the feeling they were walking into trouble.

Rendezvous: 0400. That meant they still had several hours to hook up with the Black Hawk that would ferry them to Clark AFB. There they'd hop a C-130 to Guam, where a medical detachment and government officials would take over.

Max checked his watch and nearly cursed. Too much terrain to cover. And civilians who'd endured weeks of imprisonment. . .

"Keep moving!" he gritted out, trying to push his voice as far as he could with as little sound as possible. No telling what lay about to trap innocents. He assessed the stream of bodies working through the thick, lush vegetation ahead. Although they'd hiked several miles without confrontation, they were still too close to be safe. No doubt the Higanti or Abu Sayyaf radicals had transportation. The close proximity worried him, forcing him to check his six. Clear. But the foreboding clung to him heavier than the humidity.

At his twelve, the lanky missionary mumbled encouragement to his wife, who'd insisted on carrying their daughter. "Kimber, let me take her. She's heavy."

"I'm fine," the woman grunted.

Max looked at his GPS. Another five hundred yards or so would intersect their path with Cowboy and Legend's. Once the full light of day hit them, they'd have to be more strategic and keep under the canopy of leaves. A strange tickle worked through the soles of his boots. "All quiet," Max called. "All stop!"

Midas and Fix stopped, the native girl between them. Midas glanced back. "Chopper!"

The vibration seemed to emanate from his bones. The helo must be right over them.

"Take cover!" Max dropped low as the branches overhead swayed. Moonlight glinted off the hull of an attack chopper. The bird tore up the sky, heading straight toward them. He rolled into a thick tangle of bushes and low-crawled to the others.

Midas had the young girl secure, his body stretched over hers for protection. "They're too close," he growled.

They know. It wasn't just a hunch now. The proof whirled in the sky.

Max scrambled to the missionary and his wife, who lay huddled behind a large tree stump. Even with the green glow of the NVGs, he could see the fear in their eyes. "Stay low, keep moving," he whispered.

They nodded.

Wind whipped against them. Like a giant bird of prey, the chopper swooped in circles. The branches snapped back and forth, smacking and lashing Max's skin.

Lightning broke the void of early morning.

Max grunted, slamming his eyes shut against the brilliance that flashed through his goggles. A smart SEAL would trade these in for auto-adjusting goggles. He'd put that on his next req list.

Thwat-thwat-thwat-thwat!

The sound of the bullets pelting the palm branches drove Max rolling into the brush, bringing his weapon skyward. He blinked rapidly, trying to refocus, but couldn't see the chopper. "Where is it?"

"Pulled high. Everyone, move. Go, go, go!" Midas waved the group past himself.

The husband caught his wife as she stumbled, but the native sprinted with Fix. As they pushed hard to the rendezvous point, a concern lashed at Max. The missionary woman. Her uneven steps and clumsy gait. What was going on? Exhaustion? Regardless of injury, they couldn't stop. Taking a break meant a permanent one—death.

"Frogman," Midas said in a low voice, angling the imager attached to his wrist so that Max could see it as they hiked. "I've got three readings on thermal, ahead twenty meters."

Jogging behind the others, Max prepped for a confrontation. Since Cowboy and Legend should be more than thirty meters away and weren't supposed to backtrack, that meant one thing: trouble. Of the fully automatic kind.

"Split up," he said as he aimed upward, tagging the missionaries with him and motioning Midas to go low. With his weapon pressed to his cheek, he kept his ears trained, his eyes on every twitch and rustle of branches. The darkness worked against them. Predawn in a jungle varied little from night. Until the sun rose high and streamed in through branches, they'd need to rely on the NVGs and thermals.

"Why'd we split up?" the husband asked from behind.

Without answering, Max trudged onward, hoping the guy would stay quiet. A word spoken at the wrong time could kill them. Traversing the rugged slope parallel to Midas's path, he kept a close eye on the others, waiting for the soldier's signal.

Midas raised a fist.

"Hold." Max crouched, watching his guy who had the thermal readout.

Slowly, a sound filtered through the suffocating humidity. Quiet at first. Footsteps, hushed and hurried. Stealthily, Max craned his neck and peered through his scope. Every distraction filtered out, all senses trained in the direction of the sound.

A whistle rent the tension. The Nightshade signal.

He huffed and eased back just as two forms manifested between two large palms. He stood and stepped in front of the two. "You're about twenty meters off course."

Cowboy grabbed his hand and pulled him into a brotherly hug. "We were being tracked. Had to move and shake them."

"We need to haul butt," the Kid said as he stepped around the two MARSOC guys. "Those hostiles are, well, hostile."

"Picked up police chatter on the radio." Legend exchanged a glance with Cowboy before rubbing a hand over his buzzed head. "They know we're here just as we suspected."

Max's left eye twitched as he considered the two tough guys before him. "What aren't you telling me?"

Legend huffed. "Chatter reports an American journalist on the island is the new target."

Journalist. Max's gut turned to ice. "Sydney." She'd been tracking them. What were the chances she'd found them?

"That's what we thought." Legend sipped from his camelbak. "We'll have to keep a watchful eye out, try to intercept her—and she's probably not alone, not out here—before *they* do." He nodded toward the missionaries. "They look haggard. Think they got what it takes to get 'er done?"

For the first time, Max glanced at the civilians' faces. Of the four they'd rescued, the husband seemed most alert. Head down and mouth clenched tight, the native girl didn't move far from the wife, who wiped a hand across her face and seemed to sag even more.

"No choice. We have to make rendezvous, or we're going to have to hoof it another day's journey without getting killed." But his mind slid back to Sydney. If she was truly out here, if that journalist was her, she had no clue what she'd walked into. His team had tactical skills. She had nothing.

God surely wouldn't do this, would he? Sydney had always been a faith follower. She'd held hard and fast to the scriptures, unlike him. He slid the pack off his shoulder. "Hand out nourishment. We can relax when we get to rendezvous. Let's get them under way."

"Agreed."

The team quickly distributed foodstuffs to the captives. Max found himself watching the couple, the way the man crooned over his wife. Had they been married long? They looked young and acted young in love. His mind skipped to Sydney, to the thought of helping her through this rough terrain. With the only morsel of spirituality he had in him, he silently prayed she wasn't on the island.

The missionary woman sagged. She'd probably sleep a month once they got back home. "Midas, take the baby. Give the woman a break."

"No," she objected—but her voice was weak. And strained.

Max silently ordered his man to obey his command.

Midas worked at removing the special baby carrier they'd rigged to the woman. He lifted the soundly sleeping infant and paused, his hand on the inner bottom portion of the unit. With a glance he spun toward the woman.

That's when Max saw it, too. A dark stain spread over the blanket.

He looked at the wife—her eyes slid shut. She drooped forward.

Max lunged, catching her and easing her to the ground. "Fix," he growled, trying to keep his voice tight and controlled. He shifted aside to let the medic work.

"Kimber! Kimber! God, no," the man cried out.

"Quiet, or you'll get us killed!" Planting both hands against the man's chest, Max nudged him back several feet. The missionary's heart thundered under Max's palm as they watched the tragedy playing out before them.

Kneeling at her side, Fix clamped his hands over the wound. "She ate a bullet." When he pressed on her side, she yelped. Dark liquid squished between his fingers.

Too much blood. She was bleeding heavily. Max swallowed hard. If she'd been shot, that meant it had happened during the chopper attack, which meant she'd hiked for the last hour with her baby and that injury. Guilt swam a mean circle around his mind.

"It's bad," Midas mumbled as he knelt beside Fix and the woman.

Fix dragged his bag closer and dug through it. "Light. Now." Green bathed him as Midas and the Kid turned on their torches. He ripped the woman's shirt open and peeled it back.

Even in the darkness, Max saw a glimmer of liquid pooling just above her hip. This wasn't good. Wasn't good at all. Max shifted. He should talk to the husband, get his mind off this. But that felt hollow. Besides, what would he say? The guy had a direct link to God. What would he need from Max?

Silently, Fix worked on her. He tucked a needle into a vial and withdrew liquid. He thrust the needle into her thigh. With a shake of his head, he grabbed more tools and bandages. The light shifted away from the emergency surgery, and Fix snapped at the men with the torches.

The lanky missionary all but crumbled against Max. "Whoa, easy there, chief," he said, swinging an arm around the guy's waist and steadying him. "It's going to be okay."

"Is she. . .is she. . ."

"She's alive, but. . ." Fix cursed. "She's on the edge."

Eyes wide with horror, the man turned to Max, staring blankly. "We were going home."

"It's not over yet." Max tried to encourage him. But in light of the wound and Fix's frantic reaction, he knew she probably wouldn't make it. "We'll get you home." He glanced around the camp.

To the side, Legend and Cowboy huddled around the Kid, whispering. The cowboy's voice scraped with hoarseness and emphasis as he whispered between the two. Something was up. Something they weren't happy about.

"Hey," Max said, stepping closer. "What's going on?"

Cowboy and Legend hung their heads.

The Kid looked down, then to Max, then back down. "More chatter," he finally said. "The radicals found the journalist. Sounds like they're setting up an ambush."

Legend slapped the Kid on the back of the head, as if reprimanding him.

"Hey, what—"

Cowboy's blue green eyes fastened on Max. "We don't know it's her. It could be anyone."

"No." Everything in Max shut down. "She found us." With her tenacity, there was no doubt in his mind Sydney had managed to track them all the way to the Philippines. How had a simple human interest story taken such a wicked turn—straight into the heart of his team? If she found them, she'd make her report. Which meant the team would be exposed. Worse, it meant she would walk into an ambush. She would die.

Maybe they could sabotage her trip. Cripple her before she got far enough out. No. They were too far away, and they didn't know what hotel. He'd need time to track her down. Time he didn't have. Or did he?

He blinked. Looked back at the Kid. "Where? Where's the ambush?"

"No way, no how, Frogman." Legend's stoic face grew stern.

Ignoring him, Max hedged closer to the Kid. "Where?" He gripped the guy's shirt and drew back a fist.

The Kid's eyes widened. He cowered, a trembling hand held up in defense. "B–base of the mountain, outside the city. A f–fruit market."

Without a word, Max turned and started in that direction. He wouldn't leave his wife in a jungle with extremists and radical natives who had a thirst for her blood. He could hoof it down there, get there in time to save her life. Could he avoid exposing his identity? He'd try, but that was the least of his worries.

"Frogman," Legend called in a terse voice. "You can't do this."

As he stepped over a fallen tree, he glanced at the GPS reader.

Legend caught up and moved in front of him, their noses almost touching. "I'll try to explain to the general why you abandoned the mission, why you left these people to die."

"I'm not going to let my wife walk into an ambush and get riddled full of holes."

"Your job is to the team. To the mission."

"He's right, Max." Cowboy's solemn words sifted through the confrontation. "You can't do this. No side missions. Stay focused. We don't have the proof."

Legend's expression remained unchanged, his wide nostrils flaring. "You're in command, so command. Do it right. Dedication to the mission, *for* the mission. Go off on some half-cocked mission, you get everyone killed, *including* your wife."

"Max," Cowboy spoke in a softer tone, but there was no missing the adamancy. "You don't know it's her; it could be any journalist. Come on, man. What are the chances, right? We have a mission to finish, people to protect."

What if it wasn't? What if he went off and did this, only to find some journalist bent on destroying Nightshade? Suddenly, the idiocy of rushing out on his own to find Sydney revealed itself:

no backup, no plan. They'd die. The missionary woman would die. The others could be set upon by terrorists.

And it'd be his fault.

But if he did nothing, and it *was* Sydney, and she died? Somehow, he had this sense. . .a warning that she really was here on the island. He spun and drove a hard roundhouse into a nearby tree. "I can't leave her out there."

"Even if it was her, you can't go," Legend said. "What's the creed say, Frogman?"

Muscles taut, Max fixed his gaze on the man several inches taller than him. Even as he did, the words of the SEAL creed rang through his mind. *We expect to lead and be led. In the absence of orders I will take charge, lead my teammates and accomplish the mission. I lead by example in all situations.*

Accomplish the mission. "I'm not leaving my wife to die." Wrestling with the monster inside who wanted to rip down the mountain and rush to Sydney's rescue, he stuffed balls of truth into its mouth—they didn't know if it was her. They didn't know her position. They didn't know. They just didn't know!

Legend huffed, his words hardening as he spoke through tight lips. "Right here, right now, these people and this team are your responsibility."

Both hands fisted, Max drew them up. Everything in him went tight. Hard. Ready to explode. "My *wife* is my responsibility!"

"I'll go." Cowboy's gentle words carried a phenomenal punch.

Stunned, he stared at the cowboy, feeling a puncture in the balloon of frustration that had cocooned him. "I can't let you do that." He gulped the adrenaline squirting into his throat. "Y–you don't know it's her. I can't let you."

Cowboy grinned. "Don't have a choice."

"I'll back up Cowboy." Legend raised an eyebrow at Max. "Are we good?"

They'd do that? Sacrifice their lives to save someone who might possibly be his wife? A wife who should be curled up at home watching soaps or something? The revelation of his team's dedication rolled through him. He forced himself to relax, to trust the team to operate the way they should. He gave Legend a sharp nod.

"Wait," the Kid said. "If you go after that journalist—whoever it is—how are we going to do that? We can't let this person know who we are. Won't that blow everything sky high?"

Max wanted to curse. "He's right. Keep a tight lip. Don't tell them anything."

Cowboy patted his shoulder. "I don't intend to, partner."

"Guys?" the Kid's nervous voice drew them all around. His eyes slowly came to theirs, mortified. "They hired a driver—" He stopped. Blinking, he pressed a finger to his earpiece and listened to more radio traffic. He sucked in a sudden breath. "The driver! He's in on it. Has orders to kill the Americans if the ambush fails."

Frozen as if ice had doused her entire body, Sydney stared at the dark form spilled across her floor. The towel shifted and unwound, thumping softly onto the bed. Her hair dumped against her back, making her flinch.

A soft moan jolted her. "Lane!" She darted to his side as he pushed up on all fours.

"What hap...pened?" he asked, his words slurred. He reached for his head and staggered to his feet.

"I don't know."

He groaned and eased into the chair by the small dresser. "It feels like I tried to stop a semi with my skull."

"Let me look." She tugged his hand away. Running her fingers over his head, she winced at the lump rivaling a golf ball. "Looks like you've got a nice souvenir, but there's no blood."

Banging at the door jerked them both around. "Sydney!"

Holden. She hurried to the main door, unlocked it, and flung it open.

He urged her back and slammed it shut again. When he turned, the yellow glow of the light bathed the small handgun he held. "Are you okay? Are you hurt?"

Startled at the weapon, she recoiled then shook off her reaction. "I'm fine—Lane was attacked. Where did you get that? And how did you know something was wrong?"

"No time to explain. Grab your stuff, and let's go. I hired a guide, but he'll leave us if we're too long in coming. We have to take a boat to the other island." He smirked at Sydney. "Nice hairdo."

"It's not even daylight." Combing her fingers through her hair, Sydney glanced at the bed. Something—papers—fluttered under the tease of a Mindanao breeze that pushed back the curtains. "What is that?" She plodded over and lifted the pages. A stack of photos.

Both men joined her. Lane reached around her and pointed. "Look, the patch on his arm." He plucked the photo from her and slumped onto the bed, still cradling his head.

"It's them, the star." Sydney flipped through the others, her mind whirling. Photo after photo of the men working. "Look, look! This woman—it's Mangeni!" She turned to Holden, bewildered. "Why would someone give us—"

"The better question is who. If these guys are black-ops, who's ratting them out?"

She stopped on the last page. Numbers and locations. "What are these?"

Holden lifted Sydney's pack and handed it to her. "Grab your stuff. We can decipher them later. Our guide's waiting."

Sydney peeked out the now-open window and tried not to think about how the last ten minutes amounted to a heap of trouble. Dangerous, deadly trouble. A man breaking into her room, knocking Lane out, and leaving clues—a horrifying thought skidded into her. She stilled—had the man spoken the Insh'Allah she'd thought she heard in her dream? Was he telling her that the elite team was doing God's will, or was he saying that revealing the team was God's will?

"Syd." Holden prompted her.

"Sorry," she mumbled, as she started for the door.

Awareness of how easily the man had infiltrated her life without her knowing kept her head down and her thoughts racing as they wove through the busy street toward a jeepney. Mentally she groaned, hating the thought of the jarring ride they were about to endure.

Holden helped her in and paid the driver. In seconds they were barreling through the city. The way he drove, their jeepney driver seemed like a guided missile—only without the guidance. Trounced. Bounced. Rolled over curbs—and feet! Around cars that nearly broadsided them.

Holden smiled at her. "Want to close your eyes?"

"How about I vomit all over you?"

Flinging around a corner, the driver seemed oblivious to the marked lanes and normal flow of traffic. Soon he whipped to the side of the street and braked hard, nearly tossing Sydney out.

"There he is," Holden said, snapping her attention to the end of a darkened alley.

A short man waited, dressed in a torn, dingy white shirt and soiled khakis. He darted a glance around then frantically waved them toward him.

Sydney's knees buckled as she walked, but Lane slipped an arm around her waist. "You doing okay?"

She twisted out of his grasp. "Fine."

Why did this gig get worse at every junction?

Lane's hand on the small of her back pushed her forward. Would he never get the hint? She skipped a step to move out of his reach, but there was no such luck. With his long strides, he remained right next to her, guiding her. She guessed he meant to protect her and be chivalrous. And that wasn't a bad thing, but. . .

When they turned the corner, they both stopped.

A beat-up old Jeep sat in the alley between two apartment buildings. Idling, the thing rattled and shuddered as if it had a bad cold. It wasn't the banged-in side door or the broken windshield that bothered her. It was the pin-striped-style holes. Bullet holes. Sydney glanced nervously at Lane.

"I'm sure it's safe." He didn't sound convinced.

Just go home, Sydney. Just go back home, crawl under the covers. "Holden," she said, hating the whimper in her voice.

He came to her side, tucking his head. "I know it might look bad—"

"You could say that."

"Trust me. I did some casual asking around, and it seems your guys are on one of the small, nearby islands. Back-channels report an explosion up in the mountains there. The only way to get to your guys is with him." He planted his hands on his belt. "It's your call, Syd. I won't force you to go."

But you'll go without me, right? Steal my story. Did it matter anymore? Was it worth it?

The photos in her bag seemed heavy as bricks. They were key to finding the men. Given their camo-painted faces, she couldn't tell who was whom, but it was a huge leap forward. No, she wasn't going to shrink from this story.

Yet something niggled at her. She just didn't know what.

Suddenly, the man screeched and pointed to Sydney. In a lively voice, he prattled in Tagalog, apparently refusing to let Sydney come. Maybe this was divine intervention, an answer and confirmation to the really bad feeling taking root in the pit of her stomach.

Holden strode toward him, tossing his pack in the Jeep as he did, and spoke in the man's language. Several times their would-be guide shook his head and flashed his hands emphatically, as if signaling *no way*, which only had Holden reaching into his pocket for more money. Soon the objections ceased.

"Get in," Holden said through gritted teeth.

Sydney climbed in the back of the Jeep, her pack nestled between her feet, and buckled in. She cast Holden a furtive glance as she adjusted the belt under her enlarged belly. "Are you sure this is okay?"

With a cheeky grin, Holden winked. "If you are dissuaded that easily, you'll never get your story. Don't worry. Like I said, I won't put you in danger."

Yeah right, Pinocchio. Had he forgotten about Keighley? About the chopper, the plane, and her waking up in a foreign hospital with no identification? Then the FBI stuffing them on a plane bound for London? And just how long had Holden been sounding like a used-car salesman without her noticing? Next thing she knew, he would offer to throw in a case of grenades with that life-threatening ride into the mountains.

A man stepped through a nearby door and shouted something as he pumped a fist in the air. The driver shouted back, his own fist relaying a silent conversation. Sydney watched the anger in his face as he hollered. But as they rounded the corner, the man at the door smiled at her. A smile that said she wouldn't be coming back.

Really. She was an idiot. Her son, jostled and trounced as the Jeep hit ruts and zigzagged up the winding roads, gave her the swift kick she needed. Something deep and harrowing wrestled within her, warning her to go back home. A bitter, acrid taste coated her tongue. She gulped past the apple-sized lump in her throat.

As they tore down the roads, heedless of the potholes and in some places where there was no road at all, she had to duck and protect her head from the palm fronds slapping at her. "God, please," she whispered, hoping nobody could hear, "get me home safely, and I'll never want another adventure. I like quiet. Quiet is good. I know You hear my prayers—but if You never hear another one, please hear this. For my baby."

The vehicle lurched to a stop by the water, and the man waved them to a boat that looked more like a rotting log than something that should hold four people. In the boat, she gripped the sides, hating the way her stomach rose into her throat. Not good. Within minutes, they were delivered to a frond-encrusted shore, ushered up a small embankment to where a structure offered another vehicle, almost the twin of the one they'd left on Mindanao.

By the time feeling had left her legs and a pounding headache made coherent thought impossible, they pulled a sharp right—and the truck lurched to a stop. The driver rattled off to Holden, who shifted around to them. "He says this is the last market stand. If we need bathrooms or water..."

Anything to get out of the Jeep. To remind her land really existed and didn't move. She unbuckled, and for a second, she considered taking her pack but opted to leave it. She could just see herself wrestling that in a cramped bathroom with her big belly.

A few minutes later as her land legs slowly returned, she came out of the hut and walked the market of fruits. Even without the early morning blues streaking the sky, she could tell the fruit was ripe by the delicious scents wafting up to her. The pineapple smelled wonderful and made her taste buds pop at the tart but sweet scent. She paid for bottled water as she considered a mango.

"You holding up okay?" Lane bought his own water and uncapped it.

She sipped the liquid and looked toward the skyline, where golden hues hid behind a mottle of early morning clouds. "I find myself missing superhighways and my SUV with amazing suspension."

Chuckling, Lane nodded. Then paused and stared at her.

"What?" She guzzled more water.

"You don't wear your hair down often." He smiled, a tenderness filling his face.

She straightened, closing her bottle. "Look—"

He held up his hand. "Hey, don't bother, Syd. Even I know I can't compete with his memory."

Bristling, she rubbed the skin on the mango. "It's not that." Liar. "I'm just not ready for a relationship. Other things need my attention." She pointed to her belly. "Case in point."

"But that's just it," he said earnestly. "I want to be there for you, help you with the baby." He swept a hand along her cheek. "All I care about is you and making sure you're taken care of."

Taken care of. Yeah. "Thanks, but I'm going to take care of myself, Lane."

A flurry of excitement erupted around them. A shout. A scream.

As they turned, Lane pulled her closer, and this time she didn't fight him. She scanned the road and small area. The shop owner darted back into the building and shut the small bamboo door. Then the windows.

"Stay here," Lane said, nudging her into a small alcove next to the building.

Was this how she took care of herself? Hiding in a corner? Irritated with her own cowardice, she pushed herself out and watched Lane half jog to their vehicle. Holden sat in the front seat next to the driver, obviously making sure the guy stuck around.

A woman's whimper yanked Sydney around. Huddled under a stand, the woman motioned Sydney to join her. What...?

Then the woman pointed.

Sydney looked in the direction the woman indicated. A man at the end of the street. In the *middle* of the street. What was he looking...? No! He had something on his shoulder—a launcher!

She jerked to the right. He was directly in the path of—

"Lane!"

A whistle screamed down the road. Smoke and fire pierced the engine.

Boom!

Fire burst out at her.

CHAPTER 23

Birds flew out, screeching and mirroring the panic that lit through Max. Flames licked the trees and devoured the foliage in an angry, hungry circle. The explosion had been big. He strained to make out details through his binoculars. But the distance proved too great.

He keyed his mic. "Ghost One, this is Delta One. Come in."

Nothing.

"I can't see a thing for the smoke," the Kid said.

Below him, Midas squatted with a long-range scope. "Looks like someone took out a vehicle."

Repetitive snaps echoed through the mile that separated them from the raging ball of fire.

"Sounds like they're not done with whatever they're trying to kill," the Kid said. "But ya notice? Nobody's shooting back."

"Think maybe the bad guys caught up with those journalists?" Fix offered, peering through his own scope.

Max resisted the urge to stomp the guy's head. "Ghost One, come in."

"This is Ghost One," came the hushed reply.

A kink in the tension ball in Max's stomach released. "Please tell me you're there."

"Negative. One hundred yards northeast."

The kink tightened again. "Get in there and find out what happened."

"Roger, going in."

It'd be just like her, with all that tenacity and fire that had drawn him like a moth to the flame. His nostrils flared as he tried to think past the thrumming of his heart that rang in his ears.

He'd never forgive himself if she died tracking him down.

"We need to get under way." Though the words came from his mouth, Max barely heard them. He blinked. Right. Get moving. "On your feet." Mind still on the explosion and the possibility that Sydney had just been buried in a burning ball, he returned to the missionary who held his wife's IV-rigged hand.

On his haunches, Fix fisted a hand over his mouth, staring at the woman's ashen face. For several minutes he stayed like that then shook his head and pushed to his feet. He met Max's gaze.

Had they come all this way, gone through one trap after another, only to have her die? He bobbed his head to the side, drawing Fix over. "Can you sedate her?"

"Already did. She'll be out of it in a few." Fix glanced back at Kimber Harris on the ground, her husband steadfastly at her side. "I don't know how much longer she'll hold out. She's emaciated and weak. She's lost a tremendous amount of blood. A low-grade fever is complicating it. Her blood pressure is scary low. Even with the stretcher the guys made, every time we move her—" He pushed his gaze in the opposite direction, and in a very low voice, he said, "I doubt she'll make it."

Max watched as Jon Harris cradled his daughter in one arm and gripped his wife's hand in the other. With the explosion down the mountain, would he be holding Sydney's hand as she bled out and died?

This mission had tanked in a big way. Disgusted, Max returned to the missionaries. Sweat and stench spiraled up from the man as he hovered over his wife and whispered soothing words to her.

Max patted his shoulder. "We have to go. It's going to be rough. I don't know if. . ." Of all the—

He clamped his jaw tight. Max couldn't say it. Couldn't tell the man the truth. "Your wife—"

"Kimber's strong." Blue eyes darted to him with defiance. "She'll make it."

Max gave himself a mental shake and shifted toward Midas. "Get your gear. We gotta make tracks."

With a curt nod, Midas slung his pack over his shoulder.

"Uh, Frogman?" The Kid's voice cracked. "I think we got trouble." He spun and scrambled up the slight incline, shoving his NVGs toward Max. "Check it out—two o'clock."

Snatching the goggles from the Kid, Max glared at him, daring him to add to this colossally screwed-up mission. He peered through the lenses. And cursed.

A dozen unfriendlies crowded the screen, green and entirely too close. Sizing up their weapons, he cringed. His gut coiled. Machetes, axes, spears. Higanti.

"Scouting party! Take cover," he hissed, pointing to the dense vegetation and knowing that although they could easily take a dozen village warriors, it'd be the hundreds prowling the jungles for them that would complicate things. "Midas, get the girl. Kid, behind the rocks. All quiet!"

Beside him, a strange gurgling noise.

"No," Fix growled as he lunged toward Kimber Harris. "She's not breathing." He pumped his hands against her chest, then blew into her mouth.

"No time, Doc. No time," Max said between gritted teeth. "Twelve mean and ugly coming our way."

"She's dying!" Fix continued, panting and counting.

Jon Harris huddled over his wife, holding her hand tightly.

"Please. . .please, God—Kimber. Please don't die. Please, sweetheart. Please. Stay with us."

They didn't have time for this. If they stayed out in the open, they'd be dead. The team would be dead. The missionaries, the girl—everyone.

But what kind of cad would stop the medic from working on a missionary woman?

Jaw ground, Max balled his fists, watching the futility of the resuscitation attempt. What good would that be if they all died?

Why? Why in the name of all that was holy and just would God put him in this situation? Was God going to force him to kill one of His children?

A whistle stabbed his thoughts. The Nightshade signal. The Kid, it was the Kid warning them the Higanti were close.

Max clamped his hands on Jon Harris's shoulders and jerked him back. "Get under that bush and do *not* move." With a thrust, he shoved the guy in the direction.

"My wife—" he yelped, pressing his hands against the pouch containing his daughter. He started back toward the woman.

Ruger snapped up, Max stared down the barrel to the man, his chest tight, his pulse thundering through his head. "I will put you down myself."

The man froze. . .then wilted. "She's dying."

Max lowered his weapon a fraction "We all die if we don't hide." An unfamiliar pressure pushed down on his shoulders. "I—I'm sorry, but. . ."

Where had his soul gone? How could he be this calloused? He wiped the sweat from his face as the man turned, walked to a cluster of trees not far from his wife, and lay down on the floor with his daughter in the pouch, then covered them with jungle litter. All too clearly, he watched his wife battle for her life.

Being hacked into a thousand pieces by the Higanti paled in comparison to the million pieces of his heart held together by sheer willpower. With a quick glance around the area to make sure the team wasn't overtly visible, Max realized he didn't even have the strength of heart to curse God this time.

He tucked himself flat amid a bramble of weeds and bushes and pulled his M4 up so he could yank it up at will. His gaze probed and poked the darkness until he finally spotted Fix burrowed in next to the missionary woman, still working. Fingers digging into the cool soil, Max groped for control, for something to go right. Yet every quiet *thump* of the medic's hands over her heart sounded as a gun blast to Max's trained ears. A bitter taste burst across his tongue, and he swallowed the squirt of adrenaline and fear.

The crunch of leaves and twigs silenced his morose thoughts.

Fix hesitated and glanced in Max's direction then lowered himself to the earth.

Gradually, a dozen forms solidified in the small clearing. The way they walked through the jungle, as if they were a part of it, not as if they were trying to get out of it, unnerved Max. They were too familiar with the hills—would they recognize the odd rises and color patterns in the terrain that were screamingly obvious to him?

He eyed Fix and the woman lying sandwiched between two trees and a line of small palms. It was impossible to tell if grief or the all-quiet imperative kept the medic's head down. A trickle of light danced over one side of Kimber Harris's face. . .and revealed her slow descent from this world.

He swallowed, hoping the Higanti couldn't see her and panicked that he'd be forced to watch her die.

Her lips parted then closed. Again. . .opened.

Seconds pounded through his skull as she lay there without moving. Fix's gaze crawled to Max. His shoulders sagged, and he finally lowered his head.

No! Max coiled his fingers into the soft dirt, squeezing. . . wishing he could reach across the open space and hand-pump

Kimber Harris's heart. Keep her alive. She deserved it. Deserved to live with her husband who loved her so much and the adorable child so much like her mother. He squeezed again, mentally prodding her to live.

Do it! Live!

He tightened his hand around the dirt until the strain almost shook his arm.

Snap!

Max flinched and peered up at the sound. An oak of a Higanti warrior approached. With legs that seemed thicker than cannons, the guy swung a long-handled scythe loosely at his side. Each step brought the *tsing* of that blade closer.

Closer.

Max's finger eased into the trigger well. Fury licked through him that these whacked-out villagers had put Kimber Harris's life on the line. Possibly pushed her into eternity. Forced him to do something that shredded his soul.

A flurry of words shot out, and the Higanti paused. His heart rapid-fired as one snuck toward the Kid's position and poked a spear at the earth. Max's gut clenched at each jab. *God—?*

The Higanti near him turned back. Swung his scythe wide.

Metal and fire sliced Max's cheekbone, the *tsing* of the scythe ringing in his ears. He fisted his free hand and bit through the pain. Warmth slid down his jaw and neck. Behind the cluster, he saw Midas throw something down the incline.

Seconds later, birds screeched and shrieked, breaking the deadly silence, and erupted through the jungle. Branches swayed and palms *thwapped*.

The Higanti warriors raced in the direction of the birds.

The team waited as silence once again gaped and yawned. Finally, Max wiped the blood from his face and gave the all clear.

Jon Harris scrabbled from his hiding place and rushed to his wife. A half gulp, half sob burst from the missionary. "No..."

Max cringed, unable to remind the man to keep his voice down so he didn't draw the Higanti back. *Let them come.* He shivered, recognizing the bloodlust that coursed through him.

Sorrow clung to the man's face. He shook his head and sighed. "Oh God, I wasn't ready." The man crumpled against his wife. "Kimber, we need you. Maecel needs you." With his daughter sandwiched between him and his dead wife, he cried. Sobbed.

Max shifted away, the turbulent emotion ricocheting through his chest. Too bad he couldn't sedate the man just like his daughter, anything to quiet that gut-birthed sob.

You're a jerk!

No, he had a tight lid on things, and that kept him topside, above the emotional squall. If he could just deaden his feelings the way he had twenty-plus years ago when his father had walked out, he might be able to put a coherent thought together and get out of here—without any more fatalities.

The Kid and Midas moved off to the side.

They needed to move. *He* needed to move. Put a lifetime between him and this nightmare. His gaze drifted back to the scene. The sleeping babe's head rested just under her mother's chin. One asleep for now, the other forever.

Max shook his head and turned away. And yet. . .wasn't this what he'd always done? Deadened the pain—no, *killed* the source so he didn't have to feel. *This is your fault.*

No. He'd done everything he could think of—he hadn't invited the Higanti.

You let her die. Made Fix stop.

What else could he do? Their necks would've been severed if the warriors had found them. Why did it matter? Fatalities happened. Missions were dangerous and deadly. That's why he and the Nightshade team were trained and sent.

"I'll take good care of Maecel," Jon said with a shuddering breath. "I'll never let her forget your smile or your love for her."

Lips pressed tight, Max drove his gaze to the ground. Worked to keep his chin from quivering as he watched the man hold his dead wife. Heard his quiet cries. Whispered promises. *Bury it. . .bury it.*

He clamped his jaw. *You did this.* Breathed harder. *You killed her.* Max forced himself to shoulder his pack, ignoring the weight that seemed to descend on him, leaving him exhausted and aching. Why couldn't he shake this off? He hesitated, his gaze trekking over the scene with Jon, Kimber, and Maecel Harris. He had to remember this, because in some tripped-up way, this was his fault.

A strange glow glittered through the trees. With its first golden rays, dawn stretched from the horizon and kissed Kimber Harris good-bye.

Concealed under the slats of a raised hut, Sydney burrowed in as far as she could and pressed her back against a large support. Warmth dripped down into her right eye. The concussion had thrown her back and smacked her head against one of the market stands. It'd been enough to blind her for a second—but that didn't stop her from scrambling to safety at the sound of shooting.

Trembling wracked her body as she stared out the two-foot space toward the road. Heat plumes rippled through air from the burning Jeep. Holden. Lane. Where were they? Had they been killed? Pain radiated through her neck and shoulder, but also around the small of her back and into her hips. Come to think of it, she hadn't felt the baby moving since the explosion. Had the concussion. . .? Oh no. She couldn't say it. Couldn't think it.

"My baby," she mouthed, hot tears streaking down her cheeks. "Please, God!" Still, she didn't allow a sound to escape her moving lips. Had she, in her own foolishness, killed her son? Rubbing her belly, she willed the little guy to let her know he was still alive. *God, forgive me. Forgive me.*

Nothing. Silence. Emptiness. *I've killed him. Oh sweet Jesus, I killed him.* Grief strangled her. She didn't care if she died. She deserved to die. What kind of mother traipses around the world, willingly walking into danger zones for a story?

Fear wrapped its long tendrils around her chest, squeezing tightly. Thick smoke billowed in under the boards, reaching for her with hungry, greedy fingers. She wouldn't cough. Couldn't cough and give herself away. Breathing resisted her every attempt. Thick ash found her in the hiding place and coated her dark clothes.

Crackling and popping of the fire worried her, reminded her of the blaze she'd set to her own life. What she wouldn't give to go back in time, to show Max more love, to be more patient, to remain on American soil for her story.

Crunch.

Sydney's heart seized.

Crunch, crunch. . .crunch.

A boot slowly moved into view, its movement methodical. Heel touched the wood and wreckage-strewn sidewalk first, rolled through the instep to the toe. Left foot next. He was searching for her.

Crunch.

The grittiness sifted into her mouth and nostrils. Down her throat. Her body convulsed to cough—but she stopped it.

A knee dropped into view.

Thump! Thud!

The man splayed out, his face turned toward her, blood streaming down his temple. He'd been shot! But who had killed him?

Hurried steps rushed closer.

"Americans, let's go!"

It's a trick. Didn't matter anyway. She didn't deserve to live. If her baby was dead, so was she. Never would she be able to face Max knowing what she'd done.

"You have five seconds, and we're out of here." Another voice, gruff and terse, shattered the obnoxious quiet of the now-empty market. Two sets of black boots stormed into view. One crossed the road toward the Jeep. Another paused in front of the hut where the dead man stared back at her. A dark hand slipped around the man's neck, apparently checking the pulse.

"They're all dead." The gruff voice called. "Nobody's left."

"Then who were they shooting at?" the one closer asked.

Movement across the street caught her eye. Lane! He crawled out of a house on his hands and knees, gagging and coughing. "Help! Help! Don't leave me."

The two men sprinted and helped him to his feet. "Is there anyone else?"

"I—I don't know," Lane said, his voice almost inaudible.

Don't tell them. *Just leave and let me be.*

"How many in your group?" Gruff asked.

"F–four. There were four of us. Me, two other guys, and a woman. A pregnant woman."

"A preg—" A growl emanated from one of the men. "You sure are some special kind of stupid to bring a pregnant woman into an environment like this."

"Let's find her."

Silently, she willed them to leave. Leave here. Leave her. She didn't want to go back home to normal things. She didn't deserve anything. In her attempt to find purpose, she'd found death. Now she had nobody. Her mom was dead. Her husband she'd legally signed out of her life. Bryce—that was another story.

No, she was alone. All alone. In a strange country. Her brother didn't even know she was here. They'd hopped that flight without notifying anyone.

"Here! She's under here!" Lane's shouts echoed through the early morning. "Sydney, are you okay?"

She tried to curl in tighter, but her bulging belly wouldn't cooperate.

A hand clasped her foot and pulled.

She kicked out with her other, screaming. "Leave me alone!"

Still, they hauled her out as she scraped and clawed at the dirt. If she could just stay hidden, maybe they wouldn't know what she'd done to her own baby.

The large man towering over her clamped a hand over her mouth. "Quiet." He seemed to scowl at her, even under all the lines of green and black smeared over his face. "You injured?"

Lane cradled her face. "I was so worried about you. I couldn't find you. . .and I thought. . . ." He sobbed. "I thought you were dead."

The two soldiers shifted awkwardly.

Irritation clawed at her. She batted Lane away. "Leave me alone. Just go away." The larger man drew her to her feet. Swallowing the bitter taste that glanced off her tongue, she wiped the blood dribbling into her eye.

The soldier tilted her head to the side. "It's not gaping. We'll fix it when we rendezvous."

Everything in her wilted. "I don't want to go back."

"Are you crazy?" Lane exclaimed.

She'd come here, hadn't she? She might as well die here. And she'd bolt the minute the soldier turned—

A viselike grip wrapped around her arm. He held a finger to his ear, and only then did Syd notice the ear mic and the rolled up sleeve—and tattoo.

She'd found them! The team she'd been hunting.

And look what good it did.

The ache around her back and stomach hadn't lessened.

"Delta One," the soldier said, tightening his grip as he led her into the thick of the jungle. "This is Ghost One. En route, plus two friendlies."

Friendlies. Why did that sound wildly contrary? She glanced at the man dragging her through the high grass and bushes. He stood taller than her by nearly a head and a half, with broad shoulders. Of course, the armor that wrapped his body seemed to enhance his chest several inches. The camo rag over his head shielded his hair and the shape of his head, but something seemed oddly familiar.

Insane.

After several long minutes, he finally stopped, tugging her aside. The other guy and Lane huddled up. "We have a hard hike ahead of us. Only a mile, but it's rugged, and we have to make it fast." He held Syd's arm again and peered down at her. "Can you handle it?"

"Does it matter?"

"Not to us," Gruff barked.

Ghost One held up his hand. "Is there something we should know?"

Those hazel eyes seemed to see right through her the way Max always did. And somehow, in some strange way, it twisted right into her heart. A tremor worked through her lower lip. The avalanche of emotions overtook her. She buried her face in her hands.

Warm hands pulled her in an embrace. Lane was so sweet, so understanding. She let him hold her as the tears wracked her. "I can't do this. I was so stupid to come out here, looking. . ." She choked off her confession. The soldiers would leave them here if she admitted searching the world over for them.

"Everything's going wrong. The man last night. The driver. The explosion. Now Holden's dead. My baby's dead. I don't want to live. I want to die. Right here."

The arms tightened around her. Warm breath tickled her ear. "Sydney, God didn't bring you this far to abandon you."

The words sounded familiar yet different. She pulled back. Hard. Surprise pinged through her. It wasn't Lane comforting her. The soldier caught her shoulder, his expression solid and sincere.

"You don't know that. I killed my baby! I can't feel him moving. God won't forgive me for that. I should've never come here."

"You got that right," Gruff snapped. "Move it or lose it."

Again, the soldier held up his hand as he turned to her. "We have a medic. He can check you and confirm that your baby is just fine."

She whimpered at the way her heart leaped, snatching that ultrathin thread of hope he dangled in front of her.

With a nod, Ghost One took her arm and guided her up the mountain. A medic would have a stethoscope, right? The fifteen minutes proved grueling, but Sydney rearranged her thoughts and determined that each step brought her closer to hearing her baby's heartbeat. Would God really grant her mercy?

His mercies are new every morning.

A small smile pricked into her depression. She glanced at the sky, feeling the warmth of the golden hues spread into her chest. With a shuddering sigh, she refocused on treading closely behind the soldier who'd shown her more kindness and consideration than she deserved. What she *did* deserve was the treatment Gruff had delivered.

What felt like an hour later, the men crouched. Sydney struggled, unable to crouch comfortably. Ghost One let out a long whistle, followed by a warbling sound. Seconds trickled through the noisy jungle. Soon a matching whistle bounced back at them.

They stood and crossed a small path of swampland. As they did, Sydney saw shadows skittering over the water. Her heart plummeted at the sign of a half-dozen people gathered in a small grouping. A man her height, astonishingly short against the towering giant beside her, ambled toward them, a machine gun cradled in his arms. The two men clapped hands and patted backs.

Ghost One glanced around. "Where's Delta One?"

"Headed downstream. Seems our chopper isn't coming. He's

trying to plot our route."

No chopper? Sydney's heart lurched. How would they get out now?

"Where's the Fix?" Ghost One twisted and held a hand out toward her.

The shorter man nodded to the side. "The woman died. He's with the husband."

A knot formed in her throat as she spied the skinny man holding a still form against him. Another soldier sat nearby, his head down.

"Stay with her," Ghost One said to the man.

Coldness swarmed around her, leaving her chilled and frightened as the burly man left. A man had lost his wife in this jungle. Holden had died. Several others in the fruit market. Seemed that's all this jungle was good for. Death. The skinny man sobbed as he lowered his dead wife to the ground. Tears sprang to Sydney's eyes as he bent and kissed her face.

"Ma'am?"

She jerked from the heartrending scene and turned toward Ghost One.

"This is our medic, Fix. He'll take good care of you."

The man, about a head taller than her, nodded. "How are you feeling?"

Wiping her tears, she smiled weakly. "Exhausted."

"I've got a tarp set up over here. Why don't you let me check you out in the light?" Without waiting for a response, he stepped around some trees and bushes then shifted back and waved her closer.

Sydney swallowed her courage as the moment of truth came upon her. She dragged herself to his tent, and he instructed her to lie down. On her back in the cramped, hot space, she wondered why she'd complied so easily with a stranger. Maybe it was the presence of Ghost One lingering just outside.

"How far along are you?" Fix knelt and set a stethoscope

around his neck.

"Almost six months." Even through her shirt, she could feel his cold hands as they probed her abdomen.

"When did you last feel the baby move?"

So, Ghost One had told him what she'd done. "Just before the explosion."

Without a word, he examined her, gently pushing on her belly on all sides. Her heart thundered that her son wasn't responding to the intrusive pressure. He'd given her heck for bending over to put on her shoes. Tears streamed down her face.

He tucked the plastic tubes in his ears. "Lie still and stay quiet." Carefully he peeled back her shirt.

In her periphery, he flinched visibly. Their eyes met.

"Where did you get this?" His words rushed out in a single breath.

Unnerved at his reaction, she struggled to know how to answer that. He didn't need her entire history. "Long story, but I honestly don't know. Just woke up with it." Palms flat against the ground, Sydney stared up at the dark tarp as the medic resumed his task.

I beg Your mercy, God. Even though she'd struggled to understand why God would allow her to get pregnant when her marriage fell apart, and though she'd wrestled with being a single mom, right now she knew without a doubt she wanted this baby. He was a part of her.

In that moment she realized she'd never really had to trust God for anything. Her salvation—age six. Her father had died when she was three, but Bryce had always been there, being a father to her and a man of the house for her mother. That was rough, but she'd made it through her teen years unscathed. She'd married Max young, enamored by the Navy SEAL and his bulging muscles. His passionate intensity. His smile.

Like the gift of salvation, she didn't deserve this baby after trekking into a dark heart of the world. *But please. I want my baby.*

More tears streamed.

The stethoscope lifted, and he placed it against her left breast, snapping her attention. "Your ticker's running a little fast there. Try to relax; take it easy."

Take it easy? He wanted her to take it easy? Why? Was he about to say her son had died? Was he trying to brace her? She squeezed her eyes shut as more tears threatened.

"Hey," he said in a soothing voice. "Easy there. Here, take a listen."

She opened her eyes, surprised to find him handing her the stethoscope. She accepted it gingerly, her fingers shaking as they wrapped around the cold metal. Once she placed the buds in her ears, he set the scope against her belly. A flurry of static bled into her ears. "I don't—"

Whoomp, whoomp, whoomp, whoomp.

She gasped hard, her lips parting as wild hope danced through her chest. Her eyes darted to the medic, a laugh bubbling through. "He's. . ."

"Quite healthy." Fix smiled. "And first order of business is getting you hydrated to get your BP up. Then make sure you sit at every op. Stay put." As he pushed out of the covered area, he joined Ghost One, who seemed to be waiting for a report.

Lane eased in next to her with a broad smile. "I heard."

"I've been so stupid coming all the way out here," she said, watching as Ghost One whispered to the medic before disappearing around the side. The medic glanced back at her with a lengthy stare. He then signaled to someone, and a second later another soldier stood outside the door as the medic left. It was as if they were guarding her.

What was going on?

DAY TWENTY-SIX

Later

She wasn't supposed to leave him like this. They were supposed to live to an old age, growing closer in wrinkles and heart. Till death do us part. Jon smoothed back Kimber's hair, her forehead still warm in spite of the fact her heart no longer worked to thrust blood through her veins.

Emptiness consumed him, deep and starving. If that fool leader hadn't ordered him to lie down like a dog and watch his wife die, they might've saved her.

I didn't want to leave. Through a crooked smile and raspy words, Kimber had tried to encourage him, to tell him that she was okay with dying here. But he knew that. She wanted to stay here. Even with the bustling around the camp, the return of the soldiers with two more civilians, Jon sat in his own grief, unable to release her.

Anger flowed free and raw.

The medic had already promised they'd carry her out so she could have a burial back in the States. Only Jon knew Kimber wouldn't want a ceremony with pomp and flair. She was a simple woman. Loved the people of this island. Loved this island. If their family wouldn't object so loudly, he would ask the soldiers to dig a grave and bury her here.

"Her body leaves," Kezia whispered next to him, wide brown eyes darting to his. "But her heart always here."

Although grief held him tight and made it difficult to breathe, he couldn't regret this or regret staying when the warnings came to get off the island. "If he'd just let us try..."

"Not even a soldier can defy God's hand."

Startled by her words, Jon stared at her wide brown eyes...and realized she was right. He hung his head. "You're right." A piece of him wanted to blame Frogman for the decision that sent them hiding like cowards and left Kimber to die. But he had seen the torment in the man's face despite the paint and tough facade. *He's as much a man as I am.* Could he forgive the man? That he wanted someone to hate tore at him almost as much as his wife's passing. Kimber had battled the dengue fever valiantly, and in the end, that's probably what left her vulnerable to death's grip—not the fact that the medic had been ordered to stop compressions. Even Fix had said she'd been too weak to fight. Maybe if she hadn't had the fevers.

If "ifs" and "ands" were pots and pans... How many times had she'd quoted that to him, hinting at the difference between wanting and having? *Ifs* did nothing to help the circumstances. Only God could control what happened. But why had God let Kimber die?

Jon tucked aside the questions. He'd learned long ago that those questions served no purpose other than to create a wide chasm between man and God. It was impossible to understand the ways of God. And Jon certainly wasn't going to try to drag God's divine actions down to something understandable. Kimber was gone. On her beloved island. A hole gaped in his soul over the emptiness of life without her.

Bittersweet sorrow laced his pain into a box. He tucked it into the inner recesses of his heart. If only he could be as strong as Kimber had been, maybe he would handle this better. Maybe he'd even rescue the man who'd come to rescue him.

CHAPTER 24

Cursed. That's what he was. Completely cursed. Max clenched his fist. Everything that could go wrong had gone wrong. They'd encountered one obstacle after another, all ones that shouldn't have existed. The chopper couldn't show up for whatever reason. Probably got run off by the attack chopper that clipped the life from the missionary woman. Now they'd have to hike down the mountain, risking injury and exposure, to reach a secondary extraction point.

Pray.

He grunted. Right. He'd made it this long without it. *Yeah, and look how that went.*

Shoving aside the niggling thought, Max trudged up the slope back toward the falls, wincing at the fresh pain in his cheek. Fix had stitched it, promised a souvenir scar and all. But for Max, it was a reminder. A reminder that he'd failed. That he had let Kimber Harris die.

But he hadn't had a choice. They would've all died!

If it were Syd, if she'd been shot or if she'd died in that explosion, he'd go ballistic. Take a flying leap straight into heaven just to have it out with God. Why would God let a sweet missionary woman, a wife and mother, die so needlessly? Nightshade had arrived in time. Where were the angels who were supposed to intervene and protect God's children? He didn't get it.

Just as he crested the hill, he stopped short. Jon Harris stood next to the small pool where water plummeted down the mountain to the bay. The churning, foaming wake of where the falls met the pool seemed to mirror the turbulence of this trip. Yet that turmoil was absent from Jon Harris. Why wasn't the man railing against the injustice? Was he mad at Max, angry for the call he'd had to make?

Jon shifted and looked at Max then hung his head. "I. . .I want you to know I don't blame you."

The revelation impaled him. The man should be punching his lights out. Why wasn't he? This didn't make any sense.

"I know you had to do what was best for the team, that your mission is Kezia and getting her out of here." Jon's voice hitched. "I. . .I forgive you."

"For—" Max bit his tongue. Balled his fists. "I killed your wife!"

Watery blue eyes came to Max's. Then a slow smile. "No." He wiped a hand under his nose. "She died here in her beloved jungle. Sure, it hurts something fierce. . .but we both know she was already dying."

Max considered the man, heart whooshing.

"I know you don't like what you did, and I appreciate your anger over her death."

"You appreciate my anger?"

Jon grinned this time, stuffing his hands in his pockets. "It's a masking emotion, anger." He shrugged. "I was a psychology major before coming out here. Anger masks fears." He sniffled. "Kimber probably would've died before the helicopter came, but I just. . .kept hoping. Praying." A cool mist rose from the water and seemed to enshroud the man. "You shouldn't blame yourself. You made—" His chin quivered. But he drew himself tall and sighed.

"You made the right decision, Frogman."

Max darted a glance to the makeshift camp, shaking his head, frantic to get the guy to understand. . . .

"You should forgive yourself, too. It was out of your control."

Max snapped his gaze up then yanked it down. Forgive himself? Out of his control? Wasn't everything these days? His gaze pinged to the camp, to Midas and Fix placing the woman's body into a bag.

"I, uh, asked them not to cover her face."

Teeth clenched tight, Max stood rigid. He didn't want to hear this. Didn't want to be the man's confessional. Didn't want to play church in the middle of a deadly jungle. Didn't anybody get that he didn't do emotion?

The ability to control my emotions and my actions, regardless of circumstance, sets me apart from other men. It was right there in the SEAL creed—he didn't do pain.

He ran from it.

The truth stung and startled him. Was it true? No, he faced ugly head on. Except. . .guilt clawed at him. The chatter of jungle life pecked at his conscience. Why else would he so readily head into the wild, the deserts, the places of extreme danger?

To get away from what was inside him.

"I never thought this would happen," Jon said, snatching Max from his internal diatribe. He stretched on his tiptoes, his head tilted back as he stared up at the canopy of palms. "Trusted God, came here. We were so happy."

Happy never lasts. Max could relate. "Then God yanks her out of your arms."

Jon snapped his gaze to Max, a yellowish tint from the dawn sky on his skin. "No, not really," he said, his voice soft but strong. "Kimber loved this island. Loved the people. She never wanted to leave. I always knew she'd die here. Just. . .not this soon."

Stupefied, Max stared at the man. Was he really not angry?

"I mean, don't get me wrong." Jon sniffled and wiped his nose. "I'm devastated over Kimber's. . . . Grief is a long process." A not-so-brave smile. "There's a piece of me already missing, but no." He again shot a clear, focused gaze in Max's direction. "I'm not mad at God. Or you. Kimber loved Him and loved serving Him. I'm not going to waste time being angry when it's nothing I have control over—she taught me that."

Max's mind sped to the story of King David when his son with Bathsheba died under a move of God's hand for David's sins. When word came that the boy had died, David got up from his grieving and praying, dusted himself off, and went back to work, saying he could not change what had happened.

But that was then. Old Testament. Eons ago. How could Jon Harris—

"I spent my youth angry, rebelling." He smiled, a distant haze taking over his eyes. "Then I met Kimber. That's when I knew God had given me a second chance. Now? Now I just want to remember the good and raise our daughter in honor of her mother's memory."

"I think I'd be on a rampage." The thought coiled around Max's gut, remembering how close someone had come to murdering Sydney and knowing that she could've been the one in that house explosion—not her mother.

And why hadn't Cowboy reported in yet?

"Anger doesn't solve anything. She's still gone." Jon considered him. "Do you have a wife?"

Max dropped his gaze. "I did." He blew out a hot breath. "She filed for separation five months ago."

The missionary pivoted, his hands in the pockets of his torn pants. "Do you still love her?"

"It's over. Too late for second chances."

A slow smile filled Jon's face. "It's never too late. With God, anything's possible."

"Time ran out on me two years ago. She didn't deserve what I dished out, but I couldn't stop myself. Didn't know how." Why was he telling this stranger his darkest secrets?

"But you do now?"

Shrugging, Max considered the rippling water. "Would've tried a little harder." Any other time he would've said that was an easy answer. But this morning, under the tease of the dawn's first rays, he wondered what it really took to make a marriage work. And what gave Jon Harris so much strength, the ability to accept his wife's death? It wasn't that the man didn't love his wife—he could see the fat tears and grief that pushed down on him. But there was something—more. Deeper. "Can I ask, how did you make it work?"

"Make what work?"

"Your marriage. Out here in the jungle with hardships—and no doubt you've seen things you probably didn't want to see."

Jon shrugged. "It's a choice. You have to decide it's worth it. She's worth it."

Too easy. Max regretted asking.

"You just decide that no matter what it takes, you're going to make it work. You're going to see it through."

"Frogman!"

The call drew him around. His heart leaped when he spotted the cowboy heading his way. He excused himself as he turned and clasped Cowboy's hand. "What'd you find? Anybody alive?"

"Fix is checkin' 'em out."

"Good, good." So if the cowboy wasn't telling him anything shocking and grim, then he could assume everything was cool. That it wasn't Sydney. He tried to nudge his thoughts toward the mission, toward getting to safety. But his gaze surfed between the trees and bushes looking for whoever "them" included. "We've, uh, got about a day's journey down the worst terrain you've seen yet."

"Max—"

A swell of adrenaline swished through his veins at hearing Cowboy use his first name. "I just want to get out of here." He grunted, roughing a hand over his face. "And remind me to tell the Old Man our next mission will not be on a mountain or in a jungle."

"Max, she's pregnant."

"Who—?" He stopped short and drove his gaze to the medic's tarp, where a man and woman stood just outside. A faint glow from within the tarp silhouetted her significant bulge. "*Who* in the name of all that's holy was stupid enough to bring a pregnant woman into this?"

Cowboy stood by silently.

Agitation plowed through him. He wanted to punch something or someone. Were the fates aligned against him? Or had God had enough of him and now wanted to annihilate every hope of getting off this putrid island? He wanted to say he didn't care, that the woman would have to tough it out. And she would. They didn't have time for frequent breaks. Then again, he wasn't going to be responsible for another death. "Where's Fix?"

Cowboy pointed toward the Kid, who sat by the baby's carrier as Fix administered another sedative.

Max stomped over to his medic. "Fix, what's with the woman?"

He strung an IV into the baby's hand and set a pouch on the edge. "Watch that. She needs to stay hydrated." He stood, hesitation guarding his eyes. Then he darted a glance to Cowboy. "We'll need regular breaks for the woman. It'll slow us down."

Max scowled. "Clock's ticking. We'll be dead meat by tomorrow morning. How often do we have to stop?"

"As she needs it. Her BP is low, the concussion has her vitals whacked, and her baby's heartbeat is slower than it should be—I think. I'm not a pediatrician, so I could be wrong." Fix started back toward the tarp and the couple.

Cowboy shifted into view. "Max, you need to know—" His

friend sighed and looked down. Slowly, he brought his gaze back to Max then glanced toward the woman and man. The man touched her shoulder, and she moved toward a rock and lowered herself. So they had lovers footing it into the jungle. Max would think the guy would know better than to let a pregnant woman into a terrorist-infested jungle.

"It's Sydney."

"What's Sydney?"

"The woman," Cowboy said, motioning toward the couple. "It's your wife. She's here."

Buzzing started at the back of his brain and slowly spread into his awareness. Hot. Then cold. It all flashed through his nerves, barreling down and back with lightning speed.

"No," he said, his voice catching. The fog of panic cleared. Couldn't be. "Sydney's not pregnant."

"It's her. I wouldn't lie to you."

Not possible. Why would she be on this side of the world? And with another man!

Wait! Max narrowed his eyes, suddenly recognizing the long-legged gait. Lane Bowen. She was here with that weak-kneed yuppie. They sure looked cozy. Which is why he'd knocked the guy out cold months back. Were they a couple now that she'd filed for separation? Is that why she'd filed? Because she knew she was pregnant with Lane's baby?

Curse the dogs! God had it in for him. *A choice*, Jonathan Harris had said. Well, there was no choice here. Sydney had decided for both of them. Max stomped toward where he'd set up some supplies.

"Frogman?"

Max spread his hand-drawn map over the rock and held up a muted flashlight. "We're here. By nightfall we need to be there, or we might as well be dead."

"Max." Cowboy's tone pleaded with him as he tried to turn Max toward him.

Freeing himself of the grip was easy. But avoiding the man's stare wasn't. "Let's just. . .get out of here." He tapped the map, trying to restart his brain on what route to take. "There are a half dozen villages along this spread. The only one we thought would be helpful is the one we almost didn't escape from."

After a sigh, Cowboy traced his finger over a spot. "What's this?"

"Basically, a twenty-foot drop. We'll have to hike around it, but it's going to be tough negotiating the area."

"What's our projected ETA at the base?"

"Oh hundred hours. If we push them, we can make it."

Cowboy shook his head. "It's not wise to push her, Max. She's already worn down and traumatized. She needs to rest."

"She'll have to do that at the base. We don't have time to baby"—he about bit his tongue on the word—"someone through this. Each minute here we're one breath closer to death. Look at the missionary's wife."

"Max—"

"Get everyone on their feet." Back to business. Get out. Get away from her. "We're out of time." He wouldn't think about the fact that their divorce wasn't even final and she was already carrying someone else's child. His heart thumped so hard, he staggered.

Cowboy cornered him between the rock and a palm. "You should talk to her, let her know you're here."

"No!" The growl ebbed through Max. "Just. . ." Eyes closed, he balled his hand. "Don't tell her it's me, that I'm here. Let's just get this over with." He rubbed his eyes, fighting back the confusion, the torrent of feelings. Some new feeling worked through him that he couldn't quite place.

His eyes drifted to the body of Kimber Harris. Death. That's it. Death. His marriage to Sydney was dead. What surprised him more was the realization that he'd still held an atom of hope that he could fix things, himself, their marriage. But now, the tiniest element had been obliterated. And the impact felt nuclear.

Cowboy blocked his path. "We're friends. So I'm going to cut it straight. You're screwing this up. God's givin' ya a second chance. She's your *wife!*"

"And she's carrying someone else's child! *His* child!" No wonder she so quickly filed for the separation. "Everyone, on your feet. Move." Then a thought speared him. "Cowboy."

Cowboy turned, his brows drawn tight.

Max set his pack down, worked his way out of the interceptor vest, then tossed it to the guy. "Have her put that on." He returned the pack to his shoulder and set out. Their marriage might be over, but he'd do everything he could to make sure her life wasn't.

Weariness slunk through Sydney as the sun rose high overhead. At least she thought it was overhead. With the clouds and thick ceiling of palm fronds and other tree limbs, she couldn't tell—except for the oppressive heat that glued her shirt to her back and stomach. Blisters worked into her boots. Boots designed for fashion. Boots not designed for hiking. When had she become so insensible?

Moisture from the early morning dew that settled over the soft grass made the hill seem like one long, slick banana peel. More than once her feet slid forward—and Lane caught her. As they hiked down one particularly tough spot, Ghost One and Midas assisted her.

"Keep it moving," Gruff called, patting the drill sergeant's shoulder.

Sydney wanted to spit on the man. Let him saddle an extra twenty pounds around his waist, then add this stupid vest that wouldn't even cover her belly and rubbed her underarms, and see how quickly he moved. Every soldier seemed to be concerned about her welfare, except him and the drill sergeant. All he wanted was to get where he was going.

Okay, yeah, that wasn't a bad thing, but she wanted to arrive alive.

She snapped her thoughts closed, remembering the missionary whose wife lay on the stretcher in a bag, her gray, lifeless face staring up at the sky. In a strange, twisted sort of way, she looked peaceful.

Sydney maneuvered closer to the missionary. "I'm sorry for your loss."

He glanced at her and smiled. "Thanks." His gaze fell on his wife's still form. "She wanted to die here, so I'm glad."

Glad?

"At least I still have a piece of her with me," he said, nodding to the pack strapped to him. White wisps of hair rustled under a breeze.

Sydney smiled, her hand going to her belly. "How old is she?"

"Fifteen—sixteen months."

"Quiet! Keep moving," Gruff hissed from a few feet away as he slogged toward the front.

She hated the paint streaked over their faces. It blended their faces and identities into a camo smoothie. She could only differentiate one from another because of the size differences and because Ghost One had a Southern accent, the medic was Latino, one was African American, and one had a bad attitude.

"He's a sour pill."

"Maybe because we're lost," Lane mumbled.

With a start, she looked at him. "What do you mean?"

"We're not lost," Ghost One cut in. "We came under fire, so the chopper couldn't come in." He led them to a grove of gum trees. "Move into the shade and rest. Fifteen minutes." With that, he handed out small protein bars and removed a slim pack and passed it to her. "Sip slowly and only a little. This has to get us through the day."

After a bit of liquid refreshment, Sydney tried to get comfortable with the armor vest, but no matter how she sat, the thing pressed against her stomach. "Hey, what's with the drill sergeant and Gruff?" She opened her bar and gave him the wrapper when he held his hand out for it.

Ghost One grinned. "Gruff, as you call him, is always like that."

The first bite could've been confused for a mouthful of baking power, but she wasn't going to complain. Then again, after a few more nibbles, she could almost sense the protein and nutrients seeping into her cells. "And the drill sergeant, the guy calling the shots?"

Ghost One paused then stuffed the wrappers in his larger pack. "Lot on his mind. Hasn't slept in about three days, one of his objectives just died, he's been tasked with two extra civilians now, and we're all but walking into a trap."

"A trap?"

"The whole island is a trap, but the route to the coast is laden with terrorists. It'll take a miracle to get us through."

Something in Sydney turned to iron. "I believe in miracles."

Ghost One's gaze popped to hers. He smiled. "Me, too, ma'am."

What if the drill sergeant didn't believe in God? Would that doom them? "Yeah, but does he?"

"I think he used to."

Sydney watched the guy through the trunks of the trees. He'd never ventured more than a dozen feet from her or Lane, yet he barked at them like dogs. Of course, he did all his barking in a tight, controlled manner, never loud enough for anyone but those in this little troupe to hear.

Lane moved off to take care of business.

"So, how's your boyfriend holding up?" Ghost One asked.

She sucked in a breath—the food flinging to the back of her

throat. She coughed and gagged. After a sip of water, she wiped the tears from her eyes. "He's *not* my boyfriend."

The guy shrugged. "How's he doing?"

"He'd probably rather be on a jetliner right now."

"Wouldn't we all?"

Distinct and chilling, the feeling of being watched washed over her. Sydney rubbed her neck then skated her gaze around the area. Her gaze hit the drill sergeant, who swiftly bent and dug in his pack. When he straightened and slung his backpack over his utility vest, he stretched his neck, the morning light accenting the paint on his face. She thought it odd that the paint wasn't glossy the way she'd seen in movies. Flat. Matte, with streaks across the brow and—

Wait.

Sydney cocked her head. With narrowed eyes, she watched him.

Something hit her leg, snatching her attention from the drill sergeant.

"You need a bathroom break?" Lane asked the all-too-private question.

The heat murdered her good sense, because she wanted to do nothing more than smack him. How could he be so loud and pointed with a question like that? And she detested the way he behaved as if she were his—so often, apparently, that the soldiers thought he was her boyfriend. Never more than now did she realize how much the thought sickened her. Besides, she'd already been humiliated once in the last four hours having to stop and squat. Even though her bladder pushed against her, she wouldn't go through that again just yet.

"Time to go," Ghost One mumbled as he returned his gear to his back.

Sydney pushed to her feet, reminding herself if she wanted to live—and she did—she had to endure this day. She had a new appreciation for what Max had gone through when he was in the military.

Over the next six hours, they had managed only one other break. Rumors rumbled through the line that they'd take a break just after the pass. Whatever that meant. Belly burning, she rubbed it and yawned. This day wouldn't be over soon enough. She might even call Max when she got back and apologize for not under-standing more. . .better. And what she'd experienced here prob-ably paled in comparison to his years as a SEAL. Holden was right—a new perspective dawned on her protected and isolated American mind.

Life in war was brutal. Those words didn't even begin to cover it.

The feet in front of hers shifted to the side. Sydney looked up, surprised to find the drill sergeant working his way to the back of the line. As he swept past her, something. . .familiar drifted into her awareness. She paused, trying to pin down the elusive trigger. With his head tucked, the camo stripes weren't as distracting. His nose. . .those cheekbones. She followed him with her gaze. The square shoulders. So much like. . .Max.

It wasn't possible. Was it? Her heart sped a little faster as she kept moving. The baby kicked. Palm over her belly, she glanced back to the drill sergeant as she walked.

"Watch out!" Lane said, his hands on her shoulders, swiftly turning her.

Skimming the wall she'd nearly collided into wasn't easy with her baby bulge. She focused her attention back to the path. But when she craned her neck to the side to see around the group in hopes of looking at him again—it just couldn't be—the breath dropped from her lungs.

To the right, nothing but mist swirled up from the chasm below. Directly ahead, a narrow path not more than two feet wide snaked around a rocky cleft. Barely wide enough for one person to negotiate. The path disappeared into bamboo shoots and palm fronds. She tried to ignore the suffocation that gripped her. She lifted her chin a bit and drew in a long, steady gulp of air. She wouldn't die here. She'd be fine.

A hand landed on her waist. "You're slowing down," Lane prompted.

She shifted, trying to dislodge his hold and his irritating comment. Instead, she concentrated on putting one foot in front of the other. But that was the problem. She couldn't see her feet!

"Don't stop." Now both hands guided her—by the hips.

Sydney stopped. "Quit telling me what to do." She wrenched away and pivoted toward him, batting rogue strands of hair from her face. "Keep your hands to yourself, Lane Bowen!" she hissed. "I don't need your help or your orders to get me down this mountain."

Lane drew back—and when he did, she saw the drill sergeant behind him, smiling.

That smile! That crooked, endearing smile. Her heart hitched. Deep, dark eyes sparkled. Warily and slowly, she shook her head. "No. . ." She took a step back. "Max?"

"Syd!" Eyes wide, Max lunged—

Crack!

The ground fell out from under her. Gravity yanked her down.

CHAPTER 25

Temples bulging as he two-fisted Sydney's arm, her body dangling below the rocky ledge, Max strained. Her screams over the roar of the gorge pierced his heart. "Help," he growled to the others.

Arms wrapped around his waist, anchoring him. Others groped for a grip on her as she kicked.

"Hold. . .still," he said between clenched teeth.

"Help me!" Her cries snaked up the ravine and into his mind. Fingers clawed against his as she tried to reach with her free hand.

His feet skidded forward, her weight pulling him. Closer. To the edge.

No.

Couldn't lose her. Wouldn't. Not like this.

In his periphery, Max saw Cowboy get on his knees and reach for her other arm. "Grab my wrist, Sydney!"

Sweat worked against Max. His grip slackened. *No!* Would God help him, just once? Max had ignored Him for years, too disgusted with himself to venture a prayer heavenward. But if there was a time—

"God!" was all he could manage.

His footing caught. Those holding him cinched their grip. But sweat slid down his arm. . .between his hand and her arm. Slipping.

Sydney dropped an inch. She screamed.

The sound went straight into Max's soul. He clamped his eyes shut and focused on holding her, dragging her up. *The baby.* His gut clenched. "Come on," he growled, trying to take a step back and draw her to safety.

"On three, pull," Cowboy grunted. "One. . .two. . .three!"

Mustering the last of his strength, Max yanked up—and she came. The group stumbled backward—he barreled into them, his knees buckling. They righted him, and he bent, gripping his knee with one hand as the others steadied her. Only then did he realize she still had a death grip on him. The realization drew his gaze to her eyes.

Brilliant blue green eyes stared back. Shock. Relief. Her chin quivered.

Although everything in him wanted to pull her to himself, hold and never release her until they were on American-controlled soil, he wouldn't. It wasn't him that had her chin quivering—it was the adrenaline rush of nearly dropping to her death.

"You okay?" he braved.

She nodded, trembling.

His fingers itched to hold her. To whisper that he'd never let anything happen to her again. To comfort her. But then again, she'd already found someone to comfort her, hadn't she? Even now, Lane tucked an arm around her. He'd punched Lane out cold six months ago. Maybe he should've finished it.

Max slowly disentangled himself from her. "Let's get moving," he grumbled, brushing the dirt off his pants.

"Max?" The hurt spiraled through her voice and thudded into his chest.

He paused, unable to face her. "We can talk later," he mumbled.

Not in front of a team he had to lead. If he got his head out of the game, they'd get killed.

But his steel-reinforced defenses wavered like walls of Jell-O. He hated the pained rejection glued to her face. Her faltering composure haunted him as he warned the team to toe the rock edifice as they negotiated the pass. Even with feet scraping against rock and the occasional crunching and dribbling of rocks raining down on them, her soft sniffles carried to him like deadweights.

In spite of his every effort to push the thoughts and guilt aside, he failed. The only thing he was good at these days. Guilt harangued him. He should've taken her in his arms the way he'd wanted. He'd let his anger, his stupidity, get in the way. Again. Marvel of all marvels that he could lead a skilled team successfully but couldn't navigate the turbulent waters of a relationship. A relationship that meant the world to him.

Or did it?

We make time for what's important. How many times had his mom said that before she'd abandoned him and his older sister when things got too tough? And look at how Sydney had abandoned hope for them when things got tough.

No sooner had they cleared the twenty-foot drop than the skies let loose their bounty. Rain pelted them as they slid and skidded down the rain-slicked mountainside. When they came upon a swampy area, the team formed a human chain, making it possible for the civvies to traverse the swollen swamp.

Next to him, Cowboy aided the passing of the stretcher from one side to another. "And here I thought you had a brain hiding behind that thick skull."

Max glared. "Don't start with me, Cowboy."

"Yeah, 'cause the Lord knows nobody wants to find out what's really in that steel trap of yours." Cowboy closed the line as Fix and the Kid carried the stretcher over the murky water. "After all," he said, towering over Max with a fierce expression, "we all know there's no compassion for your own wife."

"What's that supposed to mean?"

Pausing, Cowboy seemed to be reeling in his frustration. "You're pushing us through the hardest parts of this jungle. I can handle it. The guys can. But her? It's like you don't care how much of a strain it's putting on her. What? Are you trying to kill that baby?"

Heart pinging off his ribs, Max tensed. "No. We have to get to the coast."

"Alive, or dead?" Cowboy shook his head, sludge collecting around his ankles as he stepped up out of the slick vegetation.

A heavy weight pressed against Max as he ducked his head, avoiding the rain that drenched them and brought a frightening chill. He was tired. They'd been on the move for three days straight now. Exhaustion weighted his limbs.

But that wasn't what weighted *him*.

Guilt. Like boulders around his neck. He *was* pushing them too hard. Wanting them to feel what it was like to be him, to battle insurgents and fight through hell and not get singed, yet still have to face life and society unaffected and with a smile. Maybe. . .just maybe after this, they'd understand.

The team pulled aside and took shelter as the downpour became too thick to see through. Legend and Midas quickly set up a tarp for temporary shelter. With Sydney and Lane cozily situated under the cover, Max wanted nothing to do with it.

He dragged out his own tarp and stretched it between two trees, lodging rocks into the spot to support it. Under it, he tugged the camelbak straw over his shoulder and took several long drags. As he burrowed into the wet spot, he closed his eyes.

Seconds later someone joined him. Why couldn't they leave him alone? He didn't want or need another lecture. He already hated himself and his life.

"Max, can we talk now?"

The sultry voice that had always heated his chest forced his eyes open. Sydney knelt next to him, her ocean eyes staring up at him softly.

Molars pressed together, he scooted over on the rock and let her sit. He couldn't look at her belly and talk to her. Couldn't accept she'd been with another man.

The monotonous thump of rain against the canvas beat into his muscles as they sat in silence. Bent forward, he rubbed his hands over his knuckles, wishing she'd get on with what she wanted to say. When she placed a hand on her belly and gave a soft laugh, he couldn't take anymore. "What are you doing here in the Philippines?"

"Searching for a team of elite soldiers working the globe."

"How did you find us?"

She shrugged. "God, I guess. It's really too much coincidence to be anything else."

The words soured in his stomach. "You're going to tell me God is putting you through this?" He clicked his tongue and shook his head. "Sorry, don't buy it."

"Why?" she asked, a quiet challenge in her question. "Why can't God use this to get our attention? He's certainly gotten mine."

Without straightening, Max peered up through his brows to the storm-darkened jungle. "There are better ways to get our attention."

"Well," she said, wiping the water from her hair, "sometimes when He uses the small things, we are so deafened by the world and our own desires, we can't hear Him."

"Yeah, I guess He'd have to be talking to us first."

"He talks if we listen. Just like me. I'll listen, Max. You looked really angry out there, on the pass. It. . .scared me."

"Don't worry. We'll get you out of here, and you won't have to worry about seeing me again." The words burned all the way down.

Her eyes glossed. "I'm not sure what I've done to make you so angry. Something changed. Is it because of the baby?"

The word hit, center mass. "You could say that."

"I...I was scared to tell you—" She shifted and bent awkwardly toward the side and fidgeted with her boots—and that's when he saw a gold necklace glimmering against her black T-shirt. Not just any necklace. The one he'd had Cowboy deliver to her. The anchor.

What did that mean, her wearing the necklace?

Max nudged aside the question. He'd asked too many questions for too long. "Ya know, I don't care, Syd. Don't care that you came out here with your boyfriend, the father of your baby. Just don't rub it in my face, okay?"

"What?" Her question breathed disbelief and anger. "What did you say?"

Had a northerly shifted their way? Why did it feel chilly? "Look, I have a team to lead. Just. . ." Keep talking. That's all he had to do. But why? What was the point? "We can do this later. I have to maintain my focus on the team and getting to the coast."

"You seriously think—" She pushed off the rock and stood just outside the cover of his tarp, rain splattering her face. She blinked, water bouncing off her lips. "Of course." Her cheeks flushed. "God forbid you focus on me. Your wife. Our marriage. But that's always been the problem, hasn't it, Max? You're too worried about what you want to protect, that you forget *who* you promised to protect."

Fire burst into his chest. He stomped to his feet. "Sorry, I learned a hard lesson from my mom—that I can't expect anyone to hold to their word. I learned that everyone walks out eventually, no matter how many times they promise not to. Just like my dad. Just like my mom. So, yeah, I do protect what I want."

Sydney stared at him, her mouth open. "You never told me that."

One side of his fortress collapsed. He bit back the curse on the tip of his tongue. She'd finally seen into that dark vault he'd sealed fifteen years ago.

"But you did tell me about your father." She stepped closer, the tarp covering her again. "And you also told me you'd never be like him. So, tell me, Max. When are you going to make good on that promise?"

The gall! "You're the one who forced me to leave. I didn't want to leave."

Her chin quivered again. "Your body was there, but your heart hasn't been in more than two years."

Right about the time he returned from that tour.

"If you didn't want to leave so badly, why didn't you fight for me, for our marriage, the way you fought for your job?"

"You have no idea what I've fought. How hard—"

"You're right! I don't." She batted the hair from her face. "I don't know because you stopped talking. Each night you'd jolt awake, drenched in sweat, having shouted and wrestled with ghosts. I was so worried about you, but you'd only tell me to go back to sleep as you dragged yourself to the bathroom for an hour-long shower. Why won't you tell me what's eating at you?"

"You don't need to know." He tried to stem the furious tide. "I don't want you to know."

Her brows knitted, nostrils flaring. "Why? Why are you shutting me out?"

Everything in him closed down. He'd tried to be open, and it had backfired. A tight lid slid into place, vacuum-packing all the anger and violent images. "Just leave it alone. Okay? I can't change. . . ." He couldn't say it. Not anymore.

"You can't change who are you are," Sydney said the words for him, sarcasm coating her tone. "Yes, Max, you can. If it ever becomes important enough, you can. The man I know, the one I love, can do *anything* when he focuses." Her throat processed a swallow. "I want to be important enough."

When he took a step toward her, everything in him railing that she would think that, she stopped him. And left.

Scolded and feeling like a schoolyard bully, he stood under her reprimand, somberly. The places he'd have to open up, explore, and face were so heinously dark, he didn't think light could penetrate them. If he went into that black jungle of his heart, he wasn't sure he'd make it out alive.

DAY TWENTY-SEVEN

"P urpose. Purpose defines us."

"Huh?"

Jon worked his way around a large gum tree and glanced at the soldier everyone called Frogman. He hadn't meant to speak his thoughts. "Sorry, just thinking out loud."

Frogman shrugged.

But a stirring deep within Jon told him not to drop this train of thought—and to keep talking to the wounded soldier. *Wounded?* He sure didn't look wounded, not with the toned, muscular build and the umpteen pounds of gear on his back. But even though there were no visible scars, Jon could well imagine the internal ones screaming for help. Supernatural help.

"In Old Testament times, each person within a tribe had a duty. Some were shared on a rotating basis, some were permanently assigned, like Aaron as the priest." Jon smoothed Maecel's hair, noting the IV bag was low. He'd have to mention that to the medic. "Those familial duties passed from generation to generation. So one always grew up with training and a sense of purpose."

A purpose. How he longed to know what *his* purpose in life was now that being on this island and being a husband and lover to Kimber were over.

"But we don't live in tribes," Jon said with a smile. "Our purpose is found in Christ." Where he'd expected derision, Jon found thoughtful consideration, which he tossed back at the special ops soldier. "Take you, for example. Clearly, God has given you a military purpose, a warrior's heart. Did you know that David was a warrior before he was a king?"

The man grunted. "Yeah."

Surprise seeped into Jon. "Have you found salvation in Christ?" He'd heard others whispering that the pregnant woman was the soldier's wife. She'd shared her beliefs with Jon earlier as she encouraged him and tried to offer comfort regarding Kimber's death. Anyone with eyes could tell their marriage was in trouble. And it burned a hole straight into Jon's gut.

With a nod, Frogman picked a piece of fruit from a durian tree. "But even God considered David's work too violent—He wouldn't allow him to build the temple. The one thing David wanted to do, and God said no." Frogman wouldn't look at him as he carved the fruit in two pieces.

"But don't you get it?"

This time, Frogman looked up.

"Your sins are covered in the blood of Christ."

Frogman slowed, apparently thinking this through. He ate the fruit, his expression still grave and discouraged. He pursed his lips then shook his head. "I've screwed up too much."

"Ah." Jon chuckled. "Then it's not God holding your sins over your head. It's you."

Frogman cut him a sharp glance, dark eyes blending with the paint that covered his face, neck, and hands.

"Forgiveness starts here." Jon tapped his chest and stopped in front of the man. "It's never too late."

" 'Too late' came and went." With a gentle but firm nudge, Frogman moved him out of the way. "Coming up on enemy territory. All silent."

Give him hope.

"Frogman," Jon whispered, garnering a heated stare. "God hasn't given up on you."

CHAPTER 26

She needs a break. We all do," Cowboy said in a stage whisper, falling into step.

"No time." Teeth gritted, Max pushed forward, focused on one thing—getting to the coast. He could smell the salty spray, feel it sticking to his skin. Ignoring the blisters forming in his boots and under the place that rubbed raw on his shoulder as his pack shifted during the thirty-six hours of hiking, he encouraged himself with the thought that this was almost over.

"Frogman, your anger is pushing everyone, and too fast. Just let it go."

Yeah. They all had the answers.

With a snort, Cowboy picked up his pace, inching ahead. "I expected more from you."

A branch snapped behind him. He mentally cursed whoever was behind him. He slowed, the realization rushing him that there wasn't anyone behind him. Or there shouldn't be. He dragged his gaze to the back. Jungle flickered and waved under the guide of an ocean breeze.

"If you'd do the math—"

All stop. Max fisted the signal up, probing the variations of greens and brown around him. He eyed the clearing they'd just entered. Silently, he cursed himself for hurrying them into an open area. Should've gone around. Should've used Fix and the Kid as point. He ground his teeth. It was too late now. Someone was out there. Following them.

He eased into his grip, back-stepped, and circled a finger in the air. Behind him he heard the team closing up. A quick check confirmed the civvies were surrounded by his men. They'd take out whoever had found them. Get moving. Hustle it to the beach.

Chills slithered down his spine as he searched the canopy, then to the side. There! A darkened shadow wobbled.

He snatched up his M4 and took aim.

The foliage came to life. Men oozed from the pores of the jungle. His stomach plummeted. Firefight with this many would be a bloodbath—for the good guys. Shouts erupted as roughly twenty men dressed in old school jungle camos stalked them, pushing the group closer and closer.

"This isn't good," Fix mumbled. "We can't just go down like this."

"Quiet," Max said. If he fired, at least four of them would shoot him. Dead before he hit the ground. Wasn't worth it. They had to have been waiting in ambush. He eased his weapon down and released it, raising his hands out, but not too far from his weapon.

A scream whipped Max around.

While a dozen or more radicals broke up the team, penetrating the tight circle they'd just formed, two wrangled Kezia from the group.

"Max!"

"No!"

Pop! Pop-pop!

The chaos—and Sydney shouting his name—spun Max around. In the blur of the instant, the data rushed through his brain. Fix was down. Midas knelt beside the fallen medic. Legend,

Cowboy, and the Kid were all sweeping their weapons toward the radicals. The leader held Sydney in a choke hold.

And Max had the man in his crosshairs. "Hold," he growled to this team. "Hold your fire."

A man moved from the foliage and stood facing Max. The radical shouted out in a language that left Max sick. Arabic. Max didn't need an interpretation. He understood their language. Understood they intended to take Kezia and Sydney and kill them before anyone could take them from the island and provide testimony against their leader.

"Lower your weapon," the tall, well-built leader said, his tongue smooth as a viper's. He motioned to Sydney. "Or everyone will die."

I want to be that important. Sydney's whispered words only hours earlier locked Max's gaze on her. Seeing the terror bulging her eyes, her face red under the strain of the radical's stranglehold, a machete against her throat, he couldn't move.

Because she *was* that important. That and so much more.

Fingers burning to gun down every radical left his mouth dry.

Regrets numbering thousands whistled through his mind. Should've let go of his anger, his past, long ago. Suddenly that the baby in her belly was another man's, that she'd shoved him out of her life and given up on him—none of it mattered. *Sydney* mattered.

Whatever it takes, God. Whatever it takes. Just don't let it go down like this.

His finger twitched, the M4 bobbing.

"I would be very careful," the leader said as he waved his hand—and the radical drew her up tighter. Her belly arched toward Max, as if reaching for help, for salvation. The sun peeked through the clouds, glinting off the blade of the machete that rose to her throat.

"Let her go," Max said, peering through the crosshairs.

Sydney whimpered—a small trail of blood slid down her neck toward the black T-shirt and disappeared.

"You're killing her."

"Please!" Kezia's young voice burst into the chaos. "Trust God. He will save us. Trust God!"

Yeah, right. Faced with M16s trained on his men and a machete against his wife's throat, he was supposed to just trust God? Sorry, but an M4 worked faster.

Sweat dribbled into his eyes, forcing Max to blink and break the lock with Sydney's terrified gaze. He couldn't deny the heinous odds. They were hugely outnumbered. If he didn't stand down, he'd kill everyone.

His anger would be his undoing again. *God. . . ?*

With every measure of restraint he could muster, Max vowed to kill these hostiles. If not here, then later. He'd come back. Make sure they paid. Nostrils flaring and his heart rat-a-tat-tatting like his M4, he slowly lowered the gun.

"Good," the man said in English. "Kill the soldiers. Take the women."

"Wait," Midas shouted, as radicals worked to drag him backward. "Sydney, show them the mark."

What mark?

She whimpered, both hands on the man's arm that held the machete. Her right arm muscle flinched, as if she struggled to obey.

"What mark?" Max hissed.

"Stop with the games, Americans." The leader stomped toward Midas.

"Sydney, trust me. Do it."

Her hand released and went to the hem of her shirt.

The leader turned. "It is improper—" His words stopped short as the bulge of Sydney's white belly glared at them all.

A brown-tinged symbol with a knife through it stunned Max

into silence. Where had that come from? He frowned as he craned his neck forward, suddenly connecting the dots. The man holding her bore a similar symbol on his right forearm.

"What is this?" Enraged, the leader stomped toward Sydney and grabbed her face. "Where did you get this? Do you mock my people?"

A slow breath filled Max's lungs as the machete moved away from her throat. But now she hung in the hands of the leader. He wasn't sure which was worse.

"No," she groaned out, clawing at the hand squeezing her face crimson. "I met a woman. She painted the symbol on my stomach."

Seconds hung like anvils.

"It's the mark of your people. You cannot harm her," Midas said, fierceness cutting a hard line into his words. He winced as the men holding him jerked his arms behind him, bringing him to his knees. "If you do, you forfeit your position. And your life."

The man whirled, eyes dark and narrowed. With a round-house kick, he drove a boot into Midas's face. His head snapped back, and he dropped against the ground, unmoving.

"I know the laws of my people. I do not need an American to tell me anything!"

Adrenaline urged Max forward, but he caught himself.

God will save us. His eyes bounced to Kezia. A serene expression soaked her face—and served as a lifeline to Max's soul. He felt the peace, the serenity.

"Take the other girl," the leader ordered.

Sydney rushed to the girl and held her. "She is under my protection."

"Syd!" Max lurched, but hands clamped onto his shoulders.

"Give her a chance," Cowboy said, then gave Max a pat on the shoulder and a look that conveyed a message. A message to be alert.

The leader slunk closer to Sydney, sneering at her before he slowly dragged dark eyes to Max. Through his thick brow, he stared at Max.

And in that second, that silent challenge, Max knew. Knew this wouldn't end peacefully. Knew the man had no intention of letting her go—or letting her live.

The leader lifted a knife from a scabbard on his belt and poked the tip against Sydney's side, watching Max. "I could carve that symbol off her fat body, gut that infidel child from her womb, and finish this. For good."

"And your guilt would remain." Sydney stared up at him defiantly.

"Sydney!" Heart pumping sludge, Max watched everything as if in slow motion. The oversized bad guy's hand balling so tight his knuckles turned white. Kezia's eyes fluttering closed, her lips moving—he hoped in prayer. Cowboy using his expert stealth skills to steal into the vegetation as he ever-so-slowly raised his Remington 700.

Max's gut churned. No way the leader would walk away from this. He had too much at stake. That meant Kezia and Sydney were in danger. What about the team? Were they ready?

Max eyed Legend, who slithered to the side, unnoticed by the radicals. He slanted a gaze to Midas, who lay on the ground still unmoving but looking directly at Max. He fisted his hand as if to say, "Let's do this." The Kid's lips were pulled tight, determination etched into his face. The team knew it was coming. They were ready.

Kezia turned a gentle face to the man intent on her death. "Allah will not forgive you for breaking your own laws, but the voices you try to silence serve a God who will."

"Our symbol may protect you, but there are those coming behind me who will not care. The Higanti will eat you for dinner!" The leader turned, considered the Nightshade team who froze from their repositioning, then took one step, swung around with brute force, and backhanded Sydney. She flew backward and landed on her backside. Almost as quick, he hooked an arm around Kezia's neck and raised the knife to her throat.

Crack!

A split-second later, red streamed down the man's face. His knees buckled. Nailed by Cowboy's expert marksmanship, the leader dropped at the girl's feet.

In that stunned instant, as the radicals stared in confusion at their fallen leader, Nightshade responded. Max snapped up his M4 and pegged the men behind Sydney, the sound of his weapon firing mingling with the flurry of gunfire and shouts. Midas dove at Kezia, pinned her down, and fired at two tangos rushing the girl. The crackle of the firefight echoed through the early morning.

The Kid darted forward—then stumbled, gripping his leg as he grunted and fired to the side. He'd taken a bullet, but nothing life-threatening.

Max scrambled to Sydney as more rebels emerged. He lunged toward her, easing back on the trigger. Two rebels fell while their three buddies skidded to a halt and sprinted past two date palms. Max fired into the bushes. On his knee, his gaze surfing the dense foliage, he reached toward her. "Sydney!"

She rolled onto her hip and pulled up, a stream of blood sliding down her chin.

Quiet rustling in the jungle kept his attention and adrenaline sharp. "Secure the perimeter. Verify the body count," he shouted to the team. Once he saw them in action, he turned to Sydney.

Wide blue green eyes watched him nervously. He helped her to her feet, feeling the trembling in her fingers, and pulled her into his arms. Kissed the top of her head. He cupped her face, holding her close. "Are you okay?"

She nodded, tears glossing her eyes.

Relief washed through Max. He would've done anything for

her not to have to see him kill a man or to be in the line of fire. She clung to him, the fingers of one hand digging into his left bicep and the other into his side. She sniffled, cried.

He tried to hold her closer, tighter, but it just didn't seem enough.

Half his mind gathered the data from the men: fifteen dead radicals, Fix was dead, and the Kid bit his first bullet. But Max tried to smear from his mind the image of what had happened to Sydney.

He gazed down into her beautiful eyes. Her beautiful face. Wiped the trail of blood from her chin. "I don't care." He took in her face. "I don't care if it's Lane's baby. I'm ready. To do whatever."

Easing back but not out of his hold, she blinked. Hesitation and hope jockeyed for first place in the eyes that had always made his mind numb. "You'll go to counseling?"

He swallowed hard, knowing the team listened. He didn't care anymore. Pride had cost him too much. Almost cost her life.

"Whatever it takes. I want us together." He shrugged, knowing there was only one way to say this, no matter how lame it might sound. "You're worth it." He captured her mouth with his, savoring the sweetness of all that was Sydney.

Then, all too soon for his liking, she pulled back. She smoothed a hand over his face, almost as if she were at a loss for words. Tears streamed down her face again, and she shuddered. With a smile she said, "*Your* son is worth it."

He stilled, uncertainty rushing through him. He bent closer. "*My* son?"

"You dope." She nodded, dislodging the tears from their hold. "I wanted to tell you. But you were so angry. I'm so sorry, Max." Arms linked around his neck, she buried her face in his neck. "I would never betray you. It's your baby. He's your son."

With her nestled in his arms, he let the revelation dig deep into his heart and mind. *Your son.* His pulse spiked. He looked at the others. With a stupid laugh, he announced, "I'm going to be a father!"

"What a genius." Cowboy popped the back of his head.

"Yeah, like you had it figured out."

"Actually," Cowboy grinned, "I did. When you had me deliver the gift, I noticed her belly. And any sane man—and I do qualify that with *sane*—can see this fine woman is as loyal as she is beautiful." He winked and hugged Sydney. "Right, darlin'? Or should we test my theory?"

"Bug off," Max said, pushing Cowboy away from Sydney. "She's mine." With that, Max honed his attention in on the love of his life. Tracing the side of her cheek, he knew he'd screwed up way too many times to deserve even this one instant in time, let alone that she carried his son. "I love you, Syd." He swept his lips over hers, relishing her softness, tasting her sweetness when she returned his kiss.

"Hate to break up the lovefest," Legend said. "But we're down one man, another will probably be seeing double for a while, not to mention the Higanti, and—"

The Kid whooped and thrust his fist in the air at the sound reverberating toward them. "Chopper!"

Elation worked a magic tonic on her heart and mind, even seemingly erased the pain of the scrapes and bruises that left her stiff and achy. Sydney had seen the light in Max's eyes, one she hadn't seen in a very long time. Years. And that kiss. . .oh, how she missed Max. His strength that always seemed to pour into her at his touch. She tucked Kezia close as the men retrieved Kimber Harris's body. Jon walked close to the stretcher as they headed to the beach.

Sydney glanced back to where Ghost One assisted Max in carrying the body of their fallen comrade. In spite of the reconciliation that had occurred between her and Max, she saw how the loss of one of his team members weighted him. And in the haze of euphoria and grief, she tried to grapple with the fact that she'd spent the last three months hunting down an elite team, a team led by her own husband!

Fresh tears worked through her composure. He'd been through so much. All these years, all these battles. Just as Holden had said. Max was a warrior. Pride filled her, watching her husband—*husband*—as they plodded toward the lapping ocean.

Although Max's anger had erected a virtually impenetrable barrier in their marriage, God had knocked it down. While she knew he bore responsibility in their marriage, she secretly wished she could've had this firsthand knowledge of his career sooner. Then maybe she would've been a bit more understanding. More accepting of him.

The heavy thuds of the rotors thundered as the helicopter roared closer. Sand and harsh wind whipped into her face. Long strands of hair stung her face, and she closed her eyes against the grains peppering her cheeks and eyes.

"Syd, let's go," Max shouted over the din.

He guided her, Kezia, and Lane into the Black Hawk. The chopper crew assisted her toward a small vinyl seat straddled over a canvas hold. They buckled her in and then secured Kezia. Lane sat next to her, his face awash with fear and yet relief.

They were going home. Alive. Reconciled. Her baby would have his father. She'd have her husband back. Things were going to work out just fine. Sydney averted her gaze as Gruff unloaded one of their own from his shoulders. The man had died for her. The harsh reality stung.

Bamboo grated against the steel floor as two soldiers worked to secure the gurney at Jon's feet. He stroked his baby's head, his gaze on his wife's body, now zipped head to toe. For the first time since Sydney had joined the group, the little girl awoke. Screaming and disoriented. Good. At least she had enough bearings and vitality to protest.

Ping! Ping!

The chopper veered to the left sharply—up and away. Sydney grabbed the edge of her seat and thrust a hand in front of Kezia as someone shouted, "Taking fire! Taking fire!" The girl clung to her. What was going on? Was everyone already on board? She scanned the black-clad bodies near the open door. Where was Max? Maybe she'd missed him. With the paint and everyone dressed alike.

"He's down, he's down!" Ghost One sat on the edge, his weapon pointed toward the ground. No, wait—he was firing at something!

Her stomach tightened. Weapons' fire tore through her hearing. Shots errupted from all directions, by all the soldiers.

Where was Max? As the chopper swung back, she saw the spread of brown beach. . .and a black form stretched out over the sand.

Her breath backed up into her throat. Then rushed out. "No! Max! Stop, he's not on board!" The chopper devoured her screams.

Gruff motioned the pilot back to the beach as others provided suppressive fire. The chopper slowly swooped back down and hovered over the sandy stretch. Amid the plume of sand swirling around them, she spotted Max.

He lay on the beach, his tactical gear a stark contrast against the sand. He wasn't moving.

Face down.

"Maaaxxx!" Her scream mingled with Maecel's.

Seconds later, Ghost One leaped out, followed closely by Gruff and another of their team.

Sydney tried to wrestle free of the belt.

"No!" The Kid stopped her, a hand over hers. "They'll get him.

Stay." When she started to object, he shook his head and shouted, "He'd kill me if you got off and got hurt. Stay!"

As if everything swirled into one slow-motion movie, Sydney squinted through the sheet of sand to the men sprinting toward Max. Two bent and hoisted him off the ground. Another fired shots into the trees. Tiny explosions of sand erupted as the three hurried back to the chopper. Max hung limp between them.

Two soldiers lifted Max's shoulders and set him on the steel floor of the chopper. His head lobbed to the side, facing her. Gravity pressed her to the side as the chopper veered off. But nothing could pull her gaze from Max's closed eyes and limp body. Tears found their exit again, choking her with the fear that she'd lost him. He'd just promised that they'd get back together and work on their marriage, and now. . .now he was gone?

She cupped a hand over her mouth, disbelief choking her.

"Where's his vest?" Midas shouted as he ripped open Max's shirt with a knife. Blood spread down from his shoulder and chest.

"A medic should do that," someone shouted.

"Our medic is dead!" Gruff shouted back.

Sydney sat back, fingering the multistrapped vest Ghost One had given her. It was Max's! If he'd been wearing it, the bullets would've hit the body armor, not him. He'd not said a word about his missing vest. But that's the way he'd always been. Sacrificing. Quiet strength burning brightly in his eyes.

As the chopper roared across the ocean and Midas worked to stop Max's bleeding—Sydney stared at his face, disbelieving. Hot tears streaked down her face. They'd just agreed to make things work. They were going to be a family. He couldn't die. He just couldn't.

A hand patted her leg, jerking her from the woeful thoughts.

Ghost One wiped a rag over his face. "He'll make it."

Gulping the fear back by the mouthfuls, Sydney stared at

Ghost One. "How do you know?" she shouted over the growl of the engine and rotors. She silently begged him to give her a reason to hope, to tell her they weren't going to be ripped apart permanently.

"He's too thick-headed to die."

A half-choked sob escaped as the man wrapped an arm around her. "You must really know him."

"Like a brother."

GOING HOME

Tiny fingers wrapped around his as the soldiers respectfully loaded the oak coffin up the ramp of the C-130. With plane engines roaring as loud as his heart, Jon lifted Maecel into his arms. A longing, tight and constricting, wormed through his chest. Tears, unbidden and sudden, lurched to his eyes. How he ached to wrap his arms once more around Kimber. To see her sparkling blue eyes smiling at him. Hear her laughter and the always encouraging words that sang from her lips.

"Mama," Maecel said, pointing to the box.

How excruciating to try to help her understand. Of course she didn't.

She stuck two little fingers into her mouth and sucked on them. Any other day, he'd have stopped the habit, but today he granted her whatever measure of comfort she needed. If only God would grant him some measure, too. Something to ease the wicked pain threatening to send him to his knees.

Tears blurred his vision as the casket disappeared through the back hatch. In the jungle, carting the remnant of the woman he loved through the damp, mucky terrain, it hadn't seemed real. As if she'd been sleeping.

But now, standing alone on the tarmac with his daughter, it was far too real. He buried his face in Maecel's shoulder and sobbed.

CHAPTER 27

The soldiers of Max's team lined up on either side of the ramp leading into the C-130, fingertips pressed to their temples in a final salute to their comrade as a steel coffin rolled into the transport. Behind the casket came Kimber Harris's.

Watching through the window overlooking the airstrip as tears streaked down her face, Sydney cried for Jon Harris, for the fallen soldier. The pain was too great. And too close.

Would Max die, too?

Slowly, she turned and slumped against the hard plastic chair. Hanging her head, she wiped her nose, silently praying God would guide the surgeon's hands in the operating theater. Max's operation had been going on for hours, and still no word. She shifted on the vinyl chair, rubbing her neck.

"What were you doing on that chopper, Midas?" she heard Gruff demand of the green-eyed team member.

"Saving his life."

"You're not a medic."

The guy looked down then back to Gruff. "Actually, I am. Fully vetted."

"And why didn't we know this before?"

"Nobody needed to know. They took away my certification."

"Sydney?"

She blinked and looked up.

Lane's smile didn't make it past the mole next to his lip. "I...I hope he makes it."

She drew back, uncertain whether to scoff or accept the words that seemed empty in light of the way he'd pursued her these last few months.

"I'm serious." He raked a hand through his sandy blond hair. "If you're happy, that's what matters. And I know you've wanted Max to come around. I mean..."

Awkward silence hung between them.

Clearing his throat, he stood. "I–I'm going to get something to eat." When he turned and took a few steps, he grazed shoulders with Ghost One.

"Sorry," Ghost One mumbled.

Almost immediately, Gruff fell into step with Lane and hooked an arm around Lane's bony shoulders. "We need to have a little talk."

The not-so-subtle messages—Ghost One's shoulder bump and Gruff's "little talk" with Lane—told Sydney these men were serious. And spoke of the imperative for complete anonymity. They would do everything and anything to protect that.

She considered Ghost One as he handed her a bottle of orange juice and eased into the chair across from her. "Midas says you look pale, probably need the sugar."

Uncapping the bottle, she found her gaze once again on Jon Harris. He'd go home without his wife. With painful memories of watching her die. She tensed her jaw, trying not to explore the possibility she could do the same. Instead, she forced her mind to the juice and took a sip, ignoring the way the man across the aisle from her watched her without watching. A guardian, of sorts. Max's friend.

Movement outside the building caught her attention. A man

in military uniform strode from the building toward Jon, shook his hand, then spoke into his ear.

"Who's that?" Sydney mumbled.

"Our guardian. He'll make sure our presence here is kept quiet."

Sydney met Ghost One's stare evenly.

He winked then tapped her leg. "Hey, there's the doc."

Sydney came to her feet awkwardly as a man in green scrubs shuffled toward her.

"Mrs. Jacobs?"

"Yes?" She straightened the too-tight shirt across her belly. The strength she lacked in her body she felt in the support of Max's team. As she stood before the doctor, she glanced back. The fact that the team huddled confirmed what she'd sensed.

"I'm Dr. Tomzyck." He considered her then took her by the elbow. "Why don't you sit?"

If he wanted her to sit down, did that mean Max was dying? "No. Just tell me."

"I'm sorry. I didn't mean to alarm you," Dr. Tomzyck said. "You just look a bit worse for the wear."

"I'm sure we all are." Her respect and admiration for the men around her swelled.

"Please," the doctor said. "Let's sit."

Acquiescing, Sydney eased into the seat, gripping the arm tightly. Ghost One sat next to her, a silent sign that she wasn't alone. The others clustered nearby.

"Your husband is stable but serious."

A breath whooshed out of her. Ghost One nodded.

"I believe he's stable enough to be ambulatory. Since that C-130 hasn't left, I'd like to get him on that and deliver him to Okinawa, where they're better suited to continue treating his injuries."

"What's the damage?" Midas asked.

"Three bullets across the chest. One narrowly missed the carotid. But one splintered off his rib and punctured his lung. We've repaired the tear, but I'd feel better if he were checked at a facility equipped to handle combat injuries."

"Agreed," Midas said, then peeked at Sydney. "Sorry. Didn't mean to intrude."

She smiled. "No, it's okay. You're right." She returned her attention to the doctor. "We do agree, Doctor. Can I go with him?"

"Of course." He stood. "They're prepping him for transport now. I need to call it in and make the arrangements."

As the doctor started away, the man from the C-130 who'd talked with Jon Harris appeared. He greeted the doctor, and together they disappeared.

Relief dripped like a nice oil massage over her shoulders and back. Max made it. *He's going to live.*

"Told you he was too thick-headed to bail."

Sydney smiled, grateful when the large guy wrapped an arm around her shoulder, offering comfort. "I'll never forget seeing him face-down in that sand."

He gave her a hug. "You and me both."

Doors flapped back and a gurney emerged. Sydney bolted to her feet, watching. Buried amid crisp white sheets, boards, straps, and tubes, Max was wheeled into the open. She hurried to his side and bit back the tears at his pale face. "Oh, Max," she whispered. She kissed his cheek, grateful for the warmth she found there.

She wanted his eyes to flutter open, to show her he really was alive. But with the heavy sedation for surgery, she wouldn't see those riveting eyes for a while. The medical staff gave her a nod then pushed him out onto the tarmac. An ear-piercing thrum from the engines screeched through the air as they ran the gurney up the steel grate.

Sydney walked behind the team, noting that Lane kept his distance. Beside her, she felt Ghost One pause and step back. She caught his hand. "You're coming with me, right?"

He hesitated then nodded. "Of course."

But when she looked around, the others were gone. Like a flash of lightning. Enough to crack the night but be untraceable afterward. Yeah. That's the way it should be. She'd bury this story. Thankfully, the photos were incinerated in the explosion. "You should know, there were photos of you, of the team. I don't know where they came from. My copies were destroyed, but the film is out there somewhere."

Ghost One's features darkened. "Thanks. I'll pass the word along."

Sydney glanced around. "Where are the others?"

Again he hesitated. "They don't exist, so it'd be funny if they all showed up at another military hospital." He urged her into the plane. "They'll find their way home. It's what we do. All of us. Even Max. We find our way home."

In his own gentle way, he made sure she understood she had a secret to keep. She placed a hand on his arm. "Don't worry, Ghost One. I understand."

"Thought you might." Slow and small, his smile warmed her. "And for a nosey reporter, I'm surprised you don't know my name's Colton Neeley."

"My husband has a friend by that name." She watched the techs secure Max's gurney to the left side as Colton guided her to the right, where she lowered herself onto the red web seating. Not exactly comfortable, but she didn't care. "I won't be tracking down any more stories. All I want to do is go home, buy a house, have our baby, and fall in love with my husband all over again."

Hollow laughter trickled into his awareness. Max pried his eyes open—and white light shot into his vision. He grunted and turned away.

A soft gasp. "Max? Max, can you hear me?"

Sydney's voice lured him from the greedy claws of sleep. "Where—?" Something stuck in his throat, severing his question.

"Shh, you have a tube in your throat. Colton, get the nurse," Sydney said. Then he felt her breath against his cheek. "I'm so glad you're back, Max." Warmth pressed against his forehead. A kiss. A guy could get used to this. Except for the pain that made him feel like he'd been beaten to a pulp.

He battled to see her face, to take in the fact she was really here, that he had survived that cold-blooded attack intent on wiping out the team. Muffled shouts had pulled him around at the last second on that beach, just as the gunmen had emerged. If he hadn't turned, everyone would've been killed.

"This is going to hurt, Mr. Jacobs. Just hold on."

Max willed himself to relax; it wasn't the first time he'd had a feeding tube. He gagged once as it came out, leaving his throat raw and sore. The nurse handed him a lidded drink with a straw. "Sip slowly." He squeezed his eyes shut then pushed them open.

When he tried to elevate his head, pain tore through his shoulder. He stiffened and dropped back, dots sprinkling his vision.

"Yeah, might wanna take it easy there. Seems you tried to bring home a few souvenirs."

Cowboy. The man's voice made Max smile. Shouldn't be surprised that of all the team members sent to check on him and report back to Lambert, it'd be Cowboy. The guy probably volunteered. Closest thing to a friend.

"What's a vacation without souvenirs?" Max croaked out, wishing he hadn't.

The burly guy bent over the bed and gripped Max's hand tightly. "All right, buddy. I'm going to jet. You get better. We aren't a team without you."

Once Cowboy was gone, Max rolled his gaze to Sydney. Daylight streaming through the side window made her look like an angel. Her hair hung loose past her shoulders, thick and dark. Her beautiful eyes sparkled.

"Hey, handsome." She smiled, a tear spilling over her lid.

With the IV hand, he waved her closer. "No tears." He touched her face. "I meant what I said." His throat seared. He winced.

"Shh, we can talk later. Just get better. Please."

"A little pain isn't going to stop—" His words caught on the dry, stinging portions of his throat. He forced a swallow that stung all the way down. "Whatever it takes, Syd. I don't want to lose you again."

She held his hand against her face. "You won't, Max. We're in this together."

Another thing leaped to his mind with urgency. She'd been there for one reason—to find Nightshade. "The team—you can't say anything." He tried to show his sincerity, but heaviness and weakness quickly overtook him, pulling his arms down and eyes closed. He pushed them back open. "No reporting. . ."

Through her tears, she bent toward him. "I found what I was looking for." She kissed him with a small laugh. "And I'm not sharing him with the world."

EPILOGUE

A steamy haze filtered through the bathroom as Max toweled his hair. He dropped the towel on the side of the tub and adjusted the string on his shorts. Rotating his arm, he thanked God for the wonders of hot water after a rigorous physical therapy session. He almost had full rotation in his shoulder now. He'd beat the odds and recovered in under ten weeks. Next week he'd have his checkup with Lambert's doc and shrink to verify his ability to return to combat. Months ago he'd have jumped at a chance for a new mission. Today he'd rather have a few more weeks with his wife.

Grabbing a black compression shirt, he glanced around for Syd. Not finding her, he headed into the kitchen, threading his arms into the sleeves. As he banked left toward the living room, he spotted her standing behind the large island in their new kitchen. She stood there, a glass half raised to her mouth, eyes wide.

"Your brother called last night. Again." He shrugged into the shirt, vowing he'd prove Bryce wrong, that he could be a good—no, a *great* husband and father. No. He didn't care what Bryce thought as long as he convinced Sydney. He'd laid his anger and his life on the altar, as the counselor had said. "Hey, don't forget about the appointment with Pastor Roy."

She blinked and set down her glass. "I don't think we're going to make the appointment."

He chuckled and opened the stainless steel fridge then pulled out a protein drink. "That's a line I'd expect to come from me, not you." When he turned back, she hadn't moved. "Syd?" He took a step closer.

Then he saw. A puddle around her feet. Frozen, his gaze traveled back up to her tan capris, darkened along the inseam. He widened his eyes. "Oh."

"Yeah."

"Let me get a look at that kid." Griffin strode toward Sydney, dressed in swim trunks and revealing a large creature tattooed on his toned and muscular right pectoral.

Sydney angled three-month-old Dillon toward the large man. "This is Dillon Brian Jacobs."

A meaty brown finger wiggled into her son's grasp. Dillon's large dark eyes flashed toward the big guy, clear and sharp under a mop of thick black hair. His legs kicked.

"All right, now." Griff grinned. "This boy's going to be spec ops. And strong, too."

The medic had a ready smile. "Hey, that can't be Frogman's kid." He laughed. "He's too pretty."

"Bug off, Canyon." Max laughed as he joined them, wrapping an arm around Sydney from behind. He kissed the side of her neck.

A muscular guy a little taller than Sydney ambled from the barbecue grill where smoke spiraled up into the clear blue sky. Marshall Vaughn had been dubbed the Kid, and the poor guy probably took a lot of flak from the warriors, but he didn't seem fazed. "Look at those fists!" He held up one of Dillon's balled hands. "Yep, that's Max's boy."

With a fake lunge, Max teasingly growled for the Kid to shove off.

Cowboy came over and gripped Max's hand, tugging him into a one-shouldered hug. "What'd the doc say?"

"Yeah, what's the word, Frogman?" Griff asked, holding his bottled water.

A smile lit Max's face. "Clean bill of health."

Griff's wide smile was quickly followed by a bear-sized laugh that echoed across the lush green park. "Boys!" he shouted. "Nightshade is back in business."

ABOUT THE AUTHOR

An Army brat, Ronie Kendig married an Army veteran. They have four children and two dogs. She has a BS in Psychology, speaks to various groups, is active with the American Christian Fiction Writers (ACFW), and mentors new writers. Ronie can be found at www.roniekendig.com or www.discardedheroes.com.